Patric

Virginia Street

Oakdown

Praise for Patrick Easter

'Patrick Easter is a find. A first rate historical thriller, particularly memorable for its evocation of the Georgian underworld . . . it's fortunate for us that there is more to come.'

Andrew Taylor

'Wonderfully atmospheric. Carries you along on a floodtide of excitement.'

Rory Clements

'Easter has chosen his setting wisely, creating what I think may be a new sub-genre – naval, historical, crime and he should find a readership in all three camps.'

Eurocrime

'A historical thriller brimming with atmosphere and colour and is an exhilarating read . . . Rarely has a modern novelist evoked the fascinating London of this era with such pungency and vividness as Easter does here.'

Daily Express

'Overflowing with atmosphere.'

Daily Mail

'Great on period detail. Easter conjures up a satisfyingly creepy atmosphere of fear and menace in the filthy, overcrowded streets by the docks . . . for fans of historical fiction and crime novels alike.'

The Guardian

'Brought alive the alleys, dives, waterways and dank doings of the Port of London in its swarthy prime at the tail-end of the 18th century.'

Wharf Magazine

Also by Patrick Easter

The Watermen

The River of Fire

The Rising Tide

Cuckold Point

First published in Great Britain in 2018 by Oakdown Publishing

Oakdown Farm Burwash TN19 7JR

A CIP catalogue record for this book is available from the British Library

ISBN 978 1 9996466 0 8

www.patrickeaster.co.uk

Patrick Easter is the author of the Tom Pascoe series of novels. He is a former police officer who spent part of his service on the River Thames. After leaving the Met he became a journalist writing for both international technical journals and the national press.

His first novel, *The Watermen*, was published in 2010 to widespread critical acclaim and was followed by *The River of Fire, The Rising Tide* and *Cuckold Point*.

His keen interest in 18th Century history together with his extensive experience of the criminal justice system make him the ideal author for this subject.

He lives in East Sussex with his wife and two dogs.

He can be reached through his website at **www.patrickeaster.co.uk**.

Virginia Street

By Patrick Easter

For Jack and Mia

London – February 1800

Henry Arthur Teeling limped up the broad expanse of the Ratcliff Highway, a mile or so east of the City. It was snowing, the thin soles of his shoes crunching softly on the white flakes that lay in his path. He stopped at the junction of Virginia Street and peered along its length, searching for any sign the men had returned. He was early. The street was deserted. But he knew the respite couldn't last. Sooner or later they'd catch him. He wondered how much more he could take.

He shuffled down to the next corner, his right shoulder rising and falling with the effort of his gait. He still had a little way to go before he could feel safe. Another twenty-five, perhaps thirty yards to the door of the squat building that was his destination. He breathed deeply, and searched the lane to his right.

The men were there; five of them.

They'd seen him, of course. There was no denying that. He could see one of them nodding in his direction. His meaning was obvious. Teeling broke into a fractured run, the pain from his thigh raging up his spinal column to the back of his skull. He had no illusions about what would happen if he was caught. He risked another glance at the men. They, too, were running, their speed increasing with each step. He peered at the door he was heading for, and then back at his pursuers. He might just make it. Then he remembered the door was always locked, a precaution against unwelcome visitors.

He knew then it was hopeless.

He felt a hand grab hold of his coat. Another gripped his elbow, the fingers thick and powerful. A hard shove in the small of the back sent him sprawling. It was quickly followed by a blow to the back of his head, a weapon of sorts; heavy, hard and unyielding. Teeling tried to curl himself up into a ball, his arms over his head. He could hear their jeering voices as if from far away. The pain from his leg was excruciating but no worse than that caused by his present beating. Someone kicked him. Once, twice, three times. He felt the heavy boot striking his body. He tried to protect himself but the blows kept coming. One of the men had bent down. Teeling could see his face close to his own, spittle dribbling from between his lips and over a pockmarked chin. The face moved closer. It was shouting, the rancid stench of its breath billowing over Teeling's face, its mouth twisting this way and that, the words unintelligible but for the flow of obscenities. Teeling peeped out from under his arm. He knew the man.

Suddenly, it was over. Teeling opened his eyes, his vision blurred by the swelling of the flesh. The men were leaving. He lay quite still, the melting snow seeping through his tattered clothes. He felt something warm trickle down by his right eye. He wiped the blood with his fingers and tried to get up. A sharp pain shot up his back and he slumped down, shivering with the cold.

A shadow fell across him. He shut his eyes and brought both arms up around his head. A hand, small and gentle, took hold of his wrist.

'Let me see.'

Teeling moved an arm and peered out. A hazy image of a young woman in a faded blue dress, kneeling in the snow beside him. She reminded him of his late wife. The same oval features, the same pale skin. And the same smile. She released her grip and stroked his forehead.

'Can you stand?' she said.

He started to shake his head and promptly stopped as yet another spasm of pain passed up the back of his neck. More people arrived. He could hear the jumble of their voices. There was one in particular, one he recognised, but couldn't place. Whoever it was appeared to have taken charge, was issuing a string of orders. Teeling felt himself being lifted out of the snow and carried up some steps and into a building. A door closed and some bolts shot home. Then he was lowered to the floor.

'Will he be all right?' said the woman who'd been with him in the street.

'Too early to say.' A male voice. The one in charge. A pause, then, 'Joseph, go fetch the apothecary. No, not that one. I don't trust him. See the one in Market Hill.'

Footsteps pattered on the stone floor as someone left. A door opened and then closed. Silence. It was as though time itself had stopped. Teeling twisted his head and tried to open his eyes. A series of hazy images. He recognised no one.

'Do you know him?' someone asked.

'No,' said the young woman. 'I was passing. I saw what happened. That's all.'

Teeling felt in his pocket and took out a crumpled piece of paper. On it was a single word, written in charcoal. He knew he was taking a risk. This place might not be where he'd been heading. These people might not be who he hoped they were. Handing over the piece of paper to the wrong folk could well result in another beating. And he doubted he'd survive another one of those.

The paper was taken from him.

A pause, then, 'Looks like he's one of us. Anyone know him?'

Another face appeared. Teeling tried to speak but no words came. He felt a damp cloth wiping away the blood from his eyes and mouth. The face withdrew.

'It's Teeling.' A pause. 'It could have been any of us. Poor fellow. He's suffered enough already.' The voice trailed away.

Teeling felt suddenly drowsy, as if the need to remain awake and alert had passed. For the time being, he was safe. He closed his eyes.

Chapter 1

Three weeks later

Emanuel Lazaro walked east along Narrow Street, Limehouse, close to the banks of the River Thames. He was a short, strongly built man in his early fifties, his thick black hair, streaked with grey, hung loosely about his shoulders to merge with a long and untidy beard. It was early morning and the winter sun had not yet risen, the sky overcast with the promise of rain. He shivered and tucked his hands under his armpits. Despite the hour, he wasn't alone. The street was filled with men trudging wordlessly through the half light, their shoulders bent, their lined and unsmiling faces encased with grime. Now and then a pair of hostile eyes would stray in his direction and then sweep away. It wasn't unusual. His presence was frequently the object of resentment, even of outright hostility. He knew the reason, of course. His olive skin and prominent nose marked him out as different, a foreigner, an outsider and irredeemably a Jew. As so often in the past, he fought to control his resentment. Losing his temper would solve nothing.

He branched right onto a grubby street lined with chandlers, blacksmiths, rag merchants and a couple of run-down taverns that led down towards the foreshore and, from there, ran along beside the river to Limehouse. No sooner had he joined it than he became aware of a commotion a little way ahead. A small crowd had gathered at the edge of one of the many docks that populated this stretch of the tideway. Emanuel walked over. Others were doing the same. People were pointing at something he couldn't yet see. He eased his way to the front. Twenty feet below him and some way from the dockside, two men were leaning over the side of a skiff, struggling with something below the surface of the water. Suddenly, a man's head appeared, quickly followed by the rest of his inert body as he was dragged onboard and dumped between the thwarts of the rowing boat. There was no doubt, even from this range, that the man was dead.

The crowd fell silent as the corpse was brought up the dock steps and lowered onto the stone apron. Its mottled black skin had, in places, peeled away to reveal a sodden mass of grey flesh while its thin, bloodless lips stretched tight against the black stumps of its teeth. If the cadaver had ever possessed a pair of boots, there was now no sign of them, its blackened feet protruding beneath a pair of three-quarter length slops, the toes stripped of their nails and skin, exposing the bones beneath. The stench of decaying flesh was everywhere.

'Anybody know the cully?' One of the watermen who'd brought him ashore was looking enquiringly at the surrounding faces.

The crowd shuffled as though embarrassed by the question. For a long moment, no one answered.

'Could be Collins,' said a voice.

A murmur rose from the crowd, although whether in agreement or not, it was impossible to say.

'No. Don't look nothing like him,' said a second voice.

'Could be him, an' all,' said a third man. 'I ain't seen him this past fortnight. Wondered where he were.'

Another murmur, this time louder. A kind of agreement seemed to have been reached. The body had, in life, been Collins.

Emanuel stared. He knew Collins. Had known him, on and off, for many years although the ravaged features of the corpse looked nothing like the man he remembered. Yet… He looked more closely. The clothes were certainly familiar, the distinctive blue jerkin and the red and white striped slops that Collins always wore. It could be him.

Emanuel's thoughts were cut short. The mutterings of the crowd had suddenly changed, become more aggressive. A man's name was mentioned, and then quickly taken up by others. It was a moment or two before Emanuel understood why. A wound on the dead man's forehead had been seen. It wasn't obvious. Not to the casual observer. A welt of grey flesh amongst so much else was easily missed – until it was pointed out and the supposed culprit named. After that it hadn't taken long for the charge of murder to be laid at the suspect's door and the guilty verdict handed down.

The name made perfect sense to the crowd. Three weeks ago, Henry Teeling, an Irishman and undoubted Papist, had been given a beating by Collins, a Protestant, who now lay dead on the dockside. The search for his killer was over before it had begun. Teeling was guilty, defined by the country of his birth and his faith, the case against him established beyond doubt.

Emanuel looked at the faces of those around him; saw the spreading anger in their eyes and knew he should leave. There would be those within the crowd who might know him. It would not be sensible for him to remain in the present climate. He had turned to go and then stopped, aware of a sense of being watched. His eyes tracked round and caught the woman staring at him. She was young, and extraordinarily beautiful, her large dark eyes flecked with gold, her fair hair tucked beneath a mob cap. She looked away, a faint blush rising in her cheeks as though embarrassed by the encounter. There'd been none of the antagonism he'd been expecting.

#

Sara Payton stared into the early morning sky where streaks of white and pink and grey lay across the eastern horizon. Soon the sun would be visible, its bright red orb appearing from beyond the flat lands of the Isle of Dogs. Away to her left, columns of thick black smoke were already rising from the chimneys of Limehouse and Shadwell, while above her head gulls swooped and wheeled and cried. A new day was beginning.

She glanced down at the body lying on the quayside, a puzzled look in her eyes as though aware for the first time of the stench of death. She reached up and untied a brightly coloured handkerchief she wore about her neck, and held it to her nose. She hadn't intended to be here. Her duties as a lady's maid meant her hours of freedom were relatively few and her choices limited. This morning she'd intended to cross the Thames and browse the Borough market on the south side but had changed her mind at the last moment. If truth were known, anywhere was preferable to the house to which she seemed anchored.

Her life had not always been so regimented. She was not from London. Her family came from Norfolk where she'd been born and where her parents still worked on the estate of Lord Howard, the Earl of Ardingleigh. She'd also worked there for a time, initially as a kitchen maid and, more recently, as her ladyship's maid. It was a job she'd enjoyed and would have continued to perform had not events conspired against her. In the autumn of 1799 the eldest son of the earl, a young man with a fiery temper and an interest in women, had resigned his commission in the army and returned home to the family estate.

Within weeks he'd made it abundantly clear that his long absence had done nothing to diminish his unwelcome interest in Sara. And when his frequent advances were rebuffed, his frustration had grown and his behaviour towards her had morphed into a desire to inflict humiliation on the young lady's maid. When, finally, his conduct had come to light, it had been Sara, rather than the Honourable James Grenville, who'd been required to leave family and friends and take up employment in London. She'd had no say in the matter and, within the week, she had left all that was familiar to her.

But if she had imagined that her move south would, at least, rid her of the attentions of the young man, she was mistaken. Within months, Grenville had discovered the identity of her new employer and had travelled south in his relentless pursuit of her.

Sara felt herself being jostled. A small crowd had formed around her and was pushing for a better view of the corpse. She looked down at the bedraggled shape lying on its back, its mouth open as if in the act of screaming for the help that never came. The renewed sight of it brought her out of her reverie.

She turned to leave and again noticed the man she'd seen earlier, the one who'd caught her staring at him. A foreigner, from the light dusting of his skin, perhaps from southern Europe. She remembered seeing him before, in Virginia Street, Shadwell. She'd been helping a man who'd been beaten by a gang of bully-boys, when this foreigner had appeared with a few others and quickly taken charge of the situation.

Her thoughts drifted. It was a pity about the corpse. Perhaps the men in the crowd had been right. Perhaps he'd been murdered. She turned to leave. It was nothing to do with her.

Chapter 2

Emanuel walked up Virginia Street. A week had passed since the finding of Collins's body. The image of it being brought up the dock steps and laid out for the world to see had played on his mind. He'd long suspected that something like this might happen, that Collins's end, if not the means, had been entirely predictable. If, as seemed probable, his death had been the result of some violent act, it was surely the consequence of a life he'd chosen for himself; a life where a difference of opinion was all too often settled at the point of a knife. Collins had known no other way. In truth, there had been no other way. Not for him. Not on the streets of Limehouse where he'd lived for most of his short life.

And if what he'd overheard at the dockside was right, he hadn't far to look for the identity of the man responsible. Yet everything Emanuel thought he knew about the supposed culprit suggested the improbability of the claim. He wondered where Teeling was now and what he was doing. Doubtless he'd find out soon enough.

He turned and mounted the steps of the small, barn-like building in front of which Henry Teeling had been beaten all those weeks ago. The few windows it possessed appeared as though an afterthought, forming a narrow line below the eaves, while a heavy oak door seemed a needless extravagance. Emanuel stared at the faded wood set in the white-painted stonework. Nothing about the building gave any hint of its purpose.

It was all a far cry from another building before which he'd often stood as a young child. He felt the sudden tug of a life gone by, a yearning to be back in the country of his birth, where his family and the friends of his childhood still lived. Despite the passing of the years, he was still a stranger here. He had no friends in whom he could confide. Only acquaintances. And with these he had to be careful. The casual chatter, the confidences shared, the warmth of intimacy were all now absent from his life. He knew he could blame no one but himself, could tell no one of the secret he'd harboured for thirty years. Yet hardly a day passed when he didn't think about the consequences of its discovery.

The mood quickly passed and, unlocking the door, he entered a large vaulted room that seemed to occupy the greater part of the whole. From high up by the eaves, light spilled through the windows into an otherwise gloomy interior. A large stone table occupied the far end of the open space and, in front of this, a few benches now stood. To the left of the table, a red lamp hung from the side wall.

He sat down on one of the benches. In a few minutes others would join him but for the moment he was alone. His thoughts drifted back to memories of childhood. He smiled inwardly. Older than the others, he'd been the leader of a small group of boys who'd roamed the back streets of the Alfama district of Lisbon, close to the Sé de Lisboa. More often than not, the little gang would find itself embroiled in fights with the boys from other neighbourhoods. Looking back, it seemed to him that most of these childish battles had been to protect one particular lad, a skinny youth who'd never learned to look after himself and who, in consequence had proved an irresistible target for the bigger boys. He'd often thought of going back. Just for a month or two. Meet again the friends of his childhood.

But that was impossible. He could never go back. Not since he'd made his choice to renounce the traditions by which he'd been raised. From that moment he'd been shunned by his community, a pariah in their midst. At thirteen he'd left home. At twenty he'd come to England.

He sighed and, getting to his feet, strolled to a side door. In the small room beyond he dressed carefully. He could hear the others beginning to arrive, the outer door opening and closing, the subdued chatter of voices, the occasional laugh as they waited for him. This had been the pattern of his life since he'd arrived here from Portugal thirty years ago to take up the life of a Roman Catholic priest.

He looked at his watch. It was time for the Mass to begin. He opened the door into the chapel, wondering if Teeling would be there. It was hardly likely, given he was now a marked man.

But the Irishman *was* there, occupying his usual place near the back of the chapel, his head bowed as if in prayer. He still bore the marks of his beating, great welts of blue-black skin covering his pale, narrow face, his clothing heavily stained with blood.

Emanuel climbed the steps to the stone table. Someone had covered it with a white cloth and placed a crucifix in the centre with a lighted candle on either side.

'*In nomine Patris et Filii et Spiritus Sancti...*'

The Mass had begun.

Emanuel couldn't rid his mind of Teeling or Collins or the darkening mood of the crowd when the dead man's injury had been spotted. He could still hear its murmuring growl of disapproval, the simmering threat of violence.

'*Corpus Christi*,' Emanuel intoned, offering the host to those who came forward for Holy Communion. Teeling was not amongst them, the Irishman still in his place, his face buried in his hands. There had to be a reason for not receiving the host, a feeling of unworthiness. Emanuel's stomach tightened. Not for the first time he thought of the injury to Collins's head and wondered if the rumours were not, after all, founded on fact.

#

Teeling felt the priest's gaze boring into him. He didn't move. Time seemed to drag before he heard the rustle of the chasuble as Emanuel turned back to the altar. He wondered if the priest had heard the rumours about his involvement in Collins's death. Perhaps he should have publicly denied the stories but there would've been no point; not once people had made up their minds. He winced as a spasm of pain tore through his body. He'd not fully recovered from the thrashing he'd received that morning three weeks ago. It reminded him of the first time he and Collins had met. His head fell forward into his cupped hands and he felt the sharp sting of his tears.

'Will you hear my confession, Father?' he asked, a few minutes later when the Mass had ended and the rest of the congregation had gone. It didn't take long. A matter of minutes. At the end of it he got up and returned to his seat, a feeling of emptiness inside him. There were things he'd omitted, things he'd not had the courage to tell the priest. The realisation haunted him. The words of absolution spoken in the confessional rang hollow in his mind. He thought about returning and starting afresh. But he didn't. He'd deal with the consequences – if that were ever possible. He climbed to his feet and walked out through the main door onto the street. A fresh fall of snow had already covered the tracks of those who'd left before him.

At the bottom of the steps, he paused at the spot where he'd been attacked. He thought of the young woman who'd helped him that morning. A stranger. No one he knew. He walked on. At the corner of the Ratcliff Highway, he turned right towards Limehouse and the room he shared with around a dozen others. He'd already decided it was for the last time. He couldn't stay there. Not since the rumours had started. He wasn't even sure why he was going there now. There was nothing in the room that belonged to him. Even the moth-eaten blanket under which he slept was not his own. The room was just a place to go to rest his head. Now he would move on.

He searched the road ahead of him. As he always did. He didn't have to think about it. His eyes roved the distant scene as a painter might view the hills and valleys in which he walked, noting the presence of trees and rocks and clouds. He'd been in London a matter of months but already the routine of care, born of the need for survival, had embedded itself in his head. The glance that turned into a stare, the hardening of a stranger's eye, the whispered asides behind hands cupped to the mouth – these were the signs that he searched for, the warning of approaching danger. He had learned to keep his mouth shut, to keep himself to himself, to speak only to those who he knew to be his fellow countrymen and his co-religious. To do otherwise was to invite trouble.

It hadn't been much different at home, in Ireland. He'd seen the nation tearing itself in two, neighbour against neighbour, father against son, Catholic against Protestant. Men and women hacked to death on the strength of a rumour, or hanged from the bough of a tree, their bodies left as food for wild animals, children dying for want of food. Yes, it had been tragic. But was it any better here, living in a land which was not his own, where the sound of his voice was enough to invite a whipping – or worse – and where he was forced to work for pay that couldn't keep a dog alive?

He peered over his shoulder at the imaginary horde pursuing him and quickened his pace, the pain from his injured thigh a constant reminder of what he'd left behind. The image of his late wife appeared in his mind's eye. She was looking down at him from a great height, willing him on, giving him hope. The image faded.

Chapter 3

It was almost six in the evening when Emanuel walked in through the door of the coffee house, on the corner of Bow Street. He stopped and looked round the crowded interior, the multiple candles barely penetrating the darkness, thin wisps of black smoke rising in columns from each lick of flame. In a far corner of the room, a man sat by himself, his face partially obscured by a cloud of tobacco smoke, a dish of tea and a copy of *The Times* on the table in front of him. Emanuel grinned and strolled across.

'Joy, Walter,' he said, pulling out a chair.

'Give you joy, my dear Lazaro,' said the voice from inside the cloud. A hand waved away the offending smoke to reveal a round, pink face out of which two enormous brown eyes looked out. John Walter had been a journalist in his day. He was retired now, responsibility for the newspaper he'd founded passing to his son. Not that that seemed to make any difference. He was one of those men to whom information seemed to flow of its own accord and there were few subjects about which he did not know something. 'May I order you a drink?'

'Thankee. A coffee if you will.' Emanuel settled into his chair and looked round at the huddled groups of men seated at each of the tables, the din of conversation like that of a hovering swarm of bees. A few faces glanced in his direction, their disapproval of his presence obvious. He tried to ignore them. There were not many places he felt completely at ease.

'I hear there was a bit of excitement in your neck of the woods.' Walter's voice broke in on Emanuel's thoughts.

'Really?' said Emanuel, looking puzzled. 'Oh, you mean the body that was fished out of the river. Yes, sad business. I was there when they pulled him out.'

'Were you, now?' said Walter, his face brightening. 'I hear he died from a blow to the head.'

'So it would appear.'

'Why, sir, I do believe there is something you're not telling me,' said Walter, leaning forward expectantly. 'Come, now. Tell me everything. You know I shall winkle it out of you eventually.'

'His name was Collins,' said Emanuel. 'From the look of him, he'd been in the water at least two weeks and maybe more.'

'And the blow to the head? What of that, sir?'

'Yes, there appeared to be a wound above one eye. There was some suggestion it had been caused by a man with whom he'd had a fight some weeks before.'

'Did you know him?' asked Walter.

'The dead man? Yes, since he was a boy. But I'd not seen him for the last few years. I heard he'd been pressed into the army.'

'And the other fellow?'

'Yes, I know him too, although not so well. He comes to Mass most days.'

'A Papist?' Walter whistled softly. 'Does anyone know?'

'If you mean, is it common knowledge that Collins may have been killed by a Catholic, yes it certainly appears so.' Emanuel dropped his voice, conscious of the continued glances coming his way.

'Has he been arrested? This fellow?'

'It hasn't got quite that far,' said Emanuel. 'At the moment it's simply talk based on, oh, I don't know what.'

'What's his name? The one suspected of the dirty deed?'

'That I can't tell you,' said Emanuel. 'I fear I've already said too much about him.'

'Well, these things can very quickly get out of hand; particularly where a Catholic is thought to be involved.'

'Yes, I agree,' said Emanuel, anxious to steer the conversation away from the personalities concerned. 'And yet the minister chooses this moment for Parliament to debate the issue.'

'The Catholic question?' said Walter, raising his eyebrows. 'You do surprise me, sir. I would've thought you'd have welcomed his attempts to give your people greater freedom.'

'Oh, I do, I do,' said Emanuel. 'But I get the feeling Mr Pitt is using the issue as a means to achieve something else and, in the process, making things worse.'

'Something else? You mean union with Ireland?' Walter paused for a moment while he sucked noisily at the stem of his pipe. 'The situation with Ireland is an impossible one, but the Minister has to try and resolve it. Every difficulty in recent years that's involved the Irish can be traced back to the religious question. The Catholics want greater freedom. The Protestants don't want to give it to them.'

'I thought most of the population of Ireland was Catholic,' said Emanuel. 'I would have thought it a simple matter for the Irish Parliament to grant its own people what they want.'

'That's exactly the problem,' said Walter, tapping the table with the tip of his index finger. 'It's not the people who object to greater religious freedoms, it's the Irish Parliament. And since all its members are land-owning Anglicans, it has no interest in Catholic emancipation. Indeed, they see it as a threat to their own way of life.'

'And the debate on becoming part of the United Kingdom?' said Emanuel, a baffled expression on his face. 'What has that to do with the religious argument?'

Walter snorted. 'Because union with the United Kingdom would result in the abolition of the Irish parliament and with it the power to prevent reform of the Catholic question.'

'So Mr Pitt is stuck.'

'He certainly faces a few difficulties,' said Walter, waving away a fresh cloud of tobacco smoke. 'And it's not helped when one of his most influential colleagues opposes him.'

'Is there nothing he can do about that?' said Emanuel.

'I believe he's tried all the usual means at his disposal; knighthood, peerage, land, that sort of thing but it's had no effect on the man. He's known as a staunch Anglican, is very popular with the public and in a position to do great damage to the Administration if things don't go his way.'

'In the meantime Catholics are assaulted in the street and their churches attacked and set on fire,' said Emanuel, a trace of bitterness in his voice. 'What's his name, this orator?'

'Fielding, Mr David Fielding, the MP for West Kent,' said Walter. 'He is something of a rabble-rouser and that's always a problem if you're the minister with a different view on the world. Fielding's already suggested there could be serious rioting if Pitt tries to force through his reforms. He sees the issue as a threat to the country.'

'By *issue*, you mean the Catholic Church?'

'It's not what *I* mean, sir. It's the view of those who blame Popery for all their misfortunes. People like Fielding point to the authority of Rome and the supposed conflict of loyalty as between the King and the Pope. They see Irish Catholics coming to this country and taking the work away from the English. I'm afraid the arguments carry weight amongst a significant number of people.'

Emanuel stared at the ceiling. He knew how easily the mob could be stirred. He remembered the riots of twenty years earlier. He could hardly have forgotten them. Something like three hundred deaths and several churches, including his own at Virginia Street, destroyed. 'Do you have any more details?'

'In what regard?'

'Who might be involved and what they're planning.'

Walter hesitated and looked at Emanuel for a second or two. 'I regret it extremely, sir, but there are any number of men against whom such an accusation might be levelled. I suppose one might include David Fielding. He has an estate in Ireland which might help to explain his opposition to the emancipation issue. Like most of his kind, he's terrified of what might happen if Catholics are given the vote. But in spite of his reputation as a fiery orator, I doubt he would want to be involved in violence of any kind. Two others I've heard mentioned are Sir Peter Westlake and someone called Grenville. I rather fancy that must be the Honourable James Grenville, eldest son of the Earl of Ardingleigh. If that's true, he is a particularly odious character and someone you should try and avoid. Sir Peter is also someone you should try to steer clear of. As to what's being planned, I have no idea except to suggest it likely it'll involve the deaths of many.'

Emanuel stared at the table, slowly shaking his head. 'You think it could come to that?'

'From the little I know, I think it highly likely. You might want to speak to the Reverend John Rippon,' said Walter. 'He is, as you probably already know, the leader of the Protestant Association. I don't say the Association is involved in any of this but Rippon might be able to add something to what I've already told you.'

'I hardly think he would wish to see me,' said Emanuel. 'His reputation as an anti-Papist is well known.'

'I think, were you to meet him, you'd be pleasantly surprised,' said Walter. 'Particularly where the reputation of the association might be at issue. However much you might disagree with his philosophy, he will certainly wish to disassociate himself from anyone seeking to further a cause through violent means. If anyone knows what's going on in that area, it's him.'

'Then I suppose I'd better try and see him,' said Emanuel.

Chapter 4

Emanuel was in Castle Street, Holborn, when, a week after his meeting with Walter, he was surprised to see a familiar figure standing on the opposite side of the street. He hadn't seen Teeling since the day he'd heard the fellow's confession. He remembered watching him leave the church that morning, hearing the sound of his footsteps in the nave and the gentle closing of the front door as he went out into the street. When he'd failed to come to Mass for the following two days, Emanuel had begun to worry he might have fallen victim to a mob convinced of his involvement in Collins's death. Now he watched the Irishman limp across the street, glad to see him alive.

'Will it be you, Father?' Teeling smiled and held out his hand.

'Give you joy, Henry. What brings you to this part of London?'

Teeling glanced away and Emanuel had the feeling this was not a chance meeting. Teeling had known where to find him.

'Can I talk to you, Father?'

Emanuel nodded and led the way back to the drab, three-storey red brick house from which he'd just emerged. Entering, he led the way across the hall to a wood-panelled room smelling of polish and the faint tang of worn leather. A crucifix hung above the fireplace.

'Sit you down,' said Emanuel, pointing to one of a dozen chairs grouped around a long oak table in the centre of the room. When they were both seated, he said, 'Now, what can I do for you?'

'It's an apology I'll be owing you, Father,' said Teeling, avoiding the priest's enquiring gaze and running a soot-encrusted hand through an unruly mop of hair.

'Why's that?'

'The last time I saw you, I left without saying goodbye. It were wrong of me. To tell the truth, Father, I knew…' Teeling broke off for a moment. 'Will you be remembering the fight outside the chapel, Father?'

'Yes,' said Emanuel. 'I do.'

'I knew one of the scrubs what flogged me,' said Teeling, an angry look in his eyes. 'His name were Collins—'

'You already knew Collins?' interrupted Emanuel. 'How did you meet him?'

'Two years ago he were with the army when they came to Wexford, near where I lived with my wife,' said Teeling. 'There'd been trouble in the town. The rebels had come in and…'

'Massacred a large number of loyalists,' said Emanuel, recalling the story he'd read in the English papers. The killings had been savage even by the brutal standards of the time.

'Aye, well, I didn't know nothing about it at the time. The first I knows about it were when I saw some soldiers coming across the fields where I were working. Three of them, there were. Two of them went to my house what were close by while the third one, Collins, came towards me.'

'Tell me what happened,' said Emanuel.

For a minute or so Teeling said nothing, his hands covering his face. Slowly, his fingers slipped down to his chin and he said, 'Collins were screaming about how I were a croppy what murdered folk in cold blood. He said I didn't deserve to live. I tried to talk to him but he weren't listening. All of a sudden he stabbed me in the thigh with his bayonet. I must have lost me senses 'cos I didn't see him after that. When I woke, the men had gone but I knew something bad had happened. I crawled back to the cottage and saw me wife lying on the floor. She were dead, Father.'

'The next time you saw Collins was in Virginia Street?' said Emanuel, after a moment's silence.

'Aye, so it was, but I didn't know his name then.'

Emanuel leaned back in his chair and again considered the possibility of Teeling's involvement in Collins's death. What stronger motive could he have had than the murder of his wife? He wanted to ask if the rumours were true, if he'd killed Collins in revenge. It seemed inconceivable Teeling had sought him out merely to tell him about the circumstances of his meeting with Collins. There had to be more. He waited for the Irishman to continue.

'A few days after I were attacked outside the chapel, I saw him again,' said Teeling. 'He were with another of the soldiers what came to me house outside Wexford. A cully what's called Bristow.'

'Erasmus Bristow?' said Emanuel, his eyebrows arching in surprise. The name brought back unpleasant memories. He'd known Bristow for years. Used to see him and his mother from time to time when she would visit him on one pretext or another, usually for the few coppers that he was able to give her and for the opportunity it provided for her to pour out her heart over her young son's wayward behaviour. It had never made for easy listening, the boy, it seemed, growing increasingly resentful of what he'd regarded as his mother's dependence on the help of the Jewish priest.

As time passed and the boy grew into early manhood, his surly attitude towards Emanuel gave way to bouts of extreme anger and threats of violence. Perhaps for that reason, the visits became less and less frequent, and finally stopped. He'd often thought he should have made greater efforts to find common purpose with the young man as much for the mother's sake as her son's. But his occasional efforts in that direction had invariably ended badly, the young man's animosity towards him creating an unbridgeable gulf.

'Aye, Erasmus Bristow,' said Teeling. 'I've known the name – and Collins's too, for a while – but couldn't put faces to names until I saw them both, here in London, and recognised them.'

'Are you saying Bristow was present when your wife was killed? That he might even have been responsible for her death?'

'I don't know about that. All I know for certain is that he were there,' said Teeling. He glanced up, a curious look in his eye as though something the priest had said had only just registered. 'Will you be knowing him, Father?'

'I used to,' said Emanuel. 'I haven't seen him in a while. He and Collins grew up in the same street. Whereabouts in London did you see them?'

Teeling hesitated. 'It were in a coffee house in Exchange Alley. I saw them come in with some others. It were a shock, I can tell you. I wanted to put a knife into Collins. I asked one of the waiters if he knew their names. He didn't know but said he thought they were soldiers. He pointed to one of the other waiters and said I should ask him on account he were a soldier, too.'

'And did you? Ask him, I mean.'

'Aye, cost me a drink, mind. But it were worth it. He gave me the names I wanted.'

'And that was the first time you were able to put names to faces?'

'Aye.'

A feeling of inadequacy swept over Emanuel, a sense that there was nothing he could do or say beyond a few words of sympathy. Perhaps that was all Teeling expected. He sat in silence watching the agony on the younger man's face.

'There's trouble on the way, Father,' said Teeling, suddenly.

'To do with the death of your wife?' asked Emanuel.

'Aye, but only in a manner of speaking,' said Teeling. 'What happened to me and me old woman happened to thousands of others during the troubles and it'll take more than a year or two for us to forget. Seems the English don't want to forget, neither. They treat us like pigs and call us bog brothers and Papist bastards. Seems they don't like what Mr Pitt is doing to help us.'

'What sort of trouble are you talking about?' said Emanuel, remembering his recent conversation with John Walter.

'Don't know much, Father,' said Teeling. 'Just a word here and there. Whatever it is, they say there'll be trouble a plenty.'

'No names?'

'Bristow were mentioned. That's all I know.' Teeling paused and looked away as though an idea had occurred to him. 'No, wait, you could talk to the waiter what I saw at the coffee house; the one I told you about. His name's Rob Smith. I reckon he might know something.'

Chapter 5

It was raining the following day when Emanuel turned in through one of the many entrances leading to Garraway's and climbed the stairs to the first-floor coffee room. His meeting with Teeling the previous day had worried him. He had, over the last few years, come to believe that opposition to Catholicism was on the wane and sunnier days lay ahead. Now that view had been challenged, first by his friend Walter and now by Teeling. Elements within the Administration and outside it were, it seemed, planning some kind of atrocity which, if successful, would lead to the widespread loss of life with ramifications for the whole of society.

Passing through a set of double doors, Emanuel found himself in a large, high-ceilinged room filled with noise and movement and smoke. Groups of men were huddled at tables, talking, laughing, drinking coffee or eating their breakfast while others read newspapers or played cards. And all the while waiters rushed to and fro, their laden trays balanced above their heads on the tips of their fingers.

Emanuel wondered if it had been a good idea coming here. He knew next to nothing about the man he'd come to see, apart from what Teeling had told him. It was entirely possible he would refuse to say anything, particularly if he retained any sense of loyalty to his former colleagues in the army. And then there was the question of his faith. While Catholics had, in recent years, been allowed to join the army, it was probable that Rob Smith was a Protestant with no love for what he might call Popery.

'Mr Smith?' said Emanuel, holding up his hand at a passing waiter.

'Over yonder,' said the man jerking his head at a distant figure.

Emanuel weaved his way through the tables.

'Mr Smith?'

'Aye,' said the man, turning to look at Emanuel, a startled expression on his face, the smell of drink on his breath.

'I believe you know a friend of mine. He tells me you were in the army.'

Smith frowned as he looked round the crowded room. 'What friend was that, then?'

'Henry Teeling. He was telling me you served in Ireland with a couple of men I know. Seems you saw them here in this coffee house a few weeks since. I was hoping I could talk to you about them. Their names are Bristow and Collins.'

Smith's eyes narrowed a fraction. 'Aye, I remember those villains. I told your friend they was with me in the Second of Foot. What of it?'

'We can't talk here,' said Emanuel, aware he was already drawing curious glances from across the room. 'Is there somewhere quieter?'

'There's a yard at the back,' said Smith, jerking a thumb over his shoulder. 'I've got me victuals in ten minutes. We can talk then, if that's what you want.'

It was with some difficulty that Emanuel eventually found his way through a labyrinth of corridors to a small enclosed yard at the rear of Garraway's. The rain had stopped, the scent of damp earth mingling with the acrid stench of smoke rising from a score of chimneys.

'What did you want to know?'

Emanuel spun round. He hadn't heard Smith's approach.

'Thankee for coming,' he said, recovering quickly. 'What can you tell me about Bristow and Collins and what happened in Ireland?'

'Like I told you before, they was a pair of right villains. They joined the regiment just before we was shipped across to Belfast in the summer of '98. Didn't take no notice of them. Not at first. But it weren't long afore I could see they was trouble.'

Smith shook his head and walked away for a few paces, his hands jammed into the pocket of his apron. When he turned, his face wore a sombre expression. 'I were a soldier, and proud of it. I were used to fighting. Don't mean I weren't frightened though. What man ain't when facing death? There's no quarter given or asked for on the battlefield and oftentimes things get messy and brutal and a man can lose sight of his humanity. But when it's over, it's over. Bristow and his mate Collins weren't like that. They was evil. Proper scoundrels, the pair of them. God help any man in a brown coat what they caught within two or three miles of the battlefield. Mind you, it weren't only them. There's an officer from the regiment, a lieutenant. Comes in here regular, like. Young fellow he is. Never knew his name. Anygate, he and Bristow and Collins were always together. I reckon he were as bad as them, maybe worse, on account he were an officer.'

'Go on,' said Emanuel.

'As I were saying, some bad things happened over there,' said Smith. 'The loyalists distrusted the unionists and the unionists distrusted the loyalists, but men like Bristow and Collins sowed the seeds of hatred what'll take years to forget. Every day I'd see men hanging from trees or speared through with a lance, their bodies left at the roadside to rot. I ain't saying the fault were all on our side. Both sides did some terrible things and called it justice. No one could be trusted. The only truth was what your people told you. Everything else was lies. For all that, most of us in the army did our duty. But it only takes a few to do the damage. I'll warrant them three took a pleasure in the suffering they inflicted.'

'The officer who was with them. Was he never disciplined?'

Smith gave a short, derisory laugh. 'Disciplined? There weren't much in the way of discipline. Not then. Not in Ireland. Nobody took no notice. Besides, that officer were a titled gentleman from what I heard, and who's going to argue with a gentleman what's got a title?'

'Did anything happen that might have caused the soldiers to behave like that?'

For a minute, Smith said nothing and Emanuel thought he meant to stay silent. When finally he spoke, it was to utter a single word.

'Wexford.'

Smith's face had assumed a kind of mask and it was as if he'd been transported back in time, to an event in history through which he'd had the misfortune to live.

'I didn't know Collins nor Bristow before they joined the regiment,' said Smith. 'Don't know if Wexford were the only reason they was like they were. It just seems that way to me. We hadn't been in Ireland more than a day or so when we was ordered south to where the main rebel army had massed at

Vinegar Hill. The name meant nothing to me. As far as I were concerned it were just another battle, although some said the rebels meant to make a stand of it. We was almost there when there were a change to our orders and we was sent to Wexford, about twenty miles south of Vinegar Hill.'

Rob Smith paused, shaking his head from side to side. When he next spoke, his voice was quieter, more sombre.

'First I saw of the town,' he said, 'were the smoke; great black clouds that hung in the dawn sky. We were still a long way off and it were another hour or two before I saw the flames. They was thirty, maybe forty feet high, great sheets of yellow coming from the roofs of the houses. I were near the back of the column so it were a while afore I saw the rebels. They was gathered in front of the town, guarding a bridge over the river. There must've been ten, maybe twenty thousand of them. Some of them waving green flags, others with pikes or pitchforks or flintlocks in their hands.'

A sheen of sweat had formed on Smith's face. He wiped it away with the hem of his apron and Emanuel guessed what must have been going through his mind. He remembered the newspaper reports of the period; of the all-too-often slaughter of militia columns at the hands of the rebels.

Smith was speaking again.

'I heard our horses coming up the line towing their gun carriages. I'd seen cannon in action many times before. I knew what they could do to a man. But this time it were different. We was going to shoot at men who'd never faced artillery before; wouldn't know what to expect. They weren't no soldiers. Just farmer lads with a pike in their hands. Then it started. The noise were terrible. But I could see nothing. The smoke from the guns hid everything. It were all the same, though. When six pounds of solid iron hits a man, it don't leave much of him, or the cully behind him, neither. After a while, the shooting stopped and we was ordered to fix bayonets.'

He paused again and Emanuel had a renewed sense of the anguish he must have suffered, and continued to suffer. 'You never forget the rattle of six hundred bayonets clicking into place. There weren't a man what were smiling no more. The rebels knew what were coming, and all. I see them running back across the bridge to the town. Not all of them, mind. Many stood their ground, poor fools. They must have known we was going to charge; that they'd all be cut down…'

A head appeared at the back door of the coffee house and called out for Smith. Someone wanted to see him. He seemed not to hear, his face expressionless, his eyes staring at the blank wall opposite. The face at the door disappeared.

'I heard the order to advance,' he continued, his voice trance-like. 'We walked forward. No one ran. There was plenty of time to die. The artillery were silent and we walked through the smoke. I saw more of the rebels break and run, their dead and their dying left where they fell. Still we walked, one step following another, taking us closer to the hordes what stood opposite us. A hundred yards, ninety, then eighty, separated us. That were when the whole rebel line broke and they raced for their lives across the span of the estuary. I felt nothing. No relief or exhilaration, no fear or pity.

'When I reached the bridge over the Slaney, me boots stuck to the boards. I looked down and saw the blood. Then I saw the bodies. At first I thought they was the rebels what had died in the fighting. But then I saw they been run through with pikes and I knew then they had to be loyalist prisoners what had been murdered. They were heaped by the side, against the parapet, their mouths open, as if screaming. The sickly smell of blood stuck in me nostrils. Still I felt nothing. They weren't humans no more, those what lay by the side of the bridge. To think of them as humans was to see them as husbands or brothers, fathers or sons, and I couldn't do that. I'd not be able to do me job if I'd allowed himself to think of them and how they'd suffered in the last moments of their lives.'

Smith paced up and down the narrow yard muttering to himself, his hands clasped in front of him. Eventually he stopped, his face pale. 'There was no holding our lads, especially the loyalist militia boys what were mad with grief and anger at what they'd seen. When the fighting were over and the town were taken, the militia boys was sent back to the other side of the river and confined to camp on account they might have done some killing, else. The town were left to the Second of Foot – my regiment – to look after. We got orders to send out patrols to search for the rebels and bring any we found back to the town. I saw the orders with me own eyes. Collins and Bristow weren't included but I saw them go out with a patrol in the charge of the officer I were telling you about. I didn't know where they was going but I reckoned, from what I knew of them, there'd be trouble. I heard later that a woman had been killed and her husband hurt bad. Wouldn't surprise me none if it were Collins and Bristow what were involved.'

A haunted look invaded Smith's eyes. He turned towards Emanuel. 'He were a bully, were Bristow. There ain't no doubt about that. It didn't matter none that some poor bugger weren't near any battle. He'd be slaughtered just the same. It sickened me to see how some of our lads behaved. But Bristow were the worst. Him and Collins and the officer. They'd bayonet a cully for the fun of it. I saw Bristow once, when he thought no one were watching him, catch hold of a young lad what had been working in a field and hang him from the branch of a tree. He were no more than ten or eleven, I reckon. There weren't nothing I could do to save the poor little bugger.'

'And Collins?' asked Emanuel, in the silence which followed.

'Bristow treated him like he were his personal valet. He was a hard bastard and no mistake. Collins did everything for him. I reckon he were frightened of him.'

'I'd understood they were friends.'

'Not Bristow. Don't reckon he had any friends.'

'What about the officer? What did he look like?' said Emanuel.

'Only young, maybe twenty-two, twenty-three,' said Smith. 'Tall, fair-haired and a toff, like the rest of them.'

'But you don't know his name?'

'No. We called him "sir", same as all the others.'

'So why did he and Collins and Bristow start coming to Garraway's?'

'Ain't got the first notion,' said Smith. 'After I left the army I didn't see no one from the old days for close on two years. Then, six months ago, the officer started coming here with another, older, gentleman. He didn't recognise me and I never said nothing to him. Then, after a bit, they was joined by Collins and Bristow and a few others what I didn't know.'

'Soldiers, were they? The ones you didn't know.'

'Aye, seemed that way to me. Might 'ave been from another regiment.'

'You mentioned an older gentleman who came here with the young officer,' said Emanuel. 'Do you know him at all?'

'Saw him, often enough. Looked like he were in charge. But I never knew what he were called.'

'What did they talk about?' asked Emanuel.

'Couldn't say, sir. Mostly they met in one of the private rooms on the second floor. I—'

He was interrupted by the door of the coffee house again opening and someone calling his name, the voice more impatient, more insistent. Smith shrugged and started to move away.

'Can we speak again?' asked Emanuel.

Smith didn't answer at once and had almost reached the door of the coffee house before he again spoke. 'If you want to know about the army in Ireland, then best you find the only man who'll tell you the truth.'

'And who's that?'

'Colonel Ramsay,' said Smith. 'The Earl of Dalhousie. Served under Major General Moore at Wexford. He were one of the finest soldiers it were ever me privilege to serve under.'

'Where would I find him?'

'Last I heard he were at Woolwich.'

The next moment he'd gone and Emanuel was left alone in the yard staring at the door through which Smith had passed. Nothing made sense. Nothing the waiter had told him could explain why the meetings between Bristow, Collins, their former officer and a number of others had taken place. Perhaps they were simply old comrades enjoying each other's company. It was possible.

But he doubted it.

#

Emanuel hadn't been concentrating. His breviary lay open on the bench in front of him, the Divine Office only half read. He glanced round the gloomy interior of the chapel and thought again of his conversation with Rob Smith earlier in the day. It seemed impossible to contemplate the idea of men so inured to feelings of pity as to allow the degree of brutality of which Smith had spoken. Yet there seemed little doubt that such a stage had been reached by Bristow and Collins and the young, unnamed officer. The question was whether Wexford had been the cause of their behaviour or simply its catalyst. And in either case, did that necessarily mean they were guilty of plotting an event that might yet result in the deaths of many?

He closed his breviary and headed out through the side door of the chapel into Virginia Street. A solitary figure was standing, half hidden, in the doorway of a house opposite. It wasn't unusual. Places of shelter were hard to come by. Emanuel hurried towards the main road, the memory of the figure in the doorway lost.

The last of the daylight had faded from the sky, the crimson and white and gold of the sunset now turned to a mottled purple as he joined the main thoroughfare and passed between rows of gaily decorated stalls. Faces would appear out of the darkness, their features caught by the glow of oil lamps suspended from canvas awnings, then vanish, never to return.

Emanuel shivered. He had a sudden feeling of being watched. He stepped to the side of the road and peered at the faces of those closest to him. No one was looking in his direction. No one threatened him. He shook his head; had obviously imagined things. Yet the Highway could be a dangerous place. He knew that better than most. He was, after all, hewn from the stock of Abraham. And life was dangerous for such as he.

On an impulse, he looked to his left. Again, there was nothing. Only the passing and re-passing of the crowds and the agile scampering of a half-dozen barefoot children, bent on mischief.

And a cripple.

The man was staring at him. It was, he realised, the same person he'd seen ten minutes before in the doorway opposite the chapel. He was standing with the aid of crutches, his right leg missing above the knee, the massive bulk of his frame bent forward. Emanuel began to walk away. He wanted to dismiss the man's presence as a mere coincidence.

But couldn't.

He looked back. The cully was following him, the empty trouser leg flapping uselessly as he came closer, his face still in shadow, his body pivoting on the point of his crutches, an easy, almost graceful movement that belied his bulk. A lantern on one of the stalls flared, its light falling on a hollow face scarred with the effects of the pox, its lower jaw sagging as though under its own weight.

Emanuel felt his heart miss a beat.

He knew the man.

His name was Erasmus Bristow.

#

Bristow leaned heavily on his crutches and saw the look of pity in the other man's eyes. It was no more than a blink, quickly dissolving into the pupil of the man's eye as though it had never existed. But he'd seen it and recognised it for what it was. For a moment he felt the crushing weight of the priest's moral presence, an unbridgeable gap, a sense of his own inferiority. It had always been the same. The Jew had always looked down on him. He remembered the times his mother would insist on taking him with her to visit the scrub. She'd always said she needed to talk to him about spiritual matters but more often than not, she'd come away with a few extra coppers in her hand.

Even in those early days Bristow had rebelled. It was as though his mother hadn't trusted him to provide for them both and had needed to beg from the priest, stroking his arm whenever her pleas for help seem likely to fail. His mother's behaviour on these occasions had occasioned in him a sense of acute embarrassment bordering on rage. But for reasons he would have been unable to explain, his bitterness had been directed almost entirely at the priest. It was him, and not his mother, who was the author of all that was wrong in his young life.

Bristow's mother was dead now; had been for years. And with her death, the memories of those days had slowly dissipated, crowded out by later events, but never fully extinguished. He'd always intended to avenge his mother's memory, to make the Jew priest pay for what he believed he'd done.

'I've been waiting for you, mister.' Bristow rubbed the palms of his hands over what had once been the scarlet coat of a soldier, now black with grime and filth.

'What can I do for you, Erasmus? It's been a while,' said Emanuel, his eyes giving nothing away.

'I want a word with you, all quiet like.' Bristow hopped closer, his huge bulk towering over the priest.

'What about?' said Emanuel, rearing back from the foul stench of the other man's breath.

'Don't piss me, mister.' Bristow reached forward, his giant fist closing round Emanuel's neck, his eyes narrowing to mere pinpricks of anger. 'I ain't stupid. You think I don't know about what you did to me Ma?'

'Let go, Erasmus,' gasped Emanuel, clutching the hand at his throat. 'I can't breathe.'

'You's coming with me, mister. I told you I—' Bristow stopped suddenly, a startled, almost comical look of disbelief on his face, trying to make sense of a sudden and very rapid change in his fortunes.

#

Emanuel struggled to keep his anger under control. Remaining calm in the face of provocation had always tested the outer limits of his resolve. There'd been a few lapses over the years but he had, in large measure, managed to put behind him the fighting days of his youth. It was just unfortunate for Bristow that he should have failed to recognise the danger signals that his action had provoked and was now reaping the consequences. In a swift upward movement, Emanuel had brought his right knee into contact with the man's groin with as much force as he could muster. The result had been immediate and predictable.

Emanuel stepped back, rubbed his neck and glanced down at the still groaning Bristow. Despite what had just occurred, he was shocked by the physical wreck the man had become. He'd not seen Bristow since the death of his mother ten years ago and while news of the boy had, for a time, continued to find its way to Virginia Street, it was clear Bristow himself had felt no need to maintain the link. And without the moderating influence of his mother, his life had inevitably been set on a downward spiral. As the months passed, the flow of news of his adventures had grown more sparse. Three years ago there was talk of an appearance at the Old Bailey alongside his long-time associate, George Collins. The subsequent conviction for larceny had led to both men being pressed into the army. Since then no more had been heard.

Until Smith, the waiter at Garraway's, had reintroduced the names of both men.

And now this.

Emanuel remembered Bristow's words: *You think I don't know about what you did to me ma?* Was that what this had been about? Emanuel had always known of the young Bristow's lingering resentment of his presence in the life of his family, of the boy's conviction that the relationship had overstepped an invisible line. But he'd hoped the passing of the years and the imposition of military discipline might have mellowed Bristow's sense of antipathy towards him.

It seemed not.

Emanuel looked round. A crowd had gathered and was staring silently, first at Bristow and then at him. It was only a question of time before someone decided to get involved. He pushed his way clear. Bristow wasn't badly hurt. He'd soon recover, at least physically. The mental scars were another matter. Emanuel resisted the temptation to look back. Nothing good could come of it.

A minute later, he heard a bellow of rage. He knew whose it was. Despite his reservations, he glanced behind him. He could see nothing but the blur of movement that was the crowd moving up and down the Highway. He hurried on.

'Hello, dearie.'

A female voice interrupted his train of thought. Emanuel turned to see two gaudily dressed women standing in a doorway, fixed smiles on their painted faces, their fleshy arms folded across their chests. One of them beckoned him over. He shook his head and was about to walk on when he heard Bristow's enraged voice shouting not far behind.

Emanuel glanced over his shoulder. The shouting was getting closer. Another fight with Bristow was not a good idea. He might even be accused of taking advantage of a cripple. He had to lose the fellow somehow. He looked back at the two women and made up his mind. He'd wait in their house for five minutes, until Bristow had gone.

'Not so fast, dearie.' One of the women was blocking his path, her outstretched hand on his chest as he tried to slip past into the house.

'I'll be but a minute,' said Emanuel.

'Oh, I'm sure you will, dearie,' said the woman, picking her teeth with a grimy fingernail, her unwashed hair hanging loosely about the generous folds of her neck. 'I'll be thanking you for five shillings afore you go any further.'

'But—' said Emanuel.

'What's your game, mister?' The smile had gone from the woman's face. 'You trying to rob us poor girls what earn a pittance? Is that what you want? You ought to be ashamed of yourself, so you should.'

'No, I…' said Emanuel, the reality of the situation slowly dawning on him as he caught sight of a large, rat-faced man standing in the hall behind the women, staring at him. Suddenly, he caught a glimpse of Bristow barging his way through the crowd with surprising speed. Time had run out. He quickly delved into his coat pocket and took out his notebook. 'Five shillings, you say?'

The woman led the way down the unlit corridor, at the end of which she opened a door and stood back. Emanuel looked from her to the open door and back again.

'What…?'

'In there,' she said, in a voice that brooked no argument.

#

Emanuel felt a large hand push him through the door and was conscious of the smell of urine and stale sweat and damp that met his nostrils.

'This 'ere is Willing Annie,' said the woman who'd so recently relieved him of his money.

A child of no more than twelve was sitting on a straw mattress, her forced smile pulling at the sides of her small, thin mouth, her dark brown hair, matted with grease, hanging limply about her shoulders. She was shivering with the cold.

Behind him, Emanuel heard the door close. He looked round. The room was bare but for the single flock mattress on which the child was sitting. A small window was set into the far wall, the glass panels largely missing or cracked and through which a chill wind was blowing.

'Don't leave, mister. Please. Leastways, not yet.'

Emanuel glanced down at the child. She looked frightened.

'They'll beat me on account of I ain't given you no satisfaction,' she wailed.

He considered her for a moment, ashamed that his first thoughts had been for his own safety rather than the girl's. But he couldn't ignore the probability that Bristow was still in the vicinity and might yet find him.

'I'll stay for a little while.' He pointed to the window. 'What's on the other side of that?'

'Only the back yard,' she said, glancing behind her. 'You ain't thinking of leaving that way, sir, is you? They always have a bully-boy in the yard to catch them as don't pay.'

'Ah,' said Emanuel. It didn't seem the right moment to tell her he'd already paid.

'How d'you want it?' she said.

'Want it?' said Emanuel, frowning.

'I can do it whichever way pleases you, mister. It's up to you.'

'Thank you, child, but I'll not trouble you for anything.'

‘I’ve seen you before,’ said the girl, her eyes widening. ‘Ain’t you the Popish priest from down the Highway?’

‘Aye, I am, child,’ said Emanuel, suddenly curious. ‘Have you been here long?’

‘About a six month, sir,’ she said.

‘And before that?’

‘I were in service but I were caught thieving so I ran. I met a man what said he could look after me but after a while he brought me here and forced me to work.’

‘What of your parents, child? Do they not wonder where you are?’

‘Maybe they do. Maybe they don’t. I ain’t not heard of them this past twelve month. Don’t reckon they care none. Me father were a tenant farmer in Dorset and when the crops failed, he didn’t have no money for food or the rent. Leastways, not enough for all of us. I had to leave. That’s when I went into service.’

Emanuel looked uncomfortable. There was nothing he could say, no practical help he could offer. He plunged his hands into his coat pockets and looked towards the door.

‘You can go now,’ said the girl. ‘If that’s what you want.’

‘Aye, it would be for the best.’ Emanuel pulled open the door and looked out into the corridor. The two women were no longer by the front door. He paused and looked back at the girl. ‘Should you ever wish to talk, you know where to find me.’

Leaving the house by the front door, Emanuel checked for any sign that Bristow might still be in the vicinity but finding none, he turned west and was quickly swallowed up by the crowd.

Of Willing Annie, he thought no more.

Chapter 6

Erasmus Bristow swung in through the doors of Garraway's and made his way to the second floor. The encounter with Emanuel two days before still rankled. He'd been publicly humiliated. He tried to brush it aside. The Jew had got lucky. That was all. It would be different next time. Next time… Bristow stopped at the door of the private room and prodded it with the point of a crutch. The door swung open.

'Ah, there you are, Bristow,' said the Honourable James Grenville, late of 2nd Regiment of Foot. He leaned back in his chair, steepling his fingers under his chin. 'You're late.'

'Came as quick as I could, didn't I?' said Bristow, barely suppressing his contempt for his former officer. For the moment, the scrub was useful to him; was paying him to be here. He glanced at the remaining three men seated round the table. Two of them he didn't know while the third, older than the others, was something to do with Parliament, a thin specimen of a creature who wore a single eyeglass and had a superior air that irritated him. Bristow couldn't recall his name.

He returned to the two he'd not seen before. They were both in their early twenties, had the bearing of soldiers and looked as if they could handle themselves. Doubtless they were here to provide the muscle. Something he'd been able to do once. Bristow was conscious of a sour streak of envy coursing through his mind, regretting the passing of his own youth and agility. He sat down in one of the empty chairs and contemplated the stump which had once been his leg, his mind drifting back to the day he'd lost it.

The regiment had arrived in Ireland the month before. The men were still jumpy after Wexford, unsure of what to expect. The armed rebellion against the Crown had cost the lives of hundreds, perhaps even thousands. Now the regiment's orders were simple – find the croppy rebels and their weapons by all necessary means, and deal with them.

On this particular day it had been raining for hours, the narrow country lanes reduced to thick mud that clung to his boots, making every step more difficult than the one before. He'd been tired even before the patrol had set out. He'd argued against going. He and Collins had, after all, been specifically ordered to remain in camp – he'd never been told why - but his protest had been to no avail. Now he was drenched and cold as well. By mid-afternoon they had visited three villages and were now approaching the last one of the day. It seemed deserted. He wasn't surprised. Word of their coming would have spread from place to place and whatever weapons there might once have been would now lie buried in the hedgerows or in the surrounding fields.

It didn't stop the search. The army was nothing if not thorough. And when the initial sweep produced no more than a single pitchfork and an ancient firelock, Lt. Grenville had ordered the pitch-capping of several of the villagers. Bristow had enjoyed watching the tightly fitting cloth caps forced onto the heads of the terrified victims and heard their agonised shrieks as boiling tar seeped through the cotton weave onto their scalps. It had seemed a fitting punishment for their lies when, at last, the caps were torn off, bringing with them the hair and scalp of the victims. Yet, to his disappointment, the capping had produced nothing of interest.

They should have moved on after that. Only a fool could have failed to see the hatred in the eyes of the villagers, their desire for revenge. They should have left and returned to their barracks before the onset of night.

But they hadn't.

Lt. Grenville had found himself a woman and when, at last, he had finished with her, it had been too late. The patrol had no choice but to march through the darkness, along unfamiliar lanes, lined with high hedgerows, easy targets for the infuriated villagers.

They hadn't travelled more than a mile or two before it happened. Bristow didn't see the ghostly shapes that lay in wait for them amongst the rocks. It would have made little difference if he had. There were too many of them to count, their hideous screams splitting the air as they fell on the men in the column, the glint of their pikes cutting and thrusting at the bellies of the soldiers. There was no time to load, prime and fire their muskets. No time to defend themselves.

Amidst it all, Bristow saw a sudden movement close beside him, a shape blocking the light of the moon. Then the flash of steel arcing towards him. He swerved to avoid it but it wasn't enough. A savage, searing explosion of pain passed up from his right leg to a single point in his brain. He felt himself fading, the pain easing. From somewhere far away a bugle sounded. Help was coming.

The attackers melted into the night. He closed his eyes.

When he awoke, it was to find himself in a small, bare room smelling of hay. He was lying on what appeared to be a door resting on wooden ammunition boxes and surrounded by men he didn't know. Someone offered him a brandy. He gulped it down, his hands shaking uncontrollably. Time passed. Some more of the comforting, stupefying liquid was offered and accepted. He swallowed greedily – anything to ease the pain in his leg, to dull the senses. If only he could sleep, the pain would go. But that was impossible. He clamped his teeth and thought of the bastard who'd cut him. He'd find him and make him pay; cut him slowly, painfully so he'd know what he'd done. And then he'd kill him.

Suddenly he felt rough hands catching hold of him and holding him down while a disembowelled voice ordered him to open his mouth and bite down on an oaken wedge. That was the moment when he'd known they meant to sever his leg; that his life was about to change forever.

It was three weeks before he was discharged from the Dublin hospital to which he'd been taken after the operation. Days later he was told the King's shilling had stopped on the day of the ambush. As far as the army was concerned, he had, as of that moment, ceased to exist as a soldier.

Embittered and angry with a world that had rejected him, he'd come back to the only place he knew. For the first few weeks he'd survived by begging for whatever people had felt inclined to give him, his sense of injustice growing with each passing day. By the end of the third week he'd returned to the more profitable methods of earning a living that he'd learned as a boy: robbing the dandies and inebriated sailors who daily paraded up and down the Highway.

But the loss of his leg had meant a refinement of the methods he'd used all those years ago. In place of the speed which had allowed him and his fellow rogues to take what they wanted before escaping amongst the crowd, he had now to use a degree of cunning, combined with the huge strength of his arms, to achieve his ends. It wasn't difficult. A swift strike with one of his crutches across the shins would usually incapacitate the victim for long enough to enable Bristow to put a knife to his neck. After that, relieving the cully of his worldly possessions was simplicity itself.

Towards the end of 1799, Bristow's childhood partner in crime, one George Collins, left the army and returned to Shadwell. Within days, the two men were again engaged in the violent plunder which had, several years before, nearly cost them their lives dangling on the end of a judicial rope. As their reputation had spread, they attracted others who saw in Bristow an opportunity for depredation (and, therefore, profit) that was unlikely to be repeated elsewhere. Before long, his authority unchallenged, he controlled an area stretching from the Tower of London in the west to the hamlet of Mile End in the east.

Yet while this activity allowed him to obtain the food and drink necessary to life, there was another, stronger force that drove him on. The loss of his leg and the events that led to it had left him with a burning hatred of the Irish and, by extension, those who practised the Catholic faith. It was during this period of his life that he had begun to think again of the priest he and his mother used to visit years before. In the months that followed his return to Shadwell, his bitterness towards the man had grown and he'd begun to see in him the embodiment of all that he most despised about Popery.

But it was a chance meeting with Lieutenant the Hon. James Grenville, the officer under whom he'd once served, that finally set Bristow on the course that would again bring him into contact with the priest.

Bristow looked to his left. The toff in the eyeglass was still talking. He'd not heard a single word the prick had uttered and he'd no intention of starting now. His thoughts drifted back to Emanuel. He was still smarting from his encounter with the scrub earlier in the day. The physical pain in his groin had gone but the mental torment of having been bested was still there. Few men had ever got the better of him and he wasn't about to let a Popish Jew do so. He hadn't seen the scrub since… he thought for a moment… since shortly before his mother had died.

A smile flickered across his pallid, grime-ridden face at the memory of his mother, how she'd looked at him, the love she'd shown him and the stories she'd told him. He'd rarely paid any attention to the words, preferring instead just to hear the sound of her voice. Yet one story had caught his imagination. It had been about the Jew priest. Bristow stared at his hands and tried to recall her words. The detail was missing, hidden behind the fog of time. Small snatches came to him. A word here and there. Not enough to make any sense: *… came from Portugal… bishop… trouble…* He let it go. It might come to him in time. Then again, it might not. It probably wasn't important. Not after all these years.

'Are you listening to me, Bristow?'

Bristow looked up. The eyeglass was looking at him. The impatient look on the cully's face irritated him. He had no time for men of his kind. They knew nothing and were nothing. With an effort he curbed the temptation to tell him what he could do with his question. The man continued to glare at him for a second or two.

'I understand from my colleague here,' said the eyeglass, indicating Grenville, 'that you and he served in the army with a man named Smith.'

'Rob Smith? Aye, he were in the Second of Foot, right enough. What of it?' said Bristow, a look of faint surprise on his face.

'Find him,' said the eyeglass. 'He's been talking of matters that don't concern him. Find out the name of the man he was talking to. A Jew, I believe. Then deal with them both. The fewer people who know about us and our affairs, the better.'

Bristow nodded.

Chapter 7

Emanuel was alone in the chapel on Virginia Street, when he heard a footstep in the nave behind him.

'Mr Emanuel?'

He looked round. A young woman was standing at his shoulder.

'How...?' Her sudden appearance had startled him. The doors to the chapel were usually locked.

'How did I get in?' The woman smiled nervously and looked behind her. 'I told the man at the front door that I wished to see you, and he let me in. May we talk?'

'Of course,' said Emanuel, quickly regaining his composure.

'My name is Sara Payton, I...' She hesitated. 'I saw you by Limehouse Dock when they brought that dead body ashore.'

'Ah, yes, now I recall,' said Emanuel, remembering the woman he'd caught staring at him. He smiled. 'What can I do for you?'

She stood for a moment, glancing back towards the main door and chewing her bottom lip as though unsure of what to say. Suddenly, her face cleared. 'They say the man they found in the river were murdered by a Papist.'

'So I hear,' said Emanuel.

'Only, it couldn't have been him, sir.'

'I see,' said Emanuel. 'May I ask how you came by that conclusion?'

'I...' Sara shrugged.

'Come and sit down, child,' said Emanuel, patting the bench next to him. 'Then you can tell me what this is all about.'

'I'm employed as a lady's maid,' said Sara, perching herself awkwardly on the end of the bench. 'When my lady has no need of my services, I'm obliged to carry out other work in the house. A few days since, I was at work in the library of my master's house when I see him enter together with another gentleman. They didn't see me and before I could leave, they began talking. I couldn't hear everything but it seemed like they were planning something. I think it were connected with a debate in Parliament about the Papists. They said it had to be stopped at all cost.'

'Did they say how this was to be achieved?' said Emanuel.

'Not as I heard,' said Sara. 'But they spoke of a cully what was causing them some trouble. Seems like he'd been talking about things what he weren't supposed to talk about. My master asked if he'd been taken care of. The other gentleman said, "Funny you should ask. His body were found in Limehouse Dock a week ago."'

'He was saying the death wasn't an accident? That it was planned?'

'Yes. Leastways, that's what it sounded like to me,' said Sara.

'What's the name of your master?'

'Sir Peter Westlake.'

'And the gentleman he was speaking to? Do you know his name?'

'Master James,' said Sara, her face suddenly reddening. 'The Honourable James Grenville.'

Emanuel leaned forward on the bench, his elbows resting on his knees, a puzzled frown crossing his face. He'd heard of both men before. John Walter had mentioned them as being virulently anti-Catholic. But Collins had been a Protestant, not a Catholic. Why kill him? The stated reason was that he'd been talking too much. But about what? What was so important that merely speaking about it warranted the forfeiture of a man's life? Emanuel felt a shiver of fear as he thought of the implications of what he was being told.

'There's something else. I nearly forgot,' said Sara. She plunged a hand into the pocket of her dress and brought out a scrap of paper. 'After Sir Peter and Master James left the library, I found this on the floor. It were dropped by Master James as he were leaving. It don't make heads or tails to me but I thought you might know.'

Emanuel took the paper and smoothed it out. It appeared to be a map of sorts, with two or three streets or paths meeting in one corner. He was about to hand it back when he saw what appeared to be two crosses close to one of the streets and, in front of the crosses, some marks as if the tip of a pencil had been jabbed at the spot. There was nothing else. No writing and no indication of the area the map purported to show.

'Was this drawn during the conversation you overheard?' said Emanuel.

'Aye, it was. It were Master James what drew it but I couldn't hear what he were saying at the time.'

Emanuel stared at the paper in silence.

'May I keep this?' he asked.

She nodded.

He studied it for a moment longer. He had the feeling it could be important.

Chapter 8

It was late by the time Rob Smith had finished clearing away the cups and dishes, wiping down the table tops and sweeping the floor of the coffee room at Garraway's. He'd seen Bristow leave earlier in the evening with the rest of the group but hadn't spoken to him. There'd been no reason to. They'd never been friends. In fact, quite the reverse. Bristow was a part of Rob Smith's life he would've preferred to forget. As far as he was concerned the scrub had, through his behaviour in Ireland, brought shame not only on the British army, but on his country as well.

He took a final look round and headed for the kitchen. The rest of the staff had already gone for the night and, in a couple of minutes he, too, would be on his way. He removed his apron and walked down the stairs to the ground floor where he locked all but one of the street doors and extinguished the last of the candles. Emerging into the darkness of Exchange Alley, he shivered as a sudden chill passed down his spine. It was over in a moment. He stopped and waited for his heart beat to slow, wondering why he felt suddenly nervous. It unsettled him. He considered going back for a lamp but decided against it. He was being foolish. Cornhill was only a few yards away. He could see people crossing and re-crossing the mouth of the junction, going about their business. There was no need for a light. No reason to be fearful.

Yet something had triggered his unease. He tried to shake it off. Then he turned and locked the final door.

A faint noise. So slight he might almost have imagined it. It had come from further down the passageway, a scraping sound as though something had been dragged across the surface of the alley. He searched the gloom. Could see nothing, the silence mocking him. Something brushed against his leg. A shriek rose in his throat and died. He watched the cat slink away and disappear.

Smith shook his head, annoyed with himself. He was a former soldier. He thought he could handle most situations. There'd been a time in his life when little would have frightened him. Yet still he hesitated, afraid of the unknown, his breathing quickening, coming in short, shallow gulps. A minute passed by. Then two. Nothing happened. What he'd heard had probably been an animal, perhaps a stray dog, scavenging for food. It was hardly unusual. He clenched his fists and forced himself to calm down. He'd worked at the coffee house for over a year. Had been there ever since he'd been discharged from the military. Not once had he felt the least concern about the late night journey home. Slowly, he stepped away from the coffee house door.

'Hello, Smithy. I've been waiting for you.' The voice was harsh, almost guttural.

'Who's that?' Rob Smith spun round, peering into the night.

There was no answer.

A shape appeared. A man, certainly. But too indistinct to be recognised. He came closer, making an odd tapping noise as he approached, his gait seemingly awkward, almost unbalanced.

'Who are you, sir?' said Smith. 'Do I know you?'

Again, no answer.

Every instinct told him to go, to be away from here, to have nothing to do with the advancing stranger. From somewhere behind him he heard a sudden babble of voices; people passing along Cornhill. Smith's hopes soared. Nothing bad could happen to him now. Not when there were people about. It stood to reason, didn't it?

As quickly as it had come, the voices faded and were gone. He looked back at the stranger. He was close, too close, his face clearly visible.

'Why, it's you—' He felt a sharp discomfort in his stomach. He gasped, put out a hand to steady himself. But there was nothing to hold onto. He bent forward, trying to ease the pain, his other hand pressing against his stomach. It felt warm and sticky. The pain was unbearable. He looked for the man. The image was blurred as if the cully had stepped back. He seemed to be smiling.

Rob Smith was finding it hard to think. He felt dizzy. Then he fell, his head striking the cobblestones.

Chapter 9

The idea of a meeting with the man had never appealed to Emanuel. Nothing he'd heard about the Revd John Rippon had ever suggested the existence of an open mind, particularly where the subject of religion was concerned. The Protestant Association, the organisation he led, was nothing if not antagonistic towards the Catholic faith and the idea that he might be able to help seemed far-fetched.

A steady wind blew in from the south-west, carrying with it the familiar cacophony of sounds of the port as Emanuel crossed the Thames to the south bank. Here he turned left and dropped down the steep slope of Tooley Street, lined with warehouses and shops and taverns, each one catering for the needs of their maritime customers. Pushing his way through the crowd, he reached the comparative quiet of Carter Lane and saw, ahead of him, the Anabaptist Meeting House to which he'd been heading.

'Mr Lazaro? Welcome to you, sir,' said the Revd Rippon a minute or so later as he opened the door to his visitor. He was a slightly built, round-faced man of about Emanuel's age, with piercing grey eyes below heavy black eyebrows. 'I've been meaning to call on you for some considerable time but something always gets in the way. Never mind, never mind, you're here now. Do come in.'

Emanuel followed him across a stone-flagged hallway to a small, neat parlour overlooking an apple orchard at the back of the house.

'Sit you down, sir,' said Rippon, waving towards a comfortable-looking leather armchair. 'May I offer you some refreshment? Tea, perhaps? Good. That's settled then.'

Tea ordered, Rippon sat down and pointed to a small table that stood beside him and on which lay some manuscripts. 'Are you familiar with the works of Isaac Watts, Mr Emanuel? He is a great favourite of mine.'

'I am aware of your interest, sir,' said Emanuel. 'But I regret my knowledge of him and of his hymns is, to say the least, scant.'

'Pity,' said Rippon, his face brightening as a tray of tea and some cakes was brought in and set down on the table. 'But I make no doubt the works of Isaac Watts are not what you came to see me about. How is it that I may be of service?'

'May I, sir, speak freely?' said Emanuel.

'Naturally,' said Rippon inclining his head.

'A while ago,' said Emanuel, 'there was a fight outside my chapel in Virginia Street. Several men set upon and beat a man. Two or three weeks later, one of those involved in the fight was found floating in the Thames in circumstances that suggested he'd been murdered. The finger of blame was pointed at the victim of the original assault and, for a while, it seemed he might, indeed, have been responsible. But I've since been given information that points in another direction…'

Emanuel stopped as the housekeeper came in with a jug of hot water and some more cakes.

'Pray continue, sir,' said Rippon, after the servant had left.

'You are, of course, aware of the widespread opposition to Catholicism in this country and the occasional disturbances that result. It seems, however, there may be a secretive organisation whose ultimate aim is the total and violent destruction, of the Catholic faith in this country. I—'

'I trust you are not, sir, suggesting the involvement of the Protestant Association in murder?' interrupted Rippon, his face reddening.

'I don't, sir, for one moment, suspect the association,' said Emanuel. 'I regret it extremely if I gave that impression. Nevertheless, it is possible that some former members of the association may have taken a more extreme position than the association itself might tolerate. Were you to know of the existence of such men, I'd be grateful for anything you might wish to tell me about them.'

'Perhaps I was too hasty,' said Rippon, his anger fading. 'D'you have anybody in mind?'

'There are several. The first to come to mind are George Collins and his friend Erasmus Bristow. Collins is now dead. His was the body found floating in the Thames.'

'Murdered by the fellow with whom he'd fought weeks earlier?'

'That is certainly the view of the mob,' said Emanuel. 'I simply don't know if it's true or not. The injuries he sustained during the original assault were such that I doubt he would have had the strength to do what is alleged.'

'And the second man? Is he still alive?' said Rippon.

'Bristow? Yes, he is.'

'How, sir, did you come by these names?' asked Rippon.

'I've known both men since they were boys. Both served in the army and both were sent to Ireland during the rebellion. I've reason to think that their minds might have been turned by what they saw over there. Both were, however, known for their dislike of Catholics even before their deployment to Ireland.'

Rippon leaned across to where the tea things had been placed. Pouring two cups, he handed one to Emanuel, a thoughtful look in his eyes.

'Help yourself to milk and sugar,' he said, settling back in his chair and stirring his tea. 'I don't know either of the two men personally but their names are familiar to me. Their reputation for violence goes before them and is said to go well beyond what might be considered reasonable and proportionate. Indeed, there is some talk Bristow was seen by the Watch in the vicinity of a murder outside Garraway's. It did not, I'm sorry to say, surprise me.'

Emanuel's heart missed a beat. 'Do you know the name of his victim?'

'No, I was never told but I gather the poor fellow was a waiter at the coffee house. Good lord, sir, you look as though you've seen a ghost. Are you quite well?'

'Yes, yes. I'm quite well, thank you,' said Emanuel, pausing to gather his thoughts. 'Tell me, what do you know of a man named Sir Peter Westlake?'

'Sir Peter?' Rippon's head jerked up and his eyes fixed on Emanuel with an unblinking stare. 'Why do you ask?'

'Something I was told.'

'I know him moderately well,' said Rippon, putting down his teacup. 'He is, as you probably know, a member of parliament and, as such, exerts a good deal of influence on a range of issues, including any future reform of the law in respect of the Papist – I beg pardon, sir, I meant to say the Roman Catholic Church. I assume you mention his name because you suspect him of being involved in some way with this covert organisation so I shall attempt to answer you with that in mind. Sir Peter was, for a time, a member of the Protestant Association but his views, as they were expressed, had no place within the group and he was asked to leave. That was towards the end of last year and I've not seen him since.'

'Have you known him long?'

'About ten years. Why?' said Rippon.

'I'm curious to know whether his views have altered in the time you've known him.'

Again, the searching stare. 'He's changed in the last two years.'

'In what way?' said Emanuel.

'I'm sure you know where I stand in relation to your faith, Mr Lazaro. It's no secret that I'm strongly opposed to Popery. To put it bluntly, I believe the loyalty of Catholics to the King and the country are suspect and it is for this reason, amongst others, that we oppose any relaxation in the laws governing those who look to Rome. But, as you may have gathered, neither I nor my colleagues within the Protestant Association hold with violence. Sir Peter appears to have taken a different view. And it's comparatively recent.'

'Anything specific?' asked Emanuel, a little shaken by the vehemence with which Rippon had spoken.

For a moment or two Rippon stared out of the window to the orchard beyond, his lips moving as though in silent conversation with himself. At last he looked across at his guest. 'I want to be frank with you but much of what I've been told is hearsay. That is to say, it was said to me by persons who had themselves no personal knowledge of the facts and I've been unable to verify its truthfulness for myself. Nevertheless, I think it is right that I should give you the opportunity to seek out the facts such as they are.'

'I should, sir, be grateful for any help you feel able to give me.'

'Well then,' said Rippon, taking a sip of tea before returning the cup to its saucer, 'I told you Sir Peter's views have changed in the last two years, and so they have. At first I took little notice of his outbursts and assumed that they were no more than those of a politician unable to get his own way. But it soon became apparent that his attitude towards Popery was almost entirely based on self-interest.'

'You are, I assume, referring to his estate in Ireland?' said Emanuel.

'I see you know about that,' said Rippon. 'What you may not know is that the estate was attacked in the summer of '98 and the local magistrate, a friend of Sir Peter's, was murdered by what was assumed to be the Papist rebels. Sir Peter now regards all attempts to bring Ireland within the United Kingdom and the resultant abolition of the Irish parliament as madness, a reward for the violence of 1798. In his view, it's a betrayal of the very people who have done most to help that benighted isle and is a poor return for what he regards as his loyal service to the Crown.'

'How did all this manifest itself?' said Emanuel.

'I'm told he's become a bitter man,' said Rippon, looking suddenly wary. 'Some of what he is reported to have said to those about him could be viewed as treason.'

'Like what, pray?' said Emanuel.

'I'd rather not say.'

'Is it possible he might be planning some atrocity?'

'I've no direct knowledge of the facts, sir. It would be improper for me to say anything further,' said Rippon.

'Yet what he is reported to have said could possibly be regarded as treasonable,' said Emanuel.

'Yes, it's possible,' said Rippon. 'But it wouldn't be him who wielded the axe. You have to remember, my dear Emanuel – may I call you Emanuel? – you have to remember that Sir Peter considers himself a gentleman but one who shares many traits with Machiavelli. He will do what is necessary to achieve his ends, but always from the shadows.'

'There is, sir, one other name I'd like to put to you,' said Emanuel. 'Do you know of a gentleman named the Honourable James Grenville?'

'Grenville, you say? No, I've not heard the name.
'

#

Walking back over the Thames in the gathering gloom of early evening, Emanuel knew he'd barely begun to scratch the surface of what was occurring. And while he now knew a little more about the events that had shaped the attitude of Sir Peter towards the Church, it wasn't enough to link him to any plot.

He thought for a moment, recalling the conversation said to have taken place between Sir

Peter and the Hon. James Grenville in the library of Sir Peter's home. The comments had originally seemed to him no more than the frustrated thoughts of a politician unable to influence policy. Even the scrap of paper given to him by Sara had seemed of doubtful importance. Yet the meeting with the Revd Rippon had exposed a little more of the character of the MP for East Looe and begun to raise the possibility of his involvement in an act of subversion.

But he needed more information. And getting it meant seeing Sara again.

Which meant going to the home of Sir Peter Westlake.

Chapter 10

Emanuel woke the next morning to the sound of rain beating against the window of his room. He lay still for a while, his hands laced behind his head, his thoughts running over his plans to visit the home of Sir Peter. He wasn't relishing the prospect. The idea, which had seemed so self-evidently sensible yesterday evening, was now losing much of its appeal, the risk of detection a little too high. It was not any fear of the physical consequences of being caught that was exercising his mind. Of that, he cared little. It wouldn't be the first nor, he supposed, the last fight he'd be involved in, but if he could avoid the unseemly spectacle, it would be better for all concerned – particularly the reputation of the Church. He grinned at the thought of the bishop's reaction to the news of one of his priests scrapping on the streets of London. The grin faded. If Collins – and now Rob Smith, the waiter at Garraway's – had been killed to prevent details of the supposed plot becoming known, it was likely the same fate would be visited on anyone else making enquiries about its existence – including himself.

Emanuel pushed his concerns to the back of his mind. He knew the answers to his own questions; knew there was a chance he might lose his life. Of course, he could choose to do nothing. No one would blame him. And if the truth be told, few would care one way or the other. But that wasn't the point. The point was that *he* knew. There was credible evidence that trouble was brewing and that if it wasn't stopped, people would die. He could no more stand back and let that happen than deny his eternal soul. Frightening though the prospect of detection might be, he had little alternative but to go through with what he had planned.

A little over an hour later, he was standing outside the home of Sir Peter Westlake at 25 Cheapside, in the City of London. It was a large, double-fronted, three-storey building which, like its neighbours, was faced in white Portland stone dotted with high, sash windows glinting in the morning sunlight. Emanuel glanced up and down the broad avenue. A carriage drawn by a couple of bays stood outside a neighbouring property, apparently awaiting its owner, its driver asleep. Apart from that, few people could be seen and those that there were took little notice of the solitary, olive-skinned man standing on the south side of the street, seemingly deep in thought.

Getting here had been the easy part. What he now needed was a plan on how to engineer a meeting with Sara that didn't involve compromising either his own or Sara's safety. Certainly, knocking on the front door of the house wasn't the answer. He searched for another, less public, point of entry.

About fifty yards to his left he saw a woman emerge through a gap in the building line. Waiting until she'd gone, he walked to the spot. A path led between the houses before appearing to fork left and right. Checking that he was alone, Emanuel ducked between the houses and had soon reached the point where the path branched. Here he turned right and was soon at the rear of Number 25 facing a locked gate. He knocked and waited. There was no reply. He felt oddly relieved. He'd tried. It wasn't his fault no one was in. He started to walk away when, suddenly, the gate was wrenched open and a stout woman of about thirty looked him up and down.

'Yes?' she demanded.

'I wish to speak to Miss Sara Payton, if she is at leisure,' said Emanuel.

'Leisure? That's a good one,' she snorted. 'Who shall I say wants to speak to her?'

'My name is Emanuel. I'll not detain her long,' he said, beginning to wish he'd taken greater note of his reservations concerning this adventure. Too late, it occurred to him his visit was likely to cause Sara some embarrassment, if not censure. The other servants were bound to talk and it would not take long for word to each Sir Peter's ear. 'But perhaps I may call some other time.'

He turned away. He would have to think of another way of getting the information he wanted.

'Mr Emanuel?'

Emanuel stopped and looked back. Sara was standing in the gateway, a quizzical frown on her face. 'You wished to see me?'

'If that's possible, Miss Sara.'

She gave a hurried glance at the departing figure of her fellow servant. 'My lady leaves in an hour. I cannot talk until then.'

'May I wait?'

'Not here. Wait for me outside the Jamaica Coffee House. It's in St Michael's Alley. You can't miss it,' she said, closing the gate.

Emanuel listened to her departing footsteps, unsure whether he'd made the right decision in coming here. A movement caught his eye. He looked up to see a face at an upper window.

And it was watching him.

#

Emanuel saw her hurrying along the narrow alley towards him, a shawl over her head, her hands clutching it to her throat. She seemed distracted, her eyes searching from side to side as if wary of some unknown danger, a threat of which he knew nothing. Once or twice she stopped, looked behind her and then hurried on. She had almost reached him when he called her.

'Thank you for coming,' he said, taking her elbow and guiding her into the adjacent coffee house. Finding an empty table away from the front door, they sat down. 'Would you care for a coffee?'

She didn't answer, her eyes scanning the room. After a moment she looked back at him. 'I were seen leaving the house.'

'Who by?' said Emanuel, recalling the face at the window. 'Are you not permitted to leave?'

'No, not without the butler says you can,' she said. 'I must go afore I get into trouble. The servant what saw me doesn't like me.'

'And you think he'll try and make trouble?' said Emanuel.

'It's possible,' she said. Then she looked up, a question in her eye. 'What is it you wanted to speak to me about?'

'When you came to see me some time ago you spoke about a conversation you'd overheard between Sir Peter and another gentleman, the Honourable James Grenville. Do you recall what you told me?'

'Yes, of course,' she said.

'Can you tell me if your master has since met with Mr Grenville?'

'Aye, they see one another almost every week,' she whispered, glancing at the next table where two men were deep in conversation. Satisfied she'd not be overheard, she said, 'He and Sir Peter often take the coach and go out together. Sir Peter don't tell us where they go.'

'Does anyone go with them?'

'Only the coachman. Once or twice I've seen a third man with them. Looked to be a proper bully-boy. It frightened me just to see him.'

'Do you know his name?'

'No, but there ain't no mistaking him. He's a cripple.'

'You mean he limps?' said Emanuel.

'More than that,' said Sara. 'He's only one leg.'

'Can you describe him?' said Emanuel, looking up sharply. 'What he looks like, the colour of his hair, what he wears. That sort of thing.'

'No more than thirty, I reckon. Heavily built. Broken nose. Got no hair except black stubble on his face. But that don't begin to describe him. It's his eyes I remember most. They was evil. Black as pitch. Don't reckon he's got a soul.'

'Was he the only one?'

She paused while the waiter put down two dishes of black coffee. When he'd gone, she said, 'There was someone else, but he's dead now.'

'Would that be George Collins?' said Emanuel.

Sara stared at him. 'How did you know?'

'You've mentioned him before, when you came to the chapel. You told me your master had known about his death. It wasn't difficult to guess who you were talking about.' Emanuel sipped his coffee. 'Has your master spoken again about the subject you overheard?

Anything that might indicate what the drawing you found might relate to?'

'No, nothing about the drawing. But sometimes I hear him talking to her ladyship about Mr Pitt. He says he don't agree with the Minister and there'll be trouble if the Papists are given what they want. He said he were going to do something about it.'

'He said all this in front of the servants?'

'He doesn't see us. It's as if we're invisible.'

'Did he say what he intended to do?'

'No. Leastways not that I heard.'

'What of Mr Grenville? What sort of a man is he?'

Sara frowned and looked down at her coffee, as if wrestling with some inner emotion she had no wish to share. 'He's no gentlemen, is Master James. He…' She stopped and glanced at Emanuel. 'It ain't important.'

'But you know him. Is there anything you can tell me about him?'

'I see him give Collins a flogging. The other servants reckoned it were because he was suspected of talking about something what were meant to be secret. I thought he were going to kill him.'

'Mr Grenville did that? When was this?'

'About four, maybe five weeks before Collins's body was found.'

'Do you know what Collins had been talking about that got him flogged?'

'No, only that it was supposed to be about what Master James and Sir Peter were planning.'

'But not the details?'

'No. Master James were carrying on something fearful. The whole house could hear him. He—' She stopped, her face paling. She was staring at the door of the coffee house. 'He's here. I must go.'

Emanuel turned to look. A tall, well-built man in his early twenties stood in the open doorway, a silver-topped cane in one hand, his head turning from side to side appearing to look for someone. There was no doubting the Hon. James Grenville.

Sara scurried in the direction of a side door, her face turned away from Grenville, her passing mostly hidden by the several dozen folk drinking, talking, moving between the tables. She had almost reached the door when Emanuel saw the man's eyes flicker as though registering Sara's presence. Then he went after her.

Emanuel threw some coins onto the table and followed. Opening the side door, he found himself in a narrow, rubbish-strewn footpath bordered on either side by high stone walls. Of Sara there was no sign. Grenville was standing at the far end, at the corner of St Michael's Alley, his head turning to left and right.

'He's lost her,' muttered Emanuel. Yet even as he said the words, it seemed impossible that Sara could have covered the thirty or so yards to St Michael's Alley without being seen by her pursuer. He glanced at the walls bordering the path. The one on the right was the side of the coffee house and offered nothing in the way of a hiding place. On the opposite side, the stone was overgrown with laurel bushes whose roots had found their way into the mortar. Here and there, partially hidden by the vegetation, a door had been set into the stonework. Before he could investigate further, he saw Grenville coming back along the path. Quickly darting behind a nearby shrub, he waited for the aristocrat to go back into the coffee house. Then he turned his attention to the overgrown wall and the partially hidden doors he'd seen.

There were four. He walked the length of the path, stopping at each one and trying the rusting handles. None would open for him and he doubted they would have done so for Sara. At the corner of St Michael's Alley he stopped and looked back. Perhaps he was wrong. Perhaps Sara *had* made it to the junction, although it seemed highly unlikely. He retraced his steps and again tried each door. The result was the same. He thought of returning to Sir Peter's house in case she'd gone straight there but immediately abandoned the idea. Nothing good would come of it.

Reluctantly, he walked back to the side door of the coffee house. He blamed himself for what had happened. It was he who'd suggested a meeting, he who'd exposed Sara to the risk of discovery. There had been little justification for his actions. Certainly he'd heard rumours of impending trouble for the Church but such stories had been around for years. There was nothing new in the virulent hatred felt by many towards Catholics. It seemed to increase with each successive Act of Parliament that sought to give them greater freedoms. Each one had sparked fresh scenes of outrage by a people convinced of their disloyalty.

A sudden noise, like that of a stone falling to the ground, stopped him. He looked round, his eyes searching the empty lane. Lying in the path, close to the wall, he saw the freshly broken stem of a laurel bush. He walked over and ran his hand over the foliage from which the fragment appeared to have come. It parted to reveal a collapsed section of the wall.

Checking to see he was alone, he eased his way through the gap and found himself in a small yard. To the right was the shell of an abandoned house. To his left, he could see another building, equally decrepit, its roof long since collapsed, its door standing ajar. Emanuel walked towards it, stopped and listened. From inside came the sound of heavy breathing as of someone out of breath.

'Sara?' he called. 'It's me, Father Emanuel.'

There was no reply.

Emanuel stepped through the doorway. The building was not large. Perhaps twenty feet square, its floor littered with rubble and decaying lengths of timber.

'Sara?' he called again.

Again, no reply.

He was about to leave when, 'Are you alone, Mr Emanuel?'

He turned to see Sara's frightened face peering out from behind what remained of the back wall of the shed-like structure.

'Yes, child, I'm alone. Are you quite well?'

'I couldn't be sure it was you, Mr Emanuel,' said Sara, stepping over the jumble of bricks towards him. 'I was afraid Master James was with you. I thought perhaps he might have forced you to come. He'd know I would've stayed hidden, else.'

'He knows you are employed by Sir Peter, does he not?'

'Aye, he does. I make no doubt he'll tell Sir Peter what he saw.'

'What of it?' said Emanuel. 'He didn't see us together. If you are asked, tell Sir Peter you'd gone to fetch some sugar for her ladyship's tea. Who is there to contradict you? Come now. It's high time you were returning to your master's house.'

They parted company at the corner of St Michael's Alley and Emanuel watched her hurry away, an anxious look in her eyes, and with good reason. There seemed little doubt Grenville would try and make difficulties for her. He wondered what form it would take.

Chapter 11

On the south side of the Thames, opposite the entrance to the White Hart Inn in Borough High Street, Henry Teeling stood watching the world go by. The midday coach from Dover had come and gone. So had the late-running coach bound for Tunbridge Wells. The inn wasn't particularly busy. Perhaps a dozen customers in the last quarter of an hour. He thought of joining them for a quick drink but discarded the idea. He might be on the south bank but he was still too close to Limehouse for comfort. He could still be recognised. He looked up the main thoroughfare towards London Bridge. Several hours had passed since he'd sent a message asking for Mr Emanuel to meet him here. He was beginning to think the message hadn't been delivered. He'd give him another half-hour. His thoughts drifted.

He missed the friends he'd made while working the ships in the port. He'd been one of the lucky ones. Some men never worked. He'd not known why. A few of the lads reckoned it was because they'd fallen out of favour with the gangmaster or the landlord of the tavern where the workers were chosen. In the end it made little difference. If he got paid – and that wasn't always the case – the landlord took it all to pay for the drink he'd already consumed. He'd soon learned the only way to avoid starving was to take advantage of his perquisites, the coal sweepings that he was able to sell. That and the odd sack of coal that accidentally fell over the side of the ship. Everyone did it. Those that worked.

Teeling gulped a mouthful of air. His breathing had become more difficult over the last few months. There were times when he struggled to fill his lungs. He'd noticed, too, the black phlegm that came up when he coughed. It didn't surprise him. There was always a thick cloud of coal dust hanging over the ships he worked on and it was impossible to avoid breathing it in. All the lads suffered to a greater or lesser extent. He shrugged. It was nothing a mug of beer couldn't solve.

There was still no sign of Mr Emanuel. It seemed odd referring to a priest as Mister instead of his traditional title of Father. It wouldn't happen in Ireland. But he'd gradually got used to it since his arrival in London nearly six months ago. He'd also learned to keep his religious beliefs to himself. Admitting he was a Catholic was not the most sensible thing to do. That said, most people hearing his accent immediately assumed he was a Papist.

That was the other thing he missed about living on the other side of the Thames. Many of the folk in Limehouse and the areas surrounding it had been his fellow countrymen who thought and believed as he did. He'd felt comparatively safe from the gangs of bully-boys who would occasionally come down from Mile End and Stepney and Whitechapel, looking for trouble. There had, of course, been the usual Saturday night fights. But they had been largely confined to his fellow countrymen and no one had minded giving – or receiving – a bloody nose in those circumstances. He smiled inwardly. Life had been almost tolerable then.

He suddenly bent forward and clutched at his thigh as a bolt of pain passed up through his body. He gritted his teeth and waited for it to subside. It brought back the memories of the day his wife had been killed. Of the three men who'd come to his house that morning he'd only seen Collins up close, although he'd always been confident he'd recognise the others if he ever saw them again.

In recent weeks he'd learned of the names of two men who'd been in the army with Collins. He'd initially dismissed the information as of no interest. Thousands of men had served in Ireland, many of them with Collins. But as time had gone on, the names Bristow and Grenville had begun to crop up with increasing frequency and he'd started to look with greater care at what was known about them.

There had followed several months of silence during which he'd made little progress with his enquiries. Unable to put faces to the names, Teeling suspected that fear on the part of his informants was at the root of their reluctance to speak. Pure chance had finally led him to the coffee house at Garraway's where Rob Smith had been pointed out to him, and through him, Erasmus Bristow.

'There you are, Henry.' Teeling jumped at the sound of his name. He'd not heard the priest approaching. 'I thought to find you in the tavern. Then I saw you standing over here and… well, anygate, here I am.'

'Will you be wanting a drink, Mr Emanuel?'

'No, I seldom drink. But thank you. You wanted to see me about something?'

'Aye, so I did. Will you walk with me, Father?'

They headed south along a crowded High Street, the air filled with the stench of sheep and cattle being driven to one of the nearby slaughterhouses, their frightened bleats all the louder as their herdsmen rained down blows on their backs. The town hall came and went, followed by the dark mass of the Marshalsea, its high and forbidding walls seeming to suck the light from the sky. Soon they had reached a fork in the road and branched left into Great Dover Street.

'What's on your mind, Henry?' asked Emanuel when, at last, they'd left behind the hurry and noise of the Borough.

'It's about Collins, Father.'

'What about him?'

'They say he were turned off to stop him talking.'

'So I've been told,' said Emanuel. 'D'you know what he said that got him killed?'

'As I hears it, he were drunk and shouting about a killing what was planned.'

'Did he say who was to be killed?'

'No. He said when it were all done, everyone would know about it and there'd be fighting and killing such as we ain't seen before in England.'

'When was this going to happen?' said Emanuel.

'Don't know that, Father, but…'

'But what?' said Emanuel.

'I know who turned Collins off.'

Emanuel gaped and waited for Teeling to continue.

'There's a girl what I see from time to time…' Teeling broke off, blushing. 'You know how it is, Father. A man needs his comfort.'

'Yes, yes. Go on,' said Emanuel, churning the air with his hand.

'I saw her yesterday and after… you know… after we finished, we was talking and she told me she were Bristow's girl. She works for him. Like he's her pimp.'

'What, pray, has this to do with Collins?' said Emanuel, a trace of impatience in his voice.

'She told me it were Bristow what turned him off.'

'Bristow? How would she know that?' said Emanuel.

'She said on the night it happened, Bristow went to her. She could see something were wrong. He were agitated and when she asked him what it was, he said it weren't none of her business. But later she heard him talking in his sleep. He said he were told to stop Collins from talking. But Collins refused to listen and there was an argument. He said he never meant to kill Collins. It were an accident.'

'Do you believe her? Your lady friend?'

'I don't know, Father. All I know is what I've been told. Killing don't seem to mean much to Bristow. And from what I hear he and Collins didn't always see eye to eye.'

'I knew them both,' said Emanuel, gazing across the open fields that had, by now, replaced the crowded terraces of Southwark. There was a dusting of green on the brown soil as the new crop thrust its way into the early spring sunshine. 'Yes, they had arguments and scrapped from time to time. But I never thought it would come to this.'

He broke off and watched a coach clatter past, dust rising in its wake. When it had gone, he said, 'Will your lady friend talk to me?'

'I'll ask her,' said Teeling. It was a question he hadn't been expecting. He wasn't sure he wanted the priest talking to her. 'I don't see her that often on account of Bristow might catch us.'

'See what you can do,' said Emanuel. 'It's important.'

#

There had been no obvious reason for the meeting. Certainly nothing that couldn't have waited for a day or so. Yet Teeling's request had given the impression of an urgency which hadn't been borne out by what he'd had to say. He let the matter go. Collins had been dead for several weeks and, as far as Emanuel had been able to discover, his death had had little influence on the pace of events. Attacks on the Church continued but had not significantly increased in the wake of his death. Even the belief in the minds of some that Teeling, a Catholic, had murdered Collins, a Protestant, had failed to ignite the fury of a religious conflict that Emanuel had feared.

Nevertheless, something was afoot. There was growing evidence of the existence of the clandestine group about which John Walter, his journalist friend, had warned him. If nothing else, his conversation with Teeling about the reason for Collins's death suggested a level of determination and ruthlessness on the part of those concerned with his murder that deserved his close attention. What form the supposed plot would take he couldn't pretend to know – unless it was to be a repeat of the riots led by Lord Gordon twenty years ago. That seemed doubtful. Those riots had achieved nothing except the loss of a great many lives. Another riot was unlikely to produce what the earlier one had failed to do. Besides, the government had its eye fixed firmly on Catholic emancipation as a means of bringing Ireland into the United Kingdom and was unlikely to allow a riot to dissuade it from its course. Still, the threat of large scale rioting couldn't altogether be dismissed.

The more Emanuel considered the matter, the more urgent it seemed for him to confirm the identities of those involved and what they planned. Only after that could he begin to think about his next move. Of the four names he'd been given, three – Collins, Bristow and the Hon. James Grenville – had been in the army and been responsible for acts of savagery in the course of their supposed duties in Ireland. Whether their experiences over there had been enough to turn their minds, he couldn't say. He'd known Collins and Bristow for most of their lives. They were, and had always been, violent. What they had wanted they had usually taken by force. Yet the acts for which they were said to have been responsible in the summer of 1798 had been extreme even by their own standards of behaviour. He knew he had to properly understand the likely influence of events on the minds of the people who'd been exposed to the violence, particularly in Wexford.

Crossing the river Emanuel turned right onto Lower Thames Street and passed down through the pushing, shouting, cursing multitude that was always present in the narrow street behind the Legal Quays. He thought of his meeting with the late Rob Smith, the waiter at Garraway's who'd suggested he speak to his old commanding officer, one Colonel Ramsay. Emanuel recalled his parting words: … *the only man who'll tell you the truth.*

It was the next job on his list.

Chapter 12

Emanuel's contact at the War Office had sounded doubtful. What, he had wanted to know, did a Roman Catholic priest want with a letter of introduction to a senior officer in the British army? It had required all Emanuel's considerable powers of persuasion to convince the man – a clandestine Catholic – to provide him with the desired note in sufficiently vague terms as would allow him an audience with the colonel without divulging his own status as a priest.

Emanuel smiled at the memory and touched the crisp sheet of paper in his pocket as though to satisfy himself that he had, against all expectations, obtained the precious document. He was presently sitting in the stern sheets of a rowing skiff doing his best to look interested in the non-stop flow of unintelligible clicks and hisses coming from the lips of the ancient waterman. If the fellow knew he wasn't being listened to, he gave no sign of it as he propelled his small craft down through the Lower Pool and into Limehouse Reach.

An hour and a half later, a very damp and very stiff Emanuel climbed ashore at Ship Stairs close to the main street in Woolwich, paid his fare and walked the two hundred or so yards to the military barracks in the town. Ten minutes after that he had persuaded a doubtful clerk sergeant to announce his presence to his commanding officer.

'I've been told you want to talk to me about something concerning the regiment, although, I confess, I'm not quite sure what.' Colonel George

Ramsay, Earl of Dalhousie, commanding officer of the 2nd Regiment of Foot, waved the letter of introduction his clerk had given him. 'But how may I help?'

'I gather,' said Emanuel, choosing his words with care, 'that amongst the many other places in which you and the regiment have served, you spent some time in Ireland.'

Dalhousie stiffened. 'May I, sir, ask why you are interested?'

'I understand your men suffered from the conditions and attitudes that they found over there. I see the consequences on the streets of Shadwell and Limehouse where I reside. I like to think I might be able to assist in some way.'

Dalhousie nodded slowly and once more read the letter he still held. When he looked up, he said, 'It's been some time since I thought about Ireland and what we were asked to do over there. Fact is, it was a sorry business from beginning to end. No trust on either side. There was many a time when I'd have liked to bang heads together but, of course, that wasn't possible; not with the personalities involved. Some appalling things happened that it will take years to forget.'

'I hear some of the men were deeply affected by what they had to do,' said Emanuel.

'Indeed they were,' said Dalhousie, picking up a small stone ornament from his desk and turning it over and over between his fingers. 'Quite a few have been unable to put the past behind them. The discipline in the lower ranks of the local militias was, I regret to say, frequently non-existent. This was particularly true after a major engagement. The men were often maddened by what they'd seen and would seek out men, women and children on whom to wreak their vengeance. Many hundreds of innocent people were butchered where they stood. They…'

Colonel Ramsay shrugged, a look of helpless resignation in his eyes.

'What happened to these men, the soldiers and militiamen involved?' said Emanuel, after a moment's silence.

'If you mean was any action taken against them, the answer is no, at least not often enough.'

'And after the regiment's return to England?'

'No. A lot of them left the army for medical reasons of one kind or another. Injuries mostly. I've not kept in touch with them. There were so many.' Dalhousie gave a small wave of his hand. 'Of those I do know about, several have formed an abiding and, perhaps irrational hatred of the Irish people. They appear to be wholly unable to put the events they witnessed out of their minds. If something is not done, I fear it will lead to more violence.'

'What do you mean?'

'There are many who served in the army who came to regard Catholics as the source of all our troubles. One expects a certain amount of that kind of reaction after any deployment, but this time it's been far worse than I've seen elsewhere; more deep-seated.'

'From men still in the army?'

'Army discipline tends to keep a lid on the worst excesses of the men's behaviour,' said Dalhousie, a small smile turning up the corners of his mouth. 'The main problem tends to be with men who've been discharged and over whom we have no control.'

'Is it just the men?' Emanuel asked. 'The other ranks?'

'No,' said Dalhousie, shaking his head. 'I'm sorry to say the problem exists amongst all ranks with some of the most extreme views coming from fellows who should know better. If you challenge them, they usually point to Lake—'

'Lake?'

'General Lake,' said Dalhousie. 'Not the best… Forgive me, Mr Emanuel. I was letting his tongue run away with itself.'

Again, he looked at the letter in his hand, chewing his bottom lip as though wrestling with his thoughts. Then he swung his gaze back to his visitor.

'The truth of the matter,' he said, 'is that my august leader seemed to regard the iron fist as the appropriate response under all circumstances. God alone knows how many innocent lives were lost because of his policies. And there are still some officers who justify their extreme behaviour by reference to him.'

'Do you have anyone in mind?'

'No, there are probably upwards of fifty officers I could name, given time. Most of them would probably limit themselves to talk but there was a hardcore who, given the opportunity, would, I suspect, want to take matters further.'

'Yes, I think I know what you mean,' said Emanuel, leaning forward in his chair, and choosing his words with care. 'I've heard much the same thing from a journalist I know.'

'Really? What had he to say on the subject?' said Dalhousie.

'He'd heard talk of a clandestine group bent on mischief,' said Emanuel, wondering how far he could bend the truth without actually lying. 'The group is believed to include serving and former members of the military, including a former officer.'

'I see,' said Dalhousie. 'Did he mention anyone by name?'

'Only one, sir, but I wish it to be understood that I speak in the utmost confidence.'

'Of course, sir,' said Dalhousie. 'As I do.'

'The name I was given was Grenville,' said Emanuel.

'How very odd,' said Dalhousie, fixing his visitor with a curious stare. 'Grenville was a junior officer in the regiment and someone I would not normally have had any dealings with. But his name kept cropping up at the morning briefings with my company commanders. There was…'

He stopped and, lacing his fingers together, he stared at the top of his desk in silence for a second or two. 'There was talk of his involvement in the unlawful execution of several villagers. Murder by any other name. Unfortunately, there was never sufficient evidence to bring him before a court martial.'

'And this was in Ireland?'

'Yes, a place called Wexford,' said Dalhousie. He shook his head. 'I doubt I shall ever forget it. Quite appalling acts of savagery were committed on both sides, including the incidents of which Grenville was suspected. He was eventually persuaded it would be best were he to resign his commission. I've not seen or heard of him since. It doesn't surprise me to hear of his possible involvement in mischief.'

#

It was a disappointed Emanuel who stepped out of the colonel's office and crossed the barrack square a few minutes later. While his meeting with Dalhousie had gone well enough, confirming what he already knew of Grenville's propensity for violence, it had not gone as far as he'd hoped. Grenville's junior status within the regiment had effectively shielded him from the close supervision that he might otherwise have faced from his commanding officer and, in consequence, the colonel's knowledge of him was entirely based on what others had told him. As for Collins and Bristow, their names had meant nothing to him.

Emanuel had almost arrived at the guardhouse when some hidden sense made him stop and turn about. Soldiers were everywhere, some drilling, some painting, others hurrying between the numerous huts that dotted the area. At the far end of the square a military band marched and counter-marched. But no one appeared to be showing the least interest in his presence. He walked on past the guardhouse and onto the main street, retracing the steps that would return him to the riverside.

He'd already turned into the path leading to the water's edge when he heard a man's voice call from some way behind him. He looked round. A figure in military uniform stood watching him. Wondering if he'd unwittingly broken some rule of military discipline, Emanuel waited for the soldier to speak.

'If you is at leisure, sir, I should like to speak with you in private,' said the soldier. 'It won't take long, sir.'

'Yes, of course,' said Emanuel. 'How can I help?'

'My name is Sergeant Candler, sir. I'm the colonel's clerk, sir,' said the man, walking rapidly down the path towards him. 'I heard what you and the colonel was talking about, sir. Couldn't help it, sir. The walls of them barracks is dreadful thin, sir.'

Emanuel inclined his head, wondering where this was going.

'I were with the colonel in Ireland, sir,' said the man. 'Back in '98, sir. Only I weren't his clerk in them days. Back then I were in the line with the other lads. There was some terrible things what I saw, sir.'

'How can I help, Sergeant?' said Emanuel, glancing hopefully at a passing wherry.

'I knew Lt. Grenville, sir, the officer what the colonel and you was speaking about. It weren't right what he did. Nor the men what were with him, neither.'

'What did Lt. Grenville do that wasn't right?' said Emanuel.

'It weren't just at Wexford,' said Candler. 'The killing and the pitch-capping and the beating was going on all the time. Mostly it was the local militia boys but not always. Lt. Grenville and some of the men what went with him were the worst.'

'Do you know the names of those men?'

'Aye, there must have been around ten or twelve of them. But mainly it were just two. Collins and Bristow were their names. Two bully-boys what I wouldn't want to upset. They've left the army now. I see Bristow from time to time. He comes here and meets up with some of the lads what he knows. Don't know about Collins.'

'Collins is dead,' said Emanuel. 'Drowned in the Thames a little while back.'

'I didn't know that. Don't want to speak ill of the dead, sir.' Candler paused and glanced at Emanuel.

'How d'you know that, sir? If you don't mind me asking.'

'I knew Collins from before he went into the army. And Bristow, too.'

'Be careful of Bristow, sir,' said Candler, his curiosity seemingly satisfied. 'He ain't quite right in the head, sir. Will kill a man for looking at him the wrong way, and think nothing of it. Blames the Irish for everything what's happened. If he had his way…'

The sergeant stopped and seemed to lose the thread of what he was saying.

'What would have happened if he'd had his way?' prompted Emanuel.

'What? Oh, aye, I were talking about Bristow. As I said, sir, he ain't right in the head. He thinks the Papists want to stab us all in our beds. He's got some of the lads so fired up there's going to be real trouble. He's planning something and getting some of the lads involved. Don't know much about it but I know it's trouble.'

'A riot? Burn some churches? That sort of thing?'

'No, that's what I don't understand,' said Candler. 'There ain't no talk of a riot. It's something else. Whenever anyone outside the group asks them what they talk about, they clam up.'

'Where do they meet – Bristow and the lads you talk about?'

'Mostly at the Spread Eagle, just down the street from the garrison gate. It's where most of the lads go for a drink when they's allowed out, usually of a Thursday evening.'

'What about Lt. Grenville? Does he ever go to these meetings?'

'No, but that ain't no surprise. If he went, none of the lads would go, on account of he were an officer.'

'What about the locals? Do any of them drink at the Spread Eagle?'

'Aye, they do.'

'And strangers?'

'Why d'you ask?' said Candler, his eyes widening in alarm. 'You ain't thinking of going there, is you, sir?'

Chapter 13

Sir Peter Westlake, Member of Parliament for the rotten borough of East Looe, squinted out through the library window of his home on Cheapside. There was little sign of movement in the street outside as sheets of torrential rain fell from a uniformly bleak sky. Large puddles had already formed in the rutted surface of the road, the water spilling over and flowing, unchecked, into an already full gutter.

'I'm not entirely clear what the problem is,' said Sir Peter, turning to face his guest. 'I have expended a great deal of time, money and influence in opposition to the proposed Emancipation Bill. Is it, sir, asking too much that you bestir yourself to ensure your side of the bargain is fulfilled?'

'I've not been idle, sir,' said the Hon. James Grenville, his face reddening. He removed a solid gold box from his waistcoat pocket and opened the lid to pinch a small quantity of snuff, depositing it onto his wrist. He didn't like criticism at the best of times. 'Why, only today we would, but for the intervention of the militia, have succeeded in destroying the Papist church at Soho. As it was, considerable damage was caused. You are to consider, sir, the mob cannot be directed to act as one would wish. It must be coaxed into action. Only then can we move onto the final stage of eliminating our target.'

'I know that, sir,' said Sir Peter. 'But it's imperative that we move quickly. Mr Pitt is pressing for the introduction of the Bill and, I make no doubt, he will have his way if we do not succeed with our plans.'

'I require no lessons from you on the importance of what is planned, Sir Peter,' said Grenville, raising his wrist to a nostril and snorting the yellowish-brown powder. 'I have told you what has been achieved thus far. I should be obliged to you, sir, were you to allow me to conduct my side of this affair without hindrance. Now, if you will excuse me, I will take my leave.'

He made for the door, slammed it shut behind him, and strode angrily across the stone-flagged hall towards the front door. He stopped at the sound of light footsteps running up the main staircase behind him.

'Why, if it ain't Miss Sara,' he called, his anger instantly forgotten, replaced by a tingle of excitement as he saw her halt and turn to face him. She had been an unattainable presence in his life since he'd first begun to take notice of girls. He remembered the first time he'd seen her, at work in the kitchens of his father's house in Norfolk. Even then, as a mere thirteen-year-old, she had been beautiful, her long, shoulder-length golden hair inviting his caress, her carefree laughter mocking the social mores that, for a while, had held him in check. Each time he'd seen her, his desire to possess her had grown stronger, his frustration at what he regarded as her unreasonable refusal to engage with him more acute. When, as a result of his relentless pursuit of her, she'd been sent south to London, he'd followed her.

'How can I be of service, sir?' Grenville noted the tremor in Sara's voice. He'd called her on a whim; a response to seeing her on the stairs. He'd formed no plan in his mind, and had no reason for requiring her presence. But he wasn't about to pass up this opportunity to be with her.

#

Sara felt trapped. She'd always known Grenville found her attractive and had, from the beginning, done her best to avoid any contact with him that was not strictly required of her. She'd recognised in her former employer's eldest son an excessive sensitivity that rendered any criticism or rejection of him almost unbearable to him, causing him to fly into intolerable rages and exposing the cruel streak that she'd long suspected. She glanced down at the library door, hoping Sir Peter would emerge and rescue her.

'Sir Peter has asked me to look at the servants' rooms and report on their general suitability,' said Grenville, his eyes daring her to question the truthfulness of what he was saying. 'I wish you to act as my guide.'

'Please, sir,' said Sara, suddenly frightened, 'her ladyship has sent for me. She is expecting me, sir.'

'Your mistress will understand,' said Grenville. He walked up the broad staircase and caught hold of her arm, propelling her up the remaining steps and along a corridor. A door on the right led directly onto another, steeper, narrower flight of stairs to the servants' quarters on the floor above. Up these they now went.

'We will inspect your room first,' said Grenville, as they reached the landing, his eyes mere slits of light. 'Which one is yours?'

'I think not, Master James,' said Sara, her voice trembling. 'Please leave, sir.'

'How dare you speak to me in that manner,' said Grenville, his voice low and threatening. 'Tell me which of these is your room.'

Sara glanced behind her and then at each of the doors, listening for any sound that might indicate the occupants of the rooms were present, but all she could hear was the drumbeat of her heart and the sound of rain lashing against the roof tiles above her head.

'Come now, Miss Sara, I don't have all day. Your room, if you please.'

Sara opened her door and stood back.

'I shall want you to show me,' said Grenville, pushing her into the room, his voice thickening. He followed her in and closed the door. 'Come, come, Miss Sara, it's only a little fun that I want. I dare say I shan't be the first and I doubt I shall be the last.'

She thought she detected a hesitancy in his voice, a growing excitement at what lay ahead. She sidestepped as he came towards her, ducking under his outstretched arm and running to the door. He caught her and threw her onto the bed, removing his brocade coat as he did so. He swallowed, his breathing heavier and faster than a moment ago. He lay down beside her, his hands moving to her breasts. She let out a shriek of panic and tried to roll out of his reach. He caught her again and pulled her towards him. She could feel his hand now wrenching at the hem of her dress.

'No, Master James. Please don't. Please, I beg you should not touch me.' Sara could smell the stale sweat of his clothes and felt the urgency in his movements. She wriggled away and was rewarded with a sharp slap to his face.

'Keep still, woman,' said Grenville, bringing his face down to hers and parting his lips to reveal the uneven line of his yellowing teeth.

Chapter 14

There was a sudden, loud knock on the door to Sara's room.

'Is everything all right, Miss Payton?' Sara recognised the voice of the butler. Before she could reply, Grenville had clamped his hand over her mouth. She attempted to wriggle free but couldn't.

'Miss Payton?' It was the butler again. 'Miss Payton, I must insist on your answer. A gentleman was seen to approach your room. I will not allow anyone in the servants' quarters without my authority. Be good enough to require your visitor to leave this instant.'

Grenville rolled off the bed and quickly adjusted his clothing. Almost immediately there was the sharp crack of the latch being raised and the door swung open.

'What is the meaning of this, Jones?' snapped Grenville. 'I have come to see Miss Payton on a private matter. Kindly leave us immediately, else Sir Peter will hear of this.'

'I regret it extremely, Master James, but it is I and not Sir Peter who has responsibility for what occurs in the servants' quarters. You will, sir, kindly leave at once.' The butler raised a hand and beckoned two footmen who had, until this moment, remained out of sight. 'These two will show you the way, sir.'

'You'll hear more of this, Jones. That I promise you,' snarled Grenville, walking swiftly to the door. He stopped suddenly and looked back at Sara. 'You and I are not finished, Miss Sara.'

Sara heard the door slam and footsteps fade away as she sank, trembling to her knees, her head buried in her hands. The shock of what had happened would come later. For the present she was just relieved to see Grenville go. He would try again. She knew that. She'd seen the hungry look in his eyes, his desire for her, his determination to pursue her. She knew her rejection of him would have its consequences. She lifted her head, her fingers trailing down her face. She sat still for a minute, her heart racing. There seemed no way of escaping the Hon. James Grenville.

Chapter 15

Emanuel was alone in the chapel on Virginia Street, his breviary open in front of him, the last of the sunlight streaming through the line of windows set high up close to the eaves. He was reading the Magnificat. *My soul proclaims the greatness of the Lord, my spirit rejoices in God my Saviour.* A knock on the front door disturbed him. He wasn't expecting anyone and answering the door carried an element of risk, especially when he was alone. It wouldn't be the first time he'd been attacked and beaten.

'Who is it?' he called.

'Open the door, Mr Emanuel. It's me, Sara. I need to talk to you.'

'Sara? Are you alone?'

'Yes. Quickly, Mr Emanuel. Let me in.'

Emanuel slid back the heavy iron bolts, opened the door a fraction and peeped out. He would afterwards wonder how he could have failed to notice the girl's drawn features, her pallor and her red-rimmed eyes. Perhaps he should have seen the way she glanced behind her as though afraid of something or someone. But he didn't see any of these things, his mind still occupied with his reading.

He looked beyond her, at the deserted street outside the chapel door and at the evening sky now streaked with orange and gold from the setting sun. It was too quiet, too tranquil. He closed the door, catching as he did so the distant sounds of the Highway, the strident calls of those with goods to sell, the high-pitched shrieks of the milkmaids and the general clamour of the crowd. Soon they would all depart for the night and their places taken by those in search of drink and pleasure. He wondered how long the peace would last.

'What is it you wanted to talk to me about?' he said.

'Master Grenville...' said Sara, her voice faltering. She turned to face him and for the first time Emanuel saw she'd been crying.

'Why, child, whatever is the matter?' he said. 'What's happened to you?'

'There's been some trouble, Master Emanuel,' said Sara, waving him away. 'Up Soho way. One of your churches has been attacked. I heard Master James talking about it.'

'Yes, I've heard, but—'

Sara shook her head impatiently. 'You don't understand. I think Master James knew it were going to happen. He knew the church was to be attacked.'

'How do you know that?' said Emanuel.

'Sir Peter and Master James were arguing...'

'Go on, child. I'm listening.' He stopped suddenly and peered at her face. 'Has someone struck you? The marks on your face. Who did that to you?'

'It don't matter none,' said Sara

'Was it Master James?' said Emanuel. 'Is that where the bruises came from?'

She turned away, a hand shielding her face from him. It was clear she wasn't about to tell him what had happened. He understood why. There was little could be done about it even if she were to confirm what he already suspected. She had neither the funds to pay for a prosecution nor the credibility as a witness to sustain her case against a gentleman of Grenville's standing.

'You were telling me about an argument you overheard,' said Emanuel, changing the subject. 'Something to do with the church in Soho…'

'Aye,' said Sara, wiping her eyes with the hem of her apron. 'It was like Master Grenville knew all about it. He said, the mob had to be led by the nose as it was last night.'

'Did he say anything else?'

'Not as I heard,' said Sara. 'I was just passing the library on my way to see her ladyship. That was when Master James came out and saw me. He…' She stopped, her head cocked to one side. 'What's that noise?'

Emanuel had also heard it and, stepping to the door, he pulled it open. From away in the distance came a faint sound like that of a flock of birds chased into sudden flight, their wings beating the air. It faded then came again, borne on a wind that rushed through narrow streets, rising and falling. He knew what it was, that deep-throated rumble that set his nerves on edge. He'd heard it before. Twenty years ago, to be precise. Then, as now, he'd stood at the front door of the chapel and waited for the mob's approach, listened to the unearthly howl and imagined the blind hatred in the eyes of those taking part.

He remembered the fear he'd felt that first morning, the desire to run and hide, and the physical pain of his beating heart. It had been a new experience for him, that feeling of helplessness in the face of overwhelming odds. Then as now he knew his life was a matter of supreme indifference to the heavy-jawed men who came. Then, not one brick of the old chapel had remained upon another, not a single beam of timber escaped the lick of the flames. Nothing had been left except the mounds of smoking rubble.

'Go at once to the magistrate,' said Emanuel, leading her to the side door. 'Tell him everything. Tell him he must send the militia before it's too late.'

'What of you? You can't stay here,' she said.

'Go, child, go. We've not a moment to lose. I'll be all right.' Emanuel pushed her out through the door, more frightened than he cared to admit. He saw her hesitate and then run down the alley and cross the street into King's Head Lane. Soon she was lost to his sight amongst the warren of paths and alleyways that led off that street. He closed the door and waited.

There was little else he could do – except pray.

#

Sara raced south through the maze of streets, away from the riotous mob and the chapel in Virginia Street that was its ultimate destination. She'd barely escaped. Another minute and she would have been trapped. The shouting, jeering, tightly packed mass had already rounded the corner from the Ratcliff Highway by the time she'd begun her sprint across the street and into King's Head Lane. They'd seen her, of course. There was no doubting the finger-pointing and excited yelps of those in the front rank of the crowd. One or two had broken ranks and chased after her, quickly tiring of the idea when their example had not been taken up by others.

It was a few minutes before she dared to stop and look over her shoulder. Groups of people had begun to form in the street, drawn by the sound of rioting. Their gaze directed upwards as if expecting to see smoke rising into the sky. But if that had been their intention, they were disappointed. Perhaps the smoke would come if Sara could not get the help Mr Emanuel wanted. She ran on, past an old man, a Jew from the look of him, his white, flowing beard reaching down almost to his waist, a black, broad-brimmed hat perched on his head, a tray of trinkets spread out before him, suspended from a rope about his neck. No one pursued her. She hurried on.

At the corner of Old Gravel Lane she turned towards the river. It was busier now, her progress slower. A sudden roar. She looked back and saw the heavy plume of thick black smoke rising into the air. She knew what it meant. Time was running out.

The Shadwell police office was another quarter of a mile further along on the left, next to a sailmaker's yard. She'd seen it from the outside many times, a seemingly permanent knot of people gathered at its door, their mood invariably quiet and apprehensive as if fearful of what the future might hold for them.

They were there today. She skirted round them and turned in through the open door into a small, rectangular hallway full of men, women and not a few children, some no more than infants cradled in their mothers' arms, the air filled with the fetid stench of bodies long unwashed. Sara hesitated, unsure of where to go and what to do. Then she saw a man standing beside a closed door on the far side of the hall. He had about him an air of authority. She made her way towards him.

'If you please, sir, I wish to see the magistrate on a matter of great urgency.'

'Do you now?' said the man, his eyes continuing to rove the room in a bored fashion. 'And what would that be for?'

'A mob, sir, is attacking the Papist chapel. They are trying to burn it down. The priest is still inside. They'll—'

'Stay here,' said the man, his eyes widening a fraction. 'I'll be back directly.'

He opened the door behind him and went through. A minute later he was back.

'Come with me. The magistrate will see you now,' he said.

Sara followed him into what was evidently the courtroom. A thin youth of around twenty stood within an enclosed platform, his head bent forward, his arms folded. Facing him was a second raised area from which a ruddy-faced magistrate dressed in a black coat and white ruffles was dispensing summary justice. She caught the tail end of the case.

'… fined one shilling, five days to pay. Next case,' said the magistrate.

The thin-faced youth was hauled away by a constable, his place immediately taken by an older youth.

'John Robert Wilkins, your worship. Drunk and disorderly. Fighting in Heaven Street, Shadwell. When arrested, said, "Fuck off."'

'Do you plead guilty or not guilty?' asked a bored-looking clerk sitting at an adjacent table.

'Guilty, sir.'

'Very well. Fined one shilling,' said the magistrate, not bothering to look up. 'Next…'

Sara's escort eased his way through the public gallery and out through a second entrance where he stopped and knocked on a closed door.

'Come,' said a voice. 'Ah, there you are, Jones. This is the lady you spoke to me about, is it?'

'It is, your worship.'

'What's this I hear about a riot, madam?' said the superintending magistrate of the Shadwell police office.

'Please, sir, there's not a minute to lose,' said Sara. 'The mob is attacking the chapel in Virginia Street. I fear they mean to burn it to the ground.'

'Thank you for telling me, madam,' said the magistrate. He turned to the constable standing next to him. 'The usual arrangements, if you please, Jones.'

#

A stone crashed through one of the windows set high on the west wall of the chapel. Then a second and a third, the shattered glass scything through the air, embedding itself into the half-dozen rows of wooden benches in front of the altar. The ground shook as more missiles struck the outer walls, each one accompanied by a howl of derision from the assembled mob. Emanuel crouched behind the marble altar, protected from the worst of the barrage but knowing he was still vulnerable. At any moment one of the missiles could ricochet off the east wall immediately behind him. He put the thought to one side.

Suddenly, he caught the whiff of burning wood. He crawled to one end of the altar and peered down the short nave. A burning taper lay on one of the benches.

Soon the bench itself would catch fire and then the one next to it. Doing nothing was no longer an option. The brand would surely be followed by others; far more than he could deal with by himself. He thought of going to the front door and reasoning with the mob but dismissed the idea. Showing his face would only incite it to further violence and a redoubling of its attempts to bring the chapel down. He looked again at the smouldering taper. A lick of flame appeared and died. Then another sprang up and gave birth to a third.

More tapers followed, soaring in through the broken windows to land amongst the benches. Most fizzled out. Others did not. Still he waited. Cobbles torn from the road surface continued to thud against the outside walls. A few crashed through the now broken windows. The chance of being struck by one of them was a near certainty. He had only two, real options – to escape or put out the fires before they took hold. He waited for what he hoped would be a lull in the hail of incoming missiles, suddenly remembering he'd forgotten to bolt the sacristy door after Sara.

A minute passed. Then two. The stones kept coming. He jumped to his feet, his heart racing, and ran out from behind his refuge. Another cobble crashed through a window, narrowly missing him. He ducked and continued running. Flames had caught hold on a bench near the back of the nave, a bright yellow tongue licking at the dry timber. It wasn't the nearest but it was the most dangerous, a pall of black, choking smoke rising from its centre, up into the eaves. The sacristy door would have to wait. He dragged the bench clear and beat at the flames with his coat. It didn't work.

Behind him he could hear the animal howl of the mob battering at the front door, the solid timbers shaking from the force of the blows. It couldn't take much more. Soon it would splinter and break. He thought of Sara, wondering if she'd got through; if help was on its way. She'd been gone some time.

A small breeze wafted in through the broken windows, blowing hot clouds of choking smoke towards him. He clamped a handkerchief to his face and tried to breathe. He had to get out. No one would blame him. This was a fight he couldn't win. He was beaten.

Turning to leave he saw shapes coming towards him through the smoke from the direction of the sacristy. Three, perhaps four men. Anger swept through him. Since his first days in the seminary in the Bairro Alto thirty-six years ago, he had tried to resist the temptation to answer force with force. He hadn't always succeeded but that was another story. Occasionally he'd found it necessary to resort to the law of last resort and the appearance of the strangers in his church perfectly filled this criterion. Picking up a heavy splinter of burning wood, he turned to face them.

Chapter 16

Emanuel had always known what to expect if the mob got to him. He'd seen the savagery of its behaviour, the mindless disregard of all that stood in the way. What tomorrow it might reflect on and perhaps regret, today it could not. In the heat and madness of the moment, anything was possible. Swinging the burning length of timber back over his shoulder, Emanuel aimed a blow at the leading figure.

'Don't, Father,' said a voice from the smoke. 'It's me.'

'Teeling? Is that you?' Emanuel struggled to recover from his surprise. 'What is this? What's happening?'

'Sure, I'll be telling you in a moment, Father,' said Teeling. 'Will you be hurt at all? Shall we be putting out the fire for you?'

'What?' Emanuel was only half listening, his attention drawn back to the mob. It sounded less confident than before, as though events beyond its control were changing the expected outcome. Stones no longer crashed against the wall or came hurtling through the windows. The flaming tapers, too, had stopped. A man was shouting, a single voice urging the mob on.

'That voice,' said Emanuel. 'If I'm not sadly mistook, it's Bristow.'

'Aye, it is, right enough,' said Teeling. 'I saw him heading this way a while ago.'

More voices were now joining in. Soon the noise was as great as it had ever been.

'What d'you suppose is happening, Henry?' said Emanuel.

'That'll be the lads, Father. Sure it didn't seem right to leave you here on your own.'

'What d'you mean? Has the mob been attacked by your friends? Is that what's happening?'

'They're here for you, Father,' said Teeling. 'It's—'

He was cut off by the deafening roar of gunfire. The noise had come from a little way off, perhaps the corner of the Highway.

'Dear God, did you hear that?' shouted Emanuel, his ears buzzing. He ran to the chapel door and peered out through a crack in the wood. 'The mob's running. It's leaving. Something's happened.'

Teeling joined him and pulled open the door.

'Sure, it's the militia, Father,' he said, pointing to a line of scarlet tunics and black shakos that had appeared through the gunsmoke.

'So she did get through,' said Emanuel to no one in particular.

The firing had stopped and he watched the troopers move down Virginia Street in line abreast, their pace unhurried, their muskets, with bayonets fixed, pointing forwards as they stepped over the unmoving shapes of men lying where they had fallen. He counted five bodies; those he could see. Five men who would never again see their families – and for what? He looked at the body nearest him, the face twisted into a look of intense surprise, a crimson stain of blood around its chest, a dead hand holding a cobblestone. He could not have been more than fourteen or fifteen. A child, really.

Emanuel stumbled away from the door. For a long time he stood with his eyes closed thinking of the pointless loss of life. He'd seen death before. Far too often he'd been called upon to administer the final sacrament of the Church in the last moments of someone's life. Far too often was their passing a violent one. But familiarity with sudden death didn't make it any easier to deal with. He opened his eyes to find that Teeling was watching him. The Irishman turned away and pretended to busy himself with what remained of the fires.

'Thankee kindly, Henry. All of you, thankee,' he said, looking round at the scene of devastation. 'I owe you a debt of gratitude. Had you not come, I make no doubt the chapel would've been lost.'

'Sure, it's nothing, Father,' said Teeling. He turned to go, stopped and looked back. 'Will you be sparing me a minute, Father?'

'By all means,' said Emanuel.

Teeling waved the others on their way. When they'd gone, he said, 'I told you I saw Bristow earlier…'

'Yes, you did,' said Emanuel. 'What was he doing?'

'I were having a drink with some lads what I know when I saw him. He were at the front of the mob what did all this. He were the leader.'

'Is that why you came? Because of him?' said Emanuel.

'Not entirely,' said Teeling. 'Sure, I guessed the mob were coming this way and meant to burn down the chapel. There was no other reason for them to have been in the Highway. I told the lads to go for help. As soon as they knew it was you what the mob was going to turn off, they all came.'

Emanuel nodded, wondering how many lives had been lost or destroyed during the battle that had undoubtedly raged between the two sides before the arrival of the militia. It could have only staved off the inevitable for a week or two. Maybe a month. The antagonism towards the Church could never be solved by breaking a few heads. Yet he knew he couldn't have it both ways. Left to itself, the mob would have burned the church to the ground and that, at least, Teeling and his friends had had a hand in putting off – for the time being.

'You said part of the reason for coming here was Bristow,' said Emanuel. 'What was the other part?'

'Do you remember asking me about Wexford, Father?' said Teeling. 'I told you what happened to me and me wife.'

'Yes, I remember,' said Emanuel. 'You blamed Collins for her murder.'

'Aye, but I also said there were two others there as well. Men I didn't see. Leastways not properly. I've always thought that if I ever saw them again I might recognise them.'

'And you told me you'd seen Bristow who you believed to be one of them, here in London?'

'Aye,' said Teeling. 'When I saw him again in the Highway, I wanted to find out what happened that day.'

'How did you expect to achieve that?' asked Emanuel. 'He was with the mob. If he'd seen you he'd have killed you.'

'I'd have found a way.' Teeling looked up suddenly. 'You can understand that, Father, can't you?'

Emanuel shrugged, not knowing what he was expected to say. There wasn't a great deal he could say. He sensed that Teeling's real motive in wanting to see Bristow had been to avenge his wife's death. The pain of his loss must've been almost unbearable, the urge for retribution overwhelming. What puzzled him was why Teeling should choose this moment to tell him, in a roundabout way, what he had wanted to do; perhaps still wanted to do. What had he expected from a priest? The grant of absolution for an act he had yet to perform? He would have known that was impossible. But if not that, then what?

'I understand how you feel, Henry, but you have to step back. Collins is dead. Leave it at that.'

'I can't, Father. I've tried to put it out of my mind. But I can't.'

#

Emanuel pulled open the front door of the chapel and looked out. Teeling had gone. A small crowd of the curious had gathered in the street outside, watched over by a detachment of the militia. The bodies of the dead still lay where they'd fallen while half a dozen women tended the living, binding their wounds with whatever rags came to hand. Emanuel watched them for a second or two, pondering the wisdom of offering his help. The crowd would already have seen him; noted where he'd come from. He doubted they'd accept the help of a Papist. Or a Jew, for that matter.

They were, he thought, more likely to regard him as the cause of all the trouble.

'Master Emanuel?' He spun round to see Sara standing amongst the charred benches. He guessed she must have come in through the sacristy door at the side of the building.

'Why, there you are, dear child.' He beamed. 'I see you managed to get help for us.'

'Yes, the magistrate knew of this chapel and he'd been expecting the mob to attack sooner or later.'

'And he was right.'

'Yes.' Sara hesitated as though something else was on her mind. 'Who was that man I saw leaving the chapel?' she asked.

'Teeling?' said Emanuel, surprised by the question. 'He and a few friends helped put out the fire… but of course, you know him, do you not? It was you who helped him after he was attacked outside the chapel a few weeks since.'

'Yes, that must be it.' Sara avoided the priest's gaze and walked to the front door. 'What were you looking at just now?'

'All those who've lost their lives. And those who were injured,' said Emanuel, looking back onto the street. More women had arrived and were kneeling by those who still lived. 'I'd thought of offering my help.'

'No, don't go, Mr Emanuel,' she said. 'As like as not they'll kill you for what happened to their menfolk. And don't imagine them soldiers would come to your assistance.'

'Perhaps you're right,' said Emanuel, moving away from the door.

'There was…' Sara hesitated for a moment, a look of confusion in her eyes. 'There was talk Master

Teeling had killed the man what was found at Limehouse Dock. Is it…?'

'Is it true? Is that what you're asking?' said Emanuel. 'I don't know and nor does anyone else. Certainly no one has yet come forward with any evidence to prove his involvement.'

'But that doesn't mean he didn't do it?' said Sara.

'No, child, it doesn't,' said Emanuel.

Chapter 17

It was after midnight when Erasmus Bristow finally reached the building in Gun Lane where he usually spent his nights. It had once been a glue manufactory over whose walls the powerful odour of its past still lingered. Tired and irritated by the failure of the day, he swung in through the big double doors and past one of the vast fire boxes that had once been used to boil the glue. The attack on the Papist chapel would have succeeded had it not been for the Irish. Them and the militia.

He stumbled on, the acrid stench of human waste reminding him to avoid a hole in the earthen floor. Soon he reached the narrow strip of ground he regarded as his own. There'd been someone else there when he first arrived several months ago and Bristow had needed to persuade the cully his tenure had come to an end.

Squatting awkwardly, he rolled out a length of canvas and lay down on it, still smarting from the morning's failure. It made him look weak. He clenched his fists, trying to work out what had gone wrong. The Irish had appeared from nowhere; hundreds of them. He hadn't minded that so much. He could have beaten them. It was the militia who'd done for him. Somebody must have called them.

He drifted into sleep. An image appeared to him. He was alone, surrounded by strangers in brown coats, their faces blurred and unrecognisable. One was carrying the dead body of a young woman. She'd been strangled, the fingermarks around her neck a bluish-red colour against the whiteness of her dead body. The man carrying her stopped in front of him, staring at him, holding the woman out to him. His lips moved but no sound came. Now the other brown-coated men were crowding in, carrying pikes and pitchforks. Their scalps were missing and hot tar dripped from their torn flesh. One had a length of rope in his hands, a loop in one end, and this he threw over the bough of a tree. He was beckoning. Bristow knew what was intended. He was shouting now, sweat pouring down his face. He didn't want to die. He tried to run, but he couldn't. He looked down at his feet. One leg was missing and someone was chopping at the second one. He was shaking with fright, begging the brown coats to spare his life.

Then the man holding the dead woman approached him, blood flowing from a stab wound to his thigh. Behind him was a church. More men milled around him. Someone was screaming. His eyes snapped open. The scream was his own.

Bristow stared into the night, the sweat drying on his skin, cold and uncomfortable, his body shaking.

He knew the man in his dream. But from where? Nothing came to mind.

His eyes once again grew heavy. He slept.

Chapter 18

'Yes, what is it, Dawkins?' The Hon. James Grenville looked up from his copy of *The Times*, irritated by the interruption to his morning.

'Begging your pardon, sir,' said the impeccably dressed figure of the butler. 'There is – ah – a man asking to see you, sir.'

'Who is he? Did he give a name?'

'He gave the name of Bristow, sir. Said you would know what it was about.'

Grenville looked as though an unpleasant smell had invaded the room. He had always regarded Bristow with a mixture of fear and loathing, a common thug whose only attribute was the ability to inflict pain without compunction. Yet he knew it was precisely this quality that had persuaded him to look for Bristow in the months after he'd resigned his commission and returned to London. It hadn't taken him long. He'd known enough to begin his search east of the Tower, amongst the squalid courts and alleys of Shadwell and Limehouse, Hackney and Mile End. After that, a few hours spent drinking in the local taverns had been all that was necessary for him to be pointed in the right direction. There were few who'd not heard of Erasmus Bristow.

The meeting, the first since Bristow's operation and subsequent discharge from the army, had not been an easy one. Free of the constraints of military discipline, Bristow had given full vent to his views of the officer cadre in general and Lt. Grenville in particular, none of it flattering. While little progress had been possible at that first meeting, Bristow had, on the promise of a generous remuneration (of sorts), agreed to a second meeting the following week. There were, however, to be limits in the direction and scope of the relationship envisaged by Grenville. For him it was not to be a relationship between equals, and any assumption by Bristow to the contrary had swiftly to be corrected.

Grenville climbed to his feet and ambled across to the drawing room window. He stood looking out over the pleasant lawn interlaced with formal flower beds, to a large oak at the end of the garden. Perhaps it had been a mistake recruiting Bristow. The fellow had always been difficult, if not impossible, to control; a sneering, contemptuous presence, in the face of which social rank counted for nothing. Even within the military environment, Grenville had felt the need to seek the approval of his inferior. His mind shrivelled at the thought. This was the man he had gone out of his way to find and recruit to a cause so delicate that the least suggestion of its existence would unquestionably lead to their executions. Why had he done it? Why Bristow?

Grenville puckered his lips and stared up into a sky blackened with the threat of rain. He knew the answer. He'd often thought about that night when the patrol had been ambushed, and its consequences for them both. He breathed deeply and turned back into the room as a fresh thought occurred to him. Bristow might be many things but he was not a man to come running for help. Something must have gone seriously wrong. He was not looking forward to the meeting.

'Very well, show him to the library, will you, Dawkins?' said Grenville. 'I'll see him directly.'

#

Bristow had woken early that morning, conscious of a dread feeling in the pit of his stomach. For a moment or two, he'd been unable to identify the cause. Then he'd recalled the dream. Snatches of it came back to him. A nightmare. Vivid, forceful, brutal. He'd tried to put it out of his mind but it had kept returning, each time more threatening than the last. He'd lain on his back listening to the cacophony of noise that surrounded him in the cavernous interior of the old manufactory, the vague images in his dream coming and going.

It had been a while before he'd understood the truth.

His nightmare had been more than just a dream. It had been a warning. He'd known the man in his dream, the one carrying the body of a woman. And he'd known who she was and how she'd died. He'd been there with Collins and Lt. Grenville, at the stone shack where the woman and her husband lived, close to the banks of the Slaney, a mile or so outside Wexford. He'd heard her screams in the last seconds of her life. And he'd known at once what had happened.

He'd always thought of Lt Grenville as weak, particularly in relation to women. The officer had never been able to resist them. And that, in the end, was why the woman had died.

He looked up as Grenville entered the room.

'He's on to me,' he said, his voice dull and unusually subdued.

'Who is?' said Grenville, examining the back of one hand. 'And what is he on to you about?'

'Teeling. He must've seen me that day in Wexford.'

'Who, if I might ask, is Teeling and what has he got to do with Wexford?'

Bristow told him.

'From what you tell me, it is you and Collins who this fellow saw on that day. Is that not so?' said Grenville, the faintest outline of a sneer crossing his handsome features. He waited for an answer and when none came, he said, 'The problem is yours. You deal with it. Is that all you came to see me about? Really, Bristow, I have more important matters to attend to. Now, if there is nothing else, I'll bid you good day.'

Bristow moved with surprising speed, catching hold of his former officer by the throat and pinning him against the book-lined wall. 'You ain't nothing to me no more, mister. How would it be if I were to tell the beak what you and Sir Peter bleedin' Westlake have been planning? Don't suppose it would be too long afore you was doing the Newgate dance one fine Monday morning, would it?'

'Let go,' gasped Grenville, struggling to release himself from the choking grip. 'Who d'you think is going to believe the word of a vagabond like you over that of a gentleman?'

'No,' said Bristow releasing his hold. 'You's right. I think I might just have a word with Teeling instead. I think he'd like to know who really killed his old woman – I could tell him exactly who it was, couldn't I? What d'you suppose he'd do when he found out?'

'You'll pay for this, Bristow, you scoundrel,' shouted Grenville. 'Mark my words, I'll make you regret the day you ever set eyes on me.'

Bristow's jaw muscles flexed and whatever light there might once have been in his eyes died in an instant. He swung forward on his crutches, his face close to Grenville's, the razor-sharp edge of a knife pressing against his former officer's neck.

'You threatening me, mister? I'd be very careful what I said if I were you. Why, someone might just find you in the Fleet ditch with yer throat cut,' said Bristow, releasing his grip and turning to leave. 'And wouldn't that be a crying shame?'

It was some time before an ashen-faced Grenville felt able to rise from the chair into which he'd been pushed. Pouring himself a generous measure of brandy, he swallowed it in a single gulp. In that instant he made up his mind.

Bristow would have to be dealt with.

Chapter 19

The questions surrounding Collins's murder remained uppermost in Emanuel's mind as he left his room the following morning and walked up New Gravel Lane towards the Highway. It wasn't simply his death, although that was serious enough, but rather its immediate cause. He remembered Teeling telling him of a lady friend of his, a prostitute, who in a moment of professional indiscretion had repeated something she'd heard Bristow muttering in his sleep; that he'd been told to stop Collins from talking.

While the claim had seemed fanciful, Emanuel had taken the view that he ought, at least, to see the woman and find out what else she might have to say on the subject. But his attempts to discover where the girl might be found had been a deal harder than he'd anticipated, with a reluctant Teeling initially refusing to tell him.

'I don't know, Father,' Teeling had stalled. 'It were just talk. I don't want her to get into trouble.'

Busy with his thoughts, Emanuel didn't see the approach of the tall, bearded figure dressed in the traditional black, ankle-length coat and broad-brimmed hat of an orthodox Jew.

'Emanuel? Emanuel Lazaro? What? Can it be you?' said the man.

'Aaron Malka,' said Emanuel, recognising his childhood friend, the boy on whose behalf he'd fought many a battle in the streets round the Alfama district. 'It's been a long time. I thought you were still in Lisbon.'

'Ahey,' said Aaron, raising the palms of his hands and shrugging. 'Why would a member of the true tribe wish to live in Portugal and be forced to renounce the ways of Moses? No, I could not stay there. I came to this country two years ago. To begin with I lived in Liverpool but moved to London not above six months since.'

'And you have found work?' asked Emanuel, conscious of slipping back into the comfortable relationship he'd enjoyed with Aaron in their youth. He knew it wasn't sensible. He knew the safest course was to cut short the meeting and move on. Yet he stayed. He wanted to hear news of the friends and the little community he'd left behind. And he wanted to hear about his ageing parents, to know if all was well with them. Yes, there was a danger – a danger that more might be given away than it would be sensible to contemplate. He had kept his apostasy secret in England not for its own sake but because of the inevitable questions that would follow; questions he could not answer without destroying everything he had lived for these last thirty years.

'Certainly,' said Aaron. 'The Mahamad found me a position with a dealer in old clothes not far from here, in Rosemary Lane. But you? What about you? You are well? I've not seen you in the synagogue.'

'Does that surprise you?' said Emanuel, conscious of a sudden tightness in his throat. 'London has many synagogues.'

'Ah, that must be it,' said Aaron, stroking his long beard and watching Emanuel with what seemed an unusual degree of care. 'Do you remember how our parents used to take us to the Christian church in the Alfama?'

'Aye, I do.'

'We used to go to a neighbour's house on the Sabbath where the rabbi would meet us and our friends in secret before going to the cathedral the next day.'

'Aye, we did,' said Emanuel.

'But you, you always preferred the church, did you not?' said Aaron.

Emanuel felt a weariness come over him. He was tired of hiding from the truth, of avoiding people for fear of the questions they might ask him. He'd not been able to tell anyone. He'd not been able to trust anyone with his secret. Until now. He felt a weight being lifted from his shoulders.

'Let us walk,' he said. 'We have much to talk about, you and I.'

#

Bristow was not a happy man. The hammering sensation above his right eye was getting worse. It was affecting his ability to think, a skill he'd always struggled to master even in those moments in his life when a headache could not be said to be responsible. He was a man who viewed the world about him through the prism of mistrust and the physical violence that was its natural ally. Whether this state of being could be said to be the result of his frequent headaches or simply a mentality which saw everything reduced to the power of the fist, was less clear. Whatever the answer, it was certainly true that his moods were invariably darker and his propensity to violence more in evidence during those periods when the headaches were present. His recent confrontation with his former officer in the army, the Hon. James Grenville, was a case in point. The memory of it made Bristow shake with rage.

He'd deal with the scrub as soon as the opportunity arose.

He squinted at the passing multitude in the Highway through half-closed eyes. He was waiting – none too patiently – for a suitable victim to appear. Any solitary inebriate, preferably one with obvious signs of wealth about his person, would do. Sailors were a favourite source of income for him, as were the occasional dandies – inebriated or not – who strayed so far east from their natural habitat as to invite his attention.

He looked up and down the Highway. There was nothing of interest and he was about to move off when he saw the two men approaching, deep in conversation. He watched as they came to a halt a few yards from him. Then they parted, one turning down a footpath leading to the Thames, the other continuing along the Highway. Soon, both were lost to sight.

Bristow crossed the Highway, the germ of an idea forming in his mind. It was too early to call it a plan. He would not have been capable of that. Not at the moment. Not with the pain in his head the way it was. He turned into the footpath after the taller of the two men. It was darker here, the daylight blocked by the presence of high tenement buildings that rose on either side. Bristow paused and waited for his eyes to grow accustomed to the conditions. The tall man in the long, black coat and the broad-brimmed hat was no more than thirty or forty paces in front. He caught up with him.

'It's a word I want with you, mister,' said Bristow.

Aaron Malka stopped and turned to face the man who'd called.

#

Emanuel put aside any regrets he might have had about his chance encounter with Aaron. The conversation with his boyhood friend had been like lifting a heavy burden from his shoulders, a chance to talk about the one subject he'd kept hidden from the world for longer than he cared to remember. They'd promised to meet again in a few days' time.

His thoughts returned to the subject of Collins's death and the girl he'd been on his way to see when he'd bumped into Aaron Malka. Teeling had eventually told him where she might be found – on a jealously guarded stretch of the north side of the Ratcliff Highway, east of the junction with Cannon Street, down as far as the barber's shop.

He saw her as he crossed the road and recognised the thin, scantily dressed child he'd come across on the evening of his first encounter with Bristow. She'd told him her name was Annie; Willing Annie, to be more precise. She smiled as he approached, the corners of her mouth upturned in an empty grimace, her eyes red-rimmed with tiredness.

'Why, I knows you,' she said, the smile fading as quickly as it had appeared. 'Ain't you…?'

'Yes, it's me,' said Emanuel, noting some bruises on her face that hadn't been there when he'd last seen her. 'May we talk?'

'What about?' Her voice had a hard edge to it, the result, he guessed, of the life she led and the men she'd met along the way.

'Your friend, Bristow.'

Her jaw dropped and she turned away, her eyes darting from one part of the crowd to another as though expecting to be punished for some unknown transgression.

'I ain't done nothing wrong, mister,' she wailed. 'Honest, I ain't.'

'No, of course, you haven't, child.' Emanuel saw several heads turned in their direction. 'I'm a friend of Henry Teeling. He spoke of you.'

She stared at him, unconvinced.

Emanuel tried again. 'You told him about something you'd heard Bristow saying in his sleep. Something he'd been told to do to a man named Collins. Do you remember that?'

She nodded, her eyes still scouring the crowd. After what seemed an eternity, she pointed up a side street and said, 'I'll meet you at the coffee house what's up there.'

The coffee house on the west side of Cannon Street had little to recommend it. A narrow building squeezed between other, equally narrow properties, it had the appearance of being long neglected and, but for the glow of candles in the ground-floor windows, might have been mistaken for an abandoned dwelling.

Emanuel pushed open the door and went in, the rich aroma of coffee beans helping to mask the more obvious disadvantages of the place. An elderly man was leaning against a small bar in one corner of the room, scratching his bald pate. He looked up and nodded as Emanuel came in. Down the centre of the room, a long, heavily stained table occupied most of the floor area. It was empty but for two men sitting at the end nearest the door. They looked up as Emanuel entered, their conversation faltering for a second or two before resuming. He walked past them and sat down at the far end to wait.

Five minutes passed by. Then ten. Then fifteen. He was beginning to think the girl had changed her mind and would not be coming when he saw the door open and her head appear. She beckoned him to follow her.

'He were here,' she said as soon as he'd joined her on the street, her voice low and urgent. 'Bristow was. Took me money and left. It ain't safe for us to talk. Not with him around.'

'Down there,' said Emanuel, pointing to a footpath that ran along the side of the coffee house. 'Bristow won't see us. If he looks for you, you can tell him you were with a client who ran off without paying. It's important I talk to you.'

Annie glanced nervously about her. She shook her head and seemed on the point of refusing. Then she said, 'Two minutes. No longer. You don't know what he's like.'

Emanuel followed her as she hurried down the path and stopped behind some tall weeds that offered a degree of privacy from anyone passing along the street.

'I don't talk to no one what don't pay for me time,' she said, peering round the vegetation towards the street. Suddenly, she looked up at Emanuel with a hard stare. 'What's your game, anygate? Why d'you want to know about Bristow?'

'Does he treat you right?' said Emanuel.

Annie pouted her lips and stared wordlessly at the ground.

'Where did you get those bruises on your face?' he asked, remembering the last time he'd put a near identical question to a woman. On that occasion it had been Sara.

Annie's hand flew to her left cheek, her fingers covering the reddish blue marks to the skin. 'It ain't nothing, mister. I fell and hurt me head.'

' You told me once you had to leave your father's house in Dorset,' said Emanuel, after a pause. 'Have you been on your own ever since?'

'Aye, mostly.' She laughed, a short derisory snort. 'Lived with a cully what said he loved me. But one day he weren't there no more. Then Bristow said he'd take care of me, all proper like.'

'Tell me about the night of the fight with Collins.'

Annie's head jerked back as though she'd been struck. 'Who told you?'

'You know who told me, Annie. What happened that night?'

'That's all I know about it; what I told your friend,' said Annie.

'You mean Teeling?' said Emanuel.

'Aye, him.'

'Did Bristow tell you what the fight was about?' said Emanuel.

Annie's tongue passed over her lower lip, her eyes flicking from Emanuel to the ground and back again. She appeared nervous; seemingly afraid of the consequences of answering the question. At length she said, 'When Bristow came to the room that night he were covered in blood. I asked him what had happened but he told me to mind me business else I'd be sorry, so I kept me mouth shut. Later, when he were asleep I heard him say he never meant to kill Collins. It were an accident.'

'Did Bristow say why he hadn't wanted to kill him?' said Emanuel.

'They was in the army together, that's why,' said Annie.

'But someone had told him to do it. Is that right?'

'Aye.'

'D'you know who?'

'He didn't tell me no names.'

'What else did you hear him say?'

'He went looking for him and found him down on the Thames foreshore. They argued and there were a fight. He didn't have no choice.' Annie shrugged. 'Then he left him.'

'So he killed him?'

'Aye. Leastways, that's what it seemed like to me.'

'What was Collins supposed to have done?' Emanuel asked.

'He…' Annie looked up the path towards the street, a quick, anxious glance from behind the tall weeds that hid her. Seemingly satisfied, she looked back at Emanuel. 'Bristow didn't say nothing more that night but I've heard him sometimes when he's angry. He'd say Collins weren't playing fair and if he weren't careful he'd get himself turned off.'

'Playing fair?' said Emanuel. 'What did he mean by that?'

'Collins were talking about something he didn't ought to.'

'And what was that?' said Emanuel, a rush of excitement passing through him, a hope that he was, at last, about to learn details of the supposed plot. He suppressed the mood. He'd been here before.

'It don't matter none. I got to go,' said Annie. She started to turn away.

'If we can't stop whatever is being planned, people will die,' said Emanuel.

'I don't know nothing about any plan,' she said, her voice rising. 'All I know is what Bristow said to me the night Collins died. He said the scrub deserved to die for what he'd done, that he weren't playing fair. He didn't say no more. Not then.'

'But since?' said Emanuel glancing up sharply.

The girl shrugged her shoulders, a helpless expression on her face. 'There was one time he were muttering to himself. I think he'd forgotten I were there. Anygate, he were carrying on something terrible and said he didn't agree with what were planned. He said it made no sense to turn off a cully what were a Protestant in the Parliament.'

'You mean a Catholic,' said Emanuel.

'No, a Protestant.'

Emanuel stared at the girl.

'You don't believe me, do you?' she shouted angrily. 'They's planning to kill a Protestant what's in Parliament. That's what he said.'

'But it makes no sense, unless…' Emanuel thought for a moment. 'Unless they want to make it look as if the Protestant was killed by a Catholic. That would work. You're sure Bristow didn't mention any names?'

'I know nothing more, mister,' said Annie, her eyes widening in fright. 'I have to go now. Bristow will want to know where I am.'

He watched her hurry away. He had no reason to doubt what she'd told him. But for such a plot to work, the victim would have to be a Protestant of some note whose death, supposedly at the hands of a Catholic, would inflame public opinion and have consequences that he dared not think about. Emanuel walked slowly up the path. Without knowing the name of the intended victim, without clear evidence of a plot to murder, there was little point in him, a Jew and, what was worse, a Catholic priest, attempting to inform anyone in authority about what he'd learned.

Turning into the Highway he joined the chattering horde as it meandered between the market stalls. Annie was leaning against the wall of a house, the same fixed grin on her emaciated face that he'd seen before. He'd given her a few pennies for the time she'd spent with him. It hadn't been enough but it had been all he could afford. She would have to work well into the night to pay for the supposed protection afforded her by Bristow.

He walked past her without acknowledging her presence. It would not have been sensible. Not with Bristow around.

Chapter 20

Henry Teeling was making one of his rare visits north of the Thames when he saw her. She was reading a book from one of the stalls around St Paul's Cathedral, oblivious to the jostling crowd surrounding her. A lock of golden hair had fallen loose from under her cotton mob cap. She pushed it back into place and continued to read. He studied her from a distance, seeing her smile and then frown, her hand flying to her mouth in apparent dismay as her eyes flicked back and forth across the pages. Several times, he thought to approach her but stopped, his courage failing him at the last moment.

He'd seen her once before. At least he thought he had. He stared at her, trying to make up his mind one way or the other. The problem was that on that first occasion, he'd been in no condition to take much notice of anything.

And yet he'd often thought of the fair-haired girl he'd seen that morning in Virginia Street; the one who'd come to his assistance.

Perhaps it was her sense of being watched that caused her to look up and see him. He glanced away and pretended to be examining a book on a neighbouring stall, acutely aware of her presence.

'Forgive me, sir, but have I not seen you before?' she said, stepping towards him. 'You're Master Teeling, are you not?'

Teeling felt the blood rushing to his cheeks. 'I… that is…' he stammered to a halt.

'Why, yes, I am sure of it,' she said. 'I saw you knocked down by some rough fellows in Virginia Street, some two or three months since. I tried to help but…' She left the remainder of her sentence unsaid.

'Aye, I was there right enough,' said Teeling not daring to meet her gaze.

'Well, no matter. I see I have disturbed you, sir,' said Sara turning to leave.

'Miss…?'

'Miss Payton. My name, sir, is Miss Sara Payton,' said Sara.

Teeling hesitated, searching for what he wanted to say. 'I were wanting to thank you for what you did for me.'

'It was nothing,' said Sara. 'I was passing and saw what those evil men did to you. I left you with Mr Emanuel. He—'

'Will you be knowing Father Emanuel?' said Teeling, his eyes widening in surprise. He stopped, suddenly aware of people glancing in his direction. It was a moment or two before he realised why. His accent and his careless use of Father Emanuel's title had marked him as a Papist and made them both the subjects of unwelcome attention. He glanced at Sara and shrugged apologetically. She smiled and beckoned him to follow.

'Yes, I know Mr Emanuel,' she said, when they'd walked a minute or two in silence. 'Not well, but I've met him. But you? Are you much recovered from what happened to you?'

'Sure, I'm well enough,' said Teeling, looking back along the way they'd come. He knew his response could hardly be said to have answered her question but it was all he felt able to say. The physical injuries he'd suffered that morning had, in large measure, healed. He no longer suffered the headaches that, for a while, had been a daily feature of his life. The bumps and bruises inflicted by the kicking had also disappeared. Yet the incident had reawakened in vivid detail the events surrounding the death of his wife at the home they shared outside Wexford. But these were not the thoughts he wanted to share. Not yet. Perhaps never.

'I'm glad you're well,' she said, seeming to sense his reluctance to talk. She turned to go. 'Perhaps we'll meet again, one day.'

For a long time, Teeling remained still, staring at the place where Sara had disappeared from view, swallowed up by the crowds surrounding the bookstalls of St Paul's, unable to make sense of the sudden lightness of his mood.

Chapter 21

The food stall was situated on the south side of the Highway, close to the corner of Fox's Lane. Emanuel could already see the queue of people waiting their turn to be served. More sat at the side of the road munching their way through thick slices of white bread overlaid with rashers of bacon or beef or cheese. Emanuel quickened his pace, a smile of anticipation crossing his lips. The evening meal was one of the high points of his day.

'Been waiting for you, Mr Emanuel.' Emanuel spun round at the sound of the familiar voice. Bristow was standing to one side of the stall, a malevolent grin stretching the sides of his mouth.

'What d'you want, Erasmus?' said Emanuel, doing his best to hide his distaste for the man. He envied people who were able to mask their emotions; to smile whatever their inner feelings. He'd often tried to do so himself but it never seemed quite right, the resulting contortions adding to his own sense of discomfort.

'Been talking to a friend of yours. What was his name, now?' Bristow paused, placing a finger to his lips as though trying to recall the information. 'Aaron something.'

'Aaron Malka?' said Emanuel, a sinking feeling in his stomach.

'That's the cully. We had a good natter, him and me.'

'You mean you robbed him.'

'Why would you say such a thing, Mr Emanuel? And you a priest an' all.' Bristow leaned forward and gave an exaggerated wink. 'It were charity. That's what it were. On account of me having only got one leg and can't work none. I got to eat, ain't I, Mr Emanuel? I mean, it stands to reason, don't it? Mind you, I needed to tap him once or twice as a sort of reminder that a bit of charity were called for.'

Emanuel fought to control his anger. 'Yes, I suppose you would. You always did prefer people smaller and weaker than you, didn't you?'

'He needed a little persuading to tell me what I wanted to know, Mr Papist.' Again, the malevolent grin crossed his pockmarked face. 'It were worth it, Mr Emanuel. He told me all about you.'

The sinking feeling in Emanuel's stomach took an abrupt turn for the worse. He knew it wouldn't have taken much to persuade Aaron to repeat everything he knew. He'd never been able to look after himself and it had always been Emanuel who stepped in to protect him. He tried to remember if he'd told his friend everything that had happened to him since his arrival in England. He thought he probably had.

'D'you remember me ma, Mr Emanuel?' Emanuel stared at him, taken aback by the mention of Bristow's long-dead mother, unsure where the question was leading. 'Course you do. Nobody could forget me ma. She used to come and see you, didn't she? Sometimes it were in that Papist church and sometimes…' He nodded meaningfully. 'Sometimes in your room. Ain't that right, Mister Emanuel?'

'What are you saying, Bristow?' Emanuel's patience was running thin.

'Oh, I think you's going to be very interested in what I have to say, Mr Emanuel.' Bristow's voice had dropped to a low growl. 'She used to tell me everything. I'd forgotten most of it, but your friend Aaron reminded me.'

Emanuel clamped his teeth together and tried to remain calm. His meetings with Elsie Bristow had not been at all frequent and the subjects about which they spoke had generally been limited to one-sided monologues about the difficulties of controlling her errant son. But there had been one occasion when the talk had strayed far from its usual confines. Emanuel had regretted it ever since. It was a confidence he'd hoped she would respect but he'd always known there was a risk he would have to pay for his loose tongue. And now he had repeated his mistake. He'd told Aaron the same thing he'd told Bristow's mother all those years ago. In moments of weakness he'd unburdened himself of the secret he'd carried all his adult life. He'd trusted his boyhood friend as he had trusted Bristow's mother. He could blame no one but himself.

'You've lost me,' said Emanuel. 'Why would I be interested in something your mother told you? She's been gone over ten years.'

'Never you fret, Mr Emanuel,' said Bristow. 'Your little secret is safe with me. For the time being, anygate. You just tell me where I can find your mate Teeling and we'll be all square.'

'Why do you imagine I could, or would, tell you where Teeling is?' said Emanuel.

There was a gleam in the other man's eyes that Emanuel could not quite place. Something had happened. Teeling now appeared to be of some benefit to Bristow. Why and in what way, he could not imagine.

'Let's just say I've got some information what he might be very interested in having. I ain't saying more than that till I see him.'

'I'll pass it onto him when I next see him,' said Emanuel.

'Best you do that, mister,' said Bristow, jabbing a finger at Emanuel's face. 'I ain't in the mood for playing games.'

Chapter 22

The Hon. James Grenville turned in through the white entrance portico of Boodle's, the gentlemen's club on St James's Street of which he was a member.

'Good evening, sir,' said the duty porter, touching the rim of his hat with a single finger.

Grenville nodded curtly and swept into the Morning Room.

'There you are, Sir Peter,' he said, a tight smile crossing his lips as he caught sight of Sir Peter Westlake, partially hidden behind a copy of *The Times*. 'I've been to the house and was told you were here.'

Sir Peter lowered his paper and peered at the newcomer over a pair of steel-framed spectacles. 'Has something happened?' he asked.

'Not yet.'

'What—' The older man stopped short as a black-clad steward appeared and hovered expectantly. 'Drink?' he said, raising an eyebrow in Grenville's direction.

'A brandy, thank you, Sir Peter.'

'Two large brandies, George,' said Sir Peter. He waited for the man to leave before turning back to his visitor. 'What d'you mean? Has something happened or not?'

'Bristow is threatening to make trouble,' said Grenville.

'Really? What's brought that on?' said the older man, disappearing behind his paper.

'The confounded fellow had the nerve to come to my house and threaten me over something that happened in Ireland a couple of years ago.'

'I take it you've now dealt with him.' Sir Peter shook his paper and scanned one of the inside pages.

'It's a little more complicated than that.'

Sir Peter's face reappeared. 'What is?'

'Bristow is in a position to compromise me in a way which threatens our plans,' said Grenville, lowering his voice.

'I see,' said Sir Peter, his gaze travelling round the empty room. From the far side of a connecting door he could hear the raised voices of those at the gaming tables. 'What have you done about it?'

'There…' Grenville searched for the words. 'There may have been someone who saw Bristow and Collins together on the night Collins died. I've got a couple of my fellows looking for him. As soon as he's found I'll have a quiet word in his ear.'

'To what end, pray? I'm not following you, sir.'

'Why, sir,' said Grenville, lowering his voice still more. 'It will be put to this fellow that he saw Bristow in the act of murder. Naturally, he will have to be paid some trifling amount for his trouble.'

'And then what?' said Sir Peter. 'You think this fellow's evidence will rid you of the Bristow problem?'

'I've no doubt about it, sir,' said Grenville.

'I hope, for your sake, sir, you're right, although it's a deuced nuisance and means we'll have to find someone to replace him. We've come too far to stop now.' Sir Peter broke off as the steward came into the room and set down their drinks. When the man had left, he said, 'What's happening about that Jewish fellow; the Popish priest who's been asking questions? Wasn't that a job we gave to Bristow?'

'It's all in hand,' said Grenville, waving his hand impatiently. 'There's something else I wanted to mention to you. It's a somewhat delicate matter…'

'Yes, what is it?' Sir Peter looked over the rim of his brandy snifter.

'I hesitate to raise it, Sir Peter.'

'Spit it out, man. I'd rather like to enjoy this brandy in peace.'

'It's about Lady Westlake's maid, Sara, and your butler.'

#

It was gone midnight by the time Grenville rose from the Faro table and called for his hat and coat. His meeting with Sir Peter earlier in the evening had gone well and he had every reason to expect that despite an initial reluctance on the part of Sir Peter to accept what he'd been told about two of his most trusted servants, the information would shortly bear fruit. He was also quietly confident of the Bristow situation being resolved. The business concluded, he and Sir Peter had parted company shortly afterwards, Sir Peter for home and he for the gaming tables.

Several hours later he'd drunk more than perhaps he should and while he wasn't exactly incapacitated, neither was he in full possession of all his faculties. Had he been so, he might have thought better than to walk home from his club. It wasn't so much the distance that should have informed his decision but rather the inherent risks of walking alone and at night through London. Robberies could not be said to be infrequent, particularly if the victim was seen to be a gentleman of quality who had consumed more alcohol than was good for him. And on this particular night there was an added problem of fog, a thick blanket of which now hid everything from view.

Leaving the club, Grenville lurched slowly up St James's and across Piccadilly, into an all-but-deserted Bond Street. Only two, perhaps three people had passed him so far, their spectral shapes looming out of the mist before disappearing as quickly as they'd appeared. Once or twice he thought he'd heard a tapping sound behind him. He'd turned to look and, seeing no one, had continued on his way.

The fog grew steadily thicker as he walked and, by the time he'd reached Oxford Street, he could see little beyond the reach of his hand. He slowed his pace and glanced to his right where he knew a solid line of coaches would be occupying the central reservation, parked there for the night. Sooner or later he would have to find a gap between them so as to reach his house on the north side.

Again he heard a light tapping noise somewhere behind him, so slight as to barely register on his inebriated mind. He walked on a few paces. The sound came again. Equally faint. This time there was no doubt in his mind. Someone was there. He stopped and peered over his shoulder, through the swirling clouds of white vapour. Fear crept up his spine. He shivered, his hand fumbling in his coat pocket for the pistol he always carried.

'Who's there?' he shouted, his mouth dry. 'Show yourself, else I'll shoot.'

Nothing. No sound and no movement disturbed the night

Then a twig snapped. Grenville felt a shriek rising in his throat. He lifted the pistol, aimed and pulled the trigger. There was no explosion and no lick of flame jumped from the barrel, just the dull thud of the hammer striking the plate. He gazed uncomprehendingly at the piece, his brain unable to process what had gone wrong. He rammed the pistol back into his pocket and drew his sword.

Still no movement.

Grenville wiped away a tickle of sweat from his eye. He thought about rushing whoever was there but dismissed the idea. If there *was* someone, the advantage lay with the other fellow and not with him. He left the comparative safety of the wall and sprinted across the street to the line of parked carriages. He was lucky. He'd found a gap that allowed him through. Reaching the other side he stopped and looked back, breathing heavily. Still he could see nothing but the tumbling curtain of white mist disturbed by his passing. He hurried on, past the houses of the rich, past Stratford Place, his head turning every few yards to search the emptiness behind him.

There was nothing; only the rasping sound of his escaping breath. Slowly, he began to relax. The drink had affected him. No one had been following him. He'd been mistaken.

Tap, tap. Tap, tap. It was gaining on him.

Grenville broke into a run, a frantic, headlong dash to be away from whoever was behind him. His house – really it still belonged to his father, Lord Ardingleigh, although Grenville had come to regard it as his own – loomed out of the mist. He could see the lamps that stood on either side of the wrought iron gate. They were always left burning until after he returned each night. His butler would be waiting up for him to see him safely home. Grenville opened the gate, went through and closed it behind him, his eyes scanning what little he could see of the street. For a moment more he listened. No sounds came. He began to relax. It was probably the drink that had caused the problem. He climbed the steps to the front door and rang the bell.

'Welcome home, sir,' said the butler. 'Shall I ask cook to bring you something before you turn in?'

'No thank you, Dawkins. I shall have a brandy and go up shortly.'

'I shall fetch it directly, sir.'

Picking up a lamp from the hall table, Grenville crossed to the library, a sense of relief flooding through him. He'd made it. He was safe. He sank into a green leather armchair, all thought of what had happened drifting to the back of his mind.

#

The pall of fog shifted and swirled as if disturbed. The dark outline of a man appeared from the doorway of a house and moved silently along the broad expanse of Oxford Street, his movements slow and graceful. From time to time he cocked his head, examining particular houses as he passed. He reached a building in front of which was a tall, wrought iron gate mounted between stone pillars. An oil lantern glowed at the head of each pillar. The man stopped and peered through the gate at the house beyond. Then he nodded, a slow malicious smile spreading across his pockmarked face. He retraced his steps and turned down one of the many streets that led off the main thoroughfare. He knew the way. He'd been here several times in the past few months.

Soon it would be over. The man felt a shiver of excitement pass through him. No one had seen him. No one would see him. He'd make sure of that. He slipped in through a second gate at the back of the property, reached the side of the house and tried one of the sash windows. It was locked. He took out his knife and inserted the blade between the two sashes, flicking the locking mechanism to one side. Quietly, he lifted the bottom sash and eased his powerful bulk over the sill, into the room beyond.

For a moment he stood quite still, his knife held ready in his hand. Hearing nothing, he moved to the door that he knew opened onto the entrance hall. Again he listened. He could hear someone moving around. He eased the door open a fraction and looked out to see a tall, well-built man moving towards the stairs. His route meant he would pass close to the door behind which the stranger now stood.

A sudden draught blew out the candle the man was holding, plunging the hall into darkness.

Chapter 23

Thomas Higgins squatted down by the body lying on the hall floor. He was, by trade, a butcher with a small shop in Long Lane, an occupation which barely brought in enough money to sustain his growing family. It was one of the reasons why, on two or three nights a week, he could be found patrolling the main streets of the capital with the Bow Street Horse Patrol.

The man on the floor was dead. There wasn't any doubt about that. His throat had been cut. Higgins held the candle a little closer to the body and looked at the cut with a professional eye. A single sweep of the knife. The poor bastard would not have died immediately but there would have been no sound.

'And you heard nothing at all, sir?' Higgins looked up at the gentleman standing next to him.

'No, nothing,' said the Hon. James Grenville, his face grey. 'I arrived home after midnight. I'd spent the evening at my club. When I got home I had a small brandy and then went upstairs to bed, leaving Dawkins to finish up. I found that I'd forgotten something and came downstairs to collect it. That's when I saw the poor fellow.'

'Did your butler have any enemies that you are aware of?'

'None,' said Grenville. 'He was a servant on my father's estate in Norfolk and came down with me when I opened up the London house. I don't think he knew many people down here.'

'What about you, sir?' said Higgins. 'Is it possible whoever did this killed the wrong man?'

'What...' Grenville's features took on a lighter shade of grey as the blood drained away. 'What d'you mean, sir? You cannot be suggesting that I was the intended victim.'

'I simply ask the question, sir,' said Higgins, getting to his feet. 'People rarely die in these circumstances without a reason. Somebody appears to have broken into your house, killed your butler and then left without apparently stealing anything.'

'A vagabond, sir, a worthless scrub,' said Grenville. 'I make no doubt he broke into this home with the intention of stealing but came upon Dawkins, here, took fright and murdered the poor fellow.'

'I might have agreed with you, sir,' said Higgins, 'were it not for the manner of your butler's death. You see, the man who did this has killed before. This was not an attack driven by the fear of discovery. The cut to the throat is a single hurt rather than a number of cuts that I would have expected to see from someone acting in a moment of panic. And you heard no sound because Dawkins was unable to cry out. No, sir, this was not done by your average bully-boy. It was done by someone far more dangerous than that.'

'But why?' Grenville's voice rose an octave. 'Why would a professional killer come to my house? I have no enemies.'

'None at all, sir?' said Higgins. 'Am I right in thinking you was in the army, sir? In Ireland? Someone was telling me you was over there during the rebellion of '98. Is that right, sir?'

'Why, yes,' said Grenville, tearing his eyes away from the dead body of his butler. 'What of it?'

'Just thinking, sir. Ireland must have been a rough place then. I'll warrant you saw some terrible things, what with all that were happening.'

'Yes, I did. We all did.'

'Quite so, sir. And I should imagine stern discipline had to be imposed on the locals. Just to keep them in order, of course.'

'This all very interesting, Higgins, but where is it leading?' said Grenville.

'You sure you didn't make no enemies while you was in Ireland, sir?' asked the Bow Street man. 'Quite understandable, of course. Just need to know, that's all, sir.'

'No, none at all,' said Grenville. 'Quite the opposite, in fact. Treated them all as I would my own family.'

'Well respected by your own men and the Irish as well. That's good to hear, sir. Well, I'll be going. Be back in the morning. Once you've rested, sir. Once you've had a chance to think about who might want to do you harm, sir.'

#

A fine drizzle of rain was falling out of a black, starless sky, driven here and there by an erratic north wind. Occasionally a low moan would rise above the clatter of rubbish being blown down the centre of the highway. Otherwise, almost nothing was moving at the western end of Oxford Street.

Almost nothing.

The man eased forward in an effort to relieve the slight discomfort that came from too long spent in one position. He'd been here for close to an hour, waiting for the officer to do whatever it was that officers did on occasions like this. He wouldn't find anything, apart from the body, of course. The man in the shadows was good at what he did. Had to be. One either learned quickly or one hanged. There was no middle way. And he'd made sure that he learned quickly. What he hadn't learned on the streets of Limehouse, he'd learned in the army. He allowed himself a rare smile. Weren't too many jobs where you were taught the many ways of taking a cully's life.

He stiffened as a light appeared in the front door of the house opposite and a man came out. It was the officer. He walked to the gate and swung up into the saddle. Soon he was swallowed up by the fog.

The man listened to the fading sounds of the horse's hooves clattering on the hard road surface. He was conscious of a lingering doubt in his mind. He had felt it almost as soon as he'd left the house. It should have occurred to him sooner. But it hadn't. Something had gone wrong. He'd always found it impossible in these circumstances to think as clearly as was needed, to slow his beating heart and steady his quivering hand in the moments that preceded the taking of a human life. Twenty, perhaps thirty seconds had passed before he'd been able to think. Then had come the first stirring of doubt. It had been too late to go back. That would have invited disaster. He was, however, increasingly sure of his mistake.

He'd killed the wrong man.

He glanced up into the black vault of the night sky and swore silently. He didn't like making mistakes. It meant extra work and the added risk of detection. He turned his gaze back to the house. A candle still burned in one of the ground-floor rooms. Likely it would burn for a little while yet.

He thought of the man inside that room. The scrub would know the knife had been intended for him. He would know who had wielded it. Frightening Grenville was giving him almost as much pleasure as the prospect of killing him. The prick would be looking over his shoulder for the rest of what remained of his life.

He could never relax.

Erasmus Bristow smiled happily.

#

Grenville leaned against the back of a library chair, his head bent forward, a worried frown creasing his forehead. *You sure you didn't make no enemies while you was in Ireland, sir?* Higgins's question kept running through his head. Of course he'd made enemies. He'd made enemies out of nearly every Irishman he'd ever come across while he was out there. How else was he supposed to have dealt with the bastards? It had been a hard and brutal affair and if a man needed pitch-capping then that's what he got. If that made enemies, well he couldn't help that. He'd not been alone in what he'd done. Far from it. They had all done it to a greater or lesser extent. He'd made it a rule to give no quarter when he and his patrol – and that included Bristow and Collins – went out looking for rebels.

Bristow! The mere thought of the villain's name reminded him of all that he loathed about him – and their ill-tempered meeting here in this room. The fellow had had the gall to ask for his help. Naturally, he'd refused and the scrub had threatened to expose him. It wasn't as if he'd meant to kill the woman. If she hadn't resisted, none of what followed would have happened.

But it had happened. Grenville felt his knees weaken beneath him as he recalled the events of that day. The Wexford massacre had been a ghastly affair with mutilated bodies everywhere. He'd taken a patrol and gone in search of those responsible who might still be hiding in the surrounding countryside. It was chance that brought them to the tiny cottage, half hidden amongst a stand of oaks, close to the banks of the river. Sending the rest of his men on, he and Collins and Bristow had approached the isolated cottage from different directions.

He'd seen the woman as soon as he walked in. She'd been sweeping the floor, her dark hair tied into a bundle on top of her head, her movements swift and graceful. She'd looked round at the sound of his heavy footsteps, a scream dying in her throat as he'd motioned her to be silent, her pale green eyes wide with fright, her hands covering her mouth. She could hardly have been more than about twenty yet her hands were those of a much older woman, the skin reddened and lined with deep furrows, her fingernails broken. But for all that she was still startlingly beautiful. He'd felt his heart quicken and his breathing come in short bursts. It had been a long time since he'd last been with a woman.

'Where's your husband?' he'd asked, his voice catching in his throat. She'd not replied. Again he'd asked and again she'd remained mute, staring at him in what seemed to him an insolent manner but was, in hindsight, probably abject terror. His anger had risen in tandem with his desire for her. He'd pushed her to the floor and, for a moment, had stood over her looking down at her trembling body, her dirt-encrusted hands covering her eyes, a low animal-like whimper coming from between her lips.

'Answer me, woman,' he'd shouted, dropping to one knee beside her and encircling her slender neck with both his hands. 'By God I'll teach you people to respect the British army. I'll be damned if you think any of you can get away with murder. I'll hang you and your husband.'

He remembered seeing Bristow come in to the cottage and look at the woman's body, a half-smile lifting the edges of his mouth, a knowing look in the bastard's eye. He'd known with an absolute certainty what that look had meant. It had been part of the reason why he'd chosen to keep Bristow close to him; in a sense, buying his loyalty – and his silence. But it had never worked. Bristow's warped sense of entitlement had always led him to challenge Grenville's superior status, both as an aristocrat and an officer. And witnessing the death of that woman in Wexford had seemed to relieve him of whatever restraints of discipline still remained. After Wexford, Bristow's acts of murderous brutality increased, as though the woman's murder had granted him some unwarranted authority to slice men's throats whenever he so chose.

A single sweep of the knife. The words of the Bow Street officer came to mind… *the man who did this has killed before.*

Grenville poured himself a generous helping of brandy and gulped the amber liquid, feeling it travel down his throat as the implications began to dawn on him. It had been Bristow who had entered his home and killed his butler. But it wasn't the butler who'd been the intended target. It was him.

The vomit rose quickly and spewed out over the Turkey rug in front of the fireplace. Grenville retched a second time, then a third. He wiped his mouth with the sleeve of his coat and felt a cold sweat spreading across his forehead. He tried to get up out of his chair but fell back as the retching continued to convulse him.

It was another hour before he felt strong enough to think of anything other than the nearness of his escape. He settled into his chair, his back to the wall, his eyes sweeping the room, a loaded brace of pistols on his lap. Sleep was out of the question. He could do nothing until the morning.

Then he would act.

Chapter 24

Zechariah Hobbs sat at his usual place in the taproom of the White Admiral on Narrow Street, Shadwell, a quart pot of Truman's on the table in front of him. He was not a young man. Now in his middle sixties, he had worked the foreshore of the Thames since he was a lad, picking up anything of value which had fallen, whether by accident or design, from the deck of a ship. It was never going to make him rich. But he made enough to feed himself and his wife of over forty years. Every day he'd be somewhere along the Upper Pool, doing what he did best – until the incoming tide drove him ashore for a few hours.

Today was no exception. He'd be out again as soon as the ebb tide exposed the mud of the hard – and the occasional trove of coal or hemp or bolt of silk.

He looked up as the stranger walked in through the front door of the tavern, stopped and looked about him as though searching for someone. He wasn't the usual type seen in these parts; too well dressed for that. Big cully, broad-shouldered. Not above twenty-five. Looked like he could handle himself. Hobbs started as he saw the stranger fix him with a momentary stare and then walk towards him. It was almost as though the stranger had been looking for him – had expected to find him here.

'Is your name Hobbs?' said the stranger, his strangled tones marking him out as a member of the higher orders of society.

Zechariah nodded.

The stranger sat down on the bench opposite, laying a silver-topped walking cane on the table in front of him. Zechariah noticed the perfectly manicured fingernails.

'I'm told you work the foreshore hereabouts.'

Another nod, Zechariah's curiosity awakened.

'I'm also told you saw two men fighting on the foreshore earlier this year. Is that right?'

'Might've done,' said Zechariah, one dirt-encrusted fist gripping his mug of beer. 'Seen lots of fights in my time. Ain't easy making a living for the likes of us, like when some bully-boy comes strutting down the foreshore and wants to take what's rightfully yours – well, you just got to fight to keep it.'

'The fight I'm talking about was back in February. One of the men was a cripple, name of Bristow. The other man was a fellow called Collins.'

Zechariah gave a cautious nod of his head. He remembered the fight. It had been towards the end of the day, the winter light fast fading. He'd heard raised voices and, looking up, he'd seen Bristow and Collins standing on the foreshore, close to King James stairs. They were arguing over something, their voices loud and aggressive. He'd known them both since they were nippers living in the same street as his own family. Over the years he'd seen them progress from stealing fruit from the stalls in the Ratcliff Highway to the violence of knife-point robbery. He'd never told anyone. There was no point. Even if he had said something to the beak or one of the old Charlies who occasionally walked the streets of Shadwell, nothing would have come of it. No one was ever held to account for what they did. No, it would have been madness to have involved himself in the affairs of men like Bristow and Collins. He'd be dead inside a week.

But the fight the stranger was talking about had been a minor affair, one he would probably have forgotten; an argument between friends. There had been no harm in it, not that he'd seen. But then he'd not stuck around. It wasn't until two weeks later when he'd been at Limehouse Dock and seen Collins's rotting corpse being brought ashore that he'd realised what must have happened that day.

'Aye, I saw them,' he said.

'And I hear you knew them both. Tell me what happened.'

Irritation wormed its way into Zechariah's brain. The stranger might be a toff but that didn't give him the right to come in here demanding this and that from old Zechariah. He'd not seen anything and that was an end to the matter. He looked fondly at his half-finished beer and wished the stranger would just bugger off and leave him in peace.

'Don't know what happened,' he said.

The eyes of the stranger narrowed. 'What d'you mean? You've just told me you saw them.'

'Aye, I see them, right enough. Then I left. Didn't see no fighting,' said Zechariah.

The stranger stared at him for what seemed an eternity, the palms of his hands laid flat on the table in front of him. Slowly he clenched his fists, his knuckles whitening. Zechariah forced himself to meet the fellow's angry stare, saw his teeth biting down onto his lower lip, traces of blood visible where the skin had been broken. Finally, the man spoke.

'You were there. Tell me precisely what you saw. I'll make it worth your while.'

'I…' Zechariah stopped as the implication of what the man had just said penetrated his brain. 'How much?'

'How much, what?' said the stranger with an impatient shake of the head.

'You said you'd make it worth me while. How much is you paying?'

'Depends on how much you tell me. But since you've said you saw nothing, then nothing is what you'll get.' The man swung his legs out from under the table and got to his feet.

'Well, now that I think on it, I might've seen something,' said Zechariah, rubbing his chin with the back of one hand and eyeing the stranger with renewed interest. He glanced round the taproom at the half-dozen men sitting at the other tables. One or two were taking what appeared to be an unhealthy interest in the developing conversation on the other side of the room. 'But this ain't the place to talk of such things, if you knows what I mean, like.'

For a second the man's face bore a puzzled expression. Then it cleared. 'Very well. Outside, then.'

The two of them left the tavern and walked a few yards along Narrow Street before turning in through the entrance of a court, the stench of excrement heavy in the air.

'What's your game, your honour, if you'll pardon me asking, like?' Zechariah eyed the young gentleman with a mixture of curiosity and anticipation. The good things in life were surely within his grasp if only he played his cards right.

'Tell me what you saw that day,' said the stranger. 'If I like it, I'll pay for it. If I don't, you get nothing. The choice is yours.'

'Like I said, your honour,' said Zechariah, 'I were on the foreshore same as what I am every day, looking for anything what might bring in a penny or two. It were a cold day as I recall, the wind coming up the reach something fearful. Why, I remember—'

'The fight, old man,' cut in the stranger. 'I've not the time to listen to you talking about the weather.'

'Please yourself, I'm sure,' said Zechariah, his face crumpling. 'I were only trying to help.'

'Bristow and Collins. What were they doing? What did they say?'

Zechariah shrugged and looked up and down the court, seeking inspiration. He'd seen nothing beyond a bit of pushing and shoving, accompanied by some colourful language which, he supposed, the gentleman wouldn't want to hear. He'd left the foreshore as quickly and as quietly as his aging legs would carry him as soon as he'd realised what was going on and who the two men were. Yet he had to say something – if he wanted payment.

'Bristow cut him with his knife. That were what happened,' he blurted. 'George—'

'Who?' demanded the stranger.

'It's begging your pardon, your honour. I meant to say Collins. His Christian name were George. Anygate, Collins falls down dead.'

'You are a liar and a scoundrel.' The stranger raised his walking cane and poked it into Zechariah's chest. 'Collins was not stabbed at any stage. The truth of the matter is that you saw nothing.'

Zechariah stared miserably at his feet and said nothing.

‘But what you have demonstrated is a willingness to lie. It is a quality that I intend to make use of. Here is what I want you to do…’

Chapter 25

It was late afternoon when Sara left Sir Peter's house on Cheapside and turned south towards the Thames. It was the part of the day she had always enjoyed most, when a break in her duties meant she had a few hours to wander as she pleased. But the memory of Grenville's threat was still raw. *You and I are not finished, Miss Sara.* The words swirled around Sara's mind as they had done every day since Grenville had tried to rape her. She could still see the look of fury in his eyes at the very public humiliation he'd suffered in front of the servants. She hadn't eaten or slept properly since that day, her stomach a churning mass of constricted muscle whenever she thought of that moment in her room.

Grenville's words were at the forefront of her mind now as she reached the north end of London Bridge and turned down Lower Thames Street where she would normally have lingered a while at the Legal Quays or at the Billingsgate fish dock next door, to watch the hurly-burly of activity. But not today, when her thoughts were again on Grenville's words. *You and I are not finished, Miss Sara.*

She'd almost reached the old Norman Tower of London when she became aware of the limping figure in front of her, of the way his shoulder rose and fell with the effort of each step he took. She had drawn abreast of him before curiosity made her turn and look at him.

'Why, it's you, Master Teeling,' she said. 'I didn't think to see you here.'

Teeling stopped abruptly, an uncomprehending look in his eye and, for a moment, Sara was afraid that he meant to walk away without speaking.

'I'm sorry,' she stammered. 'I should not have spoken.'

'No.' Teeling raised a hand as though to stop her. 'Forgive me, Miss Sara, I were thinking of something. You took me by surprise.'

A moment of silence passed. Sara smiled uncertainly and looked down, not wanting to leave but unable to think of a reason for remaining.

'Will you be stepping this way? I mean… Are you…?' Teeling's voice trailed away, as though embarrassed by the intrusiveness of his questions. He stared at the palms of his hands. 'I'll be going, then.'

'What is it you were about to ask me?' said Sara

'Have you… That is, I were about to take my victuals,' said Teeling, looking suddenly hopeful. 'I were wondering if you would you care to …?'

'Join you?' said Sara, her earlier, troubled thoughts forgotten, at least for the moment. 'Of all things I would like that.'

'We can eat there,' he said, pointing to a brightly painted wagon on Tower Green in front of which a dozen or so folk were waiting to be served.

She watched him join the queue and realised she knew next to nothing about the man with whom she was now to share a meal. In his mid-twenties, he wasn't handsome in any conventional sense, his slight build and thin, bony face together with the thick mop of reddish-brown hair doing nothing to enhance his physical attraction. Yet Sara felt strangely drawn to this shy man who walked with a limp and spoke in the soft tones of southern Ireland. She found herself wanting to know more about him, who he was and where he came from.

Teeling turned unexpectedly and caught her looking at him. He smiled. It was the first time she'd seen him do that. The corners of his mouth curving upwards, his eyes reduced to mere slits behind the crinkled skin of his cheeks. She hadn't meant to respond. Her smile just seemed to arrive, unbidden. She looked away, unable to hold his gaze, a hot flush invading her cheeks. And still her smile remained, her troubles temporarily put aside.

Soon he had rejoined her and together they leaned against the trunk of an ancient hornbeam and munched their way through thick slices of cold beef and buttered white bread washed down with mugs of hot, sweet tea. He asked her about her life and she told him of her family in Norfolk and of the circumstances that had brought her to London. In his turn, slowly and reluctantly, Teeling told her of his past life in Ireland and of the day the soldiers came to the home he shared with his wife on the banks of the Slaney. He'd given few details. But those had been enough. She'd seen the pain in his eyes.

'Did you ever discover the names of the men responsible?' said Sara, reaching out to touch his arm.

'It don't matter none,' said Teeling, staring up into a sky flecked with gold. 'The cully what did it ain't with us no more.'

'You mean he's dead? How did he die?'

Teeling hesitated.

'His body were found in Limehouse Dock. Leastways, that's what I heard.'

'Was it a man named Collins?' asked Sara.

'Aye, that were the villain's name, right enough,' said Teeling. He looked at her with a curious stare. 'How did you know?'

'I was there when he was brought ashore.' She turned to look at him. 'Was he not one of those who beat you so cruelly?'

'Aye, so he was,' said Teeling, a hard, cold look in his eyes.

Sara felt suddenly afraid. She'd heard the rumours of Teeling's involvement in Collins's death. Everyone knew the story. But it had meant nothing to her at the time. She'd not known Teeling's name. And Collins's death had been just one amongst many. Most of those who perished in the river would go to their graves without anyone knowing the name by which they'd lived. Death was routine, unremarked upon, something to be expected in the shifting, nameless population east of the Tower. If Collins's passing was remarkable, it was because he had a name.

Killing a man because of a beating had never seemed much of a motive. But the death of a wife was a different matter. Sara felt a wave of apprehension pass through her, not for her own safety but rather for Teeling's, the popular charge against him now infinitely more plausible. What jury would not, at the very least, ponder long and hard on its deliberations if the matter were to come to trial?

She thought about what had happened – what she'd heard from others and what she'd seen for herself. Had he killed Collins? Of course it was possible. But probable? She doubted it. The cadaver she'd seen at the dockside had been of a heavily built man who, in life, would have been more than able to look after himself. It would have been difficult, not to say impossible, for a man like Teeling to get the better of him.

'You think Collins might have recognised you?' she asked. 'From that day in Wexford, I mean. Is that why he flogged you?'

'Sure, it's possible,' said Teeling. 'But I don't think so. I used to go to Mass each morning. Often there would be men waiting to catch anyone going to the chapel. It were my misfortune that I was caught. I doubt he remembered me but I knew him as soon as I saw him.'

She realised how little she knew of the conditions under which his life in Ireland had been lived. No one of her acquaintance spoke of Ireland and its difficulties. The subject never came up. It was of no interest to the daily lives of the servants with whom she worked, a subject beyond the horizon of their lives.

After the meal the two of them strolled down to the Thames and then east through Wapping and Shadwell, past the rope walks and sailmakers' yards of Limehouse, through choking clouds of noxious smoke spilling from the tanneries and glue manufactories along the way. Here and there the Thames could be glimpsed through gaps in the buildings, its brown waters snaking south, past Cuckold Point to Greenwich and the distant sea.

'Will you return to Norfolk?' asked Teeling.

His question caught Sara by surprise and it was a moment before she understood. They'd reached the southernmost point of the Isle of Dogs, the King's fleet lying to anchor off Deptford Creek and next to it, the incongruous sight of a half-dozen prison hulks. She had told him much about her own life, of where she'd come from and where she'd grown up. She remembered him asking why she'd left and come to London and while she'd not told him everything, he must have sensed her unhappiness.

'I don't know,' she said, watching a grey plover pick its way through the darkening mud banks of the tideway. 'Norfolk is my home. My family is there.' She paused. 'What about you? Will you stay here, in London?'

'Sure, I'll be fine,' he said. 'There's nothing for me in Ireland. Not now.'

It started to rain, great drops falling vertically out of a grey-black sky and they ran to the ferry house that stood alone at the southern tip of the isle. For a few minutes they remained silent, listening to the patter of the rain and gazing over the flat expanse of the river to the splendour of the Royal Hospital and the Queen's House on the far shore. There seemed nothing left to say. For Sara it was as though the unhappiness she'd felt since her arrival in London had, for an hour or two, been lifted only for it to return.

She could see no future for them both.

#

A few miles to the east of the ferry house on the Isle of Dogs and several hours after Sara and Teeling had left that place, a man walked down the main street of Woolwich. He stopped under the sign of the Spread Eagle and, turning up the collar of his Richardson coat, leaned against the tavern wall as though waiting for someone.

On the other side of the street, Emanuel watched the man's arrival. He knew who it was and why he was here. Why would someone like Bristow choose to travel so far if not to further the conspiracy in which he was involved? He remembered being told as much.

'He's planning something and getting some of the lads involved,' Sergeant Candler, the colonel's clerk had told him.

Almost immediately Emanuel caught the sound of approaching voices and a moment later a group of half a dozen men came into view from the direction of the barracks. Seeing Bristow, the group stopped to talk to him before they all went into the Spread Eagle.

Giving them a few minutes, Emanuel followed them to the door of the tavern and peered in. The bar was crowded, the din of conversation deafening, but of Bristow and the men with him, there was no immediate sign. He looked round for a vantage point from where he might search the room without attracting attention to himself. Looking to his right he saw the huge shape of a stuffed bear standing on its hind legs, its teeth barred, its front paws outstretched as though about to attack. It wasn't perfect but it would certainly serve its purpose. He slipped in behind the animal and looked down the length of a rectangular room, on both sides of which were placed a row of low boxes, each one furnished with a table and benches. At the far end was the bar and behind this a row of brass-hooped barrels rested on wooden cradles. To the left of these he could see an old blue curtain.

Still there was no sign of Bristow either in one of the boxes or amongst the dense throng of men occupying the centre of the room. He turned his attention back to the blue curtain he'd seen. It had to have some purpose and he made up his mind to have a closer look. Moving out from his hiding place, he edged through the crowd. One or two heads turned in his direction and the hum of conversation momentarily faltered before again resuming. He ignored them and recalled something his father had once said to him. *Is it not written on my face, even as it is on yours, that you are a Sephardim?* Emanuel smiled inwardly. His apostasy had not altered the truth of his origins. He thought of his parents. They'd be in their mid-seventies now and no doubt wondering how he was. He pushed the thoughts away. Just as soon as he was able he'd write them a letter. It had been too long since he'd been in touch.

He reached the curtain and leaned against the wall next to it as though waiting for someone. Slowly, he moved the material to one side to reveal a door. As casually as he could, Emanuel put his ear to the door and listened. He could hear nothing. It didn't make sense. His options were closing down. He could either give up and leave or open the door. Neither option appealed. But of the two, going through the door without knowing what was on the other side seemed reckless in the extreme.

He turned to leave, a sense of defeat enveloping him. He'd reached the street door when he suddenly remembered something he'd seen earlier. It had meant nothing at the time.

He walked out into the street and looked back at the tavern. A light burned in an upper room. It hadn't been there when he'd first arrived. He ran back to the tavern door and sidled his way back to the blue curtain. He checked no one was paying him any attention. Then he slipped his arm behind the curtain, felt for the iron door latch and pressed the thumb plate. The latch shot up with a loud crack. He looked at the nearest group of drinkers. If they'd heard anything, they were taking no notice. The door opened inwards. With a final look at his nearest neighbours, Emanuel slipped through and found himself at the bottom of a flight of stairs. Up this he now climbed, careful to use only the ends of each tread to minimise the risk of creaking boards. At the top he stopped and looked down a short corridor off which several doors led. From one of these a light shone. He could hear muffled voices, the sound coming from the same room as the light. He moved closer.

'You lads know what to do?' The sound of Bristow's guttural tones made him jump. 'We ain't going to have any foul-ups.' A pause, then, 'Where are the others?'

'They'll be here soon enough,' said a voice. 'Got banged up in the guardhouse. Got pissed last night. They—'

He was interrupted by yet another voice. 'Never mind about that. Someone's been asking questions—'

'What's that?' Bristow's voice again. Louder than before. 'What's that you say?'

'Word is, a cully were in to see the colonel a while back. He were asking questions.'

'What about?' Bristow's voice. 'Colonel knows nothing about us.'

'That's not what I hear. The colonel had plenty to say. Reckoned the discipline weren't up to much.'

'So?' Bristow again, his tone angry, impatient. 'We all know that.'

Laughter.

'Your name were mentioned,' said the same voice. 'Yours and Collins's and Mr Grenville.'

'Who was he? This scrub what's been asking questions?' said Bristow.

'Some cully what nobody knows,' said the first voice.

Another silence. Then Bristow again, 'Ask around. See the colonel's clerk. I want to know who the scrub is and what he knows.'

A pause, then a scraping noise, like that of chairs being pushed back. The meeting had ended.

Emanuel stepped through an adjacent door and closed it softly behind him. Almost immediately he heard the tramp of feet passing the door and descending the stairs. He eased the door open a fraction and looked out as the last man reached the top of the stairs and began his descent, a hand outstretched and gripping the side rail, a bright strip of material tied about his wrist.

Soon, Emanuel was alone. He stayed where he was for a few minutes, thinking of the snatches of conversation he'd heard and regretting not having been there from the start. It was clear he'd missed most of the detail – what was being planned, where and when. Without the detail he had nothing to support his suspicions. He was no further forward than he had been, except… His meeting with the colonel had been noted. There was no doubt his clerk sergeant would be asked for the identity of the visitor and the detail of the ensuing conversation. No doubt the sergeant would talk. He would have to be warned of the danger they were both in.

Emanuel came out from his hiding place and descended the stairs. He opened the door a crack. The taproom was just as he'd left it – noisy, crowded and filled with tobacco smoke. Of Bristow and his friends, there was no sign. He slipped out and closed the door. No one looked in his direction. A minute later, he was out in the mist-bound street and hurrying towards the main gates of the barracks, wondering what reason he could give for wanting to see the clerk sergeant, or even if the fellow was still in the office.

He was in luck. Arriving at the gate, he stated his business and was waved through by a bored sentry. A few minutes later he had found the low building set back from the parade square to which he'd been taken for his meeting with Lord Dalhousie. A light still shone from one of the front windows.

'Why if it ain't Mr Emanuel,' said a startled clerk sergeant, opening the office door. 'You looking for the colonel, is you, sir? It's begging your pardon, sir, but he won't be back until the morning. Can I take a message for you, sir?'

'It's you I came to see, Sergeant.'

'Is that so, sir? In that case, best you come in. What is it I can do for you, sir?

'I've just come from the Spread Eagle. You might remember telling me that Bristow would occasionally meet a few of your soldiers on a Thursday evening.'

The sergeant slowly inclined his head, his eyes fixing Emanuel with a worried frown as he waited for him to continue.

'May I ask if you have an assistant who works with you in this office?'

'Yes, sir. Trooper Dawes. May I know why you asked, sir?'

'It seems my visit to the colonel was noted and my conversation with him, including the names of the men you and I talked about, reported upon. As a result you may find some of your colleagues wanting to know about me and my interest in the regiment.'

The soldier's face turned grey. 'We were seen talking?'

'No, I don't think we were seen when we spoke by the river stairs, if that's what you mean. But somebody told them I'd been to see the colonel and had asked him about certain members of the regiment. They are going to want to know who I am and why I've been asking questions.'

'Oh, is that all,' said the man, his face visibly relaxing.

'I don't imagine,' said Emanuel, 'it will be long before they find someone who saw you follow me out of the barracks and down to Ship Stairs. When they do, I'm sure they will want to know about that meeting as well.'

The grey returned to the sergeant's face. 'I were only trying to help you.'

'Yes, I know, and I appreciate that,' said Emanuel. 'But I need to know you will tell them nothing about me. As to our meeting down by the river, tell them you were simply returning my hat which I'd left behind. Tell them what you please. But don't tell them my name. And, for both our sakes, don't tell them what we talked about. Three people have already died for speaking about what these people are planning to do.'

'They won't get a word out of me, sir.'

'I hope not, sergeant,' said Emanuel.

Chapter 26

Zechariah Hobbs stood in Narrow Street, Shadwell watching the dim shadows of people going in and out of the Shadwell police office. It was nearly ten o'clock, the sun long since gone. He'd been waiting for some time and was still no closer to making up his mind about what to do. It wasn't a question of deciding right from wrong. He'd gone beyond that stage when he'd taken the gentleman's money. No, his hesitation was more about self-preservation than any moral qualms he might once have entertained. The guinea the stranger had given him in the White Admiral tavern, and the two more that he'd promised once the task was completed, was more money than he could earn in six months scuffle-hunting on the foreshore of the Thames.

But the bargain had come with a price of its own. Zechariah closed his eyes and wished the problem would go away. The gentleman – he'd refused to give his name – had made it clear what would happen should he fail to perform the agreed task. It hadn't been pleasant. He wiped his face with the palms of his hands and stared at the building opposite. He'd been through those doors into the police office many a time in the past and had hoped, at his stage in life, never to repeat the experience. He thought again of the money. He could just give it back to the gentleman – if only he knew who he was and if only he hadn't already spent a sizeable proportion of the down payment. He was beginning to wish he'd never met the cully.

He thought back over the meeting and what the aristocrat had told him to say. ‘No one can contradict you,’ he’d said. ‘No one else, apart from Bristow, was there. You are to say that you saw the whole thing. You were on the foreshore when you saw Bristow and Collins arguing. Suddenly, and without any provocation, Bristow struck Collins on the head with one of his crutches. The blow rendered him insensible. Bristow then struck him a second time with a stone before dragging him into the river and pushing him in. When Bristow left, you tried to save Collins but you couldn’t reach him.’

The door of the police office opened and a number of people come out, walking off towards Limehouse. Zechariah ignored them, his stomach churning. He looked up and down Narrow Street one last time and then crossed to the white-painted building.

Chapter 27

Sara jumped. Someone was knocking on her bedroom door. She wasn't expecting anyone. It had been a long day and she'd been looking forward to some rest.

'Who is it?'

'It's me, Miss Sara. It's Maisy,' said the voice of the undercook. 'Mr Jones sent me to find you. The master wants to see you in the library.'

'Now? Very well, I'll be there directly.' Sara rubbed the tiredness from her eyes and tried to think what Sir Peter could possibly want her for. As her ladyship's maid she didn't normally have anything to do with the master. She dressed quickly, splashed some cold water on her face from the basin in the corner, pushed her long fair hair under her mob cap and ran down the back stairs to the library. She knocked and waited.

'Come in.'

Sir Peter was sitting in one of the red leather armchairs by the hearth, a glass of something in one hand. Opposite him sat the Hon. James Grenville. Neither man was smiling.

'You sent for me, sir,' said Sara, noticing the presence of Mr Jones, the butler, standing by the bookcases. Her mind racing, she thought through everything she'd been asked to do by her ladyship over the course of the long day. There was nothing she'd forgotten that she could recall.

'Yes, I did,' said Sir Peter, his voice putting an end to her thoughts. 'I regret that earlier today, as a result of what Master James, here, told me, I asked for a search to be carried out of your room and that of Mr Jones. That was duly done. From both rooms were recovered a number of valuable items of silverware that belong to this house.'

Sir Peter glanced at Grenville as if for confirmation of what he was saying. 'I fully expect you and Jones to deny all knowledge of how these items came into your possession so I do not propose to ask you for an explanation. You are both dismissed from my employ with immediate effect. However, in your case, Mr Jones, in recognition of your long association with his family, I will not insist on your prosecution. But you, Sara, I have yet to make up my mind about. That is all. I expect you to be gone from this house within the hour. Good day to you.'

'Sir, I had—' There was a horrified look on the butler's face.

'Enough, Mr Jones. I confess I am deeply disappointed by your conduct. Had it not been for Master James, I might never have discovered your dishonesty.' He turned his gaze to Sara and went on, 'In your case, Master James tells me he has long suspected you of being a common thief. It was, I now realise, one of the reasons why Lord Howard dispensed with your services at his Norfolk estate. It is a matter of some regret that he chose not to tell me this when recommending you to my service, but that is another matter. Fortunately, Master James saw you both removing the articles. He followed you, Mr Jones, and was in time to see you take the items into your room. As I have already said, both your rooms were searched and the items recovered. That will be all.'

Sara, her face pale with fright, glanced at the seated figure of the Hon. James Grenville. He was looking at her. She could have sworn he was smiling.

It was difficult to tell.

Chapter 28

It was nearly midnight before Emanuel got back from his meeting with the clerk sergeant at Woolwich. He climbed the river stairs and turned right onto a Wapping Street bathed in the silver light of a full moon. Here and there, dark shadows reached across the street like the tentacles of some prehistoric monster. Few people were about. Those he saw would suddenly appear out of the gloom and glide silently by to be quickly swallowed by the night.

The conversation he'd overheard in the upper room of the Spread Eagle was still playing on his mind. Word had obviously spread of his interest in what had happened two summers ago at Wexford and of his meeting with Colonel Ramsay, Earl of Dalhousie. Yet, of greater concern to him was the level of detail that was known of his conversation with the colonel, including his interest in the activities, during that period, of Collins, Bristow and Lt. James Grenville. That Bristow would eventually discover – if he did not already suspect – Emanuel's identity, was in little doubt. It could only be a question of time before the sergeant was persuaded to part with the required information.

At the corner of New Gravel Lane, he turned northwards towards the Highway, suddenly aware of a chill in the air that had little to do with the weather. He slowed his pace, immediately alert, his eyes peering into the blackness of the shadows. In the distance he could hear the crowds still moving up and down the Highway. Another fifty yards or so and he would be amongst them. He jumped as a door slammed shut behind him. He waited for quiet to return, his sense of unease persisting. It was as though a cold mist were surrounding him, hiding from him some unseen danger. For a brief moment he thought of returning to Wapping Street and choosing another route to his room. He wavered. Home was less than two or three minutes away. He was tired. He wanted only to get to his bed. And sleep. He walked on.

Suddenly the shadow of a man separated itself from the gloom and came towards him. Emanuel stopped and instinctively looked behind him. Another two shapes were closing on him, one from each side of the street. He waited for them, again searching for an escape route. There was none. One, perhaps two, he could handle. Three was a different proposition.

A torch flared into life and was thrust towards him, his stomach twisting as he recognised Bristow's contorted features. He wondered how much, if anything, the man knew of his visit to Woolwich. It didn't seem likely. Not in so short a time. He waited for him to speak.

'Seems you ain't been listening to what I've been saying to you, Mr Papist,' said Bristow, an ugly, aggressive edge to his voice. 'You's been asking questions what it ain't clever to ask. I don't care for people what poke their snouts where they ain't wanted. You understand me?'

'What are you talking about?' said Emanuel, still unsure about the extent of Bristow's knowledge. 'You're not making any sense.'

'We'll see who's making sense and who ain't, Mr Papist,' said Bristow. He looked over Emanuel's shoulder at the men behind and pointed a crutch at the priest. At once, the men took up positions on either side of him.

Emanuel felt strangely calm, his anxiety dropping away from him, his mind crystal clear. He glanced at the two men, both in their early thirties, both going to seed, their stomachs protruding to the point that he doubted either man had seen his manhood in recent years. But that was not to underestimate the damage they could do him. He'd already seen the hilts of their knives sticking out from their belts and doubted they'd have any compunction about using them. Still…

He fixed his eyes on Bristow, mentally rehearsing what might need to be done. He'd already noted the relative position of each man, the distance to each, their likely response times to any action he might take, and their points of weakness. These were basic skills he'd learned long ago as a young man growing up in the back streets of Lisbon. If it came to it, he would strike first and strike hard. There could be no hesitation. No doubt. No fear of losing. But he knew something else, too. There could be no warning of his intention. He would wait for the most favourable moment before taking his chosen path.

'You's coming with us on account I want a quiet word with you,' said Bristow, catching hold of Emanuel's arm.

Emanuel allowed himself to be propelled across New Gravel Lane and along an adjacent alley. Thirty yards later he was pushed through a doorway into a house and down the length of a short corridor. The place seemed familiar, although he couldn't for the moment think why. Bristow pointed to an open door and the four of them entered a small room. Two women who had been asleep on a dirt-encrusted mattress scrambled to their feet and hurried out, their heads bowed, their frightened eyes averted.

'You've had your little fun, Bristow,' said Emanuel, his patience dwindling. 'Suppose you tell me what this is all about so we can all go about our business.'

'My little angel, my little girl what folk round here calls Willing Annie. She tells me you been talking to her. Is that right, Mr Emanuel? You been nattering to my little Annie what were supposed to be working?'

'I talk to lots of people, Bristow, including you,' said Emanuel. 'Now, if you've quite finished, I'll be on my way.'

'Not so fast, Mr Papist,' said Bristow, pushing Emanuel further into the room. 'I ain't finished, see?'

Emanuel's temper flared and he considered swatting Bristow's hand away. It was a risk. It was likely to provoke a response. If it came to a fight, he would need the element of surprise to have any chance of success against the three of them. Even then, he wasn't sure. It had been a long time since he'd fought against such odds He let the moment pass. The time wasn't right.

'She won't be troubling you no more, Mr Emanuel.' Bristow was speaking again. 'We can't have people running around saying all manner of things what ain't true, now can we?'

'What have you done to her, you scoundrel?' shouted Emanuel, his fists clenched. He forced himself to calm down. Whatever had happened to Willing Annie had happened. Losing his temper would serve no useful purpose now.

'Never you mind about her, Mr Papist,' said Bristow leaning forward and tapping Emanuel's chest. 'But you's a different matter.'

Emanuel glimpsed the slight movement. It might so easily have passed unnoticed, the almost imperceptible nod of Bristow's head as his eyes flicked from one of the two bully-boys to the other. Emanuel knew what was coming. He could see all he needed to of the men on either side of him; their hands moving towards the knives tucked in the waist of their slops.

The time for talk had ended.

Chapter 29

Fifteen miles south of London, two men sat talking in the library of a small country house situated on a hill not far from the village of Keston. The subject of their conversation was the forthcoming debate in the House of Commons on the subject of the Emancipation Bill.

'My dear Minister, you must know that my constituents are most unhappy with your proposals,' said Mr David Fielding, Member of Parliament for West Kent. A man in his early forties, he might once have been considered handsome but a florid complexion and an expanding waistline had long since spoilt the bloom of early manhood.

'You are to consider the implications of your position, sir,' said Mr William Pitt, the King's First Minister. 'We are at war, sir. We face perils on every side. Our situation is desperate. The French ready themselves for invasion and have already made use of Ireland as a means for attacking us in these islands. So long as we continue to suppress the hopes and ideals of the Irish people, we cannot expect their support in our hour of need. You and your colleagues must know how draining of our resources is the Irish question at a time when we can least afford it. And if that were not enough, thousands upon thousands of Catholic Irishman are denied the opportunity to serve this country in the army at a time when their assistance is desperately required. I implore you, sir, to think again about your opposition to my proposals.'

'I have given the matter a deal of thought, Minister, but neither I nor my colleagues in the House feel we can support the notion of full union with Ireland,' said Fielding.

'I'm exceedingly sorry to hear that, sir,' said Pitt. 'You are, of course, entitled to your views and your right to give expression to them. However, in these special circumstances may I ask you to reconsider your decision to speak publicly on the issue? You know how easily the mob can be excited to violence and neither of us, I think, would wish to see the militia diverted from their primary task of defending the realm to the role of peacekeepers on our streets.'

'I'm afraid, Minister, I cannot give such an assurance. The public whom we both serve are entitled to know what is being done in their name.'

'Regardless of the consequences?' said Pitt.

'Regardless,' said Fielding.

Chapter 30

In the squalid back room of the house on the Ratcliff Highway, waiting was, for Emanuel, no longer an option. Moving with a speed that belied his age he brought his right leg up in a fast jabbing kick, catching the man nearest him in the groin.

He didn't wait to see the effect, didn't need to see the man's eyes widen in shock, his mouth open in a silent scream of pain and his body double up in agony. He already knew that that would be the effect of what he'd delivered. Without pausing, he spun round to face the second man. The cully was still fumbling for his knife. He'd failed to see the danger he was in.

Emanuel didn't hesitate. He drove his clenched fist hard into the man's stomach and watched him pitch forward. Judging his moment, he brought his knee up. Jaw and knee collided with bone-shattering force, dislodging the few teeth the unfortunate man had, until this moment, still possessed.

Two down. One to go. If he got out of this alive Emanuel promised himself he'd ask My Lord Bishop to hear his confession for what he'd done and what he was about to do.

He was fast.

But not fast enough.

The heavy wooden crutch struck his right leg below the knee. The shock and the pain sent him tumbling to the ground. He scrambled to regain his feet but Bristow was on him, the fingers of one hand closing round his neck. He glimpsed the other two men. They were still down. But for how long he couldn't say. The grip around his neck got tighter. He felt nauseous, his eyelids heavy. He wanted to sleep.

‘I warned you.’ Bristow’s voice came as if from far away.

Emanuel’s eyes popped open as he forced himself to stay awake, to concentrate on what was happening. Blows rained down on him, each one harder than the last. The effort to remain conscious was getting harder.

Then his chance came.

Bristow’s face was close to his own. Barely six inches separated them. He saw the black stumps of his bared teeth, his face twisted into a snarl of hatred, his eyes blazing in anger.

‘You’re going to fucking die for what you did to me ma.’ Emanuel felt the pungent stench of Bristow’s breath. ‘You understand me, Mr Jew priest. I’m going—’

He got no further.

Emanuel brought his head up with all his remaining strength and speed, his forehead smashing into Bristow’s nose in an explosion of blood and gristle. He supposed the unearthly howl that came from Bristow’s lips was more the result of shock and wounded pride than the undoubted pain the scrub was suffering. The thought was quickly replaced by the need to escape while he had the chance. He pushed the still groaning Bristow off his chest and climbed unsteadily to his feet. He felt dizzy and unable to focus, the walls of the room seeming to wave like sheets of cotton in the wind. He stretched out a hand and felt for the nearest solid object, missed, and fell to the ground, unconscious.

#

When Emanuel awoke, he was by himself, a watery sunlight streaming in through what appeared to be a small window. He was lying on floorboards beneath a sloping, tiled roof. He looked round, a hammering sensation at the back of his head. Nothing was familiar. He brought his hand up to his face and felt the swollen skin round his eyes and his lips. He still couldn't see properly and he doubted he'd be able to say much, either. He lay still and tried to remember how he came to be in this place. There'd been a fight. He remembered that. It had involved Bristow and two of his bully-boys. He had a vague recollection of someone helping him up some stairs.

He slept. For how long he didn't know. A hand was shaking him. He opened his eyes. A young woman was bending over him. He recognised her as one of the two women he'd seen running out of the room when he, Bristow and the other two scrubs had arrived at the house. When was that? Last night? The night before? The girl was painfully thin, a brightly coloured cotton dress hung loosely, her bare arms more bone than flesh. He wondered if it was she who'd brought him here and where 'here' was. She reminded him of Willing Annie – same age, same skeletal frame, same frightened look. She didn't look strong enough to have helped him.

'You all right, mister? You didn't 'alf give me a fright. Thought you was a goner.'

He nodded, his mind already elsewhere. 'Where am I? Where's Bristow?' he asked.

'He's downstairs,' said the girl. 'He's been carrying on something dreadful about what he wants to do to you when he catches you. He'll be gone soon, I reckon. Then you must leave. It ain't safe.'

'Was it you that brought me here?' Emanuel felt the swelling around his neck. His near-throttling was affecting him more than he'd realised – that and the beating.

'Aye, me and one of the other girls. We was close by and heard all the fighting. We thought they was going to turn you off. It wouldn't be the first time, sir. Not by a long way. Anygate, the next thing we see is you coming through the door and the others lying on the floor, howling like little children what wants their mother. Oh, sir, me and my friend was so happy, we was crying.'

'So you brought me here,' said Emanuel, propping himself up on one elbow and looking round what appeared to be the garret. The window he thought he'd seen when he'd first awakened and through which the sunlight had streamed was, he now saw, merely a gap in the roof tiles. He blinked and looked round. There was no furniture in the long, narrow space, only the scattering of straw on which he was lying, next to what looked to be a chimney stack.

'Aye, it were the only place we could think on, sir,' said the girl, following his gaze. 'Bristow never comes up here. On account of his leg, see?' She paused and looked at him. 'But that don't mean you's safe. We just got to hope he thinks you's long gone.'

Emanuel stayed silent for a while. He'd thought the house was familiar. Now he remembered why. It was the same house he'd run into whilst trying to avoid Bristow the first time the two of them had met since before the loss of his leg. It was here, in this house, that he'd met Willing Annie.

'There's a girl who lives here,' he said. 'I believe she is a favourite of Bristow's. You may know her. Her name is Annie.'

'Aye, I know her,' said the girl, her thick eyebrows arching in surprise. 'There's some what call her Willing Annie. She's hurt bad, and that's the truth. Bristow beat her something cruel. Don't know why. She wouldn't tell me.'

'But she lives?'

'Aye, she lives, but that ain't no thanks to that villain,' she said. 'Bristow don't care none about folk. I told you before, it wouldn't be the first time he's put some poor devil to bed with a shovel. Why, there were some cully what he flogged only the other day what up and died. One of them Christ-killers, he were.'

Emanuel looked up sharply. 'A Jew? What did he look like?'

'Only saw him for a few seconds,' said the girl. 'I were with a customer. Saw Bristow talking to this cully. Tall, he were. Not big, like Bristow, but tall. Had a long beard and had one of them black dresses what Jews wear.'

'Poor Aaron,' muttered Emanuel. 'He died because of me. I pray to God he didn't suffer too much.'

'I don't know nothing about that—' The girl stopped suddenly and pressed a finger to her lips. From somewhere below came the sound of a door opening and the stamp of feet on the stairs. 'It's Bristow. Or one of his bully-boys. I reckon they's looking for you.'

#

Bristow had always known the value of fear. It was the only currency that really mattered to him. Inflicting it on others had ensured their loyalty, support and absolute obedience. It was this thought that now ran through his mind as he stood at the bottom of the stairs holding a rag to his shattered nose. Dealing with the Jew priest was now his first – his only – priority. It wasn't just that the jumped up piece of shit had got the better of him, although that had been bad enough. What had made it infinitely worse was that it had been witnessed by his two bully-boys. A chink had appeared in his armour. He was vulnerable. He would be seen as weak. If word got out, he was finished.

'What you want us to do?' asked one of the men, standing behind him.

'What d'you fucking think?' shouted Bristow, waving an arm up the stairs. 'Find the Jew and fetch him here.'

'He ain't up there, Bristow,' said the larger of the two men, nervously toying with a coat sleeve. 'We've searched everywhere for him. Stands to reason, don't it? He ain't stupid. He's legged it.'

'You hard of hearing, cock?' said Bristow. 'Get up them fucking stairs and find the scrub; else you'll answer for it. If he ain't there, bring Annie down. I'll warrant she knows a thing or two what she ain't telling me.'

#

Emanuel listened to the tramp of feet on the stairs below. It required no imagination to guess what would happen if he was found. He prayed silently for a few seconds, reconciled to his imminent and extremely painful demise. His physical strength expended and the element of surprise no longer in his favour, he could hardly expect to prevail this time around.

From somewhere below there was a splintering crash of a door being kicked open. Someone screamed. A man swore, followed by the heavy thud of a body falling to the floor. Then silence. Emanuel guessed the two bully-boys of recent memory had finished their search of one room and were moving to the next. A pause, then more noise. The cry of a familiar voice.

Willing Annie's.

Emanuel heaved himself onto one elbow and peered round the corner of the chimney stack at the garret door. As a hiding place it wasn't ideal but he had to hope it would protect them from all but a determined search.

A dull slapping sound of flesh on flesh. Another cry of pain. A low rumble as a body was dragged across the floorboards and down the stairs, a bump, bump, bumping sound as of someone's heels striking the treads.

'It's me they want, not Annie,' said Emanuel. 'I must go. They will kill her, else.'

'They'll not kill her,' said the woman, placing her hand on his chest and pushing him back down. 'She earns more money for Bristow than the rest of us put together. But you is a different matter. He'll send you straight to the Devil himself. And me as well.'

Willing Annie's terrified shrieks got louder as the beating continued. He could hear Bristow's voice threatening, cajoling, cursing.

'Does she know anything?' asked Emanuel.

'No, she weren't here when my friend and me found you and brought you here.'

'Then how long before Bristow stops?' said Emanuel, his face creased with worry. 'She can't take much more. He'll kill her.'

'You can't save her, mister,' said the girl. 'He'll kill all three of us if you go now. I ain't never heard him so angry.'

Emanuel felt a wave of conflicting emotions pass through him – anger, regret, sorrow, relief, shame – all of them competing against one another for the doubtful privilege of his attention. He thought of the suffering Annie was enduring on his behalf and wished he had it in him to stop it, to punish those responsible for what was happening. But he knew his involvement would solve nothing. The girl was right. Going down now would result not only in his death but the probable deaths of the two girls as well. The sense of shame welled up afresh; that he was thankful of the excuse not to go down.

It was a second or two before he realised the noise from below had stopped. He looked up at the girl. She was staring at the door of the garret. Suddenly she turned and pointed to the chimney stack.

'Someone's coming,' she whispered, her face ashen with fright. 'Get back out of sight.'

A moment later the door burst open and one of Bristow's men came in.

'You see them?' Bristow's harsh tones floated up from the ground floor.

'Nothing up here.' The door banged shut and footsteps receded.

Again, the girl moved over to the door and listened. 'I think they's gone, your honour,' she whispered. 'We was lucky. The cully what came likes me but next time…' The girl shrugged, her sentence unfinished.

'Stay here while I go down and look,' said Emanuel.

'No, I'll come with you,' said the girl. 'Bristow don't live here. If he's gone, he won't be back afore tomorrow and not even then, I reckon.'

Annie was unconscious, her thin, childish body lying in the corridor on the ground floor, her face bruised and bloodied, the flesh around her eyes already showing signs of swelling.

'Get some water,' said Emanuel. 'Bathe her face while I make sure Bristow and his thugs have gone.'

He was back in less than a minute. 'They've gone. All three. But there's a man and a woman upstairs in one of the rooms. Who would they be? D'you know?'

'She's my friend. It were her what helped me get you into the garret. As for the cully…' She shrugged. 'That'll be a customer of hers. He ain't nothing to worry about.' She turned her attention back to Annie, dabbing her face with a damp cloth. 'She don't look too good, your honour.'

Emanuel knelt and put his hand on Annie's forehead. She was shivering. 'She's taken a beating, that's for sure. But I think it looks worse than it is. It doesn't appear as if anything is broken except, perhaps, her nose. Is there somewhere we can put her so she can begin to recover? It might be better if we could find another house. I wouldn't want Bristow anywhere near her for a week or two.'

'I know of a place,' said the girl.

Chapter 31

Emanuel's condition gradually improved over the following few days. And while movement of any kind was a slow and painful business, his suffering was no longer what it had been. He'd retreated to Holborn, to the home of the bishop whose housekeeper had seen it as her bounden duty to look after Emanuel's every need. Nothing ever seemed too much for her as she watched over her new charge. Whether or not this degree of attention to his recovery had any noticeable effect on his returning strength was less clear. Emanuel chafed at the restrictions placed on him and would, despite his physical discomfort, have preferred to be about his priestly business. He was also worried about Willing Annie and the possibility of Bristow discovering her hiding place. It made no difference. His frequent attempts to persuade his self-appointed guardian that he was now perfectly restored to health and vigour continued to fall on deaf ears.

It was not until the end of the week that Emanuel was grudgingly allowed to return to his room in Farmer Street, the housekeeper's shrill warnings about the need to be careful following him down Castle Street and – it seemed to him – beyond. His relief at being able to perform his duties was tinged with the knowledge that his relationship with Bristow – while always a precarious one – had now taken a significant turn for the worse. The man was not given to rational thought and was incapable of understanding the conflicting merits of a dispute. He lived his life by a philosophy that understood everything in terms of the persuasive influence of physical violence and a determination to visit its most extreme form on those who crossed him.

Emanuel turned into the Ratcliff Highway, thoughts of Bristow quickly pushed to the back of his mind as the more immediate concerns of navigating his way through the meandering – and potentially hostile – crowds, took over. The day was a warm one although the sun lay hidden from view behind dense clouds of smoke raining soot over folk, rich and poor alike. He walked as quickly as he was able, his handkerchief held to his nose, his eyes searching the road ahead for the warning signs of impending trouble. He knew many, if not all, the local villains, knew those it was safe to ignore and those he would do well to avoid. He could never be sure of his judgement. He'd made mistakes in the past – and suffered the consequences.

He saw her standing at the entrance to a court, her back to him. She was talking to someone. Probably a customer. Emanuel shook his head. It didn't seem possible she could be back on the streets so soon. A week ago, Willing Annie had seemed close to death. He watched her give a resigned shrug of her shoulders, turn and begin to walk away.

'Annie?' said Emanuel.

The girl spun round, a frightened expression on her face, a hand drawing a scarf over the lower part of her face. She saw him and visibly relaxed.

'I'd ask you why you're working,' said Emanuel, 'but I suspect I already know the answer. Bristow wants his money.'

Annie didn't answer immediately. She stared, wide-eyed, at the faces of those nearest to her as though to satisfy herself they presented no threat. 'He's been collared,' she said, turning to look at him, her voice no more than a whisper.

'Who has?' said Emanuel.

'Bristow. The constables came for him this morning. They said he'll hang for Collins's murder. Bristow reckons it were on account of you and…'

She stopped and seemed on the point of tears.

'And what, Annie? What did he say to you?'

'He said it were me what's got him into trouble with the law on account of I told someone that it were him what killed Collins.'

'I see,' said Emanuel, recalling the last time they'd spoken, close to her strip on the Ratcliff Highway. She'd told him about the night Collins had been killed.

He went looking for him and found him down on the Thames foreshore. They argued and there was a fight.

... he killed him?

Aye. Leastways, that's what Bristow said.

Emanuel looked up to find the girl staring at him.

'I didn't say nothing about you, Mr Emanuel. Honest, I didn't,' she wailed.

'Hush, child. I know you didn't say anything,' said Emanuel, his mind racing. It was only natural Bristow should suspect Annie of passing the incriminating evidence to Emanuel. He knew the two of them had met. Did that also explain the beating Bristow had attempted to inflict on him the night of his return from Woolwich? It would have made sense. It had worried Emanuel that Bristow had somehow got wind of his meeting with Colonel Ramsay at the barracks in Woolwich. Had that been the case it would not have helped.

He wondered where Bristow was at this moment.

#

Erasmus Bristow sat in the holding cell at the Shadwell police office listening to the murmur of voices on the other side of the iron-clad door. The constables had come for him before dawn as he'd thought they might. He'd been expecting them for several days. He'd thought of making himself scarce, of going up north for a few months, but in the end had done nothing to save himself. It was almost a relief when they had come. The worry of not knowing the day or the hour had begun to wear him down. He'd not slept properly since he'd been told his fight with Collins had been witnessed. He'd known then it was all over for him.

He'd trodden this path too often to have any illusions about what to expect – the appearance before the magistrate, the hearing of the indictment on the charge of murder, his committal to the Old Bailey to stand his trial. His conviction and sentence were a near certainty. It wasn't going to be pleasant. But then dying never was. He'd seen it often enough, standing amongst the jeering crowds watching the wretched souls emerge through a trapdoor in the floor of the scaffold. In those few seconds, their shocked eyes would be drawn upwards to the heavy wooden beam skewered with butcher's hooks onto which the hangman's rope would be attached. A few had strode forward as if impatient for the deed to be done. Most had needed to be pushed by the turnkeys to their allotted place, their open palms seeming to implore mercy in the face of the inevitable, their faces twisted in the agony of despair. There had been something almost comical in the hopelessness of their situation, the nightcaps perched on their heads like some ludicrous effigy, soon to be drawn down over their faces, a final insult to their dignity, the obliteration of their humanity.

He had given no thought to the mental anguish the poor bastards must have suffered in those final moments of life. For him, as for countless others who stood with him, it had been theatre of a matchless kind, where the diehards were the heroes of the moment while those who broke down and cried out for mercy provided the real entertainment. For them was reserved the hoots and cries of derision that would rent the air as, from the far side of Skinner Street, the first strike of the bell of St Sepulchre's signalled the beginning of the end of their mortal existence.

Bristow looked down at his hands. They were trembling. He didn't want to die. Not yet. Not this way. He thought of Collins. Somebody had described seeing his grey, shrivelled skin and sunken jaw lying on the dockside at Limehouse, his milky dead eyes gazing up into the sky. Despite everything, it had been a shock to learn of his death. He'd always nurtured a lingering hope that somehow Collins had survived the murderous onslaught he'd inflicted on him. It was only when Collins's body was found that he'd come to finally accept his death – and his own culpability.

He bent forward, his head in his hands. He should never have agreed to kill him. Whilst they'd never been friends in the true sense of the word, he and Collins had grown up together, robbing and pillaging at will. They had even been pressed into the army together and shared the dangers of military life. But for all that, they'd never been close. The cully had been a convenience, someone willing to join him in his chosen life, to do his bidding.

And now he was dead.

Bristow stared with unseeing eyes at the glimmer of daylight filtering in through a crack in the wicket gate. The voices he'd heard earlier had gone, replaced by the patter of rain falling against the door and leaking into the cell.

He thought again of the night Collins had died. The fight had been short and fierce. What he lacked in mobility, Bristow had made up for in a ruthless pursuit of victory that left no room for notions of fairness or friendship. He smiled inwardly, remembering how Collins had hesitated to strike when he, Bristow, had stumbled. It had been a mistake that was to prove his opponent's undoing. He'd lunged at the man's stomach with the point of one of his crutches, winding him. Another blow, this time to his head, had sent Collins sprawling, seemingly lifeless, to the cloying mud of the Thames foreshore.

Bristow remembered looking down at the unmoving shape before him, the furious rage that had driven him suddenly departing. A side of him had wanted to believe the stupid bastard was still alive. He should have checked. But what if he'd been right? What then? No, better by far that he didn't know. Otherwise he might have had to finish what he'd started. And he wasn't at all sure he could've done that.

The rattle of keys in the lock interrupted his thoughts. It was time for his appearance before the magistrate. If he was lucky, the beak would throw his case out. But he doubted that would happen. More likely he would be indicted.

And afterwards?

For almost the first time in his life, Bristow felt his heart flutter.

#

The hum of subdued chatter fell away as, the following day, Bristow climbed the steps into the dock of the Old Bailey and gripped the iron railing that surmounted the solid oak panelling. His appearance before the Shadwell magistrate the previous day had gone as he thought it would – depositions heard with indecent haste, followed by the equally rapid committal. Then across to Southwark for the hearing by the grand jury before his appearance here in the sessions house in the City.

The scene was exactly as he remembered it from his last appearance. In front of him, lounging on polished benches in the well of the court, were several black-robed and bewigged figures, chatting quietly amongst themselves. In front of them, and at a slightly higher level, was the clerk, who, from time to time would look up from his desk and peer round the room with an air of scarcely concealed boredom. Behind and above him were a row of empty chairs, only one of which would shortly be occupied by the trial judge.

Bristow looked away to his right where the twelve men who were to form the jury of his peers sat staring at him in what seemed to be no more than passing interest. Doubtless they were looking forward to the end of their day when they could return to their homes and their families, the inconvenience of jury service forgotten for a few hours. He wondered if they had already formed an opinion of him, had found him guilty before a word of evidence had been uttered.

He would have liked to spend more time searching their faces for any hint of what they were thinking but to do so might be taken for fear on his part. And he was damned if he was going to give them the satisfaction of seeing that. He'd never shown his feelings in the past and he wasn't about to start now. He bit down on his lip and wished his heart would stop beating quite so painfully, his eyes fixed on the empty chair below the Sword of Retribution. It was where the trial judge would sit. A bead of sweat formed above his right eye. He resisted the urge to wipe it away. That, too, would have been a sign of weakness. He wished the trial would begin. He hated this waiting, not knowing his fate.

A door to the left of the empty chairs opened a fraction and then closed. Bristow started, his eyes widening. He caught the faint scent of lavender and instinctively felt for the posy he'd seen lying on the narrow shelf in front of him, his fingers winding round the flowers, crushing them, letting the fragments fall to the floor. A second time the door opened and a short, nervous-looking man in a wig and an oversized black gown sidled in, his hands gripping the lapels as though to prevent the garment falling from his narrow shoulders.

'Oyez, oyez, oyez…' he intoned, the majesty of the address largely undermined when his wig fell forward and covered his eyes. He pushed it back into place and continued, in a high-pitched voice, 'All manner of persons…'

Bristow didn't hear the rest, his whole attention concentrated on the skeletal form of the judge, resplendent in scarlet robes and black scarf and girdle, entering the courtroom. He bowed in the direction of the half-dozen barristers and took his seat.

'I take it, Mr Jones, that we are ready to proceed with the next case,' said Sir John Rose, the Recorder of London, peering at his clerk over a pair of spectacles.

'Yes, my lord. The prisoner is in court. The indictment is marked as true and is before you.'

Bristow's mind was a blank. He heard little of the reading of the indictment or the question as to how he wished to plead. His thoughts were far away, in the days of his youth when he'd been able to come and go as he pleased and been beholden to no one.

'Prisoner at the bar,' the voice intruded on his thoughts and Bristow looked up to see the Recorder looking at him. 'You have been asked how you plead.'

Bristow had thought of little else but his coming trial in the days since his arrest and committal to this place. There was no question about who had killed Collins. It was him. He'd struck him and watched him fall close to the water's edge. Even if Collins had not died immediately, he would soon have done so, swallowed up by the making tide. But if he knew one thing about the law, it was that he was innocent until proved guilty. That being the case, he wasn't about to plead to something the Crown couldn't prove.

He tried to remember what had been said at the committal proceedings. He had nothing in writing, no record of the charge and certainly no record of what the witnesses had said in their depositions. He would have to rely on his memory – except he'd paid little heed to what was going on. The proceedings at the magistrate's court had passed in a blur. There had been several witnesses – the watermen who'd found Collins's body, the doctor certifying death and Collins's aged father who'd identified the body of his son.

And Zechariah Hobbs.

Bristow had been surprised to see the old man, but not unduly concerned. He remembered seeing him on the foreshore that day but had thought nothing of it. Zechariah had left before the fight with Collins had began. He'd seen nothing. Bristow was sure of that. So why he had given evidence at the police court, he had not the faintest idea. He doubted the old man's deposition had contained anything of importance.

'Prisoner at the bar…' Sir John sounded impatient. 'The court does not, sir, have all day. Do you plead guilty or not guilty to the indictment?'

'Guilty, my lord,' said Bristow.

'Very well. Do you have counsel to assist you, sir?'

'No, my lord.' Bristow had given the question of his representation no thought.

'Very well,' said the judge, his eyes turning to the barristers sitting in the well of the court. The effect was instantaneous. Men who, moments before, had been passing the time in convivial conversation, now found an absorbing interest in the mountain of papers in front of them.

'Gentlemen,' said the judge, removing his spectacles and surveying the group below him. 'I have need of your assistance. The prisoner at the bar is charged with a capital offence and is not presently defended. I should not wish to deny him every opportunity of establishing his innocence or, should that not be possible, providing some extenuating circumstance that would allow me to recommend respiting the inevitable sentence. To that end, gentlemen, I look to one of you to take on, *pro bono*, the mantle of counsel for the defence.'

For a second or two there was silence in the court save only for the shuffling of papers as the half-dozen barristers sought to avoid Sir John's gaze. Bristow's attention wandered and his thoughts drifted back to Zechariah Hobbs. Something the old man had said at the magistrate's court hadn't sounded quite right. Bristow struggled to remember what it was. Fragments swam in and out of his head. In isolation they made no sense. He wished he'd paid more attention. Slowly, the words began to merge and form sentences.

Bristow's eyes widened in shock. Was it possible the old man had fingered him? Had he claimed to have seen the fight? It was impossible. Why would he have done that? Bristow's mind whirled. More of the old man's evidence came to mind. He *had* claimed to have seen the fight. But why? He'd never done the villain any harm; the odd clout now and again but nothing serious, nothing that would explain the lies. Unless…

Unless someone had got to him.

Bristow thought for a minute. He had his fair share of enemies. Of course he did. So did everyone else. One couldn't be in this game and not upset a few people. But this? This was a joke. This wasn't playing fair. He'd kill the bastard if he ever found out who it was.

He stopped as a thought occurred to him. He recalled his visit to the home of the Hon. James Grenville and the threats and counter threats that had passed between them in the course of that evening. It had to be him. It was Grenville who'd got the old man to lie about what had happened. Bristow curled his fists in silent fury.

'I should be glad to be of service, my lord.' Bristow was dimly aware of a young man emerging from among the group of barristers and addressing the judge. 'Perhaps I may be given five minutes to speak to my client?'

'Thank you, Mr…'

'Harvey, my lord.'

'Yes, well, thank you, Mr Harvey,' said the judge, standing to leave the court. 'You have five minutes to take your instructions, after which we shall proceed to trial.'

#

Henry Teeling stood at the bottom of the river stairs, on the south bank of the Thames, the making tide threatening to catch him unawares as it crept ever higher. He was thinking – as was so often the case – of his late wife and of the man who'd murdered her, the same man who'd attacked and flogged him outside the chapel in Virginia Street.

He'd seen Collins again since that morning.

It was on a wet afternoon, a little over two weeks after his flogging. He'd been drinking with friends in a tavern on the Ratcliff Highway when he'd seen Collins walk past in the street outside. He remembered the anger that had come over him at the sight of him. He'd wanted to plunge a knife through his heart for what he'd done. Yet even then he'd been aware of a small voice within him counselling caution, urging him to a period of reflection, a moment of rational thought.

Looking back now it was easy to see he should have paid greater heed of that voice. It would have saved the weeks and months of mental anguish that had been his lot since that day. But the voice and its message had been drowned amidst the din of retribution. The urge to confront Collins had been overwhelming. He'd rushed to the door of the tavern and been in time to see the villain disappearing amongst the crowd.

Turning up the collar of his coat against the driving rain, he'd limped after him, weaving in and out of the slow-moving hordes that pressed in on him. The pain in his thigh had been almost more than he could bear, yet still he followed, stopping when Collins stopped and moving on when Collins moved on. He had no plan, no notion of what might happen when, at last, the two of them came face to face. It was enough for him that the object of his hatred was there, in front of him, almost within touching distance.

He followed as Collins turned down the narrow path that lay beside the soot-blackened walls of the church of St Paul, Shadwell. It was quiet here, the crowds and the noise left behind, only the echo of their footsteps to keep them company. Several times he'd wanted to close with his quarry, to have done with the whole sorry business. But each time he'd been thwarted by the presence of children playing in the foul surroundings of their world or the occasional woman lounging in a doorway, or the shambling arrival of a peddler..

Teeling had told no one about what had happened on that February afternoon. He wiped the beads of perspiration from his face and gazed over the crowded tideway, seeing nothing of what was before him. He took no notice of the ships making their way up towards the Pool. He was oblivious to the score or more barges jostling for a berth alongside the Legal Quays, or the shouts of the lightermen on their sweeps. Nor could he hear the raucous sea shanties coming from the throats of the treadmill gangs as they worked the quayside cranes. None of these things interested him.

He knew he had to speak and could remain silent no longer.

He had to tell someone about what had happened.

#

Bristow felt the crushing weight of his predicament. Five minutes had been barely time to explain to the barrister how he'd come to know Collins, how they'd grown up together and how they'd served their King and their country in the army. He'd struggled to marshal his thoughts, to say what needed to be said and to leave out what it would not be sensible to say. The constant interruptions by his brief hadn't helped. The fool had wasted much of the time asking questions, the answers to which would surely carry him to the gallows. What was the argument with Collins about? Why had he gone looking for him in the first place? Who had told him to kill Collins? Had he ever been in trouble before? Bristow would have preferred to talk about other things that might not have been strictly true. He would have liked to mention the loss of his leg fighting for his country and his support for the Protestant faith. But there hadn't been time for that. He felt his heartbeat surge as the clerk entered the court and bade everyone stand. A moment later, the majesty of the law swept in, bowed, and sat down.

'Are you ready to proceed, Mr Harvey?' The Recorder leaned forward on his elbows and looked around the crowded courtroom with a bored expression on his bony face.

'The defence is ready, my lord.'

'I'm given to understand, Mr Harvey that your client may wish to change his plea?'

'Indeed, my lord,' said Harvey, rising from his seat an inch or two and then sinking back with a sigh.

'And you, Mr Ponsonby? I think you appear for the Crown, d'you not?'

Mr Ponsonby, King's Counsel, a grey-haired, grey-skinned man in the middle years of his life, adjusted his monocle and heaved his considerable bulk to the upright position before also bowing to the learned judge. 'Thank you, my lord, the Crown is quite ready.'

'Very well,' said Sir John. 'Mr Clerk, I'd be obliged to you, sir, were you again to put the charges to the prisoner at the bar. It seems he may now wish to change his plea.'

The plea duly changed to one of not guilty, the first witness for the Crown was ushered into the witness box. Mr Zechariah Hobbs, a scuffle-hunter of no fixed abode, swore to tell the truth, the whole truth and nothing but the truth.

Hobbs had never before been inside the sessions house and had, on several occasions during the minutes that followed, needed to be reminded to speak up. The effect was the opposite of that intended. The hapless Zechariah gradually became so quiet as to be almost impossible to hear. Yes, he agreed, he'd been on the north foreshore of the River Thames, close to the King James steps, Shadwell, when he had seen and recognised the prisoner at the bar. Yes, the deceased, whom he'd also recognised, had been there too. The two men had been arguing less than thirty yards from where he stood. At some point he'd seen the prisoner at the bar strike the victim who had immediately fallen to the ground, dead. He saw the prisoner strike the deceased once more and then leave the scene. No, there was no doubt in his mind that the deceased, Collins, had been killed by the blow delivered by the prisoner. He, Zechariah Hobbs, had shortly thereafter been forced to leave the scene by the incoming tide.

'Be so good as to wait there, Mr Hobbs,' said Counsel for the Crown, sliding down into his seat. 'My learned friend may wish to ask you a few questions.'

'This was, I believe, towards the close of day.' Mr Harvey had sprung to his feet, his hands gripped the leading edges of his black gown. 'The sun had gone down. In a word, it was dusk. Is that not so, sir?'

'Aye, so it was, your honour,' whispered a distinctly nervous Zechariah.

'Yet you say you recognised both men who were on the foreshore.'

'I…' The witness seemed to struggle with his answer. He looked at the judge and then at counsel. 'I've seen them many times. Known them since they were no more than nippers, your honour.'

'Quite,' said Harvey, a look of triumph lighting up his face as he glanced at the jury. 'So sure were you of their identities that you did not, at any stage, feel it necessary to approach them. Is that right?'

'Aye.'

'Not even, after the accused left the scene?'

A long pause. ‘No.’

‘Why was that?’

‘I were afraid Bristow… I mean the prisoner what’s in the dock… I were afraid he’d come back and see me. Besides, there weren’t no time; not with the tide making.’

‘But from a distance of thirty yards, in poor light, you were able to tell that Mr Collins had died.’

Zechariah didn’t answer. He was sweating; his head bent forward, his eyes staring at the floor in front of him.

‘The truth of the matter is, Mr Hobbs, that you cannot possibly be certain whether Collins was alive or dead at the time you saw him.’

Zechariah stared mutely at the judge.

‘I’ve no further questions of this witness, my lord.’

‘Mr Ponsonby?’ said the judge, raising an eyebrow at prosecuting counsel.

‘I think, Mr Hobbs, you said you knew the deceased?’ said Mr Ponsonby, clambering to his feet and seeming to gaze at the Sword of Retribution high above the judge’s head.

‘Aye.’

‘And I think you have already told us that he and the prisoner at the bar were arguing about something.’ Ponsonby leaned back, one hand resting on the bench behind him while the other held some papers.

‘Aye.’

‘Was Collins alive when you first saw him?’

‘Aye.’

‘And you are quite certain, from your observation of him, that Collins was dead following the attack upon him by the prisoner at the bar?’

'Aye, so I am,' said Hobbs, looking up for the first time since his ordeal had begun.

'No further questions, my lord.'

Hobbs was followed into the witness box by the physician who had carried out the post-mortem examination on Collins.

'... the body of the deceased at the time of my examination was severely decomposed. Nevertheless, it was clear that it had sustained a number of blows to the body and head, any of which could have led to his death, my lord.'

'In your opinion, doctor,' said Ponsonby, folding his arms and gazing at the roof of the courtroom, 'would you say the injuries you speak of were consistent with blows intended to cause death?'

'Yes, I would.'

'Thank you, doctor. Please remain where you are. My learned colleague may wish to put some questions to you.'

'Do you wish to cross-examine, Mr Harvey?' said the judge, sighing heavily.

'Just a few questions, my lord,' said Harvey. He turned to look at the physician. 'Tell me, doctor, would you have expected the injuries you have described to have led to the deceased's immediate death?'

'No. He would, in all probability, have survived for some time before dying.'

'We have already heard from the previous witness that the tide was rising. In those circumstances is it possible that the immediate cause of death was drowning, rather than the blows to which he'd been subject?'

'Indeed, sir,' said the physician. 'The post-mortem examination did, in fact, reveal the presence of water in the lungs.'

'Which means the deceased was alive when he entered the water, does it not?'

'Yes.'

'In short, doctor,' said counsel for the defence, 'you appear to be saying that while the injuries sustained by the deceased were violent enough to have caused his death and could have been delivered with that intention in mind, the fact remains that the immediate cause of death was drowning rather than the injuries inflicted by my client.'

'Yes, I would say that is a fair summary of my opinion.'

'Forgive me, doctor, but you may not be familiar with the law in all its intricacies,' said Mr Harvey. 'The prisoner at the bar is charged with the murder of the deceased, a crime that, should he be convicted, carries with it the penalty of death. What I seek to show is that while my client had every intention of killing the deceased, he patently failed to do so. He is therefore entitled, in law, to be tried for the crime of assault rather than murder. This latter crime does not, of course, attract the ultimate penalty. Do you follow?'

'Yes, perfectly,' said the physician.

'Then I again ask you to confirm that, in your professional opinion, the deceased was still alive when he entered the water.'

'Yes, he was.'

'No further questions, my lord.'

'Mr Ponsonby, do you wish to re-examine your witness?'

'No, my lord.'

'Prisoner at the bar, it is now open to you to make your defence,' said the Recorder, turning his lowering gaze towards Bristow. 'This is your opportunity to put before the jury such matters as you think pertinent to your case. It is something that, as the law stands, only you may do. It is not open to your counsel to speak for you and you will not be questioned on what you say. Do you wish to say anything?'

Bristow looked wildly around the courtroom. Was he supposed to speak? And if so, what could he say? He tried to remember if his counsel had challenged that lying bastard Zechariah Hobbs who'd claimed to have been on the foreshore and seen everything. It was an important point but he didn't want to look foolish – especially if his counsel *had* asked the question.

'I ain't saying nothing, my lord,' he said.

'Very well,' said the judge. He looked to his left where the jury was sitting on a bench below the public gallery. 'Members of the jury, the case before you is of the gravest importance and upon the result of your deliberations hangs the life of the prisoner you see in the dock. Should you find the case against him proven then I will have little alternative but to pass sentence upon him that will see the end of his mortal existence. The charge of murder requires the prosecution to prove beyond reasonable doubt that the accused unlawfully killed the deceased with the intention of doing so – what we lawyers call *mens rea* or, in plain English, malice aforethought. It means that not only must the prisoner have killed but that he'd possessed the intention to kill.'

The judge paused and shuffled some papers on the table in front of him before going on. 'You have heard evidence under oath from Mr Zechariah Hobbs that he was standing about thirty yards from the prisoner at the bar and the deceased. They were arguing over some matter. The situation then appears to have degenerated into a fight. He says that he saw the prisoner strike the deceased who then fell to the ground, dead. Under cross-examination the witness conceded that he could not say with any certainty whether or not the victim was, at that point, dead or alive. At any rate it appears he was at the very least unconscious. Crucially, the witness says that the tide was rising and that, despite this, the accused left the scene without making any attempt to move the victim out of harm's way.'

Sir John paused and sipped some water from a tumbler at his side before continuing. 'We next heard from the physician who carried out the post-mortem examination on the victim. According to his evidence, the deceased was still alive when he entered the Thames since, he tells us, water in the deceased's lungs is conclusive proof that he was still breathing when he entered the water.

'I come now to the evidence for the defence. There is no dispute that the prisoner was present on the foreshore of the Thames with the deceased, shortly before the latter entered the water. Nor is there any dispute that the prisoner struck the deceased with the intention of killing him. What is at issue is whether or not the prisoner was successful in his stated attempt to snuff out the life of the deceased. If he was not, the charge of murder must fail, albeit that death by drowning followed shortly afterwards. The distinction is this. Murder carries the sentence of death. Assault with intent to murder does not. In arriving at your decision, I invite you to consider the actions of the prisoner in leaving the scene without moving the unconscious Mr Collins out of the path of the rising tide. You may consider that his failure to do so was at one with his intention to kill Mr Collins. Your task is now to consider the evidence you have heard and reach a verdict upon which you are all agreed. In doing so you should know that if you are minded to find the case against the prisoner proven, his life will be forfeit. You must therefore be quite certain of his guilt in this matter if you are not to condemn an innocent man to the gallows. You may now retire to consider your verdict.'

Chapter 32

The knock on the door of Emanuel's room surprised him if only because it was such a rare occurrence. Most people who wanted to see him for any reason tended to try and catch him at the chapel. Reluctantly, he put down the book he was reading, got up from his chair and went to the door.

'Why, it's you, Henry,' he said, surprised at the sight of an ashen-faced Teeling standing in the corridor. 'What ails you?'

'Will I talk to you, Father?'

'Yes, of course. Come in. Take my chair,' said Emanuel, waving his visitor to the only available seat in the room. 'Come, tell me. What is it you want to talk to me about? You're as white as a sheet.'

'Is it true, Father?'

'Is what true?' said Emanuel, sitting down on the edge of his bed.

'That Bristow has been arrested for what happened to Collins?'

'Yes. He appears at the Old Bailey today,' said Emanuel reaching into his waistcoat pocket and taking out his watch. 'In fact, he might already be before the court. Why d'you ask?'

'I…' Teeling's voice faltered. 'How did they find out about him? Bristow, I mean.'

'I'm not entirely sure,' said Emanuel. 'I gather there was a witness at the magistrate's court. From what I've heard, he saw everything. I assume the man's evidence was enough to convince the magistrate to send Bristow for trial.' He paused. 'Is there something you aren't telling me, Henry?'

Teeling didn't answer immediately. He rose from his chair, walked to the window and stood looking out onto the street. Turning to face Emanuel, he said, 'There weren't no witnesses, Father. Only me.'

'You?' said Emanuel. 'What can you mean, pray?'

'I saw what happened. I were there.'

'Best you tell me what this is all about,' said Emanuel.

'I were with some of the lads in the Highway when I saw him—'

'Collins? Or Bristow?' interjected Emanuel.

'Collins,' said Teeling. 'The villain what killed the only woman I've ever loved. Anygate, as soon as I saw him I ran outside…'

Over the next ten to fifteen minutes, Emanuel listened to the story of that afternoon in February, interrupting now and again to clarify a detail or two.

'And when he went down to the foreshore, did you follow?'

'No. Not at first. There's a wee lane what leads from the road to the foreshore. I waited for him in case he came back that way, but he didn't. I were just about to follow him onto the foreshore when I sees Bristow. I thought he were going to pass by but I sees him go down the same path as what Collins had gone. It looked to me like he knew Collins were there.'

'Go on,' said Emanuel.

'After a minute I went after them both. It were getting dark and at first I couldn't see nothing but a few hulks hauled up on the hard. Same stuff what you see all the time. After a bit I saw them – Collins and Bristow. They was arguing. Shouting at each other.

Then, all of a sudden I sees Bristow catch Collins a blow with one of his crutches and the next thing is they was scrapping good and proper.'

'You said it was getting dark?'

'Aye, but not so dark as I couldn't see what were happening.'

'And you're quite sure there was no one else who could have seen what was going on?'

'Aye, so I am,' said Teeling.

'Tell me again, Henry. Why were you following Collins in the first place? What was in your mind?'

Teeling let his head drop forward into his cupped hands. 'I were thinking about me wife what was murdered by Collins in cold blood,' he said, his voice hardly above a whisper. 'I couldn't stop meself, Father. I just followed him. I didn't give it no thought.'

Emanuel's stomach tightened. This was not the answer he'd been hoping for. 'What happened next?' he asked.

'I saw Bristow hit Collins again. This time Collins went down and didn't move no more. It looked to me like he were dead.'

'What happened after that?' said Emanuel.

The question appeared to agitate Teeling and he paced up and down the room, his hands clasped to his mouth, his head shaking as though wrestling with an intractable problem.

'I waited for Bristow to leave,' said Teeling, a haunted look in his eyes. 'I wanted to see if Collins were dead. When I got to him he were on his back, his eyes closed. I were sure he were a goner but then his eyes opened and he looked at me.'

'So Bristow hadn't killed him?'

Teeling looked towards the window, his fingers twisting around each other in unceasing movement, his breathing more laboured. After what seemed an age, he said, 'We'd known each other since we were little, me wife and me. Her ma and her da lived in the same village as me. After we was married I got work on an estate and were given a house for the both of us to live in. After she died, I couldn't go on living there and I came to London. When I saw Collins that day, it all came back. At first I didn't know what I were thinking but when I saw him on the foreshore looking up at me, a rage came over me and…'

'Go on,' said Emanuel.

'The tide were making, Father. He were going to die without I did anything.'

'You could have saved him,' said Emanuel. 'But you left him to die? Is that what happened?'

'No,' said Teeling.

'What d'you mean?' said Emanuel. 'Tell me.'

'I couldn't stop meself, Father. I knew he were going to die if I left him but I wanted to make sure so I dragged him to the edge of the water and left him there. Then I waited for the tide to cover him.'

Emanuel stared at him, shocked and unable to speak. He thought of Bristow who would, in all probability, go to the gallows for a crime he didn't commit. And he thought of his own role in accepting Teeling's assurance that he was innocent. Should he have pressed harder? Would it have made any difference? The answers seemed so straightforward in hindsight.

'You know, of course, Bristow will hang for what you did?' he said, his throat dry.

Teeling shrugged. 'Aye, I knows that, right enough.'

For a few moments neither of them spoke. Then Emanuel broke the silence. 'You have to tell the court what you've told me. Before it's too late.'

'I can't, Father,' said Teeling. 'They'll hang me.'

'Yes, they will,' said Emanuel.

#

Bristow felt his whole body trembling. There was nothing he could, or wanted to, do about it, his eyes fixed on the huddled backs of the jury, a glimmer of hope in his eye. He hadn't understood everything the judge had said but enough to believe that he might still escape the hangman's noose. The old cully had seemed to suggest the case against him was not as hopeless as it might have been. Something about Collins's death being due to drowning and not anything he, Bristow, had done. If that was what the judge thought, he wasn't going to argue about it. He caught sight of one of the jurymen glancing in his direction and felt his stomach somersault as he tried to read the man's thoughts. Others of the jury were now looking at him, their expressions inscrutable. He strained to hear what they were saying and caught the occasional word. It wasn't enough to make any sense. His mind wandered and he thought of his long-dead parents. He couldn't remember his father, had never really known him. The old man had been hanged for his part in the riots of 1780 when his son was about four or five. His death had left his widow to bring up the boy as best she could.

The young Bristow had never given the matter any thought as he played amongst the mud and the filth of Limehouse. Few memories survived from that period of his life but amongst them were the visits to the chapel in Virginia Street where his mother would talk to the Papist priest. He'd asked her once why she went. He remembered her saying how she drew comfort from talking to someone who was prepared to listen. Sometimes, she said, the priest would give her a few pennies with which to buy food for the two of them. It was on one of those visits that the priest had told her of his secret and his constant fear of exposure. Bristow's eyes widened. He hadn't believed it at the time and the detail had eventually faded from his memory. But he'd heard the same story repeated much more recently. It had come from a Jew. True, he'd had to beat the story out of him. Of what he and the priest had been talking about. But it had been worth it, even if the cully had died as a result of the flogging.

He had no time to think further. The clerk of the court was announcing the return of the judge. Bristow watched the foreman of the jury rise to his feet. The clerk of the court was speaking. Bristow strained to hear his words: '… reached a verdict upon which you are all agreed?'

He stared at the speaker, his heart hammering painfully against the wall of his chest and waited for the answer.

'We have,' said the foreman of the jury.

#

Emanuel sat alone at the back of the chapel, his eyes fixed on the flickering red glow of the sanctuary lamp, deep furrows creasing his forehead. His conscience was troubling him and although he'd learned not to expect immediate answers to his prayers, there were times when he would have appreciated a faster response than the Almighty seemed minded to give him. He leaned forward and buried his head in his hands.

Teeling's confession and his refusal to give himself up to the authorities were playing on his mind. It had left him in the impossible position of knowing the truth but being unable to speak of it. Yet, if he did not speak, an innocent man would die. The words of his professor at the seminary where he'd trained for the priesthood came to him from across the years: *A priest must, under all circumstances, remain silent about any matter of which he is informed under the seal of the confessional.*

Emanuel shook his head. That wasn't it. That wasn't what was really troubling him. Harsh though the injunction imposed upon him might be, there was another aspect which was disturbing him. He wondered if he'd tried hard enough to persuade Teeling to give himself up. Or had self-interest stood in the way? Had he calculated that with Bristow's death his own secret would, once again, be safe?

Emanuel knelt. 'Lord, in your infinite mercy, help me.'

The questions continued to race through his mind. Was he now to try and save the life of a man who had threatened to ruin his? Was it his duty to break the confidence placed in him? Was it not for Teeling to admit the wrong he had done? It was hardly his fault Teeling had demurred. And even if he were to bring the new facts to light, would it make a difference? Would it save Bristow's life?

He suddenly jerked upright as he recalled something a barrister friend had once said to him. *It's rare, even in the most serious cases, for trials to last more than a few minutes...*

Was it already too late to act? Ashen-faced, Emanuel got to his feet and walked slowly to the rudimentary rail in front of the altar. Again he knelt. More of what his friend had told him sidled into the outer reaches of his consciousness. He searched his memory. He and Jeremy Blythe had met, as they often did, in the Mitre tavern, on Jewry Street, not far from the Tower of London where they would enjoy a meal, and talk about matters both spiritual and temporal. On this particular occasion the conversation had turned to the criminal justice system and what Blythe considered to be its inherent inadequacies. Emanuel stared at the stone floor of the sanctuary and waited for more of his friend's words to come to him.

... convicted prisoners have to wait until the end of the day to discover whether they are to live or die... six o'clock... hear their sentences... grown men often faint clean away on learning their fate.

Emanuel looked at his watch. It was eleven o'clock. He had less than seven hours in which to act.

#

Henry Teeling turned off Virginia Street and limped down the maze of narrow alleys that led to the Thames. His confession had achieved nothing. There'd been no absolution, no comforting words, no hope of salvation. Damnation awaited him. He'd not meant to kill anyone. Not at first. It was only when Collins had opened his eyes that he'd felt compelled to finish him. He hadn't thought of the consequences for himself – either for this life or the next.

Perhaps, if matters had ended there, he might have been able to live with the fiction of Bristow's culpability. He might even have been able to convince himself it had been Bristow who'd struck the mortal blow. But not now. The appearance of a witness had changed everything. It had led to Bristow's arrest, trial and almost certain conviction. Now he, Teeling, was in the position of having killed a man and left another to take the blame. It was that, more than anything else, that tore at his conscience. It was for that that he'd sought forgiveness and absolution.

He wiped his mouth on the sleeve of his threadbare coat and thought of his old parish priest in Wexford, his sonorous voice warning him and the other children of the dangers of sin to their eternal souls; of the downward plunge into the bowels of Hell for those who did not repent. Teeling smiled bitterly. He had singularly failed to repent. What price then, forgiveness? He knew the answer. He'd always known it. The price was his own life in place of Bristow's.

A crushing weight bore down on him, unspeakable in its savagery, too terrible to contemplate. He'd reached the Thames and now stood on London Bridge gazing over the parapet at the swirling brown waters below. There lay oblivion. An end to his earthly worries. A few moments and it would all be over. He thought of Sara who'd so recently entered his life and of the hope he'd nurtured of a better, happier existence in her company. It couldn't happen. Not now. Not ever.

'It's for the best,' he said.

Chapter 33

The tide had begun to turn when Emanuel hailed a passing wherry and persuaded the reluctant waterman to carry him to Temple Stairs. Passing under London Bridge he failed to see the lone figure of a man leaning against the parapet, seemingly lost in thought.

Alighting at Temple, he hurried up through Fleet Street to Chancery Lane and on towards the main gate of the Inns of Court at Lincoln's Inn Fields.

'Yes?' A wizened face confronted him at the old stone arch guarding the entrance to the court.

'I've come to see Mr Blythe,' said Emanuel.

'Number five, New Square, sir. Across the yard and through that there alleyway,' said the man, pointing to a narrow path passing between what looked to be a chapel, and another building of dubious architectural merit. 'You'll see the gardens in front of you. Turn left and you'll soon find yourself in New Square, sir. Number five is next to the coffee house what you'll see in front of you, sir.'

A minute or so later Emanuel arrived at the front of a long, two-storey building extending the entire length of the south side of the square. A porter led him up a broad flight of steps to the first floor where a passageway led off to the left. The porter stopped at one of the several doors and knocked.

'Come,' said a muffled voice from within.

Walking in, Emanuel found himself in a large, high-ceilinged room, three sides of which were lined with glass-fronted bookcases. In the centre of the room, a red-faced gentleman of about fifty sat behind an oak desk, his presence almost entirely hidden behind a mountain of thick files, each one tied in pink or white ribbon. Beside him, on two chairs, placed there for the purpose, more files had been stacked. Yet more books, files and papers occupied the floor area surrounding the man.

'Why, Mr Lazaro! Give you joy. Sit down, sit down, sir.' Mr Jeremy Blythe, of counsel, clambered to his feet and cleared some files from one of the chairs before carefully balancing them on another stack.

'I apologise for this intrusion, sir,' said Emanuel.

'Pray, do not think of it, sir. Can I interest you in a dish of tea, perhaps? Coffee? No? Now, to what do I owe the pleasure of this visit?'

Five minutes later, Emanuel had finished his story of his meeting with Teeling, carefully avoiding any mention of his or Bristow's names. Blythe leaned back in his chair and steepled his fingers, his eyes closed.

'You say the trial of this unnamed individual is still in progress?'

'I can't be certain,' said Emanuel. 'It might already be over. But I recall that you once told me it's usual for sentence to be passed at the end of the day. Is that not so?'

'Yes, that's the normal procedure, assuming, of course, the prisoner is found guilty. But we don't yet know that to be the case. Or do we?'

Emanuel shook head.

'Well then, if he's found guilty, he will learn his fate this evening. If he is condemned then it's likely he'll be executed on Monday morning. Do you know if he is represented by counsel?'

'I regret I don't know, sir.'

'I'd be surprised if one was not appointed to act *pro bono*,' said Blythe. 'No matter. I imagine you simply want to know if anything can be done for the poor fellow. Is that right?'

'Yes.'

Blythe rose and walked to the sash window behind his desk, his hands thrust beneath the tails of his coat.

'On the facts as you have related them,' said Blythe, turning to face his visitor, 'and assuming he is found guilty, I regret there is nothing can be done.'

'Even if another man has admitted to the killing?' said Emanuel.

'But where, my dear fellow, is the evidence that this is so?' said Blythe. 'You have already told me that the supposed killer is not prepared to come forward and give evidence and you are unwilling to repeat what he said to you, even in the confines of this room.'

'I can't,' said Emanuel. 'What is said to me in the strictest confidence, I may not repeat without the permission of the person concerned. Indeed, I have already exceeded what I am permitted to say.'

'It matters not,' said Blythe, returning to his desk. 'You would not have been permitted to give evidence. At least, not evidence of something you did not know for yourself. And anyway, if the prisoner is found guilty, it will have been on the basis of the evidence before a jury and it's probably too late to change that.'

For a minute there was complete silence in the room.

'Of course, even if the prisoner were to be sentenced to death, it might never be carried out,' said Blythe. 'Indeed, in most cases where the judge considers there are grounds for respiting the sentence to one of, say, transportation, he will leave directions for a stay of execution until he and his fellow judges have further considered the matter.'

'And you think this may happen in this case?' asked Emanuel, not entirely sure he wanted to hear the answer.

'I've no idea. I wasn't there. But I say again, most sentences of death in this country are respited and the felon concerned is deported. As a general rule, where the trial judge feels there may be grounds for not imposing the sentence, he will, as I say, leave a list of those who are not to be hanged until he has conferred with his fellow judges. The decision may take a day or so to be ratified one way or the other.'

'So we have to hope that's the case. There's no other way?'

'None, unless it can be shown there was an error on the record,' said Blythe. 'And if that were found to be the case, his counsel will appeal. The fact is, such appeals are very rare.'

'Would it make any difference if the man known to have done the killing came forward?'

'It would certainly affect the sentence,' said Blythe. 'But not the finding. That cannot be challenged once the jury has returned its verdict. As regards the sentence, I suspect the judge would, in those circumstances, recommend a Royal pardon. Meanwhile, the real culprit would face trial for the original murder. But you tell me the fellow is unlikely to come forward?'

'Yes,' said Emanuel. 'I'm afraid he's made that very clear.'

'Then it's likely your man will hang unless…'

'Unless, what?'

'Unless the judge can be persuaded that hanging the prisoner would be unjust. If we move quickly it might be possible for counsel to seek an audience with him before he leaves tonight. If he is so minded he may include your man on the list of those whose execution is not to be carried out pending further consideration of the matter.'

'So there is hope for him?'

'I wouldn't, sir, put it as high as that.'

#

Nobody moved in the great hall of the sessions house. The clerk of the court was on his feet and facing the jury. 'Do you find the prisoner, Erasmus Charles Bristow, guilty or not guilty of the charge of murder?'

Bristow stared at the floor of the dock and waited for the foreman's answer. It seemed an age before it came.

'Guilty, my lord.' Bristow swayed and would have fallen had he not been caught by one of the turnkeys standing behind him. For a few seconds he couldn't focus, the courtroom seeming to spin round him, a blurred image of movement and noise. He let his head fall forward and closed his eyes, trying to stand straight, conscious that people were watching him.

'… take the prisoner down.' The words drifted through Bristow's consciousness. 'I'll pass sentence at the end of the day.'

A hand fell on Bristow's shoulder and he felt himself being pulled away from the dock railings and down the steps to the underground passage, back to Newgate.

#

The hours dragged by. Bristow tried to sleep but couldn't. It was nearly seven o'clock that evening before he heard the rattle of keys in the cell door and saw the gaoler beckoning him out. The return, along Dead Man's Walk, seemed interminable, the climb to the dock more difficult than he could remember. His muscles refused to respond, his leg too weary to take his weight. He forced himself to move forward and then upward, one painful hop at a time, the sweat of fear and exertion dripping off his body. He knew what awaited him. He pushed the thought away as he'd tried to do all day. It made no difference. Again and again the reality of what faced him loomed large in his mind's eye, the horror of his ending too much to contemplate. Behind him, one of the turnkeys urged him on, jabbing at the back of his leg with a stick. In other circumstances he might have retaliated. But not today.

He was breathing heavily when, at last, he reached the dock and was able to lean against the spiked iron rail. It was crowded now with five other prisoners, all of them there for the same reason. He looked around the courtroom, the babble of conversation temporarily stilled. Heads had turned to watch his arrival. Now the noise resumed afresh, his presence of no further interest. That would only resurrect itself when the judge returned to the court.

'All rise.'

A hush descended. The door to one side of the judge's seat swung open and the Recorder of London appeared. He seemed a little unsteady on his feet, the face flushed below his full-bottomed wig. He sat down with a jolt and looked about him as though unsure of where he was or what he should be doing. A sheet of paper grasped in one hand seemed to catch his attention. He squinted at it as though surprised by its existence. Gradually, the look of doubt in his eyes cleared. The moment had come.

Bristow was the last of the prisoners to be handed his sentence. Of the other five, three were sentenced to hang, two to transportation. The judge, who had had the black square of silk removed from his head while delivering the sentence of transportation, now signalled for it to be replaced. He looked up at Bristow.

'Prisoner Bristow,' he said, his voice slurred, though whether from the effects of a recent meal or from tiredness, Bristow neither knew nor cared. 'You have been found guilty by a jury of your peers of the crime of murder. It now falls to me to pass the sentence upon you that has been decreed by Parliament. It is that you shall return to the place from whence you came and from there to a place of execution where you shall hang by the neck until the body be dead. And may the Lord have mercy upon your soul.'

Chapter 34

Emanuel Lazaro slouched in the stern sheets of the wherry as it approached Blackfriars Bridge. The sun had long since set and the night was ablaze with countless ships' lanterns swinging back and forth in the tide, their long fingers of light reflected on the dancing surface of the river. He barely noticed them. His attempt to find a way through the legal morass surrounding the Bristow case had run its course. There had been a moment when it seemed to be within reach – a suggestion that Bristow's defence counsel might usefully seek an audience with the trial judge. But it had come to nothing.

'The time for hearing the testimony of witnesses has passed, Mr Lazaro,' the defence counsel had told him when Emanuel had met him at his chambers in Pump Lane. 'The most we can hope for is that the trial judge will consider what you have told me. But I warn you, it will have not the slightest effect on the verdict and I very much doubt it will influence the sentence of death handed down to my client. I regret it extremely, sir, but there is nothing more can be done.'

But there was.

Emanuel ran his tongue over his dry lips. His courage deserting him, his knees shaking at the implications of what he was thinking. Perhaps he'd never have to go through with what he had in mind. He stared at the tiny whirlpools caused by the boat's oars leaving the water. If he did nothing, Bristow would hang. But to act was to invite repercussions too painful to contemplate. Either way, the future looked bleak.

#

The noise was deafening, the stench of human sweat suffocating. Emanuel was hemmed in by the huge crowd that occupied every vantage point. A heavy cloth fell across his face, suffocating him. He swept it aside. Leaving, even if he had wanted to, was virtually impossible. He looked over his shoulder. Grinning faces stared out from the windows of the tavern and from the houses on either side. Before him was a kind of stage some twenty feet high, girded in black baize. The crowd was singing now. A low-throated, tuneless sound, interrupted here and there by cheering and rival chants. He let his gaze lift above the stage. A heavy beam traversed its length, supported at either end by timber struts.

Suddenly the noise of the crowd fell away. Utter silence filled the void. A dozen people now stood on the stage. His eye ran along from one to the other until he found him. His heart was racing now, painful in its throbbing motion. He wished he hadn't come. Yet he was aware of a certain light-headedness, a sense almost of relief that the moment had arrived. He looked away, ashamed of his thoughts. And yet… *Forgive your servant, Lord. I am unworthy.* The feeling of elation persisted. He would shortly be free of the torment of the past few weeks. Never again would he be troubled by the fellow. *Oh Lord, why do I have such thoughts?*

He looked back at the stage. The man he knew stood beneath the heavy beam, a rope around his neck.

Someone had placed a ladder against the beam and was climbing towards it. In his hand he held the other end of the rope which he looped over a butcher's hook screwed to the underside of the beam.

The mob was cheering now, a roar of applause.

A bell clanged, a deep sonorous sound that boomed and reverberated round his head. The crowd fell silent. Emanuel looked up at the man he knew. Then it was over.

Emanuel's eyes snapped open. Cold beads of sweat covered his body. His blanket covered his face, smothering him. He shook it free, his heart pounding. It was a moment or two before he realised he'd been dreaming, that Bristow was alive. From outside his room came the sound of revelry, drunks singing at the tops of their voices. In the distance a church bell chimed midnight.

He wasn't sure if he was relieved or disappointed.

Emanuel sank back onto his pillow. He had only to keep silent for the law to take its course, for the events in his dream to become a reality. Could he be blamed for doing nothing to save the life of a man who wished him dead? He rolled over onto his side, a wave of conflicting emotions sweeping over him – anger, remorse, disappointment, shame. He couldn't sleep.

Chapter 35

Bristow looked up at the small window set high in the wall of his cell. A dull grey light filtered in between the iron bars. A bell was tolling the hour. The realisation of where he was and what shortly awaited him came slowly. He started to shake, a violent convulsion of the body that threatened to throw him to the floor, the sweat pouring down his face, soaking the thin blanket that covered him.

Much of last night had been spent in the prison chapel with the Ordinary and another three men who were to hang this morning. They'd been grouped round an empty coffin while the priest led the prayers and the readings. Bristow knew he should have paid greater attention but he hadn't, his mind concentrated on what was to come. Now he caught the distant sound of hammering. He knew, at once, what it meant. How often had he and Collins and a few others made their way to the west gate of the prison in the small hours of a Monday morning to watch the workmen erecting the scaffold? It had never failed to excite them, those hours before the black screen was nailed into place, hiding the door through which the condemned would come and the steps up which they would climb to the place of their execution.

His mind moved on, as it often will, along random paths, to settle briefly on some topic before again speeding away to other distant times and places. He thought of the early years of his life, the ups and downs that had been the inevitable result of the choices he'd made, of his late mother, of Ireland and the army, of prison and the people he'd met along the way. All of these competed for his attention before being consigned to a kind of temporary oblivion. And in between there came, again and again, the black shadow of what faced him in the coming hours.

He rolled off the solid wood platform that served as a bed, and shivered. The night hours had sped by. Hardly had he been allowed to return to the condemned cell and lie down before the dawn had forced its way into his consciousness. He counted the tolling bell of the church of St Sepulchre-without-Newgate. Six o'clock. Outside his cell door the voice of the night duty turnkey handing over to the new guard sent a fresh streak of dread along the length of his spine. It would not be long now before they came for him.

He thought again of the hours spent in the chapel. He had never believed in God and he wasn't about to start now but there had been one task the Ordinary had promised to do on his behalf. Bristow smiled briefly. The messages he'd asked to be passed on would be a fitting goodbye. It was just a pity he wouldn't be around to see the result. The sudden jingle of keys made him jump. He spun round and stared at the door, his heart pounding, his breathing laboured. He heard the scrape of a key being inserted and the lock turned. The door swung open and two men walked in.

It was time.

Chapter 36

'Bristow?' The harsh tones of one of the turnkeys cut through him like a knife. 'Stand over there and face the wall. Quick as you like. I ain't got all day.'

Bristow did what he was told. This was no time to argue. It would do him no good.

'Hands behind your back. Spread your legs. Look lively, now.' The man paused and looked down at Bristow's leg. 'Well, fuck me old boots. I clean forgot. We won't be needing the leg irons, Bert, nor the manacles neither. Fetch them crutches what's outside the door, will you?'

The three of them walked in single file along the narrow corridor that ran past the doors of the condemned cells, and down a short flight of stone steps. At the bottom, they turned right and, it seemed to Bristow, deeper into the prison building. Another minute or so and he found himself in a part of Newgate he'd never seen before, let alone imagined. Quite suddenly, the stench of unwashed bodies was less; the corridors down which they travelled were cleaner. Perhaps most startling of all, he noticed the absence of bars at the windows.

The small posse came to a halt outside a solid oak door on which one of the turnkeys now knocked.

'Yes,' shouted a voice from inside the room.

Bristow followed the leading turnkey into a low-ceilinged room that reminded him of the cell he'd just left. At the far end, close to the small window, was a table and chair at which an elderly man was seated, seemingly oblivious to the presence of his visitors.

'The prisoner Bristow, your honour,' said the leading turnkey. 'Like what you said to be brought.'

The old man continued to stare at nothing in particular. Finally, he seemed to register their presence and glanced from one to another as though surprised by their presence. He picked up a single sheet of paper and examined it with the same air of distraction.

'Are you Erasmus Bristow of the parish of St George-in-the-East, sentenced to be hanged for the murder of one George Collins, also of the parish of St George-in-the-East?'

Bristow was having trouble concentrating. His mind was on the scene he knew to be unfolding outside the west gate of the prison. The inevitability of his demise within the next hour was all-consuming. He cared not at all what the man behind the table was saying.

'Bristow?'

With an effort, he raised his eyes.

'Answer me. Are you—'

'Aye, I'm Bristow. What of it?'

'It seems you have friends. This is an order for a stay of execution. It appears a witness has come forward.'

'Speak plainly,' said Bristow, his eyes widening in disbelief. 'What are you saying? Am I to hang or not?'

'Not today, you ain't. Maybe tomorrow. Maybe on Wednesday. Ain't for me to say.' The man turned to one of the turnkeys. 'Take him back to the cells.'

They turned to leave, Bristow in the middle. He was both relieved and frightened. While the prospect of his death had, for now, receded, it had not gone away. At least, not yet. And who was the witness who'd come forward? There'd been no one to see what happened the night he'd killed Collins; not even that lying bastard Zechariah Hobbs who claimed to have seen everything. Bristow's breathing quickened. But if not Hobbs, then who? His thoughts moved rapidly on. There was a chance he might live. He wouldn't be free. He'd be banished to some Godforsaken place at the far ends of the earth. But at least he would live.

Suddenly, his mood plummeted again, his shoulders sagging. His execution had only been delayed. They were playing with him. Tomorrow or the day after he would be taken to the scaffold and there, for ten or fifteen minutes he would dance the Newgate dance while he choked to death before a baying, jeering multitude.

The words of the man behind the table came back to him – *a witness has come forward.* Bristow rummaged through his memory. The Hon. James Grenville? It was hardly likely. They had never liked each other. Sir Peter? Why would he risk his neck? What could he or Grenville say? That he, Bristow, had simply done what they had ordered him to do? The whole idea was absurd. But who, then? And why now? Why had this supposed witness waited? If his evidence was so good that it had resulted in a stay of his execution, why had he not come forward at the trial and saved all this grief? Bristow felt a wave of illogical anger, of near hatred at the mysterious man who only now had chosen to save him.

In the distance, he caught the faint clang of a church bell. St Sepulchre's. Eight o'clock. Bristow tensed, his head cocked to one side. He didn't have long to wait. A dull roar of perhaps ten thousand throats penetrated the thick walls of Newgate. The first of the men who'd been with him last night in the chapel had entered the final moments of life.

Chapter 37

The Hon. James Grenville had, unusually for him, been up since before dawn. He had an appointment to keep and had no intention of missing it. He stood at the window of the house in Cheapside and looked up at the grey, overcast sky, his hands clasped behind his back. The coach that was to take him and Sir Peter to Woolwich was waiting in the street outside. He turned at the sound of the library door opening.

'Good morning, James,' said Sir Peter Westlake, closing the door behind him. 'You've heard the news, I suppose?'

'About Bristow?' Grenville looked up at the library clock. 'From what I hear his execution has been delayed. But it can't be long now. Never did care for the fellow.'

'No, I don't suppose you did,' said Sir Peter, pouring himself some strong black coffee. 'Apparently Bristow has asked the Ordinary to deliver a letter or two.'

'What sort of letter?' Grenville's tone was languid, almost bored.

'Nobody knows. But I think it would be wise to delay our plans. Just in case.'

'Just in case, what?' Grenville's eyes widened. 'You can't be suggesting Bristow has given us away.'

'I don't know. But I don't want to take any unnecessary risks. If we go ahead today as planned, we might find a company of the Guards waiting for us. At the moment, there is nothing to link us to anything. We just have to sit tight for a while. If it turns out to be a false alarm, then we can go ahead with the original plan.'

'What about the men? If the letters name any of them, it won't take much to persuade them to point a finger at us.'

'That's in hand,' said Sir Peter, putting his cup down on the polished surface of the library table. 'I've arranged for all those involved to be posted overseas at a moment's notice. I've got a contact who'll tell me as soon as anyone starts asking questions. That should give us time to get the men out of the way.'

'When will we know what's in the letters?' asked Grenville.

'That's where it gets a little tricky,' said Sir Peter. 'As I told you, they were given to the Ordinary.'

'So?'

'My dear boy, you know what these religious fellows are like. Any hint that we're demanding information and the reverend gentleman will just clam up. No, I'm afraid we've just got to sit tight on this one.'

Grenville felt the blood drain from his face, recalling Bristow's threat to expose what had happened two years earlier on the banks of the River Slaney, a mile or so north of Wexford. His mouth was dry as he turned back to the library window. A gust of wind rattled the sash. The memory had never left him.

He wished he'd never met the woman or her husband. It was her fault. If only she'd answered his questions, she'd have come to no harm. But she hadn't answered him and he'd been forced to take action. It was regrettable but there it was. Of course, once he'd started, she'd pleaded with him to stop and promised to talk.

Grenville closed his eyes. Often, in the stillness of the night, he'd wake as from a nightmare and hear again the screams of her agony as he'd penetrated her, of the feelings of disgust she'd awakened within him when, eventually, he had finished what he'd begun. And always, the odour of her body that so reminded him of the warm stench of the farm animals on his father's estate.

He turned away from the window and faced Sir Peter. Why he'd chosen to strangle the girl he couldn't say. He knew only that she was dead before Bristow and Collins walked through the cottage door a minute or two later.

He bit his lip and tried to concentrate on the matter at hand. If the letters Bristow had handed to the Ordinary of Newgate were what he thought they were, he was in for more trouble than enough.

'I've no intention, sir, of sitting this out,' he blurted. 'I shall see the Ordinary and demand that he hand over the notes. Why, I'll—'

'You must know that not only would you fail in your objective, but you would also draw attention to yourself – and to me as well.' Sir Peter's eyes narrowed a fraction. 'I cannot, sir, allow that to happen. Besides, we have a more immediate problem on our hands.'

'And what, pray, might that be?' said Grenville, his voice heavy with sarcasm.

'It seems the Jew priest knows more than is good for him. I told Bristow to take care of him but it seems he failed. I'm arranging for the matter to be put right but in the meantime it's as well that you know.'

#

A mile or two to the west of the home of Sir Peter Westlake, in a coffee house on Russell Street, John Walter wore a troubled expression on his face as he regarded his friend over the rim of his teacup.

'You know, of course, someone is determined to stop you asking questions. From what I hear they know who you are and mean to cause you serious harm. And anyone else who gets in their way.'

'Yes, I know,' said Emanuel. He was used to being threatened. It was part of who he was. Most of the time it amounted to little more than abusive language or the occasional attempt to tweak his beard. Yet recent events had changed all that. Bristow had all but admitted to thrashing Aaron, his childhood friend, for the information Emanuel had given him moments before. Then there'd been the killing of the waiter from Garraway's coffee house shortly after Emanuel had spoken to him. Willing Annie had also suffered for speaking to him. And all this in addition to his own narrow escape when Bristow and his thugs had caught him on his return from Woolwich. 'Bristow has already made that clear.'

'Speaking of Bristow, I hear there's been a delay in his execution…' Walter paused and looked at his friend. 'You don't, sir, seem surprised.'

'No, I'm not surprised,' said Emanuel reaching for his coffee.

'You've done something, haven't you?' said Walter, accusingly. 'This was your doing. Tell me you're not trying to save the rogue. Don't you understand that, given half a chance, he'd kill you and think nothing of it?'

'I know, but…'

'But what? Tell me. I'd like to know.'

'I regret it extremely but I can say nothing about it except what you already know; that Bristow's execution has been delayed. I understand this is not unusual and I'm led to believe the final decision will be made very soon.'

Walter whistled and shook his head. 'I'm not sure whether I admire you or pity you.'

Emanuel shrugged. 'By the way,' he said, reaching into his coat pocket and drawing out a crumpled sheet of paper, 'what do you make of this?'

Walter looked at it for a moment before putting it down on the table.

'What is it?' he asked.

'I was hoping you could tell me. It came from Sir Peter Westlake's home. He and Grenville were discussing something. That drawing in front of you was the result.'

Walter bent forward and looked at the paper again, ironing out the creases with the edge of his hand. 'If I was to hazard a guess, I'd say it was a map of sorts. But it could be of anywhere. You think it might have something to do with what we've been talking about?'

'It's possible,' said Emanuel putting the paper back in his pocket. 'If you think of anything, let me know.'

'So you mean to carry on with this foolhardy adventure in spite of everything you know about these people?' said Walter.

'I don't want to,' said Emanuel. 'I've got to. D'you think I'm not afraid of what might happen to me? Many a time I've lain in bed unable to sleep, my mind tortured by thoughts of what might happen to me. I'm not, sir, a brave man but I cannot let an innocent human being die for want of trying. Nor can I ignore the threat faced by Catholics in this country. I must carry on. Don't you see?'

'If you mean to carry on, my dear Lazaro, I will do all I can to assist you,' said Walter shaking his head in mock despair.

'By the way, do you remember my mentioning a man named Fielding, the MP for West Kent?'

'Yes, I do,' said Emanuel. 'I think you told me he was one of those firmly opposed to the emancipation issue.'

'Yes, that's the fellow,' said Walter, dabbing his lips with the corner of a napkin. 'I hear from my sources that he was invited to the Minister's home in Keston a day or so ago. Nobody is quite sure why but I think it was probably to try and persuade him to stop his opposition to the Irish question. Apparently he refused.'

'I see,' said Emanuel. 'Didn't you tell me he was a bit of a rabble-rouser?'

'Yes.'

'So we can expect trouble?'

'Yes, the usual stone-throwing, a few broken heads and the general public inconvenienced for a day or two,' said Walter.

A boy pushed his way between the tables, a bundle of broadsheets under his arm. 'Bad weather hits price of corn. Latest news on war with Bony.'

'Boy,' shouted Walter. 'Over here.'

Taking a broadsheet he paid for it and scanned the columns of tightly packed text. 'Thought so,' he muttered under his breath. 'Bony only has to sit back and wait for the allies to lose the war. I see the Austrians are blaming the Russians for the fiasco of the north Italy campaign. And they don't much care about what our lads are doing in Holland.' He lapsed into silence. Then, 'Well, well, well, it seems Bristow *is* to hang.'

'What's that you say?' said Emanuel.

'Bristow. There's a short piece in the paper. His sentence has been confirmed,' said Walter. 'He's amongst several others who are to hang the day after tomorrow. Good Lord, sir, you look like death.'

Emanuel climbed to his feet, a hand gripping the edge of the table. 'Forgive me, sir, I must leave you,' he said, bowing slightly. 'I've not a moment to lose.'

#

The news about Bristow, although not entirely unexpected, had still been a jolt. Leaving Walter, Emanuel took a carriage to Temple and from there walked the short distance to Pump Court, where Mr Harvey, Bristow's defence counsel, had his chambers.

'As you know,' said Harvey, a few minutes later, 'I went to see the trial judge, and explained the position to him as regards the information you gave me. Sir John listened to me with great attention and said he would consider the matter in concert with his brother judges the following day. In the meantime he said he would add Bristow's name to the list of those who were not to be executed until he had considered the matter further.'

'But it seems he did not believe you,' said Emanuel, a trace of bitterness in his voice. 'Bristow's sentence has now been confirmed.'

'It isn't always a question of belief, Mr Lazaro,' said Harvey. 'There are rules of evidence which must be adhered to if there is to be any certainty in the law.

In this case, the evidence presented to the jury during the trial contained no mention of another suspect, no hint that the act of murder might have been committed by someone other than the prisoner at the bar. Neither the prosecution nor I as his defence counsel raised the matter because we simply didn't have the information.'

'Yes, I'm well aware of that,' said Emanuel, his frustration threatening to boil over. 'But it was introduced as soon as its existence was known.'

'Indeed it was,' said Harvey. 'But only through a third party; in this case, you. It would have been a different matter if the person admitting to the crime had himself come forward, as I think I mentioned to you when we last spoke. The supposed culprit could then be questioned and, if believed, tried for his crime. In those circumstances I have little doubt Bristow's sentence would have been respited to one of transportation.'

'Would he not have been released?' said Emanuel.

'Perhaps unfortunately,' said Harvey, 'there are very limited grounds for appeal in our criminal justice system. It's possible, of course, that Bristow might've been granted a Royal Pardon although his admission that he intended to kill Collins meant that was unlikely. I got a note from Sir John on the afternoon following the trial in which he said that he and his brother judges were still considering the matter and he was unable to comment further.'

'And that was the last you heard?'

'Yes,' said Harvey. 'I would not have expected his lordship to keep me informed of the progress of his deliberations with his brother judges. As far as the law is concerned, the prisoner was told his sentence on the day of trial. I did not expect to hear any more on the case. It was, for me, over when I left his lordship's chambers.'

Leaving Mr Harvey, Emanuel walked out onto Pump Court and looked round at the red-brick chambers surrounding him, the morning sunlight warming the cobblestones under his feet. He wondered at the rigidity of the law and its blindness in the face of reason. He supposed minds more clever than his own had shaped and endlessly refined the precepts of what passed for justice until nothing was left but the dry words devoid of humanity and the sense of the common man. And yet… The hope he'd tried to suppress sprung up anew. He pushed it away. He'd done all he could to save Bristow's life. Right or wrong, the law would take its course. No one could criticise him for not doing enough. His conscience was clear.

He stopped abruptly as a thought occurred to him. He mulled it over in his mind. Then he hurried away.

Chapter 38

'On your feet, Bristow.' The harsh tones of the turnkey's voice echoed round the walls of the condemned cell, jolting Bristow into a state of wakefulness. He sat up, his heart racing. It seemed hardly a moment ago when he had finally dropped off to sleep, exhausted by the mental torture of the last few days, the hope and despair that had ridden in tandem with one another, his expectation of reprieve finally crushed late last night.

He swung his leg off the cot and waited for the turnkey to hand him his crutches. There was no repeat of the farce of last time. No attempt to manacle him. For the time being he would walk unfettered. He stood and slipped the crutches beneath his armpits as a second turnkey came into the cell and took up a position behind him. Then the three of them filed out onto the corridor.

Bristow saw nothing of the short journey through the ground-floor doorway and out into the press yard, the ancient significance of the narrow court as a place of unimaginable torture lost to him. Nothing mattered except his own survival. Nothing touched his awareness but the terror of what awaited him. He didn't want to die. Not ever. And certainly not like this. He found himself muttering the half-forgotten words of the Lord's Prayer, hoping something or someone would hear the jumbled words of supplication, the plea for mercy he could not enunciate. They climbed a few steps into a large room filled with people. He recognised the Keeper of

Newgate and the Ordinary; the latter dressed in the familiar black robes of his calling. The rest were a blur of scant interest to him.

'What you asked for is ready.' Bristow looked round. The Ordinary had approached and was standing at his shoulder. 'It'll be dealt with in the next day or so.'

Bristow nodded but said nothing. There was nothing he could say except, perhaps, to thank him. But he was in no mood for such courtesies. Not in the final hour of his mortal existence. Whatever hope there might once have been of his sentence being respited was at an end. There had been no explanation, nothing to indicate the cause of the original delay. Just that he was condemned to die.

Out of the corner of his eye Bristow caught sight of a row of what appeared to be white nightcaps and next to them lengths of thick rope, one end looped into the shape of a noose. His heart skipped a beat and he felt his knee begin to buckle. He steadied himself with the aid of his crutches and accepted a tumbler of brandy. Not far from him were two others destined to join him on the scaffold. One of them was a woman. Bristow had time to note her youth and beauty. He felt a stab of regret that such things were no longer of any consequence for either of them. She looked across and smiled briefly – two souls on the same journey. It was funny, he thought, how he was able to take some comfort from her presence; a fellow sufferer experiencing the same emotions as him. A bell within the prison began to toll, a monotonous clanging that he remembered from the days when he'd stood with the crowds outside the debtor's gate. Almost immediately he caught the dull roar of the crowd and reminded himself to show no weakness when the moment came.

Someone caught hold of his shoulder and was telling him to stand still while his wrists were brought together in front of him and bound with cord 'so you's can pray for your everlasting soul,' one of the turnkeys had said to him. He watched listlessly as the Keeper guided those who had been invited to watch the proceedings out of the door. Soon it would be his turn and those of his fellow prisoners.

The minutes ticked by. He wasn't sure how much more he could take. He thought back over his life, of his early childhood playing with the other children, free from all care. He wished his mother was still alive. She would have known how to comfort him in this, his final hour. One of the linen caps he'd seen earlier was placed on his head and the rope that was to hang him looped about his neck.

'Move.' A hand prodded him from behind. He stumbled forward, supported on one side by a turnkey, sweat blurring his vision. Behind him was the woman. He could hear the sound of her breathing. Quick, rasping intakes of breath as she tried to steady her nerves.

It would, he hoped, be over very soon.

Chapter 39

The note was waiting for Emanuel when he unlocked the door of the Virginia Street chapel at shortly before eight o'clock on that Monday morning. It was from Sergeant Candler, the clerk sergeant at the Woolwich garrison, requesting a meeting with Emanuel at his earliest convenience. The place chosen was the hill overlooking the town where the sergeant would wait for an hour each morning between ten and eleven, until Emanuel's arrival. No hint of the purpose of the intended meeting was provided.

Emanuel felt the now familiar lurch in his stomach. He had thought of making his way to Old Bailey, although for what purpose, he didn't quite know. The executions would already have finished. There was nothing he could have achieved by going. The note, on the other hand, suggested a degree of urgency it would be unwise to ignore. He turned about and, a short time later, arrived at Pelican Stairs on the north bank of the Thames. From here he hailed a passing wherry.

A strong westerly wind was racing up through the Lower Pool as the small boat nosed its way out into the centre of the navigable channel, its bows slicing through the choppy, white-tipped water. Within moments, Emanuel was drenched by the flying spume and regretting his decision to respond quite so quickly to the sergeant's note. Half an hour later and at the southern end of Limehouse Reach, it started to rain, large, cold drops falling from a grey sky to drum noisily on the bottom boards. On either side of the reach a seemingly endless line of ships were being buffeted, their massive hulls shielding the wherry from the worst of the wind.

Limehouse Reach gave way to Greenwich Reach, the white stone walls of the Royal Naval College and the Queen's House beyond just visible through the rain. Before long they'd turned north into Blackwall Reach, the weather now on their starboard beam, sweeping in from the desolate wastes of the Bugsby marshlands. Emanuel tucked his chin inside the collar of his coat and tried to ignore the waterman's stream of invective directed at the wind, the rain and anything else that came readily to his mind.

Then, as quickly as it had begun, the weather eased as they rounded Blackwall Point, past the big ships of the East India Company and into Bugsby's Reach.

'Won't be long now, your honour,' said the waterman about twenty minutes later. 'See them line-of-battle ships over yonder? That's where we're headed and thank the Lord for that.'

Emanuel nodded. He'd lost all sense of time and place in the last couple of hours, his clothes wet through, his mind numbed by the cold. Yet he couldn't but admire the majestic sight of the first rate men-o'-war riding to anchor two hundred yards ahead of him. There was something about the brutal power displayed in the row upon row of closed gun-ports along the freshly painted hulls that demanded his attention. Even from this distance he could feel their intimidating presence. He was still staring when, fifteen minutes later, the voice of the waterman bore itself in on him.

'Is you getting out, guv'nor, or do I have to take you back where we started?'

'What?'

'Ship Stairs, mate.' The waterman's voice dripped with sarcasm. 'What you asked for. Or has you changed your mind?'

'No. I beg pardon. I was thinking of something else,' said Emanuel handing over the fare and scrambling ashore. He turned back to wave but the skiff had already begun its return journey.

Stiff from his long confinement, he climbed the stone steps to the path leading to the main street of Woolwich. From there he turned away from the garrison, his eyes searching for the path that Candler had assured him would lead directly to their meeting point above the town. He nearly missed it, the entrance lying between two ancient cottages and overgrown with brambles. He beat his way through the tangled mass of vegetation and followed the steep path up the hill, past a small wood towards the Dover road at its summit. Candler was waiting for him under a large oak, a worried expression on his weather-beaten face.

'I cannot stay long, sir,' he said as soon as Emanuel had joined him. 'Some of the men has been talking. I reckon they suspect me of spying on them. It ain't good, sir. I've seen what some of them is capable of. Especially them what's seen some action. Lost their humanity, see? One dead man is like any other and who's to tell the difference. That's what they think.'

Emanuel waited for the man to calm himself. 'Your note suggested you had something important to tell me.'

'Aye, so I have, sir,' said Candler, looking distinctly nervous. 'There's trouble coming. I've been in the army twenty-three years and I ain't heard the likes of it before. It's the Papists. The lads don't care for them. Not since the regiment were posted to

Ireland a year or two back and saw all that killing. Now it ain't just the Papists; it's all the Irish. The lads don't agree with what Mr Pitt is doing for the Irish. They want them all back where they come from. Don't trust them, see?'

'What are they planning to do about it?' asked Emanuel.

'Don't rightly know,' said Candler. 'I don't think they know themselves. Not the detail, anygate. All I've heard is when it happens, everyone in the country will know. And it won't be long in coming.'

Emanuel was silent for a while. It was one thing for the mob to take to the streets in violent protest; quite another when the army was involved. He looked out over the rooftops of the town to the river crowded with ships of war. Away to the left, beyond the garrison, was the Royal Arsenal within whose vast acreage was to be found the military might of a proud nation. Was it possible that the very people on whom the country depended for its security were, even now, plotting death and mayhem? He remembered hearing talk of something similar happening less than three years previously when the Fleet had twice mutinied almost within sight of the Dutch invasion force. The cause was different this time but the effect would be the same – death and destruction on a huge scale.

'Over there.' Candler's voice broke in on Emanuel's thoughts.

'What is it?' said Emanuel, looking at the woods the sergeant was pointing to.

'I saw something move,' said Candler, visibly shaken. 'I reckon someone's watching us.'

Emanuel's eye travelled along the length the woods and back again. He was on the third sweep when he glimpsed a flash of red and white. He stared at the spot for a full minute but saw nothing further.

'Did you see him, sir?' asked Candler, his face grey and lined with concern.

'Not sure,' said Emanuel, beginning to doubt the whole thing. He looked at Candler, his eye drawn to the scarlet coat and the white cross belts he wore. Was that what he'd seen? Or had he imagined the whole thing? He felt suddenly uncomfortable, the sergeant's nervousness infectious.

'But you saw something,' said Candler.

'It's possible but I cannot be sure.'

'I ain't stopping here no more, sir,' said Candler, his eye still fixed on the woods.

'Before you go, Sergeant,' said Emanuel. 'Do you keep a record of everyone who visits the colonel? Name, nature of business. That sort of thing?'

'Aye, I do,' said Candler, edging away.

'So it would be a simple matter for the details to become known to anyone with access to your office?'

'Aye,' said the clerk sergeant. And then he was gone.

Emanuel stood for a while, watching him hurry down the footpath to the town. He thought of the flash of red and white he'd seen in the woods and wondered if someone had known of this meeting. It was possible, particularly if his arrival at the river stairs had been seen. Even without anyone knowing his name – and that seemed less and less likely – he would have been recognised as the man who'd been to see the colonel and therefore of interest. Emanuel cursed his carelessness. The movements of sergeants were probably as closely watched as those of the colonel. Doubly so if the sergeant concerned was on the colonel's staff and was seen to climb a steep hill to nowhere, closely followed by a man who'd recently been to see the colonel.

Emanuel's eyes strayed back to the woods. A breeze blew in from the south-west and rustled the leaves of the trees. But that was all. Nothing else moved. If there had been anyone there, he'd not show himself now. Emanuel made his way down the hill to the street below. There was nothing more he could do here but he had a feeling it wouldn't be long before someone paid him a visit.

Chapter 40

'Master Emanuel.' The woman's voice was familiar. Emanuel stopped, surprised to hear his name called. He'd taken to the back alleys through Limehouse and Shadwell on his way home from Woolwich. He looked round but could see no one. Thinking that perhaps he'd misheard, he started to walk on when the same voice again called. This time he saw a slight movement in one of the doorways abutting the fetid alley. Bending towards what appeared to be a large pile of rags, he saw a pair of eyes looking up at him.

'Is there something I can do for you?' he said.

'It's me, Master Emanuel.'

'Sara?' Emanuel dropped to one knee and took her hand. 'What's happened to you, child?'

'I were dismissed. I ain't got a job no more, nor a roof over me head, neither.'

'Why, pray? What happened?'

'Sir Peter said I were a thief. But I didn't pinch nothing, Mr Emanuel,' said Sara, her eyes bright with tears, her face smeared with filth. 'It were Master James who told him.'

'Come, you can tell me all about it later, but first you look as though you could do with something to eat,' said Emanuel, getting to his feet and holding out his hand.

A quarter of an hour later, the two of them were seated in a coffee house in New Gravel Lane, close to the corner of Wapping Street, while Sara devoured a large bowl of oysters. When she'd finished, she sat back, a mug of sweet tea in her hand, her face less drawn than it had been half an hour before.

'You said Master James was your accuser,' said Emanuel, stroking the tangled mass of his beard. 'Why would he have done that? Was he angry with you over something?'

'Aye, you could say that,' she said. 'He were angry with me for refusing him and angry with Mr Jones when he came to my aid.'

'Mr Jones?' enquired a puzzled Emanuel. 'Who's he and how did he help you?'

'He was Sir Peter's butler. He tried to rescue me from that vile Master James,' said Sara, beating a clenched fist into the palm of her hand. 'I knew he would do something to get even. And now he has. I hate him so.'

'Tell me the story,' said Emanuel.

'I've no chance of another position, Mr Emanuel,' said Sara when she'd finished recounting the events leading to her dismissal. 'There isn't anyone what's going to employ a thief.'

'Where do you sleep?' asked Emanuel, although he suspected he already knew the answer. There was hardly a doorway in Wapping or Shadwell or, for that matter, anywhere else in London which wasn't filled every evening with the exhausted forms of those without the thrupence needed for the share of a flock mattress in some flea-infested house.

Where you found me' said Sara. 'And if not there, then some other doorway close by. Where else is there for me?'

'Take my room,' said Emanuel, without thinking. 'I've no need of it.'

Chapter 41

It had been a mistake. He knew that now. The sun was making one of its all too rare appearances over London as Emanuel walked up Cornhill in the City of London deep in thought. He should've warned Sara of what might happen if she accepted the use of his room; of the risk that someone looking for him would pay a visit to the room in Farmer Street and find her instead of him. He thought of the figure in the woods above Woolwich, the fleeting glimpse of red and white he'd thought he'd seen. It seemed increasingly likely that his meeting with the sergeant was now common knowledge within the garrison. And if it was, it could not be long before his name was also known, and with it, his address.

Two days had gone by since he'd found her in the doorway of a derelict hovel in Shadwell. At first she'd refused his offer of the use of his room, only accepting when he'd told her of a spare room in the bishop's residence that was available for his use. But he should have warned her of the possibility, however remote, of the dangers involved of accepting his offer.

It was a moment or two before he recognised the man whose arrival in the Jamaica coffee house a few days before had caused Sara to run. Emanuel hung back and watched the Hon. James Grenville cross the road in front of him and disappear into Exchange Alley. Then he followed him into Garraway's coffee house and up a broad flight of stairs to the first floor, thoughts of Sara for the time being, relegated.

Reaching the landing, he opened one of the glass-panelled doors leading to the coffee room and was immediately assailed by the chattering clamour of a hundred or more voices, each one doing its best to be heard over the general din. He stopped, his eyes probing the thick clouds of tobacco smoke that hung motionless in the still air. Grenville was seated at a corner table with two other men, both young and powerfully built, their demeanour oddly deferential as though uncomfortable in Grenville's presence. Emanuel moved closer, aware his own appearance was attracting glances from several directions. He tried to ignore them and took a seat at a vacant table.

Grenville was talking. He tried to listen but was interrupted by the arrival of a waiter at his elbow. Ordering a coffee, he waited for the man to depart before again attempting to listen. He could only catch the occasional word.

'... not long... park... important... caught...'

Then it was over and the three were climbing to their feet. Emanuel waited for them to reach the glass-panelled door. Then, throwing a few pennies onto the table for the yet-to-arrive coffee, he made for the exit.

There was no sign of Grenville by the time he reached the street door and only his two companions to be seen walking towards Cornhill. He sensed a decision had been made and instructions issued. If so, it was likely the men were on their way to carry them out. He started to follow but his way was barred by a beggar, his red coat suggestive of past military service.

'Spare us a penny, sir. I ain't eaten nothing all day.'

Emanuel glanced at the disappearing figures ahead. Another few seconds and they'd be lost to sight. He sidestepped the beggar but the man caught hold of his sleeve.

'You wouldn't deny a man what's fought for his King and country, a penny, now, would you, sir?'

Emanuel sighed and decided it would be quicker to give the fellow what he wanted than attempt to escape his persistence. He fished a coin from his coat pocket and gave it to him before again looking for the two men. There was no sign of them; the interruption had done its work. He broke into a run.

At the top of Exchange Alley, a small commotion caught his attention. A man was arguing with the driver of a hackney carriage less than twenty yards away. He had his back to Emanuel and the next moment had climbed into the cab. Emanuel hesitated. The man had looked familiar but he couldn't be sure. He looked around one last time. There was no one else who fitted the bill. It had to be him. He looked round for another hackney carriage and saw one approaching. He hailed it.

'Where to, squire?' asked the driver.

'Stay behind that fellow,' said Emanuel, climbing aboard and pointing after the departing vehicle.

Holborn came and went, followed by Broad Street and the church of St Giles.

'Can you see it, driver?' asked Emanuel after an anxious few moments of lost contact.

'Never you fret, guv'nor. It'll be back in sight in no time,' said the man.

But it wasn't.

'Where to now, guv'nor?' asked the driver some ten minutes later and still no sign of the missing carriage.

'Keep going,' said Emanuel, with more confidence than he felt. 'It's up ahead somewhere. It's got to be.'

'It's all the same to me, guv'nor,' said the driver. 'But you's wasting your time. We've lost him good and proper. Can't get going, see? Too much traffic.'

They'd reached the western end of Oxford Street, at its junction with Park Lane, before the driver again spoke. 'Well blow me down if that ain't him.'

Emanuel peered over the man's shoulder. 'Where away?'

'He's just turning into Park Lane,' said the driver, pointing with his whip. 'See him? No, wait, he's going into the park. See the gates, does yer?'

'Yes, I see him,' said Emanuel. 'Pull in here and wait for me.'

Alighting from the cab, Emanuel sprinted across Park Lane and stopped behind one of the stone gateposts at the entrance to Hyde Park. Twenty yards ahead of him he could see the carriage they'd been following. It had stopped and the two men he'd seen earlier were standing close to the road that passed along the northern boundary of the park. One of them was pointing at something. Emanuel watched as they paced to and fro, stopping now and again as if to satisfy themselves on some point or other. Apparently satisfied, they walked southwards towards Piccadilly.

Emanuel thought about following them. There was little cover and the risk of being seen was high but, on the other hand, if his pursuit was to mean anything, he had to know the reason for their journey here. He waited until the two men were some distance ahead and then set off after them. Several times he was forced to hide behind the nearest tree to avoid being seen. And each time, the distance between got longer.

Then, he lost them.

The last he'd seen of them, they'd been close to the junction of Park Lane and Knightsbridge, where large houses lined both roads. The men could have been making for any one of them. He walked to the southern limit of the park, as far as the turnpike on Knightsbridge, and looked towards Green Park. No sign of them there, or on Piccadilly. For another ten to fifteen minutes, Emanuel continued his search before giving up and returning to his waiting coach.

'Thought you'd left us, guv'nor,' said the driver as Emanuel climbed in. 'Them cullies you was following? They's gone.'

'Gone?' asked Emanuel. 'What d'you mean?'

'Them two cullies you was after? They came back close on ten minutes since,' said the man. 'Did no more than get into their cab and drive off.'

'I don't suppose you heard where they were going?' asked Emanuel, feeling singularly foolish.

'As it happens I were in the park looking for you when I sees them and I heard one of them tell the driver to take them to the farmer. Didn't mean nothing to me.'

'To the farmer?' said Emanuel, puzzled. Suddenly his head jerked up. 'Could it have been Farmer Street?'

'Aye, that's what it were,' said the man. 'Farmer Street.'

'I have to get there before them,' said Emanuel. 'With all speed, driver, if you please.'

Emanuel remembered little of the journey back to Shadwell. Why the men had travelled out to Hyde Park was no longer of interest to him, their meeting with Grenville irrelevant for the moment. What mattered now was where they were going and what they intended. He thought he knew. He'd long known the likely consequences his questions would expose him to; of the chance that one day there would come a knock on his door. He'd accepted that risk.

Sara had not.

Now he had to hope he'd reach her in time.

#

Most who make the decision to jump into the fast-flowing waters of the Thames will die. For them, the end will usually come quickly, the tide forcing their flailing bodies beneath the surface, tumbling them along the underside of the thousand or so lighters moored in the barge roads of the Pool. Their torn, battered and lifeless bodies might not surface for days until, finally, they are cast up on the shore for others to find.

Teeling had known this. He'd seen the faded posters peeling from the walls close to the river stairs with their descriptions of those whose last memories had been of the swirling waters closing over their heads.

But he had been lucky. When he'd jumped he'd been seen by a waterman in a passing skiff who'd plucked him from the river and dumped him unceremoniously at the nearest landing stairs. There had been no sympathy. The man had simply told him to find his own way to whatever hovel he chose to call home.

Despite everything, Teeling was grateful to be alive. The problem which had led him to the parapet of

London Bridge had not gone away. It still needed to be resolved – if that was still possible. But he was alive.

Bristow was to hang – might already have done so – for what he, Teeling, had done. A wave of self-pity swept over him. What value was Bristow's life compared to his own? What right had anyone to demand that he give up his life to save that of a common thief and murderer? Whatever might be said about the morality of his own position, there was no doubt Bristow had intended to murder Collins when the two had met on the foreshore of the Thames. And if Bristow was now dead, of what possible benefit was the sacrifice of his own life?

But what if Bristow was still alive? What then?

He thought about his faith. It wasn't something he could pick up and put down at will. If what he'd done was wrong then, it was wrong now. He laced his fingers behind his head and stared up at the ceiling of the tavern on the south bank where he'd gone for a drink. The moral question had always defeated him, the consequence of his position brutally clear to him. He felt cold beads of sweat dribble down his back and from under his arms. He would see the priest; talk it through with him. Perhaps that would help.

He crossed the Thames and limped up Farmer Street, the black phlegm in his throat more troublesome than of late. He'd had to stop several times on his way over and rest. It was nothing. A shortness of breath. A little perspiration. That was all.

He turned off New Gravel Lane and approached the house where the priest lived. He'd not been there in a while. Opening the front door, he walked down a damp-smelling corridor to the first room on the right.

He knocked and waited, mentally rehearsing what he wanted to say.

#

The journey from Hyde Park had taken much longer than Emanuel had expected. He jumped down from the hackney carriage and ran to the house in Farmer Street. It was quiet. Too quiet. He went in and listened at the door of his old room. There was no sound of any movement.

'Sara, it's me,' he called. 'I need to speak to you. Come quickly.'

There was no answer. He pushed open the door. The room was empty, undisturbed. He'd got here before Grenville's men. He was sure of it. There would have been signs of a struggle if anything had happened. Emanuel turned back towards the door. Sara had probably gone out on some errand and would shortly return. He had to stop her.

He left the house and crossed the street into a narrow alley that lay opposite. From here he could watch the house and its approaches.

He didn't have long to wait. He recognised the hackney carriage rounding the corner from Old Gravel Lane into Farmer Street and watched it come to a halt outside his old house. A moment later, the two men he'd been following earlier climbed down and made their way to the front door before disappearing inside.

Emanuel looked up and down the street. It was deserted but for how long before Sara returned he couldn't know. Nor could he tell around which of the half-dozen side streets she might eventually appear.

Not many yards separated the house from the nearest corner, a distance she could cover in next to no time.

The minutes ticked away. Emanuel glanced at the house. The men had been inside far longer than expected. He wondered if they meant to stay until the job was done, perhaps… His musing was interrupted by a commotion further up the street – two women engaged in a furious argument. He turned back to the house and was in time to see the hem of a woman's gown disappearing through the front door.

Then he heard the scream.

Chapter 42

Two miles to the west of Shadwell, the Honourable James Grenville was holding a silk handkerchief to his nose as he followed the turnkey through the press yard of Newgate Prison, the sharp stench of urine and unwashed human flesh worse than anything he'd ever encountered. At the far end of the narrow space they passed through a small door and along a seemingly endless series of corridors, finally coming to a halt in front of an anonymous-looking door.

'The Ordinary's in the chapel, your honour,' said the turnkey, touching his forehead. 'If you don't mind waiting just a moment, sir, I'll tell him you's here.'

Grenville nodded and watched the man shamble away, his hat balanced on the tips of his ears. A few days had passed since his exchange with Sir Peter concerning the Bristow letters and the advisability of approaching the Ordinary for copies. Grenville rarely had time for the opinions of others, more especially those held by older members of the human race, their brains addled by the passing of the years, their willingness to take even the smallest of risks now beyond their imagination or wit. Sir Peter was, in Grenville's opinion, firmly within this category. He understood, even if Sir Peter did not, that the letters had to be destroyed or, if they had already been sent, copies obtained and handed over for examination. It was a simple matter of persuading the Ordinary of the logic of the argument.

'He'll see you now, sir.' Grenville turned at the sound of the turnkey's voice. 'This way, if you please, sir.'

The Ordinary of Newgate was a man of thin build, his back slightly stooped, his thinning grey hair hanging in loose strands down either side of his skeletal face. He was dressed entirely in black save only for the two strips of white cotton that hung in an inverted 'V' at his throat.

'Give you joy, sir.' The Ordinary bowed stiffly.

'Joy, Reverend.' Grenville had always felt uncomfortable in the presence of priests of whatever hue, an odd sense that they were somehow privy to his most secret ponderings. He tried to put the thought behind him. 'I am, sir, the Honourable James Grenville. I understand you knew a prisoner by the name of Bristow.'

'Bristow?' The Ordinary frowned. 'Forgive me, sir, I don't recall the name. We have so many poor souls here,'

'Yes, quite,' said Grenville, catching sight of a coffin in the central aisle of the chapel. 'Nevertheless, it is about him that I wish to speak.'

'Shall we sit?' The Ordinary waved to the nearest pew. Waiting until Grenville had seated himself, he said, 'As I've said, the name of the prisoner you mention is unfamiliar to me but be that as it may, how may I be of service?'

'I understand this man Bristow was recently executed,' said Grenville. 'Before he died he apparently dictated one or more letters with a request that you send them to the persons to whom they were addressed. Do you still have possession of those letters, sir?'

'I'm afraid I cannot help you, sir,' said the Ordinary. 'I receive so many requests for some last service. All I can tell you is that it is not unusual for men condemned to die to ask me to write a final letter on their behalf. Whenever possible, I deliver letters of this kind a few days after the soul has departed this life. You say the prisoner Bristow has been executed?'

'So I'm told,' said Grenville. 'Not above two or three days since.'

'Then it's possible the letters you refer to have yet to be delivered.'

'I'm exceedingly happy to hear you say so,' said Grenville. 'They may contain information of the utmost secrecy and it is imperative they are destroyed immediately. If they reach the wrong hands, there is every chance that men may die. I would be grateful, sir, were you to hand them into my custody forthwith so that I may ensure they do not do the damage that is intended.'

The Ordinary said nothing. Getting up from his seat, he walked to where the coffin stood on its end, the lid removed. 'You see this coffin, sir? One day we must all be placed in one of these. And on that day we shall stand before the Lord. If—'

'I regret it extremely, Reverend,' interrupted Grenville. 'But I fail to see what this has to do with the letters.'

'I'm sorry, sir. Allow me to explain,' said the Ordinary. 'If this man of whom you speak asked a service of me, then I would have given my word, as I do to all men facing the end of their earthly lives, that I would do as he asked. I have no recollection of this particular prisoner but I have no intention of going before God with the stain of betrayal upon my soul. If

I still have the letters of which you speak, I will do with them what I promised I would do.'

'I perfectly understand your position, Reverend,' said Grenville, struggling to control his waning patience. 'But this matter is one of the gravest importance. I am quite certain you would not wish to be responsible for the consequences that will follow should these letters reach their intended recipients. I urge you to reconsider your decision and let me have them.'

'There is nothing to reconsider, sir. My mind is quite resolved on the matter. The missives – if they exist – will be handed to the persons for whom they are intended. Now, if you will excuse me, I have other matters I must attend to.'

'Have a care, sir,' said Grenville, his face reddening. 'I am not one of your lost souls that you may treat me thus. Have the goodness, sir, to fetch the letters and hand them to me forthwith.'

A faint smile crossed the Ordinary's lips. He crossed to the door of the chapel and opened it. A second later, the turnkey who had brought Grenville to the chapel stepped across the threshold. 'The honourable gentleman will be leaving now. Kindly show him out, will you, Farrell?'

Grenville raised the tip of his cane and pointed it at the Ordinary. Then, thinking better of it, he turned and walked to the door. 'You've not heard the last of this, sir,' he said.

Chapter 43

In Farmer Street, Shadwell, Sara's scream hung in the air, a terrified, primeval cry for help. Emanuel was running even before the petrified sound had died away. He had no plan, no idea of how he could help. There'd been no time for that. Yet even as he raced across the street he knew the odds were stacked against him. Going in through the front door of the house was madness. There had to be a better way. He tried to think.

There was a door at the rear of the premises. It hadn't been used in years. It opened onto what had once been the scullery but which had long since been taken over as additional sleeping accommodation for the dozen or so men who now regarded it as home. Whether or not he was likely to find anyone in there now and how they would react to his sudden and uninvited appearance was equally unclear. He wasn't about to debate the issue.

Running to the rear of the house, he tried the door. It didn't move, its swollen timbers wedged tight to the frame. He pushed harder. The door creaked on its hinges, and the bottom edge scraped noisily on the threshold as it opened a crack. He peered through. Two men were asleep on the floor, each covered by a thin strip of carpet. A chair, its back broken, stood in one corner. The room was otherwise empty.

Emanuel eased the door open and, stepping over the sleeping bodies, crept to the internal door. In the corridor beyond he could hear someone moving about. He guessed it was one of the two men he'd seen going into the house. The man sounded as though he were close to the door. For a long moment Emanuel considered his options. He knew he'd have less than a second to get through the door and silence whoever was on the other side.

There'd be no second chance.

His life, and perhaps Sara's, depended on his success.

He readied himself.

#

On the other side of the door of a house in Farmer Street, Shadwell, a man leaned against the corridor wall and waited for his friend to finish questioning the woman. He smiled. He would've liked to be doing the questioning himself. Just him and the girl. Pretty little thing she was. He would've enjoyed that. He hadn't had a woman in a long time.

From somewhere came a low, owl-like hoot that might have drifted in on the wind. Except there was no wind. Not even a breeze to disturb the quiet of the house. The man spun round, his small rat-like eyes locked onto the door at the end of the corridor, his body shaking, his fists clenched. It had been like this since the regiment returned from Ireland, the demons that haunted him, the nightmares that gave no peace.

The night patrols had been his greatest fear, when the risk of ambush was at its highest. That was what continued to keep him awake at night, remembering the dark shadows of the rebels lying in wait, hearing the owl hoot that signalled the attack. The man swallowed and continued to stare at the closed door. It didn't move. He began to relax. He was imagining things. There was no threat.

Another hoot.

The same as before.

He jerked his head around. The door at the end of the corridor moved an inch, stopped, then moved again. The man drew his knife and waited.

Two, three, four seconds passed. No one appeared. The man stepped towards the door. If some cully was having a laugh at his expense, he wasn't in the mood. He reached the door and peered into the room. Two men were lying on the floor, apparently asleep. He pulled the door towards him and looked behind it. There was no one there. He crossed the room and bent over the nearest of the sleeping forms. It was the last thing he remembered. The chair hit him on the back of his neck, dropping him to the floor.

'What…?' One of the sleeping men reared up onto his elbow, looked at the unconscious stranger, then at Emanuel, an angry look in his eyes. 'What's your game, cock?'

'Hush,' said Emanuel, a finger to his lips, his head tipped to one side, listening for any movement. 'I live here. My room's along the corridor. The cully was trying to steal from you.'

'Was he, b'Jesus?' said the man. 'I'll teach him—'

'Not now,' said Emanuel, hoping his lie wouldn't be discovered before it had served its purpose. 'His mate is still in my room.'

'Will that be right?' said the man. 'Sure, you'll be needing some help.'

'No, I want you to stay and look after this cully,' said Emanuel. 'Make sure he doesn't come after me.'

Armed with the leg of a chair, recently broken, Emanuel crept to the door and along the corridor. He could hear the sound of a man's voice, low and venomous.

'Where is he? Tell me, woman, before I cut it out of you.'

Sara's cry was unmistakable, like that of a frightened animal caught in a trap. Emanuel clenched his teeth and tried to stay calm. This was not the time for anger. That simply clouded one's judgement. And he would need all of that in the next few seconds. He breathed in slowly, mentally picturing the room beyond, the exact position of the bed, its distance from the door, the likely position of his target. The door wasn't a problem. The timbers were thin and the ironwork of poor quality. He judged the amount of force that would be necessary to open it. Too much and he'd risk losing his balance, too little and he'd have to try a second time, losing the element of surprise. He crept to the door and listened. The man was exactly where he thought he would be, directly in line with the door and about four feet from it. He would have his back to Emanuel and be concentrating on the girl.

Emanuel breathed again, composing himself for what was to come. Then he launched himself at the door, hitting it with precisely the right amount of force needed to send it crashing into the room.

Sara was lying on the bed, her face twisted in fear, her eyes focused on a knife held to her throat. The man was already turning to face the coming threat, pivoting on his heel in a desperate attempt to protect himself.

He was too late. Emanuel was on top of him, swinging the chair leg with all the force he could muster at the base of the man's skull. The man jerked round, shook his head as though to clear the pain and lunged at his attacker with the knife he still held. Emanuel sidestepped and chopped down hard onto the man's wrist. There was a howl of pain and the weapon tumbled to the floor.

Emanuel knew he'd blundered as soon as he'd done it. He'd let his concentration waver, glancing down at the knife. Instantly, the man's fingers were around his throat. He felt dizzy, the room out of focus. He tried to prise loose the tightening grip but couldn't, his eyes staring stupidly at the thin blue ribbon tied about the man's wrist. He rallied and, gathering his faltering strength, brought his knee up into the man's groin. It had no effect.

Emanuel felt his life ebbing away, his hands dropping limply to his side, his sight fading. Suddenly, the man's grip loosened and there was a surprised look in his eyes. Emanuel blinked, trying desperately to focus on the new threat looming towards him.

Chapter 44

The Morning Room at Boodle's was deserted but for the presence of two men sitting at a small table on which stood a coffee pot and two cups and saucers.

'I did warn you.' Sir Peter Westlake blew out a mouthful of tobacco smoke and watched it curl up to the ceiling.

'It was the impertinence of the fellow.' Grenville gave a bad-tempered tap of his cane on the floor and stared at the wall festooned with the portraits of illustrious former members. 'I've a mind to go back and give him the thrashing he deserves.'

'Did you say he hadn't yet delivered the letters?' said Sir Peter.

'That's what he said.'

'But he intends to do so today?'

'He didn't say. Just that he delivered such letters a few days after the execution,' said Grenville.

Sir Peter rubbed the underside of his chin and gazed into space as though considering the matter.

'The problem is, he'd know it was you,' he said. 'But suppose someone were to accidentally bump into the man and, in doing so, found himself in possession of the letters.'

'I could do it,' said Grenville.

'Not you,' said Sir Peter. 'Someone else. What about one of your former comrades in the army?'

'It would take time to organise,' said Grenville. 'And we've no time for that.'

Neither man spoke for a while.

'We've no alternative. It's got to be me,' said Grenville. 'I'll cover my face. He won't recognise me.'

'I don't like the idea,' said Sir Peter, frowning. 'By the by, what's happening about the Papist priest?'

'What? Oh, him.' Grenville waved dismissively. 'I've sent two of my men down to see him. They know what to do. I've arranged to meet them tomorrow morning at Garraway's, after it's all done. In the meantime, I've some letters to retrieve.'

#

Emanuel looked at the unconscious form lying on the floor of the bedroom. It had been a close-run thing. A few more seconds and the man's stranglehold would have seen the end of him.

'I'm too old for this,' he said, rubbing his neck and turning to face the man he'd last seen in the room at the end of the corridor. 'Thankee for what you did.'

'It's nothing,' said the man, eyeing the unconscious figure on the floor. 'I were awake anyway. What d'you want done with him and his mate?'

'Take them both to the Shadwell magistrate. Ask him to hold them until I get there with the evidence to support the charge.'

He watched the man go, dragging his unconscious victim after him. Suddenly Emanuel realised he'd forgotten Sara. He swung round to see her sitting ashen-faced on the edge of the bed, staring silently at the floor.

'Are you hurt bad?' he said, walking over and putting a hand on her shoulder.

'Who were those men, Mr Emanuel?' Sara faltered, her eyes bright with tears. 'They wanted to know where you were. Why were they looking for you?'

'They work for Master Grenville. It has to do with the piece of paper you found in the library of your master's house. It's my fault. I should never have left you here alone. I didn't think they'd find out about this place so soon.'

'He threatened me with his knife,' said Sara. 'I'm frightened, Mr Emanuel.'

'Aye, I know,' said Emanuel. 'Everything is all right now.'

'I can't stop here, Mr Emanuel,' said Sara, biting her lip.

'No, of course not,' said Emanuel. 'You must leave with me. I'll find somewhere safe for you tonight. Tomorrow we can think again.'

'Your honour?' Emanuel turned to see the man who had so recently come to his rescue. He was standing in the doorway, looking embarrassed. 'Them scrubs what we were going to take to the beak?'

'Yes?' said Emanuel.

'I regret it extremely, your honour, but they escaped.'

#

An hour or so after leaving his club in St James's, Grenville was standing inside the entrance of the Magpie and Stump on Old Bailey, his eyes fixed on the west gate of the prison lost in the lengthening shadows of early evening. He hoped he wasn't too late. He'd meant to get here sooner but his meeting with Sir Peter had delayed him. He looked up into the sky, dark blue laced with strips of black cloud. Soon the light would begin to fade. A small door set within the prison gate swung open. Grenville glanced at it more in hope than expectation of an end to his vigil. A figure emerged into Old Bailey. He was dressed in what appeared to be a black soutane with a flash of something white at the collar. Grenville's eyes widened a fraction as he recognised the Ordinary. Then he dropped in behind him.

Walking to the junction of Ludgate Hill, the pair turned left up the steep slope to St Paul's and were soon pushing their way through the dense crowd browsing the many bookstalls that inhabited the churchyard. Within minutes they were out the far side and into Watling Street.

With the crowds behind them, Grenville dropped back and allowed the distance between him and the Ordinary to lengthen. It wasn't ideal, the risk of losing his quarry too great. A large group moved between them. Obscuring his view. He waited for them to move out of the way. A minute passed and still he couldn't see the priest. Concerned, Grenville crossed to the other side of the road. But the man had disappeared. He ran to the place he'd last seen him. Still there was no sign of the Ordinary.

He thought for a moment he might have passed him and, turning round, he caught sight of a figure ducking out of sight behind the corner of a building. The movement was too quick for him to be sure of who or what he'd seen and he let it pass. He had to find the Ordinary.

Turning back, he noticed a side turning he'd not previously seen, its entrance guarded by a stone arch. The priest had to be there. There was nowhere else.

Grenville hurried to the spot and found himself looking down the length of a short street bordered on either side by a terrace of around a half-dozen houses. Of his quarry, there was no sign.

Yet if not here, then where? Again, Grenville looked up and down the main street. It was getting dark now, more difficult to see the faces of the people going about their business. He had little choice but to wait and hope the Ordinary was a visitor in one of the twelve houses in the court where he now stood.

An hour passed. Then a second. Lights appeared in the windows of several of the houses as night closed in.

From further down the close, Grenville heard a door opening and the sound of men's voices. He retreated into the deep shadow of the building line and waited. A figure emerged from one of the houses and descended the steps to the roadway, his features masked by the night. At the bottom, he turned towards the main street. It was impossible to see his face but his height and build approximated to those of the Ordinary. It had to be him. And he had to be in possession of Bristow's letters. Nothing else made sense. Grenville's mood of desperation grew. He needed those letters, whatever the cost. In the wrong hands they would see him hang.

And of all things he didn't want that.

He moistened his lips, a nervous spasm turning his stomach as his hand dropped to his sword. He watched the stranger turn towards him. If it wasn't the Ordinary, who else could it be? A servant, perhaps? A neighbour? Grenville's mind alternated between doubt and certainty. He struggled with his thoughts even as his fingers tightened about the hilt of his sword and he realised he'd already made up his mind. The man whose face he could not see was to die. The choice was simple. His life or the Ordinary's. But… Again he faltered. What if the approaching stranger were not the Ordinary? He swept the doubt from his thoughts. The stakes were too high.

One last look round. There was no one in sight – only the stranger. He drew his sword, the hiss of tempered steel barely more than a whisper as it slipped from the scabbard. The man was less than twenty yards away, walking quickly, his head bowed. He would see nothing, hear nothing. The end would come quickly. Grenville would see to that.

Somewhere in the back of his conscious mind he was aware of a light tapping sound. It was getting louder. Grenville tried to ignore it, his eyes fixed on the stranger, the gap between them closing. Fifteen yards. Twelve. He adjusted his grip on the sword, flexing his sweating fingers. He hadn't drawn it since the night of the ambush.

The memories of that night crowded in. He could see the narrow country lane bathed in the ghostly hue of a crescent moon, the scudding clouds casting deep shadows over the countryside. And he could hear the hellish shrieks of the attacking horde rushing at him through the gaps in the hedgerows, dim shapes appearing and disappearing, the gleam of steel plunging, slashing, stabbing, the air filled with the anguished cries of the wounded and the dying. For the first time in his life he'd been frightened. He'd never imagined war would be like this. A shape appeared. It came towards him. He didn't want to die. Not then, not ever. He struck out with his sword and felt it sink into human flesh. Too late, he saw the white cross-belts and the shako of a British soldier fall to the ground at his feet.

He'd never told Bristow the truth about how he'd come by his injury, of the confusion of war which had led to the loss of his leg. It wasn't hard to guess how he'd react.

Tap, tap, tap. The sound was like the harbinger of doom, closer than before. If he was seen, he'd hang for what he was about to do. His mouth was dry. Even swallowing was nigh impossible. A drop of sweat stung his eyes. That, too, he could do nothing about. The stranger from the house was upon him.

Beyond the stone arch, the tapping sound stopped. A man stood on the far side of Watling Street, his silhouette sharply framed in the light of the moon.

Grenville had mentally rehearsed the detail of the savagery he was about to unleash; the single thrust of the steel blade to the man's belly, the fellow's forward motion enough to ensure his instant demise. There was to be no going back. He was committed.

But…

The doubts emerged from some buried corner of his mind. The cully had come from one of the houses furthest from the corner of Watling Street – so far away that he'd questioned the Ordinary's ability to reach it in the time available. Grenville forced away the doubt. The time for questioning had passed. The figure before him was no longer a human being deserving of thought or compassion. He was merely an obstacle to be overcome, a fly to be swatted aside, a necessary task.

Suddenly, he stopped. Something wasn't right. His mind raced, looking for an answer to the question he could not frame. He couldn't delay – yet he must. He had to search for the cause – but knew there was no time. If he was to act, it had to be now. He tried to think, to reach a decision; to kill or not. It felt as though his mind had slowed, his ability to make a choice taken from him. He needed more information than he could possibly have.

Then it came to him. It was the noise, or rather the absence of it which had unnerved him. The tapping sound had stopped. It meant someone was watching him. He was certain of it. Why else would the tapping noise have stopped so close and so suddenly? He lowered the point of his sword. He had no option. He was dimly aware of the Ordinary of Newgate sweeping past him. He paid no heed, his attention focused on the far side of Watling Street where the moonlight had caught the flash of a knife's blade. Something moved, a shapeless mass, darker than its surroundings. Grenville felt the first stirrings of fear, his pulse quickening. He remembered seeing someone duck out of sight earlier in the afternoon. He wondered if he was being followed. But why?

The shadow moved again, out into the glow of the moon, a slow, almost graceful swing of the body. Grenville started, the blood draining from his face.

'It can't be,' he gasped.

Chapter 45

Emanuel made his way along Castle Street, Holborn, the faint glow from his lamp barely enough to guide him through the black night. The escape of the two men who'd attacked Sara had been unfortunate and he'd been reluctant to leave her in the house but she'd insisted. In the end he'd agreed, promising to drop in the next morning. He stopped at the door of the bishop's residence, knocked and waited for the housekeeper to let him in.

'My dear Lazaro, give you joy, sir,' said a voice behind him. He turned to see the familiar shape of his friend John Walter hurrying towards him. 'I was hoping to find you here. Can you spare a moment?'

'In course, sir,' said Emanuel, smiling broadly. 'We can talk inside, if that suits.'

'D'you recall asking me what I knew about anti-Catholic sentiment in this country?' said Walter, as soon as they'd settled themselves in the bishop's wood-panelled meeting room. 'I mentioned a couple of names of people I thought might be involved. One of them being Sir Peter Westlake.'

'Yes, I remember,' said Emanuel.

'I've just come from Garraway's where I saw Sir Peter. He was talking to a couple of likely lads which left me wondering why someone like him should wish to keep company with such men. I tried to hear what they were saying but most of it was inaudible. I did however hear your name being mentioned on several occasions. It sounded to me as if they might have been a little put out by something you'd done. I thought you ought to know.'

'What, pray, did the men look like, sir?' said Emanuel.

'Early twenties, broad shoulders, military bearing,' said Walter. 'Looked like the sort of men I make a habit of avoiding. One had red hair tied at the nape. The other was of a darker complexion.'

'I know the men,' said Emanuel. 'I think they're both in the military. I saw them this morning with Grenville, again at Garraway's. After they left I followed them to Hyde Park…'

He quickly recounted the events of the morning and his encounter with the same men at the house in Farmer Street. 'They must have gone straight to Garraway's after their escape from custody.'

'Is the girl safe?' asked Walter, his eyes widening in shock.

'I think so,' said Emanuel. 'She insisted on remaining in the room although it can't have been easy for her.'

'No, I don't suppose it was,' said Walter. 'Nor, sir, for you. Those men were not, after all, looking for the girl.'

'The thought, sir, had not escaped me,' said Emanuel.

'Forgive me. I spoke in haste. I had not meant to cause you alarm. But the involvement of the military is a worrying development. And while I dare say the actions of these men has not been officially condoned, the mere fact of their contact with a gentleman of Sir Peter's standing is, of itself, concerning.'

'Yet hardly the cause of surprise,' said Emanuel. 'You will recall my mentioning that the men were known to Grenville and doubtless it was he who introduced them to Sir Peter.'

'Yes, of course. How stupid of me.' Walter paused for a moment. 'Do you still have that piece of paper the girl found in Sir Peter's house?'

'Yes, I do,' said Emanuel, rummaging around in his coat pocket and producing the crumpled sheet.

Walter examined it in silence, turning it over and looking at the underside before again studying the front. He shook his head and muttered to himself as though considering a number of possible explanations, before dismissing each in turn. At last he threw the paper onto the table, clasped his hands behind his head and ballooned his cheeks.

'I confess I can make no sense of this,' he said. 'I was rather hoping a fresh look would produce results but the location remains a mystery to me. You're quite sure it has something to do with the plot which is so exercising our minds?'

'I'm not sure of anything,' said Emanuel. 'Sara only said she'd found it after she'd overheard Sir Peter and Grenville talking about the emancipation question. It had apparently fallen from Grenville's pocket. It's possible it could refer to something altogether different.'

Walter leaned forward and picked up the paper for a second look. 'Aye, it might,' he said. 'Bye the bye, you've heard the rumours, I suppose?'

'What rumours are those?' said Emanuel.

'Bristow is alive. What's more, he's a free man.'

Chapter 46

It was some time before Grenville felt able to think about anything other than the shadowy figure he'd seen disappearing into the night. It was impossible for it to have been Bristow. He'd been hanged for murder. He was dead. The Ordinary had said as much.

But what if he was alive and back on the streets? There was no question but that he'd know the source of the perjured evidence that had so nearly sent him to the gallows. It wouldn't have required a genius to work it out. Grenville shuddered. He'd seen how Bristow worked, knew of his ruthless nature, the pleasure he took in the sufferings of others, especially those who'd crossed him.

A little more of what the Ordinary had said to him crept into the outer reaches of his memory. He struggled to recall the detail. *You say the prisoner Bristow has been executed?* It had been a question, not a statement. The Ordinary hadn't known if Bristow had lived or died. He hadn't even remembered the scrub. Why would anyone have bothered to tell him whether or not the fellow had been hanged?

Grenville searched the deep shadows, listening for the familiar tap of Bristow's crutches on the road surface, his nerves at breaking point. He both dreaded and longed for the confirmation of Bristow's continued existence. It would, at least, bring certainty to the chaos of his mind.

The silence was total.

He was alone.

He looked back at the house from which the Ordinary had emerged. Bristow or no Bristow, he still needed to find the missing letters. No one – except the Ordinary and Bristow himself – knew what they contained, the confidences they betrayed, the accusations they levelled. But he could guess. Bristow had had nothing to lose. For another few seconds Grenville watched the place where he'd seen the flash of moonlight on metal. Then, staying close to the building line, he crept away to the house from which the Ordinary had come. A single light shone from a ground-floor room.

Five, ten, fifteen minutes passed by. The light moved. A shadow crossed the ceiling of the room and went out through a door, plunging the house into darkness. Moments later it reappeared on the floor above, the sconce set down, perhaps by a bedside. It wouldn't be long now.

The light went out.

Grenville stayed where he was, his heart pounding, the memory of what he'd seen on the far side of Watling Street playing on his mind. If it had been Bristow – and it seemed increasingly likely that it was – the villain would have guessed what he was up to. It must have been him who'd been following him since he'd left Old Bailey behind. The thought sent a shiver down his spine. He swallowed and tried to steady his fraying nerves.

He checked the stone arch at the entrance to the court. There was no sign of movement.

A moment later he slipped silently across the street towards the house.

Chapter 47

For Sara, sleep was out of the question. She sat on the edge of the bed in the room on Farmer Street, her eyes fixed on the shattered door. She doubted the crude repairs could offer much in the way of security. She regretted telling Mr Emanuel she wanted to remain where she was; that she would be all right. She should have accepted his offer to take her with him to the bishop's house in Holborn where a bed would be found for her. She would've been safe there. It was too late now.

Her eyelids drooped. She forced them open, driving her fingernails into the palms of her hands, determined to stay awake. Her eyes travelled round the pitch blackness of her surroundings, seeing nothing. Again her eyelids drooped, grew heavier and closed.

She was instantly awake, her eyes staring up at the ceiling, her pulse racing. Something had woken her. She turned her head to the window. It was still dark outside, the night sky littered with a million specks of light. She lay still and waited.

She heard a squeak, like that of a door opening. Almost certainly the door to the street. It wasn't unusual. She knew there were around two dozen others who lived in the house. Doubtless it was one of them returning home for the night.

But she couldn't be sure. Not yet. She waited.

She heard the heavy tread of footsteps approaching along the corridor, slow, almost hesitant as though someone was groping in an unfamiliar place. A light appeared under her door and grew stronger. She waited for it to pass on down the corridor to one of the other rooms. The sound reached her door and stopped.

Sara sat upright and stared at the door, expecting it to burst open, a repeat of what had happened earlier. She felt sick, unable to move, her knuckles forced into her mouth, stifling a scream that had risen in her throat.

She heard a faint rustle. A sheet of paper appeared under the door. A moment later the footsteps retreated back the way they had come. She waited for the sound of the street door closing.

She was shaking, her eyes fixed on the paper by the door, her mind trying to make some sense of what had happened, of why anyone would deliver a note at this hour. She tried to move but fear kept her fixed and immobile as surely as if she were fettered, her imagination running free, no idea so preposterous that it could be dismissed. Rational thought was impossible for her. She tried to remember if she'd heard the street door again. Her mind refused to tell her. Sleep was out of the question. Five, then ten minutes passed. There was no sound save those of revelry in the distant Highway.

From somewhere she found the strength to move. Clenching her teeth, she slid off the bed and crept to her door. Down the corridor, in one of the other rooms, she could hear someone coughing. Nothing else disturbed the silence of the house. She looked down at the sheet of paper. Touching it would somehow confirm its existence and admit that someone had put it there. The thought frightened her. She knew of no one who could have written to her. No one knew where she was, except Mr Emanuel – and the two strangers who'd attacked her.

Slowly, she bent down and picked up the folded note. It was sealed with wax but she could see neither the mark on the seal nor the name written on the outside. She looked again at the seal. Perhaps the letter wasn't for her at all. No one had ever used red wax on a letter addressed to her. She stared at it for a moment, her curiosity awakened. She wanted to see who it was addressed to. But that meant lighting a candle and that, in turn, meant confirming her presence.

A sudden noise in the street outside made her jump. Voices. Three, perhaps four people coming down Farmer Street from New Gravel Lane. She held her breath as they drew alongside the house. Then, as quickly as they'd come, they were gone. She blew out a lungful of air, unsure of how much more stress she could take. She couldn't stay here. Anywhere was preferable to this. She listened for any sign of the stranger's continuing presence. There was nothing.

She slid back the bolts and opened her door.

Chapter 48

Grenville made his way to the back of the house. It was darker here than the court onto which the house fronted. Here he could see nothing beyond the black mass of the building against the sky. He moved closer. A window loomed into view. He tried it. It was locked. He considered forcing it but decided the noise would be too great. He moved on. A second window came into view and then, a yard or so further, a door appeared. He stopped and looked round. Nothing moved, the quiet of the night disturbed only by the distant howl of a dog. He reached for the door latch and pressed down on the thumb plate. It snapped down with a sharp crack. His heartbeat surged. He looked up at the windows and waited. No light appeared.

Pushing the door open, he stepped over the threshold into what he guessed, from the pungent smell of damp, was probably the scullery. Doubtless the kitchen would be next and from there he'd have to find the stairs up to the hall. He took his time, feeling his way past tables, chairs, cupboards and whatever else might get in the way of a rapid exit.

The stairs were at the far end of the kitchen, at the top of which was a door opening onto what appeared to be the hall, the air heavy with the scent of lavender. By now his eyes had become adjusted to the total blackness of the house and he was able to see the outline of the room. At the far end he could discern the dull outline of a fanlight over the main door and in front of this, set back about fifteen feet from it, the main staircase. Staying close to the wall, he looked for the hall table on which any household letters would normally be placed. He found it to the right of the front door and ran his fingers over the polished top, nearly dislodging an ornate glass jar in the process. Of any letters, there was no sign.

Grenville stopped and thought for a moment. The Ordinary had left this address in the last hour, almost certainly having delivered a letter written on behalf of a condemned prisoner. And, in all probability, that prisoner was Bristow. If that was the case, it was unlikely the letter would yet have been read. It would be with all the other correspondence on a table somewhere. But where? He remembered passing several doors on his circuit of the hall. He decided to check each one. The first room drew a blank, as did the second. Entering the third, he was immediately aware of the warm scents of leather and polished wood mingling with the faint smell of tobacco. His spirits lifted. It was the library and the library was where his own letters were placed in the house on Oxford Street. He looked round. A long table occupied the central area of the room while bookshelves lined each of three walls. At the far end some leather armchairs were grouped round the fireplace.

Grenville's eye returned to the main table. There was nothing on it of any interest; a few magazines, a copy of *The Times*, an empty snifter but that was all. He padded round the room. A minute passed. Then two. He'd almost given up when he saw a richly ornamented escritoire to one side of the fireplace, its desktop surface still open, some sheets of paper scattered over its surface.

He stepped over and had begun to scoop up the papers when the faint creak of a floorboard sounded above his head. A second later a door latch snapped open. Grenville crept to the library door and waited. On the floor above, the footsteps padded along a short corridor to the head of the stairs and stopped.

Grenville stood in the doorway and craned his neck out into the hall and up the stairs. He couldn't see anyone. Whoever it was had stopped out of sight. Grenville felt his heart beating against the wall of his chest. For the first time since Ireland he was afraid. This was not what was supposed to have happened. He'd not considered the possibility of detection.

Another creak of a floorboard and the pale orb of a man's face appeared over the banister rail. Grenville stepped back into the library and drew his knife, all too aware that his hand was shaking.

'Who's there?' said a male voice.

Grenville thought about making a run for it. He could just make it to the door at the head of the kitchen stairs before the householder knew what was happening. He edged his way out into the hall. The man was still peering over the rail, waiting.

Grenville readied himself to run.

Then he heard the heavy metallic click. He knew at once what it was. Cold drops of sweat formed on his brow. He looked up to see the barrel of a pistol pointing down the stairs towards him.

'Who are you, sir? Answer me directly else I shoot.' The man at the top of the stairs had begun to descend.

Grenville thought rapidly. The only question now was whether the gun would be fired. If it was, and it missed, the man would have nothing left. He'd be exposed. But the closer he got, the more accurate would be the shot.

The man descended another tread.

#

The past few days had affected Emanuel to a degree he could not have expected. Henry Teeling's admission that he, rather than Bristow, had murdered the unfortunate Collins had seldom been far from his mind. It troubled him that he'd not done more to prevent the execution of an innocent man and had, instead, chosen to rely on the seal of the confessional as justification for his lack of action. Perhaps his reluctance to act had had more to do with Bristow's discovery of a secret he'd hoped to carry to his grave.

'Bristow? Alive?' he said, unsure of what to make of the news. 'How's that possible? I thought him hanged.'

'We all did,' said Walter. 'Yet according to what I've heard, he's been seen near St Paul's. No one knows how he managed it.'

'Are you quite certain, sir?' asked Emanuel. It was all he could manage.

'I've not seen him myself but I've no reason, sir, to doubt the story,' said Walter. 'Now that I think on it, you made efforts to save him, did you not? What hope were you given?'

'None,' said Emanuel, the irony of his position not lost on him and recalling the words Bristow's counsel. 'I regret there is no appeal open to us,' the lawyer had said.

'Yet, from what I've been told, sir,' said Walter, 'you didn't agree with that assessment and took the case to the Secretary of State. I gather that Portland was reluctant to get involved until it was pointed out to him that refusing to see a Catholic priest might not sit well with the Administration's attempts to woo the Irish.'

'I'm not sure I can take any credit for what's happened, sir,' said Emanuel.

'You know he's made no secret of his intention to kill you,' said Walter.

'Yes,' said Emanuel. 'I know.'

#

Grenville stared at the pistol in the man's hand, the barrel pointing at his heart. He felt dizzy with fear, his mouth dry, his legs buckling beneath him. Of all things he didn't want to die. Yet if he moved, the man would shoot. If he stayed, it was the hangman's noose for sure. The stairs creaked. The man was a step closer.

There was no warning. A sudden spout of flame lit up the hall, white smoke billowing from the muzzle of the pistol in the man's hand followed immediately by the roar of exploding gunpowder and the hiss of a lead ball passing close to his left ear. It was all Grenville needed. He ducked and ran for the door at the head of the kitchen stairs. Behind him he could hear the sound of pounding footsteps. For all he knew the man had a second pistol and would use it at the first opportunity. Grenville raced into the kitchen, toppling a tall jar from its place on a table and sending it crashing to the floor. Then it was through the scullery towards the safety of the night beyond.

Yanking at the back door, he ran headlong into the back yard. Another explosion, another rush of air as a second pistol shot shattered the still of the evening.

Grenville kept running. He turned the corner of the house and sprinted back along the court to Watling Street, every step threatening to be his last, his lungs on fire, his muscles aching.

He stopped at the stone arch and looked back. Lights had appeared at the windows of several houses, their occupants no doubt woken by the sound of gunfire. He turned and sprinted away.

From the far side of the street, a pair of eyes watched him go.

Chapter 49

Sara eased open the door of her room and peered up the corridor towards the front door. No one was there, the corridor deserted and the front door closed. She ducked back into her room and wished once more she hadn't refused the offer of a room at the bishop's residence. At least there she would have been safe. She mulled the thought over in her mind. Perhaps she still could. One of the men in the room at the end of the corridor might be prepared to escort her to Holborn. Her resolve wavered. She didn't know the men and there'd been enough excitement for one night.

Slowly, she groped her way to the front door. The distant roar of the Ratcliff Highway was louder now with the excited shouts and screams of those for whom sleep seemed impossible. Sara hesitated. Her brief experience of street life had not been happy. She'd seldom slept, even on those occasions when she'd been fortunate enough to find a vacant doorway in which to rest. Her beauty had ensured the unwanted attention of every passing male, while a gnawing and permanent hunger had had its own way of denying her the sleep she craved. She didn't want to repeat the experience. But she had little choice. Even going to Holborn, to the bishop's house on Castle Street, would be a step too far, an imposition on a sleeping household. Perhaps she would try in the morning. But not now. Not at this hour.

She reached the corner of the Highway and paused, her arms clasped about her waist, the first stirring of doubt touching her consciousness as she surveyed the amorphous mass of humanity passing by. She wondered if she'd made the right decision in leaving her room and was not in greater danger here. She stared at the faces of the beggars, sailors, prostitutes, pimps and bully-boys strolling, shambling, bustling by. Several glanced approvingly in her direction yet no one threatened her safety. Still a feeling of vulnerability enveloped her. Several times she thought of returning to her room, to the familiarity of her surroundings. It would be better to wait there for one's fate than here surrounded by strangers.

She remembered Teeling talking about a lodging house not far from here. He'd had barely a good word to say about the place save only that it was cheap. She dipped a hand into her coat pocket and withdrew some coins. She might just have enough for one night. It had to be better than walking the streets.

Ten minutes later she'd turned off the Highway into a court, lined with tall, crumbling buildings. Here and there she could see men lying at the side of the road, their sunken features hidden behind masks of grime, their torn clothing ingrained with filth and grease. She felt their brittle, lifeless eyes on her as she walked past, their silent rebuke for a stranger's presence. From behind a shattered window came the hungry cries of an unseen child.

At the end of the court was a large yard, perhaps eighty yards square, strewn with assorted rubbish – a discarded boot, some empty bottles, the putrid remains of an animal, the detritus of life. To one side of the yard was the lodging house of which Teeling had spoken, a large, red-brick, three-storey building fronting directly onto the square. She started towards it and saw a group of perhaps eight or nine stoutly built women standing by the main entrance, and appearing to take a close interest in her arrival. She made to pass them.

'What's your game?' said the largest of the women, her thick arms akimbo, her lank hair hanging shapelessly about her bare shoulders.

Sara stopped short and stared at the woman. 'Game?' she said, her eyes widening.

'This ain't your patch, darlin'. Now, piss off afore you get what's coming to yer.'

'I mean no harm,' said Sara, stepping back a pace. 'I was looking for a bed for the night, is all.'

'Oh, aye?' said the woman. 'A bed for the night, you say? That's a good 'un.'

'No, truly,' said Sara alarmed by the aggressive tone.

'And there was I thinking you was on the game,' said the woman, her face softening. 'There ain't no room for any more of us girls, see? You ain't from these parts, is you, love?'

'No, I was in service in the City until a few days since. I was—'

'Told to go, was yer?' said the woman nodding her head in a knowing sort of way. 'Happens all the time, luv.'

Sara ignored the insinuation in the woman's voice. She doubted her story of being made the subject of a false allegation of theft would, in any case, be believed.

'Staying just for the night, you say?'

'Yes. It's all I can afford,' said Sara.

'Afford, ducks?' said the woman. 'You ain't thinking of paying, is you? You'll get us all a bad name, you will. I ain't paid for me lodging in years.

Nor 'ave the others, neither. When the time comes to pay, we scarper right quick. No, love, you don't pay nothing. It's the way it is. Most lodging houses is run by them Christ-killers and cheating a Jew ain't no sin. Leastways, it ain't in my book.'

'Is that so? Doesn't anyone stop you?' asked Sara, unable to stop herself.

'Gor' love us,' said the woman, looking round at her friends as though unable to believe anyone could ask such a question. 'They can try. Wouldn't do them no good, though. Take Kissing Kate, here,' she said, gesturing to a large woman of about thirty. 'She ain't never paid nothing though there's a few what's tried to make her. Not afraid of any man, she is. And right handy with her maulers, too. Would take a big cully to stop her leaving, and no mistake.'

'What about your chattels? Don't the owner seize them?' said Sara glancing nervously at the lowering form of Kissing Kate who now stood rather too close for comfort. 'I mean, whatever she leaves behind? Don't he sell them and get his money that way?'

'What d'you take me for?' hissed Kissing Kate. 'Think I's stupid, do yer? What d'you know, anygate? Life's hard enough without I have to answer fool questions like that. I ain't got nothing but the clothes on me back. And that's the truth. But if I did, I wouldn't take it with me so some no-good villain could take it from me, would I?'

'No, I suppose not,' said Sara, regretting she'd ever allowed herself to become embroiled in this conversation. She edged closer to the door. 'I'm sorry if I caused any offence.'

'Well, that's all right then,' said Kissing Kate, her face clearing somewhat. 'You just mind what I've said to yer. We don't want anyone getting us a bad name on account they don't know what's what.'

Passing in through the front door, Sara was met by a second door, to one side of which was a small grille built into the wall. From behind it a gaunt, sallow-skinned man peered out at her, his long side curls and Coptic nose instantly marking him as of the Root of Jesse.

'Yes?' he said.

'If you please, sir, I desire a bed for the night,' said Sara. 'If that ain't possible, then somewhere to sit and stay warm.'

'I'll thank you for three pennies,' said the man. 'Whether there is a bed or not, I cannot say. You must search for yourself. The price is the same.'

'How can that be, sir?' asked Sara. 'I pay for a bed. If there is no bed then surely I must pay less.'

'Would you steal from the poor? Did you come here to insult me?' The man's eyes blazed in indignation. 'Pay me the due amount or be on your way.'

Too tired to argue and conscious of being watched by the women she'd so recently left, Sara fished three pennies from her pocket and slid them through the grille.

'Where…' she said, but the man was already busy sweeping up the coins she'd given him and putting them in a leather purse that hung from his belt. Sara looked at the door next to the grille. 'Do I go through here?'

The face at the grille had disappeared. She opened the door and walked through where she was met by a thick cloud of smoke billowing out from an open fire in the grate. In the centre of the room was a large deal table at which several men and women were eating. Others appeared to be asleep, their heads resting on folded arms.

'New, is you?' A woman of about Sara's age was standing next to her. Sara hadn't seen her arrive.

'Yes.'

'I heard you asking old Joseph about a bed for the night,' said the woman. 'Take no notice of his manner. He's like that with everyone. There ain't no harm in him. There's an empty bed on the third floor. Turn right at the top of the stairs and it's in front of you.'

'Thank you,' said Sara. 'Best I get myself up there before anyone else comes.'

The room to which she had been directed overlooked the yard. It was small – barely eight foot square with a sloping roof. Looking round she counted a total of four rag-filled mattresses laid out on the floor, three of which were already occupied. She made her way over to the remaining bed, directly below a large gap in the roof of the building. She shrugged and hoped it wouldn't rain.

'Don't often see a strange face in 'ere.'

The woman's voice made Sara jump. She looked down to see a pair of eyes peering at her from behind a curtain of grey hair.

'Is that so?' said Sara. She wasn't in the mood for talking. She felt in her dress pocket for the letter that had so recently been pushed under her bedroom door. Taking it out, she moved over to where she'd put down her candle and squinted at the spidery handwriting on the outside of the fold.

'Your first time, is it, love?' The woman propped herself up on one elbow.

‘Aye,’ said Sara, reluctantly coming to the view that the woman wasn’t about to pass up the opportunity for a chat. She was older than most of the others Sara had seen so far. Probably early sixties, her face deeply lined, her bulbous, blood-red nose indicative of a life spent on drink.

‘It ain’t so bad in here,’ said the woman, lying back down on the mattress. ‘Course, depends on what you’s used to. In the last place I was at, it were the bugs what were the problem. I’d catch more of them in me bed than I knew what to do with. And that weren’t all. Most mornings I’d find lice in the water bucket. Lord, you should ’ave seen them – them what was still alive – paddling round and round. I reckon they dropped off the ceiling on account of the cully in the room above treading the floorboards and shaking them free. Used to crush them with the bottom of me candlestick, I did. And when it weren’t the bugs and the lice and the filth of the place, it were the fighting and the swearing and the depredations of them what don’t care about other folk.’

‘I’m sorry to hear that, I’m sure. I don’t suppose…’ Sara stopped and looked down at the woman. She was already snoring. Sitting down on the edge of her mattress, Sara again turned her attention to the letter. It was addressed to *Master Henry Teeling at the house of the Papist priest, Farmer Street, Shadwell*. She felt oddly relieved. The visitor who had so frightened her with his nocturnal visit had not been looking for her. He’d merely been delivering a letter for Teeling.

She paused as a thought struck her. If Teeling was in any kind of trouble, she wanted to know about it. Seeing his name had awakened memories of him. She broke the seal and let her eye run down the dozen lines of text to the name at the bottom. It appeared in large block capitals above an equally large 'X'. It read *Erasmus Bristow, presently residing at Newgate Prison* and was followed by the date.

She'd not known Bristow, except as an occasional visitor to her former employer's house where he would arrive in the company of Master James. As far as she was concerned that had been plenty enough. There had always been an air of menace about him that had made her feel deeply uncomfortable. Teeling had also talked about him. It had been in connection with the murder of his wife two years before, something about Bristow being one of the soldiers who'd been present when she was killed.

Sara began to read. She stopped at a sentence about halfway down the page and reread it several times. Shocked as seldom before, she stared at the paper in disbelief. Then she read the sentence once more. *It weren't Collins what did for your old woman, nor me, neither. It were Lt. Grenville.*

'Master James?' she whispered. 'Is it possible?' She was quite certain Teeling had blamed Collins for his wife's death. He'd never mentioned anything about Master James Grenville's possible involvement.

Sara sat quite still for a long time, her tiredness forgotten. At length she folded the paper and put it into the pocket of her dress.

She knew what to do.

Chapter 50

The sun was out over Hyde Park the following morning, driving the dew from the grass and raising the heads of the daffodils from their night of slumber. On a track, close to the northern boundary of the park, Sir Peter Westlake and the Hon. James Grenville were to be seen riding towards Park Lane. They were deep in conversation with one another.

'He must still have them,' said a sombre-looking Sir Peter hitching one leg across his saddle and leaning down to tighten the horse's girth. 'You're quite sure none of the letters in your possession are of any interest?'

'I'm quite sure, Sir Peter,' said Grenville.

'In which case the Ordinary must still have them or have posted them elsewhere.'

'Thank you for pointing that out, sir,' said Grenville, glaring at the older man. He'd already come to the same conclusion and didn't need reminding of his supposed shortcomings. None of the letters he had taken from the house he'd searched last night were of the remotest interest. 'The question is, what's to be done now?'

Sir Peter didn't immediately reply. The girth tightened, he sat upright in the saddle and slipped his foot back into the stirrup.

'Were you, sir, seen by anyone apart from the gentleman whose house it was?' he asked.

'It's possible—' began Grenville.

'Good Lord, man. Who?'

'I'm not sure.' Grenville fiddled unnecessarily with his stock. 'I think I was followed. I saw his shadow and, for a moment, I thought it was someone I knew.'

'You think? Pray, sir, speak plainly.' Sir Peter reined in his mount and turned to face his companion. 'Someone you knew? Who was it?'

'It was dark. I can't be sure. But it was the way he moved, as though he was a cripple. He was using crutches. I think…'

'Get on with it, man. We've not got all morning.'

'I think it was Bristow.'

Sir Peter reared backwards as though struck, his thin lips parting in a show of horror.

'How's that possible?' he said.

'I'm only, sir, telling you what I saw,' said Grenville, suddenly angry.

'What exactly did this fellow see?'

'Nothing to speak of,' said Grenville. 'Fortunately I'd seen him in time. But it did mean I couldn't get the letters off the pastor.'

'Nevertheless, I think it might be wise to postpone our plans, sir,' said Sir Peter, twirling his daffodil before his nose. 'At least until we can be sure Bristow is dead and we have the letters. I make no doubt the militia will be waiting for us, else.'

'I cannot agree with you, sir,' said Grenville. 'Certainly it would have been preferable to have found the letters but there remain several points in our favour. Bristow was never privy to all the details of our plans. Even if he is still alive or the letters fall into the wrong hands, the authorities won't believe what a convicted felon says or has written.'

'I accept Bristow never knew all the details, but are you willing to take that chance?' said Sir Peter, a doubtful look on his face. 'He knew the location. He need only say that much for the authorities to take notice, vague though the rest of his information might be.'

'What if they do take notice? What is there to link us to what happens? You'll be safely out of the way at Boodle's when the deed is done. As for me I shall be one of the crowd,' said Grenville. He fell silent. He knew the risks were a great deal more serious than he pretended. Even if the plan did succeed and they were not caught, there was no guarantee that it would lead to the outcome they wanted. He put the thought behind him. They'd come too far to stop now. 'We've spent a long time working towards this, Sir Peter. If we fail, I make no doubt the Minister will get his way on Ireland and, what is worse, emancipation for the Papists. I should, sir, rather die than see that day.'

'Very well,' said Sir Peter, tipping his hat to a passing rider. 'We'll proceed as planned. What of the man you've chosen to do the deed? Can we trust him to keep his mouth shut?'

'He has no choice. It's been made clear to him what'll happen to him and his family if he talks.'

'Good. So everything's in place for next week?'

'Yes,' said Grenville. 'I had a final word with him. He knows exactly what's expected of him. He'll be in position mingling with the crowds. The rest of the fellows will be close by in case of trouble.'

'And the escape route? I take it that, too, has been arranged? We don't want the fellow being interrogated if we can possibly avoid it. Better that he should escape detection.'

'What is planned, sir, will doubtless be followed by a scene of panic,' said Grenville, drawing the reins of his mount and preparing to turn about as they reached the end of the track. 'People will assuredly rush from the scene, frightened for their lives. Our man will use this to his advantage to slip away unseen.'

'But if he's caught?' Sir Peter paused as he, too, turned his horse about. 'What then?'

'We've already talked about this, Sir Peter. He won't talk. He knows what'll happen to him if he does. He'll pretend to be sick in the mind. At least then he won't hang.'

'Very well,' said Sir Peter, waving his crop in Grenville's direction. 'Take me through the whole programme.'

He listened intently as Grenville talked. When the younger man had finished, Sir Peter smiled and said, 'I think that should settle things for the foreseeable future. I doubt the Minister will dare raise the subject of Ireland again. Would you care to join me for luncheon?'

Neither man saw the lone figure walking down Park Lane who stopped and stared at them before continuing on his way.

Chapter 51

Evening had fallen by the time Emanuel had completed his usual round of visits to the sick and the dying, and prepared his homily for Mass the following morning. He turned into Castle Street, looking forward to his evening meal and an hour or two of quiet reading. He had, by chance, come across a Hidalgo amongst the bookstalls of St Paul's which he'd yet to open. He reached into his coat pocket and drew out the volume, dislodging a sliver of paper in the process. He stopped and picked it up. It was the paper Sara had found in the library of Sir Peter Westlake's home and which he and Walter had so far failed to make any sense of. He gazed at it for a moment. There *was* something vaguely familiar about the lines drawn on the page. He carried it over to a lantern hanging above the doorway of a shop and held it to the light. The layout was oddly familiar, as though he'd seen it recently. But perhaps the familiarity he thought he'd recognised was no more than that of an object seen many times before. He screwed up the paper in his fist and was about to throw it away, but, changing his mind, he smoothed it out and placed it between the pages of his book. He'd give it one more try in the morning.

He reached the bishop's house and went in. The housekeeper had mentioned the possibility of roast turkey when he'd seen her this morning. 'Aye, Mr Emanuel, sir, it's roast turkey right enough, with collared pig an' all. Might have some boiled hare and pheasant left over from yesterday if you fancy it,' she'd said. His mouth had watered at the prospect. He walked into the dining room and saw the squat shape of the bishop hunched over a bowl of soup, a copy of *The Times* on the table next to him.

'Good evening, my lord.' Emanuel still hadn't got used to the idea of sharing a house with the Vicar Apostolic for London. Nor was he entirely sure when it was proper to kiss the large amethyst of the Episcopal ring the bishop was wearing. He felt his eye inexorably drawn to the stone, glinting in the candlelight.

'Give you joy, Father,' said John Douglass, glancing up from his paper. He paused, then, 'I see there was some more trouble with the mob last week. They are reported to have attacked the Sardinian Chapel.'

'I'm sorry to hear it, my lord. Was anyone hurt?' said Emanuel.

'I regret it extremely but, according to the paper, there were three deaths.' Douglass put down his soup spoon and dabbed his lips with a snow-white napkin. 'The poor souls were in the chapel at the time. Apparently the mob was dispersed by the militia and no arrests were made. I sometimes doubt things will ever improve for us in this country. Certainly not until Mr Pitt can resolve the Irish question.'

'He faces strong opposition, my lord. The King is said to oppose him,' said Emanuel, ladling some soup onto his plate.

'Talking of opposition,' said Douglass, 'do you have any more news on the plot you warned me about?'

'I regret we are no further forward on that score, my lord.'

'Well, keep me informed of any developments, will you, Father?' Douglass leaned back in his chair as the rotund figure of the cook appeared and put down a plate of boiled collared pig in front of him.

'Of course, my lord,' murmured Emanuel, wondering if he still had the bishop's attention or if he should mention Bristow's apparent escape from the hangman's noose. He doubted his own role in that affair would meet with the bishop's approval, especially as it had involved a serious breach of his priestly office. Betraying what had been said to him in the confessional – even in the pursuit of saving the life of an innocent human being – was not something that was likely to be tolerated.

His thoughts moved on. Sara had not been at home when he'd called to see her after Mass this morning. He wasn't unduly concerned. Probably she'd gone for a walk. He would call again tomorrow.

'Some roast turkey and collared pig for you, Father?' Emanuel looked up as the cook hovered expectantly at his shoulder.

'Why, thankee, Mary. I think I will. I've been looking forward to your cooking all day.'

It was another hour before Emanuel was able to slip away to his room and open his newly acquired Hidalgo, happy to have avoided any mention of the Bristow affair. It would, inevitably, have led on to what was, for him, dangerous ground. He put his book down and felt a cold hand clutch at his heart. It could only be a question of time before Bristow chose to tell all he knew of Emanuel's past. There was no doubting what the outcome of that would be.

Emanuel waited for the mood of fear and depression to pass, forcing himself to think of happier times. His book still lay on his lap. He picked it up, the volume falling open to reveal the paper Sara had given him. Lifting it out he thought again of the author of the lines on the page and the circumstances under which they'd been produced. The purpose for which it was originally drawn and even the precise location were, by themselves, of scant interest. What changed everything was the identification of Grenville as the author. It had become increasingly apparent to Emanuel that if the rumours of a plot to disrupt progress towards Catholic emancipation were true, Grenville had to be involved. And if that were the case, the discovery of the location depicted by the map was of the utmost importance. He stared at it with a mounting sense of frustration. He had the clearest sense he'd seen this formation of streets before. And recently.

Reluctantly, he slipped the paper back between the pages of his book, and tried to read.

Chapter 52

Sara watched Sir Peter Westlake and the Hon. James Grenville emerge from Boodle's and turn downhill, along St James's. She'd known where to find them. Seldom would an evening pass when they could not be found at the club. The men walked slowly, talking in low tones. Now and then they would stop and face one another, each waving his arms as though to emphasis some point or other before moving off again. She let them get ahead.

She was tired. She'd hardly slept at the lodging house the previous night, largely due to the ever-present bedbugs and the nocturnal grunts and snorts of her two roommates. As a result she'd risen early and returned to Farmer Street. It had been the lesser of the two evils, her fear of again being attacked marginally preferable to the absence of sleep. Even then, the habit of early rising had ensured she was up and dressed by six. But rising early been a mistake. With little else to occupy her time and despite her fatigue she'd alternated periods of rest with walks along the north bank of the Thames, while she thought of what to do about the Teeling letter. With the approach of evening she still had not made up her mind. The clarity of the night before had evaporated. She still knew what she wanted to do. It was a question of whether what she wanted was either sensible or even desirable.

At the bottom of St James's the two men parted company, one turning left along Pall Mall and the other right towards Stable Yard. Thirty yards ahead of her, Grenville walked with the careless swagger of someone used to the deference of others, his walking cane resting on one shoulder, his gait a little unsteady as though he'd been drinking. He reached The Mall and turned towards the dark mass of Green Park. Sara smiled grimly. There was only one reason why a gentleman would choose to walk in the park after dark.

She thought of the letter she still carried, wondering if she had made the right decision in withholding it from Teeling. Fear of what he might do and of the consequences for him had, in the end, persuaded her to keep the letter a secret. But she wanted Grenville to know he'd been unmasked, that his past misdeeds were known and would not be forgotten. That, anyway, had been her plan. But now, faced with his physical presence, her plan seemed futile, even reckless. As like as not he would take the letter from her and beat her into silence. What was her word against that of a high-born gentleman? What chance was there of bringing him to account?

Suddenly her foot struck a fallen branch and she stumbled, letting out a small shriek as she did so. She saw Grenville turn and look at her, a surprised frown on his face. She knew at once he'd recognised her. Turning on her heel she fled back towards the lights of Pall Mall.

'Miss Sara?' Grenville's voice seemed a long way off. She increased her pace and pretended not to hear.

'Stop, Miss Sara. It's me, Master James.'

She could hear the sound of his footsteps behind her, closing the gap between them. He would overtake her before she could reach the safety of Pall Mall. She stopped and waited for him to catch up.

'Why, it is you. What are you doing here? Surely you cannot…?' Grenville looked back into the dark mass that was Green Park and laughed, a mocking, derisory, cackle. 'Why, I've a mind to take you for myself. How much do you charge? Here, I'll give you a shilling.'

'I'm not what you think, Master James,' she said, her voice trembling, her head bowed. 'If you please, sir, stand aside and allow me to pass.'

'Damn your insolence, woman.' Grenville slapped his thigh with his walking cane, his face close to hers. 'I'll thank you to remember your place when addressing me.'

'I'm sorry, I'm sure,' said Sara, avoiding his gaze and appalled at the situation in which she found herself.

'Answer me directly. What are you doing out at this hour? I'll warrant you offer your services to any man who cares to demand them. Is that not so?'

'I have no home, sir. I must walk until I find somewhere to lie down and sleep.'

'Then you will need my shilling. Come with me.' He caught her by the arm and pulled her in amongst the trees.

'No, sir, please. Let me go.'

'Be quiet, woman, before I beat this nonsense out of you.' He pushed her against a tree and pressed his body against hers, his lips parting for a kiss. She could smell the drink on his breath and turned aside, only to earn a sharp slap to her face. She felt his hand travel down her thigh and reach for the hem of her dress, his breathing quickening as he drew the fabric up over her knees.

'Please, sir, no. I am a virgin.'

Another stinging blow to the side of her face sent her reeling. He caught her arm and pulled her back towards him.

'I told you to keep quiet. You think I've got time to listen to your complaints?' Grenville was mumbling now, unable to keep his balance as he struggled with the buttons of his breeches. 'I'm a busy man. In a few weeks the world will thank me for what I've done. Stand still, will you?'

'No. Please, Master James, stop,' she screamed, fighting to get free of his grip. She twisted her body away from him and was rewarded by a hard punch to the jaw. Blood filled her mouth and she felt a tooth loosen from the blow. He pushed her to the ground and dropped beside her. She screamed again, begging him to stop.

'Everything all right, miss?' The man's voice seemed to come from a long way up. For a moment Sara dismissed it as a trick of the mind. Beside her, Grenville was rolling away. He was shouting, his words lost in the frenzy of his anger.

She opened her eyes. A horse stood a few feet from where she lay. She had a sense of its massive size. Her eye travelled up to the figure mounted on its back, his shoulder-length hair tied back with a ribbon, his face in shadow. A wave of relief swept through her.

'Seems the lady don't want your attentions, sir. Just stand away, if you'd be so kind.'

'Who the blazes are you, sir? Be off with you before I flog the life out of you. D'you hear me, you common oaf?'

'I shan't tell you again, sir,' growled the stranger. 'Stand away from the lady, sir, else I shall be obliged to move you myself. I'm sure you wouldn't want me to do that, sir, would you now?'

Grenville sprang to his feet, his hand flying to the hilt of his sword. 'I'll teach you to speak to a gentleman in those terms, you scoundrel.'

'I wouldn't do that, sir. Not if I were you,' said the stranger, leaning down and holding Grenville by his throat.

'Who…?' croaked Grenville, his arms flailing the air as he sought to free himself from the stranger's iron grip.

'Who am I, sir? Is that what you're asking? The name is Higgins, sir. You remember me, sir, surely? I'm with the Bow Street Patrol, sir. I were at your house the night your butler had his throat cut. Anygate, sir, I were just passing and thought the lady needed a little help. I think it's time we left, you and me, sir. Just walk beside me for a little while, if you will, sir.'

'You've not heard the last of this, Higgins,' shouted Grenville. 'I'll have you for this, you villain.' He swivelled round to face Sara. 'As for you, you common slut, there's nowhere you can hide that I won't find you.'

'Come along, sir. You's becoming something of a nuisance and I'm sure you wouldn't like the lady to think that of you, would you now?'

Sara was still shaking as she watched the two of them disappear into the night. She knew Grenville would come looking for her, determined to assuage the hurt to his pride. She could not expect to be rescued a second time. Grenville would make sure of that.

#

The answer came to him quite suddenly. Emanuel's fingers trembled slightly as he fumbled through the leaves of his book in search of the scrap of paper. He took it out and squinted at the lines crudely drawn on the page. There was the road to Uxbridge running along the top of Hyde Park. And there, at right angles to it, was Park Lane. It had to be. It all fitted. It was the place where he'd seen Grenville and Sir Peter Westlake riding one morning. And it was also the place to which he'd followed Grenville's men. For whatever reason, that part of London was of interest to them. The drawing had, according to Sara, been produced during a conversation between Grenville and Sir Peter. He recalled Sara's words: *... they were planning something. I think it were connected with a debate in Parliament about the Papists. They said it had to be stopped at all cost.*

Emanuel continued to stare at the paper. Knowing what the drawing represented was of little help. It told him nothing about what was planned, or when it would happen. And while it seemed likely it was in some way connected with a supposed anti-Papist conspiracy, the available evidence fell short of proving it. Even the presence of Sir Peter and the Hon. James Grenville at the location proved nothing. His initial excitement quickly evaporated and he put the paper down. He would think about it in the morning when less tired.

#

Emanuel woke with a start. The room was pitch dark and for a moment he struggled to remember where he was. Slowly his memory returned. He must have dozed off in the chair and left the candle to burn itself out. He wondered what had woken him. There was no sound except that of his own rapid breathing, the air rushing in and out of his gaping mouth. Perhaps he'd been dreaming. He'd go to bed in a minute, when he could find the energy.

His eyelids began to close.

Just a few seconds more. Then he'd get into bed.

A tap at the door made him jump.

'Who is it?' he called, now wide awake.

'It's me, Mr Emanuel.' It was the housekeeper, her voice drowsy as though she, too, had been disturbed from her sleep. 'There's a woman in the street outside our door. Reckons she knows you and says she must speak with you. She won't take no for an answer, Mr Emanuel.'

'Did she give a name?'

'Aye, she said it was Sara.'

'Thank you, Mrs Wilson,' said Emanuel, suddenly wide awake. If Sara had chosen to come to Holborn at this late hour, it had to be serious. 'Be so kind as to show her into the meeting room. I shall be there directly.'

Lighting the candle by his bed, he buttoned his coat, and hurried downstairs.

'Thank goodness you're here, Mr Emanuel.' Sara's voice shook as she spoke, her face bathed in sweat.

'What's happened, child?' said Emanuel, holding up his candle and noting the girl's torn and grass-stained dress. 'Are you hurt?'

'It were Master James. He… he…'

'Speak slowly, child,' said Emanuel. He turned back to the door and called out for the housekeeper. 'Mrs Wilson, be so good as to fetch a blanket and some of your excellent broth. I have a fancy both will be needed.'

Closing the door, he pointed to the burning embers in the grate. 'Sit here by the fire, child, and tell me what happened. Some food and a blanket will be here directly.'

'He saw me,' said Sara, taking her seat and looking wildly about her. 'There weren't nowhere else I could go. You don't mind, do you? He wanted to take me, Mr Emanuel. He would have done it too if Mr Higgins, the officer, hadn't come by. And that ain't all. Why—'

'Slowly, now,' said Emanuel.

'He… he murdered Henry's wife.'

'Henry?'

'Aye, Henry. Master Teeling,' she said, reaching into the pocket of her dress and handing him what appeared to be a letter. 'It's from Bristow, the cully what were hanged. He says it were Master James what killed Henry's wife. You read it, Mr Emanuel. Then you'll see.'

'Where did this come from, child?' said Emanuel, taking the note from her outstretched hand.

'It were pushed under the door of the room in the dead of night. I didn't know what to do.'

Emanuel fell silent whilst he read the letter. When he'd finished, he turned it over.

'It's addressed to Teeling.'

'Aye, I know,' said Sara. 'I thought it might be trouble for Henry… I mean, Master Teeling, so I opened it.'

'And then you took it to Master James? Is that what happened? Is that why he beat you?' Emanuel felt his anger rising, powerless to control it. 'What did you think his reaction would be? You were telling him you had evidence against him that would see him hang. He might have killed you.'

'I know that, Mr Emanuel. I'm sorry,' said Sara. 'I feel so stupid.'

'Has Teeling seen this?' said Emanuel, his anger suddenly spent.

'No. I meant to give it to him but when I read it, I knew what he'd do. D'you—' Sara stopped and looked at the closed door of the meeting room as footsteps sounded in the hall beyond.

'It's only Mrs Wilson, the housekeeper,' said Emanuel. 'What were you about to say?'

Before Sara could answer there was a knock on the door and the housekeeper came in carrying a tray of hot food. Putting it down on the table, she unfolded a blanket that she'd had draped over one arm and wrapped it over Sara's shoulders.

'Eat up now. There's plenty more where that came from,' said Mrs Wilson. She turned to go. 'I'll be in the kitchen should you want for anything, Father.'

'Thank you, kindly, Mrs Wilson. We'll not be long.' Emanuel watched her go before turning back to Sara.

'D'you remember me telling you about a plot what Master James were planning?'

'Yes, I do,' said Emanuel. 'Have you heard any more?'

'I might have,' said Sara. 'It were something Master James said to me when… well, you know, when he were trying to have me. He said, "In a few weeks the world will thank me for what I've done."'

'That's all?' said Emanuel. 'He didn't tell you what he was going to do or where he was going to do it?'

'No,' she said. 'That was all.'

Emanuel closed his eyes and thought hard. A moment later he opened them. 'Do you know if Master James often rides in Hyde Park?' he asked.

'He don't ride,' said Sara. 'Leastways he never used to when I were in service with his father, the Lord Howard. And I ain't seen him ride in London, neither.'

'What about Sir Peter?

'Oh, aye. Sir Peter rides every morning.'

'In Hyde Park?'

'Seldom,' said Sara. 'He used to complain Hyde Park weren't big enough. He said there were plenty of other places for riding what were better.'

'So, if he and Master James did go there, it would have to be for a special reason?'

'I suppose,' said Sara. 'I ain't never thought about it. Will you tell the magistrate?'

'I regret there is nothing I can tell him. We don't know what's planned or even the day. Nor is there anyone who could tell us, save only the conspirators themselves. And why should they offer their necks when there is no proof? But forgive me,' said Emanuel, changing the subject. 'In my haste I've neglected you. You must be tired. I'll call Mrs Wilson and have her make up a bed for you here. We can talk further in the morning.'

Chapter 53

Sara lay awake, listening for the slightest sounds that might suggest the approach of trouble. Four days and four nights had passed since her encounter with Grenville in Green Park, four days and four nights in which she had lived in dread that he might come in search of her. She'd stayed that first night in Holborn and might have remained longer but for her determination to overcome her fears.

Now back in the room in Farmer Street, her thoughts returned to Grenville, the sight of his flushed face inches from her own, the smell of his breath, the quick gasps of excitement as his hand had gripped the flesh of her thigh. She recoiled from the thought, disgust filling her mind, an angry, boiling sentiment that threatened to consume her. She clenched her teeth and tried to think of other things but the same image kept returning, taunting her with its presence. She slid off the bed and went to the window. Outside, the street was bathed in the cold light of the moon, the occasional shadow shifting with the movement of the clouds. Now and then she caught the sounds of voices but they were the exception. Little moved at this late hour. She stood for a while longer, cursing her stupidity in following Grenville. What had she hoped to achieve by confronting him with Erasmus Bristow's letter? What had she been thinking? That he would capitulate? Beg her forgiveness? Shame at her own foolishness flooded her mind. *He might have killed you.* Mr Emanuel's angry voice returned to haunt her. Yes, he could have done. She knew that now.

The letter would make no difference to the likes of Grenville, protected as he was by social rank and privilege. The author of the letter was dead. But even in life, the word of a common criminal would have meant nothing – except to Grenville himself. She felt for the letter in the pocket of her dress. It was still there.

In all the years she had known him, nothing affected Grenville so much as a loss of face, his humiliation in the sight of others. Such slights would send him into towering passions of rage that would often last for days. It was enough that the subject of his apparent snub was known to another, even a servant. He would not forget. The memory of it would chafe his soul, eating away at it, a little at a time, until he could bear the pain no longer. Then he would come looking for the revenge that he thought was his due. He'd done it to her once already. She wasn't prepared to wait for him to come after her again.

Slipping on her thin coat, she crept to the door and went out into the corridor. Nothing was moving. Quietly she made her way to the street door and eased herself out into the moonlight, her eyes probing every shadow, every trick of light. Satisfied the street was deserted, she made her way along a series of narrow lanes and alleys to her destination. It took a while. Perhaps an hour. She might have managed it quicker but for the frequent occasions when she'd felt the need to step back into the deepest shadows to avoid being seen by the late-night revellers and those who still searched for the comfort of a woman – any woman.

Broad Street, Holborn marked the southern border of the St Giles rookery. Here, even the smell was different from the surrounding streets, the rubbish more plentiful, the buildings more rickety than elsewhere. The man she sought hadn't long been here and doubtless would move again in a day or so.

She had walked the entire length of the street before she caught sight of the half-remembered entrance to one of the terraced houses, its doors and windows long since gone. Summoning all her courage, she climbed the steps to the front entrance and went in, her nostrils met by the stench of human sweat. Pausing, she continued on through, stepping carefully over the sleeping bodies littering the narrow hall.

The room she wanted was at the end of the corridor, a room that had once been the parlour but was now home to around twenty or thirty men, women and children.

She wasn't proud of what she intended to do. Perhaps in other circumstances she might have thought better of it; might have considered the implications – for him as well as for herself. Yet she could see no other way of ridding herself of the threat she faced.

Feeling her way, she searched the tightly packed space, each body pressed against its neighbour, each one covered with a length of cardboard, or scrap of carpet and drawing warmth one from the other. It took her a while to find him.

'Sara?' Henry Teeling rubbed the sleep from his eyes.

'Get up. Quickly, Henry. I've something to tell you.'

Teeling struggled onto one elbow and looked beyond her to the little patch of sky that was visible through the glassless window.

'What time is it?' He gazed round at the sleeping forms. 'What is it you'll be wanting?'

'Not here,' she said, glancing in the direction of a small child who'd awoken and was crying.

'What is it you wanted to speak to me about?' asked Teeling, a minute or so later, when the two of them were out on the street.

'It's about Master James.'

'Grenville?' he asked, his facial muscles tightening. 'What about the scrub?'

'I've got a letter for you. It were written by Bristow.'

'What's he to say that I'd want to take any notice? Sure, he'll be rotting in Hell for what he did to my little angel.' He turned to walk back into the house.

'Wait,' said Sara, taking the letter from her coat pocket and offering it to him. 'I think you'll want to see what he's written.'

He stopped and slowly turned to face her again. 'Then read it to me.'

'It's about what happened to you and your wife, Henry. He says there were three of them who came to your house on that afternoon; him, Collins and Master James. He says it wasn't him or Collins what killed her. He—'

'He's lying,' shouted Teeling, again turning to walk away. 'If it weren't them, then who was it? Tell me that.'

'You read it. Then you'll see.'

Teeling looked at the folded sheet of paper in Sara's hand before turning his back. 'I can't read,' he said, his voice barely above a whisper.

'He's saying it were Master James.'

'No.' Teeling shook his head as he stared at her. He swayed and might have fallen if Sara had not caught his elbow and guided him to the side of the street where he leaned against the wall of a house, his face pale. 'It can't be true. It ain't possible. It were Collins who did for me wife. Him and Bristow'

Teeling sank to his haunches, burying his head in his hands. It seemed the letter had simply reopened the painful memories he'd tried to put behind him. Sara squatted beside him, her arms about him, and waited for the mood to pass. At last, he took the letter from her hand.

'Is that what it says?' said Teeling, his eyes fixed on the page.

She nodded.

'Then it weren't only me wife what suffered,' said Teeling. 'There are two others what have died for what Grenville did that day. Sure, there's no justice in that.'

'What are you going to do?' said Sara.

#

Teeling stood quite still. The moon which had, until this moment, bathed the street in its ghostly hue, now passed behind a cloud, plunging the scene into darkness. It wouldn't be long before the light returned. He looked across the street at the line of black lacquered coaches waiting for their owners, the drivers gaudily attired in scarlet livery and gold braid. From time to time a gentleman would appear in the entrance of Boodle's, climb unsteadily into his coach and be whisked away. He stared intently as another figure emerged from the building opposite and looked up and down the street. Suddenly, a contented smile spread across Teeling's thin features. There was no mistaking Grenville.

‘Shall I be calling your carriage, sir?’ The doorman’s voice drifted across St James’s.

‘No thank you, Bates. I think I’ll walk.’

‘Very good, sir. Good night, sir.’

Just under twenty-four hours had elapsed since Sara had shown him the letter. The news that it had been Grenville who’d murdered his wife had shaken him. He’d wanted to go in search of the villain. But she’d persuaded him to wait. The hour was late and Grenville would have retired for the night. Better that he should sleep on it; consider what was to be done.

She’d been right, of course. He let his thoughts wander, unchecked. The image of his dead wife seeped in. The same one he always had. It was etched for ever into the core of his being as surely as the chiselled words on a tombstone. Awake or asleep, it made no difference. It was always there; the sight of her lifeless body on the floor of the little cottage they had shared. He’d often wake from his dreams in a cold sweat that would not leave him until exhaustion once more closed his eyes in slumber. And each time he’d experience the pain of seeing her limp body and he’d think of the terror she must have suffered in those final moments before her death. It had been the single reason for his coming to England – to find the man responsible and make him pay for what he’d done.

The weeks had turned into months and the months into years yet the rawness of his grief had never lessened. When, at last, he’d found first Collins and then Bristow, he had begun to hope that he might put the events of the past behind him and start to rebuild his life. But if he’d expected their passing to bring him some measure of relief from the torment he suffered, he was disappointed. Each of the two deaths had, in their different ways, added to the mental burden he was now forced to carry. They had, at best, meant the end of his search for retribution – until now. Bristow's letter had reopened all his mental wounds.

He'd never considered the possibility of Grenville's guilt. Perhaps it was because his mind had fixed itself on Collins and, later, on Bristow. Perhaps he had not wanted to believe he'd been wrong, that he'd killed an innocent man. Or that, in Bristow, he had let a man die for a murder that he, Teeling, had committed. But now he knew the truth.

He watched Grenville walk to the corner of Boodle's and turn down the little road that ran alongside the building. Then he followed, listening to the footsteps of his nemesis fading into the night.

Reaching the bottom of the street, he saw what appeared to be a footpath, its entrance partially hidden by a bush that had grown across its mouth. Teeling pushed it clear, the branches scratching his face and hands as he forced a way through. He stopped occasionally to rub the pain from his thigh. Suddenly, his way was clear and he could make out the outline of trees against the night sky. He'd reached Green Park.

'All right, darlin'.' Teeling turned at the sound of a female's voice close beside him. 'Want a good time, does yer?'

'No,' he said. 'But you can be telling me where my friend is? He were here just now.'

'What's it worth to you, handsome?'

'It's thrupence I have. Will you be telling me for that?'

'He passed this way not half a minute ago,' said the woman, palming the coin Teeling had proffered.

'Comes 'ere regular, like. Always goes with Gorgeous Gussy, he does.'

'Where would I find her?'

'That would be telling now, wouldn't it?'

Teeling fished around for another coin and handed it over. 'Where is she?'

'Up yonder, next to the reservoir, by Piccadilly,' said the woman, pointing up through the trees. 'Best you take the boundary path, dearie. Be quicker. Might even get to Gorgeous Gussy afore your friend.'

She cackled, and then was gone.

#

Teeling had not been alone in his long wait for Grenville to appear. A little further down St James's, another pair of eyes had been watching the entrance to the gentlemen's club on the corner of Park Place. The man shifted slightly, easing the discomfort that was the inevitable result of too long spent without movement. He was not a patient man. Waiting irked him. The longer he waited, the more irritated he became. Yet tonight was different. A weight had been lifted from his shoulders, the threat of his imminent demise removed.

Erasmus Bristow had never considered the how and the why of the change in his fortunes. He gave no thought to what might have halted the seemingly irrevocable march of justice. It was enough for him that he still existed; was free to pursue those who had sought his death.

It was a rare day when Bristow did not harbour such thoughts.

'Shall I be calling your carriage, sir?'

'No thank you, Bates. I think I'll walk.'

Bristow's head jerked up as he recognised the voice of his erstwhile officer, the Hon. Lt. James Grenville of the 2nd of Foot. Bristow slipped deeper into shadow and watched his former officer turn down Park Place. He didn't move. There was plenty of time for what he had in mind. He thought again of Zechariah and the perjured evidence he'd given to the Old Bailey jury. The old man had since paid for his mistake. Now it was the turn of the man on whose orders he'd acted.

Bristow didn't see the figure of a man detach itself from the shadows on the far side of St James's, cross the road and move silently down Park Place.

#

The reservoir the woman had spoken of was not difficult to find, its huge bulk looming up out of the gloom. Teeling slowed his pace. If Grenville had got here before him he didn't want to bump into him. Not yet, anyway. He nearly didn't see the woman. She was standing at the foot of the high bank and obviously waiting for someone. He slipped behind a tree.

A minute later he heard the sound of footsteps and saw Grenville walking quickly up the lane towards him. A rage consumed him as he thought again of his late wife and the manner of her passing. Here, finally, was the man responsible. Teeling's hand dropped to the hilt of the knife he always carried, his fingers winding round a hilt worn smooth with use. He drew it from his belt, the blade seeming to flash in the moonlight.

'Why, there you are, sir…'

A woman's voice. Close by. He'd forgotten the prostitute. He let the knife drop to his side and waited for his heartbeat to slow. In five minutes, perhaps less, the chance would come again. Grenville's little pleasure would end and the woman would leave him in search of new business. It was better this way. This way there'd be no witnesses.

'Master James?' said Teeling, stepping out in front of Grenville a few minutes later.

'Who the devil…?' Grenville started, a hand fumbling for his sword.

'I'd not want to be doing that, mister,' said Teeling, grasping the lapel of Grenville's coat with one hand while the other held a knife to his throat.

'Who are you? What d'you want?' said Grenville.

'You don't know my face? You've no recollection of me?' Teeling brushed the knife against Grenville's cheek. 'Look more closely, mister. Try harder. Turn your mind to Wexford when you and Collins and Bristow – you remember them, don't you? – when the three of you came upon a house by the Slaney. Remember that, do you? And the lady what was inside? You remember her too? Of course you do. She were my old woman. You hear me, Master, fucking, Grenville? That were my wife what you killed that day.'

Grenville's eyes widened. He struggled to free himself.

'In a minute or two it'll all be over for you. And when the Watch finds you, why, he'll think it just another cully what didn't pay his dues to the lady and got learned his lesson,' said Teeling, the point of his knife drawing a thin trickle of blood from Grenville's neck.

Quite suddenly he stopped speaking, conscious of a sharp pain in his gut. He pushed himself away from the other man and looked down to see the blade of a knife being withdrawn from his stomach, a dark stain spreading rapidly over the thin shirt he wore. He looked up, a surprised expression on his face. He felt dizzy, light-headed. He tried to think. He knew he'd been stabbed. That much was obvious. But he also knew that if he didn't do something to stop him, Grenville would stab him a second, and perhaps a third, time. And if that happened, he would undoubtedly die. He summoned his failing strength and plunged his own blade into the other man's stomach, the sharp point penetrating Grenville's tunic with the merest shudder.

Grenville slipped to his knees, both hands clutching the knife handle, unable to pull it free, blood oozing through the wound, his eyes staring straight ahead, his mouth wide open, a soft gurgling sound coming from his throat. Teeling looked down at the crumpled form at his feet.

He felt no emotion, no pleasure at what he'd done. It had been the same with Collins, something that needed to be done though he knew it would make no difference. It wouldn't bring his wife back. And that was all he'd ever wanted.

He limped away, his hand clutching at his wound, stemming the flow of blood, knowing he had to leave before anyone saw him. This wasn't the way he'd planned it. He didn't want to die. Not like this. Behind him he could hear the sound of Grenville's gurgling. It was less audible than it had been.

He wondered how long they both had to live.

Chapter 54

Sara lay on her bed in Farmer Street unable to sleep. She'd known the likely consequences of showing the letter to Teeling; had rehearsed them in her mind's eye a dozen times or more. She'd known how he would react. The same as any man would. All the same, he'd been gone a long time.

She looked out at the night sky. He should have returned by now. A wave of concern swept over her. She'd never considered the possibility of an unsuccessful outcome. She'd always assumed it was Grenville who would suffer.

She heard the front door open and someone come in. Relief flooded through her. It had to be him. He wouldn't stay. It would not be proper. He'd tell her what happened and then return to his room in the St Giles rookery. She listened to the footsteps as they approached along the corridor. They didn't sound quite right – slow and unsteady, like those of a drunkard. She swung her legs to the floor and padded across the room, ready to answer the knock on the door. A sudden crash, as of a body falling to the ground. Then silence.

'Sara.' The voice was barely audible. 'It's me, Henry. I'm hurt bad.'

She flung open the door. Teeling was lying on the floor, clutching his stomach, his face white and sweating. She knelt beside him. 'What happened? No, don't talk. Not yet.'

'I found him,' said Teeling. 'We—'

'Hush now,' said Sara. She left him, returning a few moments later with a basin of water, some rags and a lighted candle. 'Let me see the hurt.'

She moved his hand away from his stomach and saw the spreading red patch on his shirt. Tearing the shirt away, she quickly washed the bloodied area and covered the wound with a clean rag. She knew it wasn't enough but it would have to do, at least until she could summon help. There was a woman she'd heard of. Someone who knew about these matters, who had often tended to the wounds of those without the means to pay the apothecary or who preferred to remain beyond the sight of the law.

'Was it Master James who did this?' she asked.

Teeling didn't answer for a minute, his chest heaving as he sought to draw breath, his eyes closed. At length he nodded. 'We fought. He had a knife but I didn't see it until too late. He would have finished me if I hadn't got him.'

'Got him?' she asked.

'Aye, I saw him go down. I reckon he's dead.'

'But you're not sure?' she said.

'I couldn't stop and look,' said Teeling. 'There was a woman close by. The one he'd been with. I didn't want her to see me. I'd swing for murder else.'

Sara stayed silent as she tried to take in what had happened.

'If he's still alive, will he not go to the magistrate?' she said.

Teeling shrugged. 'Ain't nothing can be done about that.'

'Where did this happen?'

'Green Park, near a reservoir, up by Piccadilly. Why d'you ask?'

'And nobody saw you?' she said ignoring his question.

'Didn't see nobody except the woman he'd been with.'

'We've got to know whether he's alive or dead,' she said, a tremor in her voice. 'But first we've got to get you to bed. I know somebody who can help with your hurt. I'll ask her to come and see you while I'm gone.'

'Gone? Where are you going?' said Teeling.

'Where d'you think?' said Sara. 'If that villain lives, you'll hang, Henry Teeling, and that's for sure.'

#

Dawn was still some way off as Emanuel gulped down the last of his coffee and headed for the front door. He was up earlier than usual. The ugly mood in London meant frequent changes to the times of daily Mass and this morning was no exception. But there was another reason for his early start. He'd not checked on Sara since her return two days earlier to the room he loaned her. He meant to rectify the position on his way to Mass.

Turning into Farmer Street some time later he was surprised to see a candle burning in the window of his old room. It was early even by the standards of Sara's former occupation as a lady's maid. He wondered if anything was amiss. He went into the house and down the corridor. Everything looked to be in order. He knocked and waited.

'Who's there?' said a man's voice.

Emanuel's stomach tightened. He stepped back and readied himself for a rapid entry. Then he stopped. The voice had been familiar.

'Henry? Is that you?' he said.

A short pause, a cough, then, 'Aye, so it is. Who's there?'

Emanuel pushed open the door and stepped in. Teeling was lying on the bed, his face a dull shade of grey. 'What are you doing here, Henry? Where's Sara?'

'I found out it were Grenville what killed me old woman. We fought,' said Teeling. 'Sara's gone to—'

He leaned to one side of the bed and coughed up some blood.

'Where has Sara gone?' said Emanuel. 'What were you going to say?'

'She's gone to find him.'

'Who? Grenville?'

'Aye, him.'

Emanuel gaped in disbelief. 'And you let her go?'

'There weren't nothing I could do to stop her, Father. Sure, she were determined to find him and see if he were still alive.'

'Where is he?' asked Emanuel. 'Where did you leave him?'

Emanuel listened in shocked silence as Teeling added more detail to the events of the last few hours. He knew he had to find Sara and stop her before she reached Green Park.

'If Grenville's still alive when Sara finds him, there's no telling what harm he might do her. Or her to him. How long has she been gone?' he said.

'Not above half an hour,' said Teeling. 'But you'll not find her in time, Father.'

'I might if I go by river,' said Emanuel, glancing at Teeling's bloodstained clothes and hoping he was doing the right thing in leaving him. 'I'll be back as soon as I can.'

#

The first hint of grey had appeared in the eastern sky as Sara turned off The Mall into Green Park and walked up the boundary path towards Piccadilly. 'I left Grenville under an old oak, close to the reservoir,' Teeling had said in the moments before she left him. There was no one around. The park seemed deserted. Even the women who nightly walked amongst these trees in search of a client had given up and gone to their beds. The quiet was unnerving and she was beginning to think coming here had not been a good idea.

The high bank of the reservoir came into view. She stopped and peered in amongst the trees to her left. A tree, larger than its neighbours, appeared out of the half light. An oak. Sara hesitated, remembering the last time she'd encountered Grenville. He had thought nothing of striking her to the ground on that occasion and doubtless would do so again if he could. Only this time there would be no rescue. And yet… She thought of Teeling and the consequences for him if she were to turn back now. She had to go on, had to make sure Grenville was dead.

She stepped off the path and crept towards the oak. It was darker here, amongst the trees, more difficult to see her way, her eyes watching the ground in front of her. She was almost upon it before she saw the bloodstained body. It lay on its back, its head turned away from her, its legs splayed wide apart. There was no doubting who it was. She bent over Grenville's inert form and looked down at the patch of red on his stomach.

'Please…' Sara stumbled back, stifling a scream as Grenville's hand rose from the ground an inch or two and then fell back, his words barely coherent. 'Help me. Please help me.'

Grenville turned his head towards her, his face now screwed up in pain, his eyes flickering, seemingly unable to focus. The memory of the last time she'd seen him again reared up in her mind, his casual brutality, the smell of his breath on her face, the touch of his trembling hand tearing at the hem of her dress, seeking to possess her. And now he was asking for her help.

She felt a rage building inside her, threatening to consume her. She drew a knife from her dress pocket and looked at the dull sheen of the blade, a voice within her urging her to finish what Teeling had begun. Nobody would know who had done it. A gentleman killed for his pocket book, someone who'd come to the park seeking pleasure, like many another before him. And like many another, had paid the ultimate price. She grasped the knife, the blood driven from her fingers by the force of her grip. A swift, downward plunge would finish him.

Suddenly, she heard the rustle of leaves behind her. She leapt to her feet as fear gripped her. Someone was there, watching her. For several seconds she searched the darkness, her eyes darting first this way, then that, her muscles tensed and ready to run.

'Who's there?' she called.

There was no answer, her voice lost amongst the trees. For a while longer she didn't move, her heart racing. But there was no repeat of the sound. She began to relax. The noise had probably been made by an animal.

'Miss Sara? Is that you?' The voice at her feet was no more than a whisper.

She looked down to see Grenville looking up at her, his eyes pleading for her help. His gaze moved to the knife in her hands. She'd forgotten it was there. She turned it over, examining it with exaggerated care, feeling its weight and balance. It was as though she were looking down on herself from some high vantage point, contemplating what needed to be done. She felt no pity, no desire to relieve Grenville's suffering. Above all she wished to be rid of him, to experience the relief she was sure would follow his passing.

It was lighter now, the shapes of the individual trees clearly visible in the pre-dawn light, the dark grey of the sky slowly turning to a pale blue. Soon there would be streaks of orange in the east as the rising sun caught the clouds low down on the horizon. She would have to leave then. She remembered the rustle of the leaves that had so frightened her and she looked round. Just to make sure. There was no one in sight. She was alone with Grenville. His eyes had closed, the lines gone from his face, his head fallen to one side.

She raised the knife above her head.

Chapter 55

Emanuel's initial relief at having seen her quickly turned to concern. Something was wrong. He could see Sara hurrying towards him, down the path from the reservoir. She looked terrified, her face white, her blonde hair dishevelled and streaming out behind her, her eyes staring passed him as though she'd not yet registered his presence.

'Sara.' Emanuel held out his hand. 'Is everything all right, child?

Her eyes swivelled towards him and, for a second or two, he thought she meant to keep running.

'He's dead, Mr Emanuel. Master James is dead.'

'Where is he, child?' he asked. 'Where did you leave him?'

'Back there, under the big oak,' she said, pointing up the way she'd come.

'Tell me what happened.'

'Teeling came to my room early this morning. He were hurt bad. He—'

'Yes, I know,' said Emanuel. 'I saw him too. He told me about the fight with Master James and that you were on your way here. What happened when you found him?'

'He were alive, Mr Emanuel, if that's what you's asking,' said Sara, her shaking fingers touching her lips. He opened his eyes and saw me. Called my name. I were frightened and I wanted to kill him.'

'And did you?' said Emanuel.

'No. I were going to do it but when I looked he were already dead. Leastways, that what it seemed like to me.'

'But you're not sure?' said Emanuel.

'He looked like he were, Mr Emanuel.'

Emanuel looked across the park, still swathed in deep shadow. Behind him, on The Mall, he could hear the muted voices of people on their way to work while in amongst the trees all seemed deserted. It wouldn't last. Soon others would make their way down from Piccadilly or across from Knightsbridge, or perhaps up from the river as the city awoke to a new day. If he was to find Grenville, it would have to be done now. He had no wish to be seen. That would only serve to complicate matters.

'Go back and look after Teeling,' he said. 'I'll be along directly.'

He waited until Sara had gone. Then he walked up the path to where she'd said he'd find Grenville. He'd seldom felt more ill at ease.

It wasn't difficult finding the oak tree. Its vast bulk rose above its neighbours, its canopy spread out like the wings of a fussing hen protecting her young. He branched off the path and walked towards it, conscious that his heart was beating ever more quickly. He had to force himself to keep going, dreading the uncertainty of what he'd find.

But there was no body lying under the tree.

He searched the immediate area with the same result. There had to be some mistake. He'd come to the wrong oak. He looked round. Beech, plane, hornbeam, chestnut. All were here in profusion but only the one oak. He looked at the grass at the base of the tree. It had been trampled. And recently. He dropped to one knee and looked more closely. A dark patch caught his eye. He felt it with the tip of one finger. It was blood. Climbing to his feet he followed a trail of footprints in the dew leading deeper into the park. He doubted Grenville would have gone far.

It didn't take long to find him. His injuries had seen to that. He was lying on his front less than a hundred yards from the oak, a knife in one hand. He looked to be dead, his skin cold to the touch. Emanuel bent down and removed the knife.

'Well, well, what have we got here, then?'

Emanuel swung round. He'd heard the rumours of Bristow's reprieve but it still surprised him to hear his voice. There had never been any official confirmation of his pardon. Quite the reverse. The possibility of Bristow's release had been scoffed at. There were no grounds for appeal, no special circumstances which might have allowed the sentence of death to be respited. Bristow's death had been ordained by the law of the land. His execution had seemed inevitable.

'How—' Emanuel's question was cut short.

'How is it I ain't buried below Dead Man's Walk? How is it I'm standing here looking at you with a blade in your fist and the body of my old officer, Lt. Grenville, late of the Second of Foot lying dead in front of you? Is that what you want to know, Mr bleedin' Emanuel?'

Emanuel didn't answer. There was nothing he could say that would make any difference.

'I'll tell you why I ain't food for rats, Mr Papist,' said Bristow, his finger jabbing at Emanuel's chest. 'It's on account of a pardon what I got. Seems like a villain what I know were telling lies about me; swore on the Bible to tell the truth, he did. Then he lied, like it didn't make no difference.'

Bristow paused, took a handkerchief from around his bull-like neck and dabbed at his forehead. When he next spoke, his voice was harsh and bitter. 'I nearly swung for a murder what I was innocent of. Remember old Zechariah? He didn't know nothing about what happened. But that didn't stop him swearing on the Good Book to tell the truth, the whole truth and nothing but the truth, and then lying his bollocks off. Nearly went to meet my maker on account of what he said.'

Bristow's lips parted in a mirthless grin, his cold eyes focused on Emanuel in an unrelenting stare of hatred. 'But it's him what's in his eternity box now, not me.'

'You killed him?' said Emanuel, the words out of his mouth before he could stop himself.

'I ain't saying nothing about that, Mr Papist. Not to you. Not to nobody. But before he left us old Zechariah told me the name of the cully what paid him to perjure himself. It were Mr Grenville what's lying here, me old officer from me army days what used to order me around. 'Do this, do that and kiss my arse,' he'd say to me. And I had to jump like I were his dog.' Bristow leered. 'But it don't look like he'll be doing it no more, do he?'

'But your pardon…?' said Emanuel, still unsure of precisely what had happened to allow Bristow his freedom.

'What about it? Ain't got nothing to do with you why I got it.' Bristow sneered and nodded at the knife Emanuel still held. 'But you's a different matter.'

Emanuel waited. Sooner or later Bristow would make his move.

Then it would be his turn.

#

Nearly twenty minutes had passed since Father Emanuel had left her and walked up the broad path on the eastern boundary of Green Park. He'd told her to go home, that he would take care of Grenville's body. Sara had felt an enormous sense of relief.

She'd not thought of the implications of coming here in the first place; of what she would likely find and the decisions she might be called on to make. The reality had only struck home when she'd seen Grenville and realised he was still alive. In the sheer terror of the moment, she had wanted to kill him, to rid herself of the man who'd subjected her to so much unhappiness over the years. Yet, when the moment had arrived, she'd been unable to do it, perhaps for moral reasons or perhaps from a fear of detection. She was sure she'd heard someone moving about close behind her. Who it was she couldn't pretend to know. The park was the haunt of prostitutes and it was always possible the rustle of the undergrowth had been nothing more sinister than the sound of copulation, although she doubted that. Whatever the truth of the matter, it had played its part in staying her hand and she had run from the scene in fright.

Sara peered through the grey mist of early morning. There was still no sign of Mr Emanuel. It didn't seem right to leave him without knowing if he was all right. Yet going back into the park didn't appeal, especially when there was every likelihood she would again come into contact with Grenville – either alive or dead.

She wasn't aware of any conscious decision to begin walking up the path towards Piccadilly. That awareness arrived slowly and with it came a greater sense of the risks involved. But, by then, a more determined mood had taken hold of her. She wondered if Emanuel had found Grenville and, if he had, whether he was alive or dead. It was a dread thought. Much as she might have wished it, it was hardly conceivable that Mr Emanuel would finish him off. On the contrary, from what she knew of him, the priest was more likely to want to save him. She tried to put the matter out of her mind.

It was another few minutes before she arrived at the oak tree. She stared uncomprehendingly at the place where she'd last seen Grenville. There was no sign of him or of Mr Emanuel. She was about to leave when she heard the sound of men's voices. She recognised one of them as belonging to Mr Emanuel. The other she didn't know. She started towards them and then stopped. The stranger was speaking, his tone loud and threatening. She didn't care for it at all.

She crept forward.

#

There wasn't a great deal that Emanuel didn't understand about human behaviour in its many and varied forms. His personal well-being had often depended on reading the mood of those around him. Now, as he watched the small and seemingly innocent changes in the behaviour of the man opposite, he began to formulate his response. He would do nothing to exacerbate the already perilous position in which he found himself. Bristow might only have one leg but that didn't mean he couldn't inflict some serious damage.

'Why would I want to kill Mr Grenville?' said Emanuel. 'You know perfectly well it wasn't me that did this.'

'Makes no difference to me one way or the other, me old cock. When I've finished telling the beak what I saw, why, there ain't a jury in the land what'll save the neck of a Papist what's killed a Protestant gentleman, and that's a fact.'

'What brought you here, Bristow?' said Emanuel, suddenly curious. 'This isn't your stamping ground. It's a long way from Limehouse. You didn't just happen to be here.'

Bristow didn't reply, the fixed grin on his face finding no echo in his eyes.

'You were following Grenville, weren't you?' said Emanuel, snapping his fingers as the answer to his question came to him. 'You were hoping for the chance to kill him for the same reason you killed Zechariah Hobbs. Those were the two who got you convicted, weren't they? You found out what happened and after killing Zechariah you came looking for Grenville. It must have been a bit of a surprise to find that someone else had had the same idea. Did you see who it was? You did, didn't you? You saw the fight and you recognised Teeling. He was the fellow whose wife you and Grenville and Collins murdered that day in Wexford two years ago. This was your chance to get rid of both of them. After all, if you let them live, there was a good chance they'd come after you. So why didn't you finish the job? You could have done it and no one would have seen you.'

Emanuel waited for a response. He could see the effect his words were having on Bristow, the man's eyes narrowed to mere slits, his breathing laboured. He'd clearly been stung. It couldn't be long before his meagre ration of self-control gave out and he lashed out at his tormentor. Emanuel decided to push a little harder.

'I'll tell you why you didn't kill them,' said Emanuel. 'It's because you made the mistake of following Teeling. For some reason you thought you'd deal with him first and then come back for Grenville. But you couldn't catch him. He moved too fast for you, didn't he? After that you came back here and saw a woman standing over Grenville. So you went away again planning to come back when the coast was clear.'

'God rot your soul, mister,' said Bristow, his face twisted with rage. I'll—'

'But when you returned,' said Emanuel, ignoring Bristow's threat. 'You found me so you still couldn't turn him off.'

'Why, you scaly little Christ-killer,' shouted Bristow. 'Aye, I were going to turn Grenville off. The villain had it coming to him. As for the other cully, I never did care for them bog Irish. I'll sort him out same as I sorted out Zechariah. Come to think on it…'

Emanuel was no longer listening. He glanced at the figure stretched out on the grass at his feet.

'You hearing me, Mr Papist?' said Bristow.

'Did you say something, Erasmus?' said Emanuel and knew immediately that he'd gone too far.

#

Sara knew the stranger. She used to see him arrive with Grenville at Sir Peter's house from time to time. She remembered him for the sense of foreboding and disquiet his presence had engendered within her, his black eyes quite without pity. His name, she'd learned, was Bristow.

She turned away from him, her gaze dipping towards Grenville's supine shape lying at Emanuel's feet. She hadn't meant to look at the body yet she'd felt her eye drawn to its right hand, wondering if she could've been mistaken in what she'd seen. Then Grenville's hand moved again. She glanced at Mr Emanuel. He'd seen it too, his eyebrows momentarily arched as though in intense surprise, his attention diverted from the threat facing him.

She looked back at Bristow. He'd seen his opportunity and was swinging in for the attack, a look of hatred in his eyes.

'Mr Emanuel,' she shouted. 'Watch out.'

She saw him glance in her direction, a look of surprise on his face. Only then did he notice Bristow. It was too late. Sara closed her eyes, unable to watch. A second later she heard a dull thud followed by a howl of pain.

When she opened her eyes it was to see Emanuel flicking his hand up and down as though in pain.

'Where's…?' said Sara, looking bewildered.

'Bristow? He's down there,' said Emanuel, pointing to the bottom of a steep gradient. 'The fellow tripped and fell. His infernal crutch struck my hand. Probably broken some bones.'

‘He wanted to kill you,’ said Sara. ‘You know he won’t give up until then.’

‘Yes, I know,’ said Emanuel, looking down at the knife in his hand. ‘But your continuing presence won’t stop him trying again. Go now, before he awakes.’

‘What of Master James?’

‘I’d quite forgotten him in all the excitement,’ said Emanuel, dropping to one knee beside Grenville and putting his ear to the man’s chest. ‘His heart still beats but for how much longer, I cannot say.’

#

When Bristow finally awoke it was to a splitting headache. Cautiously, he raised his head and looked around while he tried to remember how he came to be lying on damp grass in the middle of what looked like a park. There’d been a fight. That much he knew. He remembered finding the Jew, Mr Emanuel, bending over Grenville’s body. An argument had developed and they’d fought. The precise details escaped him but he must have fallen and lost his senses. More than that he couldn’t recall. He looked over his shoulder to the place where he’d last seen Grenville’s body. It had gone.

So had the Jew.

They couldn’t have gone far. Not without help. Bristow levered himself up with the aid of his crutches and searched the surrounding parkland. It was not yet dawn but already he could see folk walking along Piccadilly on the way to work. Suddenly, he caught sight of a group of perhaps five men approaching a waiting carriage. They seemed to be carrying something heavy. Bristow stared at them. It was a body. Almost certainly Grenville's. He hesitated. Something wasn't quite right. For a minute or so he couldn't work out what it was. Then it came to him. Grenville wasn't dead. The men were carrying an injured man and not a corpse. If he had been dead they'd have used a cart to take him away.

He tried to follow but it was hopeless. The carriage was moving too quickly and was soon lost to sight. He thought for a moment. If Grenville was alive, it was certain he'd be taken to the nearest accident hospital. And that meant the one on the corner of Knightsbridge and Grosvenor Place. It wasn't far.

Twenty minutes later Bristow was standing on the north side of Knightsbridge, gazing at the large, white-painted edifice of the St George's accident hospital. In front of its main portico stood the carriage he'd earlier seen on Piccadilly. It was empty. Clearly, Grenville had already been taken inside and, for a moment, Bristow felt the urge to go in and to do what he should have done earlier. He curbed the temptation. There would, he knew, be other, and better, opportunities.

Turning to leave, he caught sight of a young woman emerging from the building. He remembered seeing her in Green Park bending over Grenville's body. And he'd seen her again, shouting a warning to the Jew. He wondered what she was doing here; what her connection with Emanuel was.

#

It was late morning before Bristow reached the former glue factory in Gun Lane that he'd come to regard as home. Most of the other inhabitants had already left for the day in search of work or sustenance or both, and the place was the quieter for their absence. Lying down on the strip of canvas that served as his bed, he stared up into the eaves and tried to put behind him his growing sense of anger and humiliation at what had happened in Green Park.

It wasn't as if it had been an isolated and minor setback in his life, something that he could forget. It wasn't. For him, it was only the latest in a line of setbacks that had begun with the loss of his leg and his discharge from the army. Robbed of the opportunities he'd previously enjoyed, he'd slipped into a downward spiral of increasing misfortune, including his near execution for a crime of which he was innocent. Dear God, how close he'd come to losing his life. He shut his eyes. Suddenly he was back in the reception room at Newgate…

He stands in line, his hands bound before him, the hangman's rope already looped about his neck. Fifty paces lie between him and the gallows. He is prodded in the back. A turnkey orders him to move. He and the others file out of the reception room and across the press yard. Another turnkey walks beside him. They have taken his crutches. He needs the turnkey's support. Inside the yard there is silence, broken only by the clink of the fetters. Even those whose day of reckoning has yet to come are silent, their faces pressed to the bars of their cell windows, high above his head, a look of despair writ large in their soulful eyes. From beyond the high walls he can hear the roar of the crowd.

A sudden shout – from whom and for what purpose he does not know. The line is halted. He feels a hand grip his arm and pull him to one side. He is ordered to stand still while the others continue on their way through the west gate and up the steps to the place of their execution. He is confused. How long must he wait? The thoughts race through his brain, his anger mounting. How much more must he bear of this inhuman treatment? He feels the nightcap removed from his head, then the rope from about his neck. He does not question any of this, his body trembling, his mind raging at the apparent injustice inflicted upon him. His crutches are thrust into his hands.

'Follow me,' says a dismembered voice. He looks around but can see no one but the slow procession of the condemned climbing the steps beyond the West Gate.

Minutes pass. No one speaks to him. Outside, the crowd is silent. The sudden clang of a church bell. He knows the sound of St Sepulchre. He flinches as the mob outside emit a low groan. The first of the condemned falls through the trapdoor.

His mind shuts down, refusing to register the detail of what is happening to him. Still less, the reason. Terror rules his brain...

Bristow woke with a start, his heartbeat racing. It took him a few seconds to remember where he was, that the immediate threat of execution was a thing of the past. Yet still his heart refused to slow, to still his trembling body. He blinked and gazed around the cavernous vault of the old glue manufactory, the majority of its human cargo gone in search of work or food or perhaps both. Only the sick and the lame and those with no reason to rise from their beds remained to keep him company. Bristow cupped his hands behind his head, his thoughts returning to the moments after he'd been dragged from the line of the condemned. Only the barest of details have stayed in his mind.

Someone – he cannot remember who – had spoken to him. The word 'pardon' had been mentioned. It had meant nothing to him at the time;. He remembered being pushed along a corridor and seeing the gate to the outside world in front of him opening as though of its own accord. And suddenly he was free to go.

For days following his release he'd wandered the streets in fear of being recalled. Barely did an hour pass when he didn't contemplate the possibility that he might yet hang for what happened on the foreshore of the Thames.

Slowly, he recovered but always, at the back of his mind, the questions remained. Why had he been spared? What had happened to secure his release? He searched for and found the barrister who'd defended him in court, eventually tracing Mr Harvey to his chambers at Inner Temple. *'A gentleman of impeccable reputation presented himself to the trial judge and vouched for your innocence,'* Mr Harvey had said. But he hadn't known the identity of the gentleman. Nor did he know what had passed between him and the learned judge. Whatever it had been it was sufficient to persuade the judge to recommend the grant of a Royal Pardon.

A gentleman of impeccable reputation...

Bristow rolled onto his side. The only gentlemen he knew were Grenville and Sir Peter and he very much doubted either of them would have moved a muscle to help him. But if not one of those two, then who?

His eyelids grew heavy. He needed to sleep.

Chapter 56

Through the mist of his pain, Grenville could hear a jumble of voices around him. He was lying on the floor, or so it felt. Faces peered down at him, some from a great height, others much closer as though bending or kneeling on the floor beside him. He tried to think. But all thought was driven from his mind by the pain in his stomach. Then the faces withdrew and he felt himself being lifted into the air.

He must have lost consciousness. The room in which he now lay was different from the one before; quieter and smaller. A man was peering down at him and removing his silk shirt. Grenville would have told the insolent fellow to desist if only he could have summoned the energy. The man withdrew and he was left alone. The pain in his stomach was getting worse, if that were possible; a kind of throbbing pain with peaks and troughs that just kept coming. Grenville wished it would end.

Another face appeared. Grenville could see his lips moving but there was no sound. Someone lifted his head and shoulders while someone else put a tumbler to his lips. He was screaming. Could not take the proffered drink. His head was lowered and Grenville waited for the pain to subside. He didn't know for how long he lay there. It might have been an hour or perhaps as little as five minutes. Again his head was lifted and the tumbler put to his lips. He took a gulp. The pain eased a little. The process was repeated and he drank some more. He felt better and looked about him.

He wasn't on the floor any more but on what looked like a table, except it was higher and narrower than he was used to. Next to it was another, much smaller table. He gave no thought about where he was or who these people were. The questions didn't occur to him. It was all he could do to manage the pain. Beyond that, nothing mattered.

Suddenly the door to the room swung open and a number of men entered, one of whom was carrying a small wooden box. They were followed by a distinguished-looking man in his mid-forties, his jet-black hair neatly tied at the nape, his long, angular face and dark grey eyes giving him the appearance of great authority. The wooden box was put down on the table next to him and opened. Grenville didn't see it at first, his view obscured by the distinguished-looking gentleman.

'What…?' began Grenville, the first stirring of unease entering his mind. 'What's happening? Who are you?'

'Nothing to worry about,' said the distinguished gentleman, gently prodding the area of Grenville's injury. 'I just need to have a look at you. We'll have you back on the ward in no time.'

'Ward?' said Grenville, turning to see the wooden box for the first time. Its hinged lid had been opened and he could now see the interior lined with red baize and holding a variety of knives, saws, forceps and sundry other items. 'Where am I?'

The gentleman didn't answer but turned instead to another man standing next to him.

'I'll perform a laparotomy. The hurt looks to be deep but I want to be as sure as I'm able. I'll begin with an incision to allow access. Is everybody ready?'

he said, taking a slim-bladed knife that had been handed to him. Then, glancing at Grenville, he said, 'There is no easy way of doing this. I regret it extremely, sir, but it's going to hurt.'

Strong arms gripped Grenville and held him down while a leather wad was inserted in his mouth. 'Bite on that,' said a voice from behind.

They need not have bothered. The shock of the first incision was the last thing Grenville was to remember for several hours.

#

Sir Peter Westlake looked out through the library window of his home on Cheapside, his hands clasped behind his back, an irritated frown creasing his forehead. Grenville was late. It wasn't like him. The fellow possessed many faults, but being late was not one of them. He removed a solid gold hunter from his waistcoat pocket, sprung open the lid, and looked at the time. He'd give the wretched fellow a little longer.

A light cough interrupted his thoughts.

'Yes, William, what is it?' he said, turning to see his butler hovering at the door.

'I beg your pardon, Sir Peter, but there is a man downstairs who wishes to speak with you. He wouldn't say what it was about but I gather it is of some importance.'

'Do you have his card?' Sir Peter held out his hand.

'I regret, sir, he does not possess a card.'

'Then who is he? Did he give a name?'

'No, sir, he did not but he was most insistent that he should see you at your earliest convenience. May I show him up?'

'Dash it all, William, I have other things to do than speak to people who turn up, unannounced, at my back door. Send him away, there's a good fellow,' said Sir Peter. He was about to turn away, noticed his butler hadn't moved, and looked back. 'What is it?'

'If I may, sir…'

'Speak up, man,' said Sir Peter.

'I think you might wish to see this man, sir.'

Sir Peter paused for a moment, staring at his servant. It was unlike his butler to question an order. 'Very well, show him in.'

A minute or so later his visitor was shown into the room. 'I'm a busy man, sir,' said Sir Peter. 'Be good enough to state your business.'

'Thank you for agreeing to see me, Sir Peter. My name is Higgins. I'm with the Bow Street Horse Patrol.'

'And what is it that I can do for you, Mr Higgins?' asked Sir Peter, his tone a little less languid.

'I believe, sir, you know a gentleman by the name of the Honourable James Grenville,' said Higgins.

'Why, yes, I do. He's the son of a particular friend of mine, the Lord Howard of Ardingleigh.'

'Quite so, sir. Can you tell me when you last saw the gentleman?'

'What's this about, Higgins? I am a member of parliament. I've no time to listen to—'

'I shan't keep you long, Sir Peter,' said Higgins. 'Perhaps you would be good enough to answer my question?'

'I saw Grenville last night at my club in St James. He left at around two o'clock. I haven't seen him since.'

'Did he say where he was going?'

'No, he didn't,' said Sir Peter. 'But…'

'What were you about to say, sir?' asked Higgins.

'Now look here, I really don't see what business it is of yours where Mr Grenville chooses to go.'

'Of course, sir,' said Higgins, bowing slightly. 'If you would be so kind, sir. You were about to say something.'

'Very well, if you must know, Mr Grenville often visits a lady in Green Park in the evenings. It's probably where he went after he left the club.'

'That would be a prostitute, would it, sir?' said Higgins.

'Since you choose to put it in those vulgar terms, yes, a prostitute,' said Sir Peter. 'Are you going to tell me what this is all about?'

'Certainly, sir,' said Higgins. 'Mr Grenville was admitted to the St George's accident hospital early this morning suffering from a stab wound. I believe he was attacked in Green Park. I don't yet know the reason. I was hoping you might be able to tell me a little more. Is there any reason you know of as to why this should have happened? Perhaps the name of the lady friend with whom he spent time? Any difficulties he might presently have? That sort of thing.'

'I regret I can't help at all,' said Sir Peter, sinking into a chair, the blood draining from his face. 'Is he badly hurt?'

'He is receiving treatment. That's all I can tell you at the moment,' said Higgins. 'Are you quite sure you know of no reason why he should have been attacked?'

'No, I'm afraid I don't,' said Sir Peter, mentally running down the list of people who might conceivably have been involved. Grenville was not the easiest of men to get on with and the list of potential suspects was a lengthy one. Among them was an Irishman whose wife Grenville was said to have murdered. And then there was Sara, former chambermaid to his wife. Hadn't Grenville mentioned some difficulty there as well? And Bristow. He'd almost forgotten about him. The list went on and on. The fellow hadn't made many friends in the army, either. Any one of these people could have been responsible, yet to mention one was to mention all. And he couldn't afford that; not with the planned operation so close to being carried out. It could prove fatal to its outcome.

'… keep me informed?' Sir Peter caught the tail end of what Higgins was saying.

'Yes, of course,' he said. 'My butler will see you out.'

He waited for Higgins to leave. There was no doubt the officer would want to see other people, with the substantial risk that one of them would say something that would have them all strung up by their necks. He felt a trickle of sweat run down one side of his nose. He remembered the letters Bristow was rumoured to have written and which Grenville had not managed to retrieve. It was now more important than ever to have sight of them. Until he'd done that, he couldn't know the extent of the danger they all faced.

Chapter 57

John Walter was sitting at his usual table in Will's Coffee House on Russell Street, reading *The Times* when he saw Emanuel approaching.

'Joy, my dear sir,' he said. 'But you look as though you've seen a ghost.'

'You could say that,' said Emanuel, pulling out a chair. 'The Hon. James Grenville is in hospital. His hurt is serious…'

'You could so easily have been killed,' said Walter, when Emanuel had finished telling him about the events of the previous night. 'And you say Bristow is involved? Yet you let him go? Where is he now?'

'I've no idea,' said Emanuel, shrugging his shoulders. 'I had to let him go. I certainly didn't want him anywhere near Grenville. He'd have finished him off and thought nothing of it.'

'And Sara?' asked Walter. 'Where is she?'

'In my old room in Farmer Street, looking after the injured Teeling,' said Emanuel.

'Does anybody know they're there?'

'Yes, there are a few who know Sara is there but no one knows about Teeling. Not yet, anyway.'

'I take it Grenville will survive his injury?'

'I don't know,' said Emanuel, shaking his head. 'I saw the duty surgeon and asked him the same question. He wasn't prepared to commit himself and said he'd know more once he'd had the fellow on the operating table. When I left, the porters were taking him up to the cutting room.'

Walter picked up his pipe that lay on the table in front of him and puffed quietly for a moment or so, his eyes fixed on some far-off point. 'And you say there was a suggestion the plot we've been talking about may take place in the next few weeks?'

'That was the suggestion,' said Emanuel. 'But, of course, that might now have to be changed in the light of what's happened to Grenville.'

'Quite,' said Walter. 'But whatever date is finally settled on, we still don't know what the plot is about or where it's supposed to happen.'

'I think we might know where,' said Emanuel. 'Do you remember that piece of paper I showed you a little while ago? We thought it was a plan or a map of sorts.'

'Yes, I do. What of it?' said Walter.

Emanuel delved into his coat pocket, and laid the drawing on the table.

'If I'm right, this drawing represents Park Lane at its junction with the Uxbridge road,' he said, tapping the paper with the tip of his index finger. 'This second road is, I think, a lane just inside the borders of Hyde Park. It's the area where I saw Grenville's men the other day. They seemed to be looking the place over. It's also the place I suspect Sir Peter Westlake and the Hon James Grenville were heading for when I saw them riding in Hyde—'

'I don't see—' interrupted Walter.

'Forgive me, my dear Walter,' said Emanuel. 'But is it not the case that riders normally restrict themselves to Rotten Row? Is it not unusual for two gentlemen to break with convention and ride elsewhere in the park? It meant little to me at the time. But now? I think it highly probable they were on their way to the point indicated by the map, the very same place where I saw Grenville's men the day I followed them.'

'Hmm,' said Walter staring at the drawing. Looking up, he removed his pipe from his mouth and pointed the stem at his friend. 'Supposing you're right, we still don't know what they're up to. What could we say? That we believe two upstanding members of society are planning something, and although we don't know what, we think it might be in Hyde Park? How long would it be before we became the laughing stock of London? I regret, sir, we need a good deal more information before we can act.'

'Better a laughing stock than the alternative,' said Emanuel. 'We know, or at least we suspect, that the plan involves the killing of a well-known Protestant in circumstances that point to his assassin being a Catholic. If it succeeds you can imagine the consequences.'

'Good God,' said Walter, snapping his fingers. 'I've just thought of something.'

'What?' said Emanuel.

'Fielding, the MP for West Kent, the fellow who—'

'The rabble-rouser,' said Emanuel. 'I remember.'

'Yes, that's him,' said Walter. 'For some time he's been whipping up opposition to the proposed Emancipation Bill and, more importantly, the Minister's plans in regard to Ireland. If anything were to happen to him it would be cause for serious concern.'

'What are you saying?' said Emanuel. 'That Fielding speaks on the north side of Hyde Park?'

'Exactly,' said Walter. 'At the corner of the Uxbridge road and Park Lane.'

Chapter 58

'Bristow wasn't executed.' The Ordinary of Newgate rested his elbows on the arms of his chair, his hands clasped below his chin as he regarded his visitor through a pair of ancient spectacles. 'You're the second gentlemen to enquire after him. Strange. Very strange.'

'Really?' asked Sir Peter Westlake in feigned surprise The two men were seated in a cramped, low-ceilinged room on the third floor of the prison. A small window overlooked the press yard far below.

'I knew nothing about this prisoner when the other gentleman came to see me,' said the Ordinary, 'but it seems he was pardoned. We don't get many of those, sir. No, not many at all.'

'How so?' Sir Peter leaned forward in his chair. He was having difficulty in hearing what the priest was saying, his voice all but drowned by the clamour of the raised voices of prisoners that seemed a permanent feature of the place.

'I don't know all the details but it appears the trial judge was petitioned by someone who apparently suggested Bristow was entirely innocent of the crime for which he was convicted. Naturally, the judge gave the fellow short shrift and no doubt thought that was the end of the matter.'

'But it wasn't?' said Sir Peter.

'That's the extraordinary thing, sir. By all rights, it should've been. But I understand that Mr Pitt himself sent word to the judge indicating that he would regard it as a singular honour should the judge reconsider his decision.'

'Why on earth would the Minister become involved?'

'That's what we all wanted to know. It appears that the petitioner who first approached the trial judge is a Papist priest. Having got nowhere with his request for Bristow's sentence to be respited, he does no more than take the matter to the Minister.'

'I still don't follow. What has the case to do with Mr Pitt?'

'You should know the answer to that, Sir Peter. Being as how you're a member of parliament.'

'You can't surely be suggesting the decision to intervene in Bristow's case was politically motivated. It doesn't…' Sir Peter clapped a hand to his forehead. 'Ye gods, you could be right. He could hardly refuse a request for help from a Catholic priest without damaging his chance of achieving Irish unification. And what better story than that the person on whose behalf the Papist was petitioning was an Anglican? And it is Ireland that is important to the Minister, not the priest and certainly not Bristow.'

Sir Peter paused for a moment. 'Before his release, and while he was still under sentence of death, I understand Bristow asked you to write some letters on his behalf. I was wondering—'

'I regret, Sir Peter, I cannot accede to your request. As I told the other gentleman who asked, the duties I perform on behalf of the poor souls in this prison are confidential. But in any case, I would have dispatched the letters concerned within a few days of the prisoner's date of execution and before I was made aware of his pardon.'

'I appreciate your position, sir,' said Sir Peter. 'And in normal circumstances I would not have asked. But the truth of the matter is that the content of the letters may already have been the cause of distress to their recipients. I merely wished to offer what advice and comfort to those people as was needed. But you no longer possess the letters. A pity. I was about to suggest a small donation to the Church. Some funds to assist in the refurbishment of the prison chapel, perhaps. Or for the poor. But, no matter.'

'Well, I may have spoken in haste, sir,' said the Ordinary. 'As I told you, the letters have now gone and it would not have been right to have shown you those. But I think I could see my way clear to allowing you to see my copybook. That, of course, contains the precise wording of every document I produce on behalf of the prisoners.'

Why, sir, I am exceedingly grateful to you.'

A few hours later Sir Peter stood by the library table of his home looking down at the bundle of copy letters in his hand. The top one was addressed to Master Henry Teeling of no fixed address, and had been written on behalf of Prisoner Erasmus Bristow, Newgate Prison, Old Bailey, London. Sir Peter turned it over and glanced at the bottom of the second page. There was no signature. Only a cross. His eye passed rapidly down the text. It appeared to deal with an incident that had occurred in Ireland two years before. It meant nothing to him. A story about some sort of massacre that had occurred in the south of the country. Suddenly his eye caught sight of a familiar name. He stopped and re-read the relevant sentence. *It weren't Collins what did for your old woman, nor me, neither. It were Lt. Grenville.*

Sir Peter read on, this time more slowly. *Collins and me were outside when it happened. I heard a scream and went into the house. Mr Grenville were standing over your old woman. I knew at once she were dead. It's him what you should blame for what happened.*

Sir Peter put the letter down. There was no reason to think Bristow had been lying. And besides, Grenville had pretty much admitted to his involvement in the incident.

He walked over to a small table on which a tray of drinks had been placed and poured himself a whisky. The letter changed everything. Grenville had become a liability, the antagonism between him and Bristow was a distraction he couldn't afford and would have to be dealt with.

Chapter 59

Grenville thrashed his head from side to side, the pain in his abdomen far surpassing anything he'd suffered in the past.

It was dark outside save only for the myriad of tiny lights that winked and sparkled in the black vault of the heavens. For a moment or two he was reminded of his childhood in Norfolk when he would often lie in his bed and gaze in wonder at the beauty of it all.

A sharp bolt of pain reminded him of where he was. He lifted the thin blanket that covered him and saw his stomach swathed in strips of white cotton. He let the blanket drop and looked down the length of the ward where he could see a table on which a single candle was burning. A woman sat there, apparently asleep. Grenville contemplated calling out for her but turned away and closed his eyes. He didn't want to die but then again he was damned if he'd admit to anyone he was in pain.

In spite of everything he must have dozed off. For how long, he didn't know. It was still dark outside and the candle, much reduced in height, still burned in its tin sconce. He looked for the woman he'd seen earlier. She wasn't at the table. He rolled his head and looked in the opposite direction. There was no sign of her there, either. He wondered what could have woken him. He looked past the table with its lighted candle and heard the small click of the door to the ward opening. Doubtless one of the night servants returning.

'Some water if you please,' he called out.

There was no reply. Grenville stared into the darkness beyond the candle. A shadow passed in front of the ward door, barely discernible against the reflected light.

He tried again, irritated at the lack of response. 'Water. I need water.'

Silence. He felt the first stirrings of unease. Something wasn't right. Why hadn't anyone responded? He tried to lever himself up onto one elbow but the pain was too great and he slumped back onto the flock mattress, exhausted. A small gust of air fanned his face as if someone were standing close to his bed. He tried to calm himself, think rationally. It had to be the night servant he'd seen earlier.

'Some water.' Grenville was aware of a single drop of sweat above his right eye. He peered through the gloom. It was odd the servant had chosen not to bring a light. 'Who—'

#

Emanuel was not unduly worried. The surgeon, when he'd spoken to him yesterday morning, had seemed optimistic. *'My preliminary examination of your friend,'* he'd said, *'gives me some hope that the hurt, while undeniably serious, is not, of itself, fatal. Provided we can avoid the fever, I make no doubt he will make a full recovery.'*

Immediately after Mass he'd taken a wherry from Shadwell to Westminster and walked up Grosvenor Place to the hospital.

'Men's surgical? On the second floor, guv'nor,' said a porter in answer to Emanuel's enquiry. 'Up them stairs, on the right.'

The door to the ward creaked as Emanuel pushed it open and entered a long, wide room with a line of beds running down either side. In the centre stood a coal-burning stove and, close to it, a desk presently occupied by an amply endowed woman dressed in an ankle-length blue cotton dress, a white apron and a mob cap. She looked up as Emanuel approached.

'Yes?' she said, brusquely, a pencil poised in one hand.

'I've come to see the Honourable. James Grenville who was admitted here yesterday morning,' said Emanuel, his eyes searching each of the beds in turn.

The woman tensed. 'And you are?' she asked.

'A friend,' said Emanuel.

A long pause. Finally, 'I regret to inform you that Mr Grenville died during the night,' she said.

'Died?' said Emanuel, taken aback. 'How did he die?'

'I weren't on duty when it happened,' said the woman. 'The body's been taken to the dead house for the post-mortem.'

'Thank you,' said Emanuel, turning to leave. Then he looked back. Something in the tone of the woman's voice hadn't sounded quite right. She knew more than she was saying. On impulse he said, 'Was it the stab wounds that killed him?'

The effect was instantaneous. 'It weren't nothing to do with me. I found him dead when I came on the ward this morning. There'll be hell to pay, that's for sure.'

'Tell me what happened,' said Emanuel.

'It were like I told you,' said the woman, an anxious look in her eyes, her words tumbling out of her mouth in an unstoppable stream. 'Your friend were in that bed over there,' she said, jutting her chin down the length of the ward. 'There were a man standing by his bed but he weren't saying nothing on account of your friend were sleeping. Didn't think nothing on it. The ward were full of visitors like it is most days. Come nine o'clock the visitors have to leave and me and me mate check all the objects before we go off. Your friend had a touch of the fever what often happens after an operation but he were all right. That were when the night servants relieve us and my friend and me went off duty.'

'What did the man by my friend's bed, look like?'

'I didn't take no notice of him,' said the woman. 'Like I told you, the ward were full of folk.'

'You saw no one else by the bed?' said Emanuel.

'No,' said the woman, shaking her head..

'What happened then?'

'I were on duty again at seven this morning. One of the servants came with me and we looked at all the objects like we're supposed to. When we got to your friend I saw he were dead. I lifted his blanket and that's when I saw all the blood. He'd been stabbed.'

'What did the night servant say?' said Emanuel.

'She were shocked. I can tell you that, mister,' said the woman. 'I ain't seen anyone that pale since the last time I were in the cutting room. She were shaking like a leaf in a storm and that's a fact. Reckoned she didn't see nothing.'

'How was that possible?' asked Emanuel.

The woman snorted derisively. 'You can't see nothing when you're sleeping, if you understand what I'm saying?'

'So you think someone might have entered the ward while the servants slept?' said Emanuel.

The woman shrugged. 'Can't think of no other way,' she said.

It didn't seem possible to Emanuel that someone could have gained access to the ward, committed the act of murder and left again without being seen. Yet, clearly, someone had done so.

He thought back on the events of the night before last in Green Park and of one man in particular, a man with a grudge to settle, a man who held Grenville responsible for his appearance at the Old Bailey, a man with hate in his heart.

'Aye, I were going to turn Grenville off,' Bristow had shouted in the midst of his frustrated rage.

#

'Your honour?' Emanuel stopped and looked round to see the same porter he'd met on his arrival at the hospital a short while before. He seemed tired and drawn but whether from worry or lack of sleep, Emanuel couldn't be sure. 'I heard you talking. In the ward, like.'

Emanuel waited for the man to continue, wondering if he'd been guilty of some minor infraction of hospital rules of which he'd not been aware.

'You was talking about the gentleman what got turned off.'

'Go on,' said Emanuel. 'I'm listening.'

'There were another object what died in one of the other wards last night,' said the man. 'I were called to take him to the dead house. After I'd done that, I were on my way back here when I sees someone coming down the stairs. It were late. The hospital had been locked for the night but sometimes there's folk what get lost and we have to let them out. So I calls out to him, all friendly like. You could 'ave knocked me down with a feather, sir. He saw me and were away without so much as a word.'

'What did he look like?' said Emanuel.

'Can't rightly say, sir. It were that dark. I didn't think no more about it till I hears you talking to the nurse. And the more I thought about it, the more I were wondering if the cully I saw weren't something to do with what you was talking about.'

Emanuel left the porter and walked down the steps of the hospital into Knightsbridge. He nearly missed the small square of brightly coloured material lying by the roadway. On an impulse, he stopped and picked it up. It was of good quality although stained with dark brown marks, its damp condition suggesting it had lain there some time. He put it into his pocket and walked on.

#

The persistent hammering noise seemed very close. Emanuel woke slowly, wishing the noise would stop. He turned to look at the door as if that might solve the mystery of who was there.

'Father Emanuel? It's me, Mrs Wilson. I've a note for you from My Lord Bishop.'

'Thank you, Mrs Wilson. I'll be there directly,' said Emanuel, rubbing the sleep from his eyes. 'Just put the note under the door, if you please.'

He waited for the note to appear before struggling out of bed and picking up the missive. Turning it over, he recognised the wax seal with the imprint of the bishop's signet ring. The note was a request that

Father Emanuel should, at his earliest convenience, repair to the bishop's private office on the first floor. Douglass, it seemed, wished to speak to him on a matter of some urgency.

Emanuel washed and dressed with that dread feeling in the pit of his stomach that always came at moments like this. He wondered what could have happened as to require his attendance quite so urgently. The bishop must have known he'd been out all day on sick visits, getting back too late even for the evening meal, and had gone straight to his room to sleep. He briefly wondered if the summons was connected with his visit to the hospital, earlier in the day.

The bishop's office was along the corridor from Emanuel's bedroom and on the same floor. He knew it well, had often been there in the thirty years since he first arrived in England. Back then the Vicar Apostolic had been Bishop Challoner but he'd been dead these last nineteen years. Emanuel could still see the old man sitting at his desk in the wainscoted room, his eye frequently turning to a large crucifix that hung above the fireplace while he listened to whatever his priests wanted to talk to him about.

Emanuel knocked and went in. Little had changed. The walls were still yellow from tobacco smoke, the same Turkish carpet lay on the floor in front of the fire. By the window, the same soot-encrusted portraits of former bishops hung on the walls as they had done for as long as he could remember. He glanced at the nearest one – Campion perhaps, or Arrowsmith, he wasn't sure which.

'Come in, Father. Do sit down.' Douglass held out his hand for Emanuel to kiss the Episcopal ring.

Emanuel would, in later years, think back on this moment as the time when he should have realised something was amiss. The bishop had always addressed him by his Christian name, rather than the more formal Father. But he assumed it had merely been a slip of the bishop's tongue.

'Thank you, my lord,' he said and waited for Douglass to continue.

'I wanted to see you because I've received a letter that relates to you,' said the bishop, opening a desk drawer and producing a sheet of paper. 'It is a letter from the rabbi of one of the synagogues in Rosemary Lane and it makes reference to two men who, the writer suggests, may be known to you. Their names are Aaron Malka and Erasmus Bristow. Are these names familiar to you?'

Emanuel felt suddenly sick. He recalled his chance encounter with Aaron Malka, a friend of his since the days of their youth in Lisbon, someone he'd not seen since leaving Portugal more than thirty years ago. It had brought back a wealth of memories and they'd spoken easily of those far-off days. It had been a pleasant interlude and he could not have known their meeting had been observed and that within the hour his boyhood friend would be dead and Emanuel's secret known to Aaron's killer.

'I know of both men, my lord,' he said.

'It appears that by some means or another, Mr Aaron Malka was in possession of information relating to you which he passed to Mr Bristow. That information was apparently forwarded by Mr Bristow to the rabbi in Rosemary Lane. It contains an allegation of the most serious kind and it is this about which I wanted to speak to you. Have you any notion of what I might be referring to?'

'I regret I have no idea, my lord. I knew Bristow when he was but a boy. His mother would often come to see me and would, from time to time, bring him along. I lost touch with him when he was sent to prison, after which he joined the army. He returned to London about two years ago but I saw him for the first time only a matter of weeks ago. Aaron Malka was a boyhood friend who I'd not seen for many years. We met briefly a little while ago.'

For a long moment Douglass stared up at one of portraits on the wall in front of him, a light frown on his face as though wrestling with his thoughts. When, at last, he turned to face Emanuel there was a look of intense sorrow in his eyes.

'It pains me greatly, Father, but I am obliged to put to you the matters raised.'

'I understand, my lord. I—'

Douglass held up the palm of his hand. 'It might be best were you to listen to what this letter has to say, after which I will ask you to respond. The writer makes it clear that he has no personal knowledge of the allegations raised against you and merely seeks to inform me for such action as I see fit.'

He looked at Emanuel, his iron-grey eyes giving nothing away. For the briefest of moments it seemed as though he might be waiting for his visitor to say something. Before Emanuel could gather his thoughts, he said, 'The story the rabbi has to tell is a little complicated and, frankly, sometimes difficult to believe. Let me, therefore, start with what I already know about you before addressing the central allegation that has been levelled.'

Emanuel nodded.

'You are a Jew, originally born and raised in Portugal under laws which required you to be baptised into the Church. According to what I've been told, you, unlike the vast majority of your fellow Jews, accepted the teachings of the Church and, at the age of thirteen, you enrolled yourself in a seminary in Lisbon. Is that correct?'

'Yes, my lord.'

'You subsequently arrived in this country approximately thirty years ago and presented yourself to Dr Challoner who was then the Vicar Apostolic for London. He sent you to Virginia Street but the following year the chapel was destroyed by an anti-Catholic mob. Largely as a result of your labours, the chapel was rebuilt with funds donated by the Royal Court of Portugal.'

'Yes.'

'Tell me, Father, why did you leave Portugal?' said Douglass, his head bent forward so that he could see Emanuel over the rim of his spectacles.

'Because it would have been impossible for me to live there as a Christian. No one, Jew or gentile, accepted the few Jews who converted to Roman Catholicism. In that sense we were always on the outside. Our Christianity made no difference to the way we were viewed or the way we were treated by other Christians. Our dress, our appearance, our mannerisms marked us out as different while our fellow Jews regarded us as apostates, people to be shunned. It was this, as much as for any other reason, that I decided to leave and come to England. I thought things would be different here.'

'But becoming a Christian was a requirement of the law, and failing to comply would result in exile, would it not?'

'Most Jews became Christians in name only; crypto-Christians, if you like; attending Mass on Sundays but observing the rituals and beliefs of Judaism at home. My mother and father were – indeed still are – crypto-Christians.'

'I see,' said Douglass, turning again to gaze up at one of the portraits. 'But you *were* baptised?'

'Yes, of course,' said Emanuel with more force than was entirely necessary.

Douglass nodded slowly. It was as if he could see into the other man's soul. Emanuel waited for him to speak. He knew what was coming. Sweat bathed his face and neck. He hardly dare raise his eyes to meet those of the bishop.

'Tell me, Mr Emanuel, where did you study for the priesthood?' The question hung in the air between them, the question Emanuel had most dreaded for the past thirty years. He supposed he'd always known it would be asked of him sooner or later. The answer, or more accurately, the partial answer was easy enough.

'At the English seminary, the Inglesinhos de Lisboa in the Bairro Alto, my lord.'

'Ah, yes, I remember, now,' said Douglass. 'You spent seven years there, I believe. Slightly more than half the expected period. Why was that?'

Emanuel squirmed in his seat and studied the back of his hands. 'I was asked to leave, my lord. I was accused of fighting with the other seminarians who accused me of being no more than a crypto-Catholic.'

'Which leads me to ask where you completed your training?'

'I regret it extremely, my lord. I did not complete it.'

'Why not?'

'I came to England to study but was told there were no seminaries here. I thought to travel to France, to Douai, but alas had not the funds to do so. By the time I had saved enough to go, the war made studying in France an impossibility.'

'So the allegation made in this letter is true?' said Douglass. 'You have never taken Holy Orders?'

'No, my lord, I haven't.'

'Although you told the late Dr Challoner that you had.'

'Yes.'

'You realise, Mr Emanuel, I have no choice in this matter.' Bishop Douglass looked suddenly old, his face grey and somehow shrunken beneath his wig. 'I'm obliged to recommend to the Holy Father that you be excommunicated. In the meantime I am required to relieve you of your duties as a priest.'

#

Emanuel remembered nothing of the following few hours, although he must have taken his leave of the bishop, packed his few belongings and made the long trek south to his old room in Shadwell where Sara and Teeling had been there to greet him. They said little in response to his tale of what had happened and, in truth, there wasn't much they could have said that would have meant anything. His mind was incapable of rational thought, a dull grey landscape devoid of meaning or purpose was before him. The bishop had given him until the following morning to vacate the room he'd occupied in Farmer Street for the last thirty years. It would, the bishop had explained, be needed for Emanuel's replacement.

'What will you do?' Sara had slipped her arm through his, her face pale and close to tears.

'I don't yet know,' said Emanuel, shrugging his shoulders and looking round the room. 'The bishop has asked me to leave this room by tomorrow. I regret it extremely but it means you cannot remain here either. Where will you go?'

He watched her glance at Teeling and sensed that something had passed between them, a wordless communication that only they could understand.

'I'll move across the river to Southwark or Rotherhithe. Somewhere I'm not known,' said Sara. 'There's work to be had over there. Maybe in a tavern or an inn. Teeling lives close by. He will look after me.'

'Are you well enough to travel, Henry?' said Emanuel.

'It's fine that I am, Father…' Teeling stopped. He was far from well. His injuries had hardly begun to heal and the black phlegm he'd been coughing up was now more noticeable than ever. 'I'll be gone shortly.'

'You can stay here for tonight, if that would help,' said Emanuel.

'No, I'll not be troubling you,' said Teeling. He looked across the room at Sara as if expecting her to say something but she avoided his gaze.

Emanuel watched the two of them set about collecting their few belongings. They looked somehow different. Sara seemed happier than she'd been for some time while Teeling, despite his ill health, no longer wore the hunted look that had so characterised his existence for the past two or three months. He studied them for a moment before turning away, content that a corner had been turned in both their lives. Soon they were ready to leave. He saw them to the door of his room and waited until he heard the front door close behind them. Then, for the last time, he walked to Virginia Street chapel and sat on one of the benches in front of the altar. The damage caused by the mob had long since been cleared away although the aftermath was still plain to see. It was no longer his chapel. In due course, someone else would take over from him and he would be quietly forgotten. He took out his breviary, opened it and began to read, more from habit than anything else. It was the only life he knew.

#

The days passed. With no work to be found, the few pennies Emanuel had saved over the years was soon gone and he was forced to give up his occupancy of the single room he'd rented in Mile End. For the past two nights his bed had been the floor of a derelict house out along the Bow road, a sheet of old canvas to keep him tolerably warm. He hadn't starved, his old flock had seen to that, but he knew the arrangement couldn't last forever. Many of them had given him what they had needed for themselves. It had kept him alive but it had been barely enough.

A light breeze scattered the accumulated rubbish in Virginia Street, and brought with it the stench of the open sewer in the centre of the carriageway. As if by silent command a pall of insects rose in unison like a small black cloud to settle a few yards further on. The stench was worse than he remembered. He didn't know what had drawn him back. Perhaps it was the familiarity of the place, the comfort of knowing every nook and cranny of the neighbourhood, of seeing familiar faces hurry by on whatever journey their life was taking them. Now and again a head would turn in his direction with the questioning stare of half-remembered recognition, someone they might have known, perhaps, from another time or place.

'Emanuel?' Emanuel looked round to see John Walter approaching, a look of intense concern on his friend's face. 'My dear fellow, I've been searching for you. I heard what happened. I… He paused, his eyes widening. 'Come, you look as if you could do with something to eat.'

A few minutes later they were seated on a bench in a cook house on the Ratcliff Highway, while Emanuel told Walter of his meeting with the bishop.

'But how did the rabbi come by this information?' asked Walter. 'Somebody must have told him.'

'Yes, he was told,' said Emanuel.

'By whom? D'you know?'

'I can't tell you that,' said Emanuel. 'In any case, it was the truth. The fault is entirely mine.'

Walter looked at him keenly.

'I think I know who it was,' he said. 'You once told me of a friend of yours who was recently murdered. A fellow Jew, as I recall, killed for the information he had about you. You didn't tell me what that information was but I can imagine it was serious enough for you to have kept it for so long. And I can guess who it was that murdered him; the same man whose life you saved; a man you have always refused to condemn although, God knows, he richly deserves to be condemned. Why d'you do it, old friend?'

Emanuel shrugged. He wasn't sure he knew the answer himself and he doubted a discourse on morality would be well received. He looked up as a waiter arrived at their table and put down several large plates laden with sliced eel, oysters and cold meats. The man returned a minute later with another plate piled high with buttered bread and a gallon jug of Truman's beer.

'Tuck in, my friend,' said Walter. He paused and looked at Emanuel over the rim of his spectacles. 'You're a good man, Lazaro. I couldn't do what you've done.'

'I'm no different to any other man but I've learned you'll never change the ways of a violent man by more violence. Yes, I'm frightened of the future, of what it holds for me, but turning to violence as a means of expression won't help me.'

'No, I suppose not,' said Walter, pouring them both some beer. 'By the by, I had a visit from an officer at Bow Street. He asked me a few questions about what I knew of the Grenville murder. I couldn't tell him much. I expect we'll hear soon enough if there's any development. Can I pass you something to eat?'

'What of the plot?' said Emanuel, nodding his thanks and forking a couple of slices of cold beef onto his plate. 'I see nothing of the news these days.'

'No, I don't suppose you do,' said Walter, wiping his mouth with a large silk handkerchief. 'It's gone very quiet. I think Grenville's death almost certainly had something to do with it. I hear whispers every so often but nothing definite.'

'What of the rabble-rouser of whom we spoke?' said Emanuel.

'He continues to rabble-rouse,' said Walter, leaning across the table and spooning a generous portion of the oysters into his dish. 'And he continues to attract increasing numbers of followers. I hear he's due to speak in Hyde Park tomorrow and again next Tuesday, ahead of the emancipation debate in Parliament the following Friday. I suppose someone might want to take a shot at him then.'

'Hardly reassuring,' said Emanuel.

'I agree, my dear fellow, but we face the same problem we have always faced – a lack of credible information without which nothing gets done.'

#

The light was fading and shadows lengthening when Emanuel reached the rope walks at Sun Tavern Fields and turned north along a route that would take him to the Whitechapel Road and, from there, across the fields to Mile End. Soon he'd left behind the crowds, their restless noise replaced by the gentle chatter of birdsong and the rustle of small animals moving through the bushes that grew on either side of the path. It was in moments like this, when the world seemed at peace, that his mind would turn again to the changing fortunes of his life and his heart would thump with anxiety for his future.

In some strange way his meeting with the bishop, though painful, had lifted the heavy burden of deceit he'd carried for the last thirty years. Punishment had been followed by a measure of relief, his conscience, at least in part, salved.

From somewhere behind him a stone rattled as though disturbed from its place. Emanuel stopped. The path was seldom used and he was surprised by the sound. On reflection the noise could have been caused by an animal – perhaps a fox or a badger. He remained still for a few seconds but the sound was not repeated and he walked on. Ahead of him, perhaps a quarter of a mile distant, he could see a light flickering in the window of an outlying farm. Another half mile beyond that was the hamlet of Old Mile End and the place he now called home. He'd be there soon enough.

A sudden, stifled cry erupted from somewhere behind him. Emanuel spun round and stared into the encroaching dusk, wishing he'd taken the longer way home. At least then he'd have had people around to keep him company. It was too late now. His fertile imagination conjured up an image of a grinning Bristow swinging towards him on his crutches. Emanuel wished he'd listened to those who'd advised him to arm himself with a sword, a knife, a cosh; anything with which he might defend himself from brigands. He'd always refused. It would not be right for a priest to be armed. But at this moment he wasn't entirely sure he'd refuse the offer of a weapon.

A few yards ahead he saw what appeared to be a small gap in the hedge. He would wait there, out of sight, and deal with the coming threat as best he could. He hurried forward only to find there was no gap, but merely a trick of light and shadow. He looked at the still distant farmhouse, a light shining through one of its windows. Whoever was behind him would surely overtake him before he could reach it. He felt his blood rushing to his head and his eyelids began to flutter as he absorbed every detail of what lay before him. He wiped the sweat from the palms of his hands and stared down the pathway.

He didn't have long to wait.

A figure appeared out of the darkness.

#

The beatings had become a daily occurrence and she wasn't sure how much more she could take. It seemed to her that everything she did or said was the cause of yet another flogging. She'd tried to leave many times, only to be found and dragged back to the hovel where he lived, close to the Highway.

Willing Annie put a hand to her stomach. The bruising was still there from when he'd punched her earlier in the day. He hadn't always treated her like this. Not to begin with. The early days had been like paradise compared to what she'd endured when she'd first left home. She shuddered. There had been no adults in the low lodging house she'd entered. At least none that had ever made themselves known – except the man who took her rent money and sat by the front door.

It was the filth and the degradation she most remembered. The children – none was more than about twelve – slept seven or eight to a bed, boys and girls alike, often naked. Seldom would a night pass without the wandering hand of a boy having to be rebuffed. It might have been different had she the means to pay. The need for money had eventually pushed her onto the streets. On some days she earned as much as ten shillings. On others, nothing at all.

She'd learned to hide her disgust from the men who sought her out on the riverfront at Limehouse. Most of them were sailors who'd just come ashore with money in their pockets and a hungry look in their eyes.

Seldom were they gentle, and many was the time she'd had to go to the foreshore of the Thames and wash the blood away from between her thighs.

But she'd known better than to complain. Several of the girls she'd known had ended their lives floating face down in the Pool. She'd never known the reason, of course, but she'd guessed. Often, on days and nights like these, she would think of her parents and wish she could return home. But that had never been possible. The family didn't have enough to eat as it was. They would have starved if she'd ever returned.

Then she'd met Bristow. He was the same age as her father. He'd taken her, of course, and given her five shillings for her time. She'd thought no more about him until he returned the following day and said he'd look after her if only she would come and live in his house and cook and clean for him.

He'd been as good as his word for the first week and she'd been content to accept the occasional flogging for failings in the bedroom and the kitchen. It was that or a return to the lodging house from which he'd taken her. By the end of the second week he had sent her out onto the streets to pay for her food and lodgings while continuing to expect her to perform her other duties. In recent months his abusive behaviour had grown steadily worse, culminating in the beating he'd given her for speaking to Mr Emanuel. She now found it difficult to walk, and the pain of satisfying her clients had become intolerable.

She stumbled, stifling a cry as she tried to save herself from falling. She had to keep going. She had to speak to him.

'Annie? Is that you?' Annie looked up to see Mr Emanuel hurrying towards her along the otherwise deserted path, a look of intense surprise in his eyes. 'What brings you out here, child? Are you unwell?'

'I'll be all right, Mr Emanuel,' she said, still clutching at her stomach. 'I saw you in the Highway. I wanted to speak with you but you was with a gentleman. So I waited but when I looked again, you'd gone. I've been trying to find you ever since.'

'Tell me what, child?' said Emanuel, still shaking from the stress of the last few minutes.

'Bristow is looking for you, Mr Emanuel, on account of the gentleman what got turned off in the hospital.'

'Master Grenville?' said Emanuel.

'Aye, Grenville. That were the name,' said Annie. 'Bristow ain't half pissed on account of you. Reckons you've been asking too many questions.'

'About what? Mr Grenville's death?' said Emanuel.

'Aye,' said Annie. She buried her face in her hands. 'He'll kill me if he ever finds out I been talking to you again, Mr Emanuel. You won't tell him nothing, will you?'

'Of course not, child,' said Emanuel. He waited a moment, then, 'Was there anything else I should know?'

'No,' said Annie. She glanced behind her as though expecting someone to appear, a frightened look in her eyes. 'I've got to go now but I had to tell you.'

He watched the girl hurry along the path that would take her back to the Ratcliff Highway. For a long time Emanuel didn't move, gazing at the empty space she had so recently occupied. Was it possible the figure seen by the night porter at the hospital had been Bristow after all? Why else would he be concerned about the continuing questions surrounding Grenville's death?

From somewhere far away a church bell chimed the hour. It was later than he thought. Certainly too late to think about food, even if he could find anyone to beg from. He would have to wait until the morning when there would, he hoped, be a better chance of finding someone willing to help him. He felt the splash of a raindrop on his face and saw black storm clouds forming in the east. It would take some time to reach the derelict house on the Bow road where he'd rested for the past few nights. Plenty of time for a drenching.

As though on cue, a streak of lightning lit up the evening sky, quickly followed by the low rumble of thunder.

He was soaked by the time he stumbled in through the open doorway of the house and stepped over the sleeping bodies in the hall. His place was in one of the back rooms on the first floor. Like everyone else, he always left something of his on the floor to show he intended to return; an unwritten rule to leave alone the sleeping area of another.

Emanuel reached the landing where yet more sleeping forms occupied every inch of floor space. There was no light and it was difficult to avoid stepping on people. He couldn't help thinking of the life he'd left behind, of his room on Farmer Street, of the comfortable bed in which he slept and the privacy that this had afforded him. All of it gone. Turning in through the doorway of the back room, he made his way to the far corner where he'd left a boot as his marker, his claim to the little stretch of flooring on which he would sleep. Except someone else had taken the space. For a brief moment he considered throwing the fellow out but knew that, ultimately, it would do him no good. He turned back towards the stairs and walked out into the rainswept night. It was too late to look for somewhere else. Every available place would, by now, have been taken. Tonight he would sleep at the roadside.

And tomorrow?

He knew the answer to that question.

He could fall no further.

#

Bristow stood at the back of the crowd. There had to be near a thousand men gathered at the north end of Hyde Park listening to the man talk. He couldn't hear what was being said and doubted anyone else could, except maybe those right at the front. Not that it mattered. They weren't expecting anything new. They'd come to see him and cheer him on, trusting that he wouldn't let them down, that he had the power to stop the government in its mad dash to give the Papists everything they wanted. The man addressing the crowd understood their concerns. He was the only one prepared to stand up for the people.

Bristow looked contemptuously at the rapt faces of the men standing around him. They were a rabble who, by themselves, could do nothing. They needed someone like him who was prepared to act, someone to achieve what they wanted but hadn't the courage to do for themselves. It had been the same when he'd been growing up in Shadwell and Wapping and Limehouse. The other boys had looked to him for leadership. Only he had understood that the good things in life had to be taken, that no one was going to give you anything. And if that meant breaking a few heads to achieve the desired end, then that was what would happen.

It hadn't taken long for the word to get round and soon nobody had dared stand in his way. As for getting caught, he'd never given it a moment's thought. When it *did* happen and he'd found himself at the Old Bailey, the judge had sent him into the army. Military service – and particularly the posting to Ireland –had allowed him greater freedom to act than ever before. As far as he knew, nobody cared what he did. And he was paid for it.

Bristow shifted his weight, leaning forward on his crutches in an effort to get more comfortable. The loss of his leg had made little difference to his activities. Discharged from the army he'd returned to London and quickly re-established his reputation for extreme violence. No one had dared challenge him.

Except the Jew priest.

Bristow could hear the scrub's voice in his head. Its irritating reasonableness annoyed him. No, it was more than that. It infuriated him, made him feel inadequate. Then there was the expression on the bastard's face. Was it pity? It had always felt that way, as though the Jew was judging him and finding him wanting, a son unworthy of his mother. A rage rose within him. He felt it sticking in his throat, choking him with its intensity. It seemed his troubles began and ended with Emanuel fucking Lazaro.

The sudden roar of the mob interrupted his thoughts and he looked up to see the speaker standing on a tree stump at the front of the crowd. Bristow thought about moving in for a closer look at him. He'd not really seen him before. He felt for the pistol tucked into his belt. It felt odd. He'd always relied on a knife to sort out those little difficulties that occasionally confronted him. Unlike the gun, a knife made no noise and always achieved the desired result. Bristow clucked his tongue. The order to carry the gun annoyed him.

He looked again at the speaker. The talking had stopped. The mob was cheering him, wanting him to go on. Bristow turned and headed south towards the river. He'd seen enough; he knew exactly what needed to be done. It wasn't difficult – apart from the timing. And there was nothing he could do about that. His heart fluttered at the prospect.

#

In later years, Emanuel would often think of that first day at the Whitechapel Workhouse. The outer door was answered by an emaciated old woman of indeterminate age who stared up at him with improbably green eyes. After listening to him in complete silence, she turned and led him through a maze of corridors to a door on the first floor. Here she stopped and pointed before shuffling back along the passage and disappearing from his view. Emanuel stared after her, undecided of what was expected of him. Then he knocked.

'Come,' said a high-pitched, almost feminine voice. Emanuel pushed open the door and went in.

Mr Jeremiah Lamb, master of the Whitechapel Workhouse, was a small, neat, clean-shaven man of about fifty whose grey eyes now cast an appraising look at his visitor.

'Have we not met before, sir?' said Lamb. 'If I am not sadly mistook, I've seen you hereabouts.'

'It is, sir, quite possible,' said Emanuel. 'I have lived in Shadwell these thirty years past.'

'Ah, that must be it. Well, sir, how can I be of service?'

It didn't take long for Emanuel to explain circumstances that brought him here.

'Do I take it, sir, that due to your Christian faith, your former brethren within the Jewish community will not assist you?'

'No, I regret they will not,' said Emanuel. 'I am regarded as an apostate. It is – how shall I put it – frowned upon.'

'And your former bishop?'

'I regret that such assistance as he feels able to give me is severely limited by the funds he has at his disposal. For reasons I can well understand, the bishop feels I have brought this trouble upon myself.'

'I see,' said the master. 'And now you wish to enter the workhouse?'

'I do,' said Emanuel, his heart sinking at the realisation of what he was asking for.

The master nodded. 'In normal circumstances, Mr Emanuel, you would have to appear before the board of guardians to determine whether or not you are a deserving case. But I can, in certain circumstances, admit people on my own authority. Since I know of you, sir, I am happy to grant a ticket of admission.'

Pushing back his chair, Jeremiah Lamb climbed to his feet and walked over to a table by the window from which he returned carrying what appeared to be a large ledger.

'Now, sir, your full name, if you please?'

When he'd recorded the few details he required, he held out a slip of paper and said, 'Give this ticket to the clerk. He will explain what we expect of you and arrange for you to be shown where you will eat and so on.'

He rang a small bell on his desk and almost at once the door was flung open by a tall, florid-faced man of about forty, sporting a handsome moustache and a full head of red hair.

'You called, sir?' he bellowed.

'Yes, thank you, Mr Jackson,' said the master. 'This is Mr Emanuel Lazaro who is joining us today. Be so good as to show him around.'

'Very good, sir,' said Jackson. Turning to face Emanuel, he barked, 'You there, look lively and follow me.'

Emanuel followed the man downstairs.

'I will tell you this once and once only, Lazaro,' said Jackson coming to an abrupt halt. 'I'm in charge here. You get that into your thick skull, we'll get along fine. Any problems, you come to me. But I ain't your bleedin' mother, see? When you want to speak with me, you will address me as Mr Jackson, sir. Understand?'

'Yes, sir,' said Emanuel.

'Furthermore, it is your responsibility to acquaint yourself with the rules of this 'ere house. Any breach will be reported to the master and, as like as not, you'll find yourself out of the front door in short order. This ain't no doss house. You obey the rules or you're out. Understand?'

'Yes, sir.'

'You see this bell what's in my hand, Lazaro? This bell is your life. Whenever you hear it, you come running, see? It rings for morning prayers, for breakfast, for dinner and for supper. It rings to get up in the morning and it rings when it's time for bed. Is that understood?'

'Yes, sir.'

'And between meals, the bell means work. If you hear it and it ain't dinner time then it must be work. No work, no food and no bed. Got that?

'Yes, sir.'

'Very well. If you wish to leave the premises for any reason you will first ask me. Same goes if you wish to report sick. You will see me first and only then will you go to matron. If you so much as fart without asking me first, you will go without your dinner. Same goes for missing work, morning prayers and everything else. No work, no food. Do I make myself clear, sir?'

'Yes, sir.'

Jackson led the way along a narrow, dingy corridor, into a large room almost wholly devoid of light where the stale odour of unwashed humanity hung heavily in the still air.

'Your bed is the third on the right. You'll be sharing with three others.'

It was one o'clock before Jackson had finished his introduction to Emanuel's new world. A bell clanged. Almost immediately there came the heavy tramping of feet and, a moment later, a silent horde rounded the corner and hurried towards him. He stood back while they passed, a rag-bag collection of the old and the infirm, most of them seemingly incapable of performing the lightest of tasks.

'You follow those men, Lazaro,' said Jackson, turning to leave. 'Someone will tell you what's what and where to sit. Work begins in half an hour.'

Emanuel tagged on the end and, entering the men's dining hall, made his way to his allotted place. Lunch that day was boiled beef, a chunk of bread and a pint of beer. It was followed immediately by around five hours in the stone yard breaking rocks and stacking them ready for collection. Then came the bell for the evening meal. At eight o'clock precisely, another clang of the bell signalled bedtime.

#

It was a long time before he slept that first night. His body sandwiched between two others, he was unable to move without incurring their kicks and curses. Even had they not objected, the constant coughs and groans of the fifty or so men in the room ensured a restless night.

A week passed, the routine of each day the same as the one before, Emanuel's body aching from the effects of the relentless physical labour demanded of him. He had no time to think. No time to regret the passing of his old life or the shame he'd felt and which had so nearly overwhelmed him. He had settled into a routine of work and sleep that allowed for little else to intrude on his conscious being.

Except the plot.

He tried to forget it. It was no longer his concern. Yet seldom a moment passed when he didn't think about the potential consequences, the death and destruction that would follow the killing of a Protestant of high standing, allegedly by a Catholic, never mind the legacy of hatred and distrust that such an event would give rise to in the minds of ordinary people.

He suddenly remembered something his friend Walter had said to him the last time they'd met. They had been talking about the rabble-rousing MP for West Kent and it had seemed increasingly likely that he was the intended target for the plotters. '… he's due to speak in Hyde Park… next Tuesday,' Walter had said. '… I suppose someone might want to take a shot at him then.'

Emanuel thought quickly. It was Tuesday today, the last Tuesday before Parliament was due to debate the Emancipation Bill. If the assassination was to take place, it would be today. But who to tell? There was little to support the theory. And even if there had been, Emanuel doubted anyone would listen to an inmate of the workhouse, someone who'd lived a lie for the past thirty years. He paused. There *was* someone who might be persuaded to listen. If only there was a way of reaching him.

'I want to see the master,' said Emanuel when, a few moments later, he caught up with Mr Jackson, the porter.

'You got any complaints, you speak to me,' said Jackson.

'No complaints, sir,' said Emanuel. 'I have a private matter to attend to and wish to leave the workhouse for the day.'

'You'll be lucky, cock,' said Jackson. 'There ain't many what ask and fewer still what's given permission.'

Emanuel was soon back. 'The master told me to show this ticket of leave to you, Mr Jackson. I've to be back here by supper time.'

'And I want to see you back on time. I'm warning you, my little Jewish friend, if you's a minute late, you'll answer to me. You understand?'

Leaving the house, Emanuel joined the Whitechapel road before turning south to cross the Highway into Old Gravel Lane. Soon he'd caught sight of the masts of a dozen brigs soaring above the warehouses and shipyards of Wapping and then the tideway itself, flashing and gleaming in the morning sunlight.

He thought about the decision he'd made to seek the help of a man he barely knew, wondering if he'd not made a mistake. For a moment he thought of returning to the workhouse. The plot had not materialised. And the suggestion it was imminent was based on – what? Yet he knew that, however little he might be believed, he could not ignore the possibility that what he feared might come to pass. The risk of doing nothing was too great to ignore.

Reaching the foreshore, Emanuel hailed a passing wherry. 'Woolwich, if you please,' he said.

'Colonel Ramsay, sir?' said Sergeant Candler when, later that morning, Emanuel stood outside the colonel's office at the Woolwich barracks. 'Why, sir, he ain't here, sir.'

'Where is he?' said Emanuel.

'He's on his way to Canterbury, sir. On account of some trouble what's happening there. He left not above two hours since. Most of the regiment went with him. Can I tell the colonel what you wanted him for?'

'No, it's not important. I'll see him some other time.' Emanuel walked to the door, his hopes fading. On a whim he stopped and looked back at the clerk.

'What sort of trouble?' he said. 'Not connected with anything we've spoken about, I trust.'

'No, nothing to do with that, sir. Seems there's been some rioting in the town. Got orders through early this morning, sir. The magistrate down there wanted the regiment's assistance. Seems like it's serious. Colonel said more troops were on their way from Knightsbridge.'

'To Canterbury? Odd place for a riot, is it not?' said Emanuel.

'Funny you should mention it sir,' said Candler. 'Colonel said the same thing. He looked like…'

Emanuel didn't stop to listen, conscious of a terrible premonition that something had gone badly wrong.

#

The tide was against him on the journey back to London, the wherry's progress along the Thames painfully slow. It was, as a result, much later than Emanuel would have wished before he reached the 'passing' stairs at Westminster Bridge.

It hadn't sounded right. Not then and not now. The coincidence had unsettled him. He'd fought against it despite the rising tide of his conviction that he was right. A riot? In Canterbury? It was hardly credible. That wasn't to say there'd never been a riot there. He supposed there must have been at some point in the long history of the town, but he couldn't recall when that might have been. And why now? If the call for the army's assistance had been on any other day, it wouldn't have mattered. But it wasn't any other day. It had come on the day of Fielding's final speech in

Hyde Park. He was popular with the mob. His message of hate chimed with theirs. If there was trouble, if he was to fall victim to the assassin's knife, the army would not be there to prevent the bloodletting that would ensue. The two nearest army units were beyond reach of recall. The mob would seek its own form of justice. There was no doubt many would lose their lives in the process.

The lobby of the Office for the Home Department echoed to the sound of a dozen or so voices. He pushed open the polished mahogany doors and walked across the marble floor to where a man was seated behind a desk.

'I'd like to see someone on a matter of the utmost urgency, if you please,' said Emanuel addressing himself to the bald skull of a man bent over a ledger of sorts. It was a moment or two before the man looked up, his disapproving gaze seeming to take in every detail of Emmanuel's appearance.

'I regret that ain't possible,' said the man, returning to his ledger. 'Not possible at all.'

'You don't understand,' said Emanuel, keeping the irritation from his voice. 'I have information of a serious and urgent nature. It is of the utmost importance that I speak to the Under Secretary. Be so good as to tell me where I might meet the gentleman.'

'Under Secretary?' said the underling. 'You'll be telling me next it's the King what you want to see. Why, I—'

'What seems to be the trouble, Morgan?'

Jones was on his feet before Emanuel could see who had spoken. Behind him was a slim gentleman of about forty, his steel-grey eyes fixed on Emanuel, a silver-topped walking cane in his right hand.

'There's no problem, Sir William. This fellow was just leaving,' said the man behind the desk. 'A Jew, by the looks of him, sir. And from the workhouse, I'll be bound. Got some cock and bull story about an urgent matter what he wants to talk about. I'll have him on his way in two shakes of a lamb's tail, sir.'

'Well done, Jones,' said Sir William, turning away. 'Glad to see you've got everything under control.'

'Mr David Fielding, the MP for West Kent, could well be killed this afternoon,' said Emanuel, his voice raised above the general clatter of the entry foyer.

For a moment there was utter silence as conversations stopped in mid-sentence and faces turned towards him. Sir William fixed Emanuel with a cold stare. He waited for the din of conversation to resume before speaking.

'That is a serious allegation, sir. I trust you are able to substantiate it.'

'I think it to be true,' said Emanuel.

'So you imply,' said Sir William. 'But the government is not in the habit of responding to every piece of unsubstantiated tittle-tattle that is brought to its notice.'

'Mr Fielding is due to speak in Hyde Park in less than an hour,' said Emanuel. 'He will speak against the Emancipation Bill, during the course of which I believe he will be assassinated.'

'And why would anyone do that, pray?' said Sir William, an amused expression curling the edges of his thin mouth.

'I understand there is every prospect the Emancipation Bill will succeed and receive the Royal Assent.'

'Yes, it's possible. What of it?' said Sir William.

'Forgive me, Sir William. I know little of the politics involved but isn't it the case that emancipation would have implications for a large number of gentlemen in Parliament and elsewhere?'

'What is your point, sir?' said Sir William, the smile replaced by an impatient frown. 'I'm a busy man with little time for idle chatter.'

'My point, Sir William, is that emancipation is a toxic subject for many people in this country, including those who wield great power and influence and who do not take kindly to the probable impact of Catholic emancipation on their estates in Ireland, their titles and their very incomes. Do you imagine that such men would be content to allow the Bill to pass into law without a murmur?' said Emanuel.

'Your fears are without foundation, sir,' said Sir William. 'Besides, I note that you have still not produced a shred of evidence in support of your supposition, particularly in relation to Mr Fielding. Indeed, I find your entire argument quite without merit. No, sir, I will hear no more of this fanciful story.'

Emanuel watched Sir William stride away across the hall. He'd wanted to tell him of the sudden deployment of troops from both the Knightsbridge barracks in Hyde Park and the Woolwich barracks on the south side of the Thames, of the supposed reason for their deployment and the doubts expressed by Colonel Ramsay. But he knew the moment had passed. If there had ever been a time when Sir William might have been persuaded of the danger that London was in, it no longer existed. Emanuel had been dismissed, his arguments of no value; certainly of no credibility. He glanced at a clock in the corner of the entrance hall.

Time was running out.

#

The hackney cab sped along Oxford Street as fast as the skeletal old nag in the shafts and the heavy weight of traffic would allow. Emanuel caught sight of a clock, high up on the face of a building. Twenty minutes to two. Just over a quarter of an hour before Fielding was due to speak. The hackney carriage slowed to a halt.

'Can't go any further,' said the driver. 'Seems half of London wants to hear a cully what's talking in Hyde Park.'

Emanuel looked over the driver's shoulder at the solid line of stationary traffic. He could just make out the trees of Hyde Park about two hundred yards ahead.

'I'll get out here,' he said, throwing some coins onto the seat beside him and jumping out.

It was slow going, the mass of bodies hemming him in on all sides. What should have taken no more than five minutes took nearly fifteen.

Crossing Park Lane into Hyde Park, he could see a large crowd formed into a semicircle facing the Uxbridge road. In front of it, a man stood on a large tree stump, stamping his feet as though to test the firmness of the block before stepping down. Others were attempting to keep the crowd from edging towards the stump. Emanuel looked around for Fielding but saw no one who might have fitted the bill.

'No, he ain't here, mate,' said the man who Emanuel had seen carrying the stump. 'You'll have to wait like all the rest.'

'I have to speak to him,' said Emanuel. 'Please inform him as soon he gets here. It's important.'

'Can't do that, cock,' said the man. 'He's too busy for all that. It's the same every time he speaks. Folk want to tell him their troubles.'

'Just tell him. Please.'

The man shook his head and moved away.

Emanuel looked round at the faces of the crowd. He knew from experience how subtle were the early signs of trouble – the fragile calm that couldn't last, a sullen and hostile stare, the low rumble of discontent. He had always possessed an instinctive awareness of danger, a perfect understanding of the changing moods of the mob. But that was of no help now. It wasn't the mob from whom the trouble would come. Not initially. Fielding was, after all, one of them. What he said was what they believed. If trouble came it would be because he, or the principles he espoused, had been attacked. Emanuel knew he had to identify the culprit before he could act. He had to watch for the telltale signs that might give the malcontent away, the classic signs that were hard to hide.

A sudden roar of the crowd signalled the arrival of the man they'd come to hear, the MP for West Kent, Mr David Fielding. Emanuel followed the eager stares of those around him. A tall, bony-faced man of around forty had stepped nimbly onto the stump, and was waving to the crowd.

Emanuel turned away. His task seemed impossible. He didn't know what to expect, where the attack would come from or what form it would take. And what if he were to see the developing threat? He belonged to a race of people shunned by a society that viewed his physical appearance as proof of his dishonesty, a man whose word meant nothing. Any warning from him would, at best, be ignored. And, at worst, he might be blamed.

He looked back at the speaker. Behind him lay a strip of parkland of perhaps twenty or thirty yards wide sprinkled with around a dozen trees – chestnuts, mainly, with the occasional plane tree here and there. Over to the left he could see a curricle, a handsome pair of greys harnessed to its single shaft. It could only be Fielding's, its driver seemingly asleep, his hat pulled down over his forehead. Beyond it lay the road to Uxbridge, empty now, but would, in a few hours' time, be filled with farmers' carts homeward bound from the markets of London. To the right of the speaker and at some distance from him stood a group of men. Emanuel recognised them as the marshals he'd seen earlier. It occurred to him the attack, if there was to be one, had to come from there, from behind the speaker, where no crowds stood and the risk of capture was at its lowest.

Emanuel's gaze returned to the curricle. Something was wrong. He stared at it, wondering what could have set his nerves on edge. 'Parliament must… the will of the people…' Fielding's words drifted across the heads of the crowd. 'Popery has no place…'

Emanuel's thoughts moved on. It worried him that he'd yet to see Bristow. Or, for that matter, any of the men from the barracks he had expected. He glanced at Fielding, his fist punching the air as if to emphasise some point or other. 'Union with Ireland… no place… must stop…'

Fielding waved to acknowledge the roar of his followers, his Adam's apple sliding up and down his throat, his messianic eyes staring, trance-like, over the heads of his supporters. '… no to popery… must fight…'

Emanuel looked back at the curricle. The driver seemed different, somehow younger than a few moments ago. He shook his head. He was imagining things. Then he saw a small blue ribbon tied about the man's wrist. Emanuel had seen such an adornment on a man's wrist only once before. He struggled to remember where.

Suddenly he knew. It was all he needed.

Chapter 60

Bristow had lain awake for much of the night. It was the waiting he found difficult. He'd always acted on impulse, reacting to the circumstances in which he found himself. He preferred it that way, where thought of the consequences played no part. The trouble came when time was allowed to intrude. Then his mind would fret and he would consider the possibility of failure. It was this which he feared most of all, for with failure came consequences. Yet these factors had not been at the forefront of his mind in the small hours of the night. It had been something else entirely.

The message had been waiting for him when he arrived back at the old glue manufactory on Gun Lane the previous evening. He barely knew Sir Peter. On the occasions when they'd been in each other's company, there had always been others present and few words ever passed between them. It was, therefore, a matter of some concern that Sir Peter's note – read to him by one of the few in the building capable of such a feat of literacy – had required his immediate attendance at Sir Peter's home in Cheapside. The interview had been short and to the point, Sir Peter's words still resounding in his head.

'*It appears our plans may be known,*' Sir Peter had said. '*My sources tell me that the person concerned is a Papist priest. While my information goes no further, I'm inclined to think the man referred to is the Jew who, I believe, is well known to you, a man I believe you were asked to deal with.*

'That villain knows nothing,' he'd replied, but even as he'd uttered the words he'd known them to be untrue. He'd been warned someone had been asking questions. Looking back, he realised it could only have been Mr Emanuel. There had been too many coincidences for it to have been anyone else.

Bristow chewed on his lower lip. He was standing on the north side of the Uxbridge road, the crowd in the park opposite growing more noisy by the minute. He barely noticed, his anger threatening to overwhelm him as he thought again of his meeting with Sir Peter. He knew he should have dealt with Emanuel a long time ago. He didn't need to be told.

He leaned against a wall bordering one of the big houses that overlooked the park. Directly opposite was the man who was to die. Bristow studied him for a moment. Killing him didn't seem to make any sense. From the little he'd heard, the cully believed in the same things he believed in. He shrugged. It made no difference to him either way. His eyes swept over the crowd and settled on the curricle parked under a tree. It wouldn't be long now.

Suddenly he was aware of having missed something. He looked back at the grinning faces of the crowd without knowing what he was supposed to find – until he saw him, his face partially hidden by others.

#

The last time they'd met, it had nearly cost Emanuel his life. He could remember little of the encounter in Furnace Street, except the sight of the man's outstretched hands encircling his neck – and the blue ribbon around his wrist. It had struck him as odd, even then, that a man should choose to wear such an adornment. Now that same man was seated in a curricle in Hyde Park, a matter of yards from where the MP for West Kent was addressing the crowd.

Emanuel edged towards him, step by careful step, and wondered at his own insanity. The fellow was probably armed and certainly dangerous. As like as not there were others close by, ready to help. It wasn't too late to draw back. He was still close to the crowd. No one would blame him were he to leave the MP to his fate. He had done all that could reasonably be expected of him. It was hardly his fault that his warnings had not been taken seriously.

It was at that exact moment the man turned towards him. Too late, Emanuel realised he'd been staring at the fellow. He looked away as casually as he could, feeling the man's gaze still on him. Ten, twenty seconds passed. He risked another glance. The man's attention had switched back to the MP, his right hand moving under his coat as though reaching for something. Emanuel was too far away to see what it was but he could guess. He wondered if he could reach him before his presence was detected. It was unlikely.

A slight movement to his left distracted him and he was in time to see the tail of a man's coat disappearing behind a tree. It was nothing. He ignored it; had other matters to deal with. He swung his attention back to the man on the curricle. The cully was holding a pistol and seemed to be priming the weapon.

There was, for Emanuel, no time for thought or consideration of the risks involved. If he hoped to prevent the shooting of the MP for West Kent and everything that would follow, he had to act. And do it now. Elbowing his way clear of the crowd, he sprinted across the open ground that lay between him and the parked curricle. Thirty yards became twenty-five, then twenty. He saw the man raise the barrel of his pistol, his head cocked to one side, his finger tightening on the trigger. Another second, two at the most, and it would all be over. The roar of the crowd would surely drown the explosive noise of the gun. In the confusion that followed, the gunman would slip away unnoticed.

He was still running when he saw the hammer on the pistol being jerked back. A second later it had begun its forward motion, striking the metal plate in a shower of sparks. He was dimly conscious of the roar of the gun, the spit of flame and the plume of smoke that came from its mouth. He saw the crowd scattering, running from the danger they hadn't seen. Over by the tree stump, Mr David Fielding, the MP for West Kent stood looking about him in a state of shock. He was nursing a bloody left arm.

The second explosion came quickly and almost immediately Emanuel felt a soft breeze against his cheek as a lead ball shaved past his head. He turned to see a pall of white smoke drifting across the park. Of the man responsible, there was no trace. There didn't need to be. It had taken him a minute or so to remember whose coat it had been that he'd seen disappearing behind a tree. And it wasn't the first time Bristow had tried to kill him.

From somewhere close by he heard the sound of a whip crack and knew he'd lost the curricle and its driver. Shaken by what had happened he could do little but watch the two-wheeled carriage race towards the Uxbridge road.

'Was Mr Fielding hurt at all?' he asked one of the stewards, a couple of minutes later.

'Aye,' said the man. 'But the hurt's not serious. The cully will live.'

'Thankee,' said Emanuel, moving away, his thoughts returning to the red-coated figure he'd seen ducking behind a tree. There were thousands of men in London who still wore the red coats of their former days in the army. But not many would consider it necessary to duck behind a tree to avoid being seen. In fact, Emanuel could think of only one.

He glanced at a clock mounted on the side of a house in the Uxbridge road. He needed to get back to the workhouse or face the prospect of being refused future requests to be allowed out.

And he needed that if he was to get to the bottom of what had happened.

Chapter 61

It was several days before Emanuel felt able to ask for another leave of absence. That it was granted owed more to the good humour of the master on that particular morning than any perceived merit in Emanuel's case. It was, if Mr Jackson, the porter, was to be believed, unheard of in the whole history of England for anyone to be granted a second ticket of leave so soon after the first one.

'I'm watching you, Lazaro,' Mr Jackson had said. 'If you ain't back before two this very afternoon, I'll chop your bleedin' legs off. Are you hearing me, Lazaro?'

Emanuel wasn't equipped for the role of investigator. He never had been. Nor, unless he were to include the frequent occasions on which he'd been subjected to the casual beatings of passers-by, could he claim any familiarity with the society of violent men. But a line had been crossed. The attempted murder of the MP in circumstances designed to suggest the involvement of Catholics was, for Emanuel, a step too far and one he was going to have to deal with.

Twenty-five minutes after leaving Whitechapel he'd reached his destination.

Bow Street was busy with the comings and goings of the market porters of Covent Garden, as Emanuel approached a white stone building directly opposite the Theatre Royal. Passing in through the front door he found himself in a large, stone-flagged hall at the end of which a man sat perched at a high desk. Emanuel approached him.

'I've come to see Mr Higgins,' he said.

'Higgins?' said the man, looking down a list of names in front of him. 'He ain't on duty. Not for another hour. Take a seat over there if you want to wait.'

Emanuel walked over to a long bench set against the outer wall and on which a half-dozen others were already seated. The hour passed quickly.

'Mr Lazaro?' Emanuel looked up at the sound of a man's voice.

'Yes.'

'My name's Higgins. I'm with the Bow Street Horse Patrol. I understand you wanted to see me?'

The officer led the way up a flight of stairs to a small room on the second floor. It was sparsely furnished with a small table and two chairs. A window overlooked the street and the Theatre Royal beyond.

'Now, sir,' said Higgins, taking up a position by the door. 'I take it you wanted to see about what happened in Hyde Park a few days ago.'

'Yes, but how did you know?' said Emanuel.

'Nothing to worry about. I'm sure we can clear up any concerns I may have and then you'll be on your way.'

'Concerns?' said Emanuel, staring at the tall figure by the door. 'What concerns might they be?'

'I understand you were present in Hyde Park when an attempt was made on the life of Mr Fielding, the MP.'

'Yes, I was.'

'What were you doing there, if I might ask?' said Higgins.

'I believed there was to be an attempt to kill Mr Fielding. I wanted to try and prevent it.'

'Alone, sir?'

'I had no choice. I attempted to tell the Under Secretary of State for the Home Department of my concerns but he chose not to believe me.'

'How did you come by the information?'

'About the intended assassination?' said Emanuel. 'There had been rumours circulating for some time. Unfortunately that's all they were so I was unable to inform anyone in authority.'

'When you were in Hyde Park did you see anyone acting suspiciously?' said Higgins.

'Yes, I saw the man shoot at Mr Fielding.'

'D'you know him?'

'I've seen him before. I believe him to be a soldier based at the Woolwich barracks. I regret I don't know his name.'

'But you'd recognise him if you saw him again?'

'Yes.'

'Did you see anyone else?' said Higgins.

Emanuel hesitated. 'I think I might've seen a man named Erasmus Bristow. I can't be certain.'

'Bristow, you say? What can you tell me about him?'

'I've known him most of his life,' said Emanuel. 'But until recently, I'd not seen him for a number of years while he served in the army.'

'So if he were to see you there would be no question of him failing to recognise you?'

'None at all,' said Emanuel. 'Is there a reason why you ask?'

'What was this man, Bristow, doing?'

'Nothing in particular,' said Emanuel. 'I mention him only because I had understood him to be involved in the planning of the attack on Mr Fielding.'

For a long minute Higgins said nothing, his head tilted back, his eyes closed.

'I have already spoken to a number of potential witnesses, including Mr Bristow,' he said, opening his eyes and looking directly at Emanuel, his manner like that of a cat playing with its prey. 'He has admitted being in Hyde Park on the day of the shooting and says he was there to listen to Mr Fielding, as were many others. He told me he had seen you at Hyde Park in the immediate vicinity of the man who fired upon Mr Fielding. In his opinion you appeared to know the suspect.'

'That's simply untrue,' said Emanuel, conscious that his voice had risen an octave. 'Why, if—'

'He has further alleged,' said Higgins, holding up the palm of one hand for silence, 'that three weeks ago he saw you in Green Park kneeling over the body of a gentleman named Grenville. He says you had a bloody knife in your hand. Is that gentleman's name familiar to you?'

'Yes,' said Emanuel.

'Perhaps I might ask you what you were doing and how it was you came to be seen with a knife in your hand.'

'I'd be happy to,' said Emanuel. 'Earlier in the evening Mr Grenville had fought with another man, both of whom were seriously injured. The other man later told me what had happened and I went to give Mr Grenville such assistance as I was able. That was when Bristow arrived. I subsequently took Mr Grenville to hospital. As to the knife, I believe it belonged to Grenville. I found it lying beside him on the grass.'

'Do you know the name of the other person?' said Higgins. 'The one you say was involved in the fight with Grenville.'

'I regret I am not at liberty to say.'

'Would you, sir, care to tell me why?'

'I am – I was – a Roman Catholic priest. I am not permitted to repeat what others say to me in confidence. All I can do is tell you what happened.'

'Doubtless you are aware Mr Grenville is now dead,' said Higgins. 'He was stabbed at some point after his arrival at the accident hospital. You are, apart from the hospital staff, the last person known to have seen Grenville alive. Is there anything you can tell me about how that might have happened?'

'I regret, sir, I cannot help you but you may wish to speak to the night porter at the hospital and ask him about what he saw late on the night of Grenville's death. You may also…' said Emanuel, his voice trailing away in mid-sentence. He'd wanted to tell Higgins about his meeting with Willing Annie on the path to Mile End. But he couldn't. Not without betraying her confidence in him and, in the process, exposing her to the risk of another beating from Bristow. He might have been tempted if he'd thought Annie could be persuaded to give evidence against Bristow but he knew that was highly unlikely. He tried a different approach. 'You might like to ask Bristow where he was that night.'

'I know where he was,' said Higgins. 'He was here, answering my questions.'

In the silence that followed, Emanuel could hear the sound of his own breath and feel the tightness in his chest. He was suspected of stabbing Grenville in Green Park; perhaps even a suspect in the case of the attempted assassination of the MP. For every answer he'd provided, there'd been another explanation, one that was unfavourable to his cause.

'Let me return, for a moment, to the supposed plot to murder the MP, Mr Fielding,' said Higgins. 'You say that your information was based on rumours. What were those rumours that you felt to so confident of your cause?'

'It began, sir, with the death of a man named Collins whose body was recovered from the tideway in February this year. It was rumoured he'd been turned off for talking about a plot to discredit Roman Catholicism in this country. It was to involve the murder of a leading Anglican in circumstances that would suggest the atrocity had been committed by a Catholic. The expectation was that serious public disorder would result and prevent the passage through Parliament of the Emancipation Bill.'

'And that was it?' said Higgins.

'Not quite,' said Emanuel, taking from his coat pocket the scrap of paper and handing it to the officer. 'I believe that that represents the corner of Hyde Park where the shooting took place. It was found in the home of Sir Peter Westlake shortly after he and Grenville had been heard discussing the need to stop the Emancipation Bill from becoming law.'

'How did you come by this, sir?' said Higgins, glancing over the top of the sheet of paper.

'It was given to me by one of Sir Peter's servants,' said Emanuel. 'A young woman by the name of Miss Sara Payton.'

'Ah yes, Miss Sara.' Higgins rubbed his chin and appeared to consider the point. 'Would that be the same Miss Sara who was subsequently dismissed by Sir Peter for dishonesty?'

'Yes, but—'

'Do you think it likely, sir,' said Higgins, 'that the testimony of a servant dismissed in those circumstances would be believed by a jury? Would the jury not be more likely to regard her evidence of where and how she found this paper as self-serving; the actions of someone bent on revenge?'

'You are, sir, to consider,' said Emanuel, angry at the direction the questions had taken, 'that the map was found and given to me well before Miss Sara was dismissed for her alleged dishonesty.'

'Are you able,' said Higgins, his tone noticeably less harsh, 'to tell me of anything else on which I might be able to question Sir Peter about his possible involvement in the attempt on Mr Fielding's life?'

Emanuel thought of what he knew of the relationship between Sir Peter and Grenville and of Grenville with both Bristow and the deceased Collins. He thought of what the Revd John Rippon, the Baptist minister, had told him of Sir Peter's extreme views and his periodic meetings at Garraway's, the coffee house on Cornhill with Bristow and others. And yet when it came down to it, he had nothing but the existence of the map to link Sir Peter to any supposed plot. Even the evidence of his meetings at the coffee house on Cornhill had been lost with the death of Rob Smith, the waiter and former soldier.

'I regret it extremely, sir, but I can think of nothing,' said Emanuel.

Higgins didn't speak for a moment, his hands motionless on the table, his eyes seeming to bore into Emanuel's skull.

'You see, Mr Emanuel, the existence of this map,' said Higgins, tapping the piece of paper with the tip of his index finger, 'has another explanation which it would be open to Sir Peter to put forward if the matter were ever to come to trial. He could suggest that far from the map originating in his home, it was in fact produced by you or someone known to you as part of a Papist plot to murder Mr Fielding and deflect the blame; the exact opposite to the picture you have painted.'

Higgins rubbed his face with the palms of both hands before continuing.

'You must understand, Mr Emanuel, that I neither believe nor disbelieve what you say. I merely put to you the questions and explanations that anyone charged with the murder of Mr Grenville or the incident in Hyde Park might wish to put.'

Emanuel stared at the officer in disbelief. The situation was unreal. There was nothing he could say that would make any difference.

#

When Emanuel arrived back at the workhouse later that afternoon, Mr Jackson, the porter, was waiting for him by the front entrance.

'You're late, Lazaro. The master is wanting for to see you,' he said, a malevolent smirk on his face. 'Don't reckon we'll be seeing you again after today. Best you get yourself down to his room quick as you like.'

Emanuel barely heard him, his mind on the questioning he'd been subjected to at Bow Street and the inferences drawn from his answers. Was he now to be regarded as a suspect in Grenville's murder? Was Bristow to be believed while his own voice carried no weight? Had Willing Annie been wrong about seeing Bristow near the hospital on the night Grenville died? And who was the person the night porter had seen wandering the corridors of the hospital that same night, if not Bristow? The questions raced around his brain looking for answers that refused to be found.

'You wished, sir, to see me,' said Emanuel as he stepped into the master's room a minute or so later.

'Indeed, I do, sir,' said Mr Jeremiah Lamb, looking up from a plate of oysters he was in the process of eating. 'I gather from Mr Jackson that you were late returning this afternoon. I remind you, sir, that you are to abide by the rules of this establishment or face the consequences.'

'But—'

'No, sir. I do not wish to hear your explanation. Good day to you, sir.'

Emanuel hardly slept that night. The following morning he was again set to work breaking rocks and had little time for his private thoughts. It was lunchtime before he was able to give some consideration to his future.

'This won't do at all, sir,' said the master when Emanuel had made his request. 'You are fed, clothed and have a bed to sleep in. If you fall ill, you have someone to care for you. All of this is at no charge to you, sir. What we demand in return is your honest labour. I will allow your absence just once more, but if you are again late returning, I regret you will be required to leave the workhouse and fend for yourself. Do I make myself clear, sir?'

Emanuel swallowed hard. He had no illusions about the quality of life that would await him on the far side of these walls. The memory of its hardships were indelibly printed on his mind. But he knew he'd have to accept the risk. He had to establish his innocence.

Or face the consequences.

Chapter 62

Sir Peter Westlake dabbed his forehead with a large silk handkerchief, removed the glass stopper from the decanter and poured himself a generous measure of whisky. It was his third drink in the ten minutes since his butler had delivered the message. He'd been expecting a call from Higgins since the unsuccessful attempt on Fielding's life.

He glanced over to his desk. The copies of the letters he'd got from the Ordinary at Newgate lay on top of a pile of other papers. He wondered if the moment had not arrived when it would be sensible to show them to the officer. But then again, perhaps not. The moment passed.

'Mr Higgins of the Bow Street Horse Patrol to see you, Sir Peter,' said the butler, standing aside and ushering the new arrival into the library.

'How may I help you on this occasion, Mr Higgins?' said Sir Peter, reluctantly waving his visitor to a chair and feeling a great deal more nervous than his outward appearance would indicate.

'I assume, sir,' said Higgins, 'you're aware of the attempt on the life of Mr David Fielding, the MP, yesterday afternoon?'

'Yes, of course,' said Sir Peter. 'In Hyde Park, was it not? I was relieved to discover my colleague was unharmed.'

'Quite,' said Higgins. 'But I believe, sir, you may be in a position to help me in regard to the matter.'

'I will, of course, do all I can,' said Sir Peter.

'Does the name Erasmus Bristow mean anything to you?'

Sir Peter's nostrils flared a fraction. He got up from his chair and walked to the fireplace. 'Bristow, you say? No, can't say I know the fellow. Who is he?'

'Are you quite sure the name is unfamiliar to you, sir?' said Higgins.

'Damn your insolence, Higgins, I've given you my answer. I'd appreciate it if we could move on.'

'Yes, of course, sir. I do beg your pardon,' said Higgins. 'It's just that this man Bristow has made certain allegations that I am duty bound to investigate. I was aware that he'd recently been released from Newgate and wanted to learn more about his background. You can imagine my surprise, Sir Peter, when I discovered that you, too, had shown an interest in Bristow and had been provided with copies of letters he had had written shortly before he'd been due to hang. May I ask, sir, why you asked for copies of letters written by a man you don't know?'

'I—' stuttered Sir Peter. 'I was concerned about what I believed to be scurrilous allegations being levelled against the son of a good friend of mine.'

'That would be Lord Ardingleigh's son, the Honourable James Grenville, would it, sir?'

'Yes.'

'What a pity you chose not to mention the letters earlier.'

'I don't see that letters about an incident in Ireland two years ago are relevant to anything,' said Sir Peter.

'You might be right, Sir Peter,' said Higgins. 'Except that the letter appears to offer the person to whom it is addressed the opportunity to avenge himself of the death of his wife. We tend to frown on things like that, sir.'

'I was going to show it to you,' said Sir Peter, rubbing the palms of his hands together. 'It must have slipped my mind. I've been very busy at the House.'

'That would be the House of Commons, would it, sir?'

'Yes.'

'What were you doing at St George's Hospital on the night Mr Grenville was killed?'

'I wanted to offer Mr Grenville my support,' said Sir Peter. 'How did you know I was there?'

'There are a number of people I've spoken to, including Mr Bristow,' said Higgins. 'He appears to know a great deal about you, sir. Strange, that. Nothing you want to say to me about him, is there?'

'I've nothing more to say to you, Higgins. I find your tone offensive,' said Sir Peter.

'I regret it extremely, sir, but I am obliged to take note of what others have told me. The fact is, sir, Bristow has further alleged that you and the late Mr Grenville had attempted to persuade him to join a conspiracy against the life of Mr Fielding.'

'Lies, lies, all lies,' said Sir Peter, jabbing a finger at Higgins. 'I've told you, I don't know the fellow.'

'That's quite all right, sir. Nothing to get upset about,' said Higgins. 'Moving on, sir, I understand you and the late Mr Grenville may not have seen eye to eye on the matter. There's a suggestion that you argued. Is that true, sir? Did you fall out with the young gentleman? Was that the real reason you visited him in hospital on the night he died? To settle the matter, so to speak?'

'What are you suggesting, Higgins?' said Sir Peter. 'That I killed him in order to silence him?'

'Did you, sir? Kill him, I mean?'

'No, I didn't,' shouted Sir Peter, a line of perspiration forming above his eyebrows.

'Nevertheless,' said Higgins. 'I'm satisfied you were present in the ward of St George's hospital at or about the time of the murder. I'm also satisfied you have information that could be useful to my enquiries into the attempt on Mr Fielding's life in Hyde Park. I must therefore ask you to come with me to Bow Street for further questioning.'

'What…' said Sir Peter, the colour draining from his face.

Chapter 63

Emanuel saw her almost as soon as he reached the Highway. She wore the same forced grimace on her bony face he'd seen before, her arms folded, her thin cotton dress hitched above her knees. She was shivering in the cool breeze of the morning as he approached.

'Hello, Annie,' he said.

She turned to look at him, the forced grin of a moment ago replaced with a wide smile of pleasure.

'Hello, Mr Emanuel,' she beamed. 'I hears you's been stirring things up a treat, what with all the hoo-ha in Green Park. Bristow is proper pissed and no mistake. He's been like a bear with a sore head these past few days. Never seen him so bad. And that's saying something.'

'It's about him I wanted to talk to you, Annie,' said Emanuel. 'Can you spare me a minute?'

Willing Annie's face fell momentarily and she peered at the crowds swirling past her, a hint of regret in her eyes.

'I got a living to earn, Mr Emanuel. I don't want another flogging from Bristow on account of I ain't earned enough.'

'I won't be long,' said Emanuel. 'Did Bristow ever talk to you about what happened that night in Green Park?'

'Aye, he told me.'

'And the following night? According to the officer, Mr Higgins, Bristow was with him. D'you remember that?'

Annie nodded, her eyes widening. 'He said it were nothing. 'He said he'd been to see the officer. He weren't best pleased about that. Reckoned if he got the chance he'd see the cully face down in the Fleet.'

'Did he come straight home from Bow Street?'

'Can't say, Mr Emanuel,' said Annie, her eyes again sweeping the crowds in the Highway. 'I ain't got no way of telling. You must leave me, Mr Emanuel. If Bristow sees me talking to you, I'll be for another beating.'

'Of course,' said Emanuel, following the girl's searching gaze. 'I've kept you too long. Forgive me.'

They parted, the girl surveying the crowd, a rigid smile returning to her pouted lips, her eyes hard and glistening. Her exchange with Emanuel might never have taken place. He watched her for a minute or two before turning away. Was it possible that Bristow had not only seen the officer at Bow Street but had had the time to make his way home via the accident hospital on the corner of Hyde Park? Certainly, the night porter at St George's had seen someone on the night of the murder wandering through the hospital long after the public should have left. *I sees someone coming down the stairs. It were late… I calls out to him… He saw me and were away without so much as a word*, the man had said. It could have been Bristow. But then again, the light had not been good and the possibility of a mistake was high.

#

Walter was waiting for him with news of Sir Peter's arrest when Emanuel returned to the workhouse later that morning.

'For what?' said Emanuel, a stunned look on his face.

'Not entirely sure,' said Walter. 'But it seems there was a falling-out between him and Grenville and things were said which, in hindsight, they might have come to regret.'

'What sort of things?'

'I don't know but whatever it was, I gather it was serious. There's some suggestion Sir Peter was at the hospital the night Grenville met his end and took the opportunity to kill him. I've heard he's likely to be charged with the death.'

'I doubt it was Sir Peter,' said Emanuel. 'He might have been on the ward that evening but the people I spoke to are sure he left with all the other visitors at around nine o'clock. There would have been no opportunity for him to do anything to Grenville. Of course, he might have returned later but…' Emanuel paused, shrugging his shoulders. 'It just doesn't quite fit. Why do it? Grenville was a dying man.'

'That could be said of whoever did kill him,' said Walter.

'Yes, I suppose you're right,' said Emanuel. He glanced back at the door of the workhouse from where he could see the lowering figure of Mr Jackson, the porter, watching him. 'I have to go but let me know what happens about Sir Peter, will you?'

After lunch, Emanuel was back in the stone yard and had little time or energy for the thoughts that swirled about his exhausted mind. It was clear to him that while Sir Peter had been arrested in connection with Grenville's death, he himself had some way to go before he could establish his innocence.

But how? There was no question of involving young Teeling in the matter. The Irishman had spoken in the belief that his confession to the stabbing would never be repeated and Emanuel was not about to betray that trust. Nor could he expect Sara to come forward in support of his alibi. He needed time to think. And time was the one thing he didn't have; not while he remained an inmate of the workhouse.

He knew then he would have to leave.

Chapter 64

Sara looked out onto the crowded yard of the Talbot Inn on Borough High Street where a coach was being made ready to leave, the noise and bustle of activity floating in through the open window. She could hear the clatter of hooves as the horses were backed between the shafts, the jingle of harnesses and the shouts of the porters. She watched as the passengers were hurried to their places, their luggage stowed and small urchins scattered with a wave of the ostler's hand. It reminded her of her childhood when she would sometimes go with her father to meet the incoming coach from London and carry back the mail to his lordship's house in Norfolk.

She turned back into the room as other, darker memories crowded her mind. For the most part she managed to keep such thoughts at bay. But it was at night, as she slept, that the dreams would come and she'd be forced to live again the events that had threatened to overwhelm her. A voice interrupted her thoughts, someone calling her name. She walked to the door and peered over the landing rails.

'Someone's asking for you, Miss Sara,' said one of the young porters looking up at her from the foot of the stairs. 'I told him to wait in the taproom. Didn't give no name.'

Sara smiled with relief. Teeling was back. She'd had no word from him in several days and had begun to wonder if he'd grown tired of her company and had moved away, perhaps to Ireland. It wouldn't have surprised her if he had. He'd lived in the hourly expectation of being arrested and charged with Grenville's murder. The strain had been intolerable for both of them and had torn away at the delicate fabric of their relationship. They had argued and he'd left.

Sara ran down the stairs and stopped at the bottom while she patted her hair and smoothed her dress. The taproom was crowded – and noisy. Sara searched for the familiar face.

'Sara?'

She spun round to see a middle-aged man looking at her, his grey wig askew, his worn and filthy clothing hanging loosely about an emaciated frame, his face and hands encrusted with grime.

'Mr Emanuel?' said Sara, her hand flying to her mouth.

'Forgive me. I'd not meant to frighten you,' said Emanuel. 'Is there somewhere we can talk?'

She nodded and, without a word, turned to walk out of the room. Emanuel followed as she led the way across the yard and into one of the storerooms, the air suddenly filled with the warm scent of hay and polished leather. She turned to face him, a worried frown creasing her forehead.

'Is it Teeling you wanted to talk to me about? Has something happened to him?' she said.

'I've been looking for him,' said Emanuel. 'I was hoping you could tell me where he was.'

Sara shook her head and sank back against the bales of hay.

'There were a place we stayed after we left your old room in Farmer Street,' she said. 'It were in Gilbert Street, in the St Giles Rookery. It were the only place he could think of but after a few days I left and got myself work here at the Talbot. We saw each other almost every day but I could see he were worried. It was then he told me he reckoned he were going to be hanged for the murder of Mr Grenville. There weren't nothing I could say to put his mind at rest. He got more and more fearful and we fought. I didn't see him for a day or two so I went to his room in the Rookery but there weren't nobody what could help me. He'd gone, Mr Emanuel.'

'And you haven't seen him since?' said Emanuel.

'No.'

'If he thinks there's a warrant out for his arrest, he's probably in hiding somewhere,' said Emanuel.

'But he didn't do it, Mister Emanuel,' said Sara. 'They fought, right enough, but he didn't kill Grenville. You know that, Mr Emanuel.'

'It's not what I know. It's what the Crown thinks it can prove that matters,' said Emanuel. 'They don't know who fought with Grenville in Green Park. They only know that someone did. They are looking at anyone who might have had a reason to want to kill him. Sooner or later they might learn about Grenville's actions in Ireland and will find out about the murder of Teeling's wife. When that happens they'll want to talk to Teeling but not before.'

'He were in your old room,' said Sara. 'You saw him there yourself. He were hurt bad and could scarce sit up. How could he have done for Grenville when he were in that condition?'

Emanuel didn't answer. He couldn't. Not without pointing out that Teeling had, despite his injuries, walked from Green Park to Shadwell. He couldn't tell her the Crown would probably suggest he was not only capable of making the journey again but would have had a powerful motive for wishing Grenville dead. Nor could they fail to be interested in the part he might have played in the death of George Collins, the man whose body was found in Limehouse Dock.

'What can be done, Mr Emanuel?' said Sara, getting up from the hay bale and pacing distractedly up and down the storeroom.

'I'll try and find him,' said Emanuel. 'After that we'll see what can be done.'

#

Force of habit took Emanuel along Wapping Street, past the dock where Collins's body had been brought ashore, all those months ago, and along Narrow Street towards Limehouse. It was familiar territory for him, a place from which many of his old congregation had been drawn. He felt safe here, amongst the Irish Catholic community, protected from the kicks and slaps that were his daily fare elsewhere in London. Familiar faces first stared and then, when recognition finally dawned, smiled their greetings and briefly passed the time of day.

At moments like this, he would often think back on his final hours at the Whitechapel Workhouse. 'Once you leave here,' Mr Jeremiah Lamb had said, 'the circumstances under which you would be permitted to return are a matter for the parish. I could not say what their decision might be but I might hazard a guess that they might wish to hear my views. I have to tell you, sir, they would not be beneficial to your case.'

He put the thoughts behind him. Several weeks had passed since he'd seen Sara at the Talbot Inn on Borough High Street and still he'd been unable to find any news of Teeling. Nobody had seen or heard from him since the first few days after he'd moved away from the rookery at St Giles, his behaviour increasingly that of a hunted animal as word spread of his supposed killing of the Hon. James Grenville. Emanuel might have searched with greater vigour had he not faced his own demons in the shape of Mr Higgins of the Bow Street Horse Patrol. The almost daily questioning about the Grenville affair had left him with little enthusiasm for his search for Teeling. It was a relief when the officer had finally conceded that he might have been wrong.

Emanuel turned away from the tideway and headed up Rope Maker's Fields past groups of women each sitting astride a pail of blackened water into which threadbare rags were plunged and scrubbed and plunged again, their hands the colour of chalk from constant exposure to water, their faces pitted with sores and blue-black bruises. They stopped their chatter for a moment or two, the abrasive, deep-throated sound of their voices stilled as they watched him go. He'd turned a corner into King Street before he heard the sound of running feet behind him.

'Will it be you, Father?' asked a breathless young boy, his face a mask of coal dust, his shirt torn and open at the chest, his trousers cut off below the knee.

'Hello, Tommy,' said Emanuel. 'Were you looking for me?'

'Me ma told me she'd seen you. She…' His voice faltered and he looked at his feet as though embarrassed. Emanuel guessed the boy knew of his fall from grace.

'And how is your mother?' he asked.

'She said to be remembered to you,' said the boy. 'She said to tell you they found Henry. Leastways, someone saw a poster what had his description on it.'

'Henry Teeling?' said Emanuel, a knot forming in the pit of his stomach.

'Aye, him,' said the boy. 'Me ma says they found his body in the tideway, close to Blackfriars Bridge, a week since.'

#

It took Emanuel close on an hour to walk to the dead house on St Andrew's Hill in the City, not far from the church of the same name.

'He's been here a while,' said the attendant, hobbling up the short path that led off the street to a small, windowless building. 'Inquest is tomorrow. Don't make no sense to me. I could tell them the cause of death without all this bother.'

'I heard he'd drowned,' said Emanuel.

'Drowned, be buggered,' said the attendant. 'His throat were cut. Plain as day, it is.'

The old man reached for his keys and unlocked the heavy wooden door of the building, an overpowering stench of rotting flesh emanating from within.

'Mind the flies,' said the old man, pulling open the door and stepping to one side as a black cloud of the insects flew out.

'Know any of them, do you?' asked the man, indicating the half-dozen cadavers lying next to one another on a marble slab that stretched down the centre of the building.

Emanuel held a handkerchief to his mouth and nose as he walked slowly past each body. Nearing the end, he stopped and looked at the grey, immobile face of Henry Teeling. He let his gaze travel down to the throat where a streak of mottled flesh had risen, wave like, from beneath the skin.

'That your friend, is it? Only you's the first to come and see him.' The attendant's voice cut into Emanuel's thoughts.

'What? Yes, yes, this is my friend,' said Emanuel, turning back for a last look.

'Coroner will want to see you at the inquest.'

'Yes, of course,' said Emanuel, his mind elsewhere. He nodded at the wound to the throat. 'Does anyone know who did this to him?'

'No,' said the man. 'But I'll you this, the villain what's done that has done it before. Many times, I reckon.'

#

The inquest into the death of Henry Arthur Teeling, an Irishman, aged about twenty-five, of no fixed address, took place in the Bricklayer's Arms close to Puddle Dock in the City of London. It didn't take long. The jury, having been instructed by the coroner, returned a verdict of unlawful killing by a person or persons unknown.

Emanuel crossed the Thames into Borough High Street and turned in through the arch of the Talbot Inn. He found Sara in the servants' quarters at the far end of the stable yard. She'd been resting but must have seen his approach because she came out to greet him, her smile of welcome fading as she saw the sombre look on his face.

'He's dead, isn't he?' she said, her face paling.

'Yes,' said Emanuel. 'I went to see him. There's no doubt it's him.'

'What happened?' she asked, her hands covering her lips, her eyes bright with tears.

'I don't know the details but it seems he was attacked. He…' Emanuel paused and gave her a handkerchief from his pocket.

'What were you going to say, Mr Emanuel?' she said, wiping her eyes with the scrap of brightly coloured cotton.

'It was nothing,' said Emanuel shaking his head.

'Tell me,' she hissed.

'He passed away,' said Emanuel. 'Would it not be better to leave it there and remember him as you last saw him?'

'Tell me what happened,' said Sara, her voice cold and determined.

'I know very little,' said Emanuel. 'But it seems he might have got into a fight with someone and died as a result of a hurt to his neck. I went to the inquest this morning but learnt no more. There were no witnesses. His body was found on the foreshore of the Thames close to Blackfriars Bridge, just over a week since.'

'Who did it? Was it Bristow?'

'I don't know,' said Emanuel. 'No one does. It would do no good to speculate.'

'Perhaps not,' said Sara, returning the handkerchief Emanuel had lent her. Suddenly she stopped, her eyes fixed on the cloth in her hand. 'Why, I do believe this handkerchief is mine, Mr Emanuel. I've been searching for it everywhere.'

He took it from her unresisting hand, a puzzled expression on his face. Then his face cleared. 'I remember now,' he said. 'I found it in the street outside St George's Hospital.'

'But I haven't—' She stopped, her eyes widening a fraction.

'You haven't what, child?' said Emanuel, his gaze straying to her neck where once there would have been a brightly coloured cloth tied about her throat. His mind went back to the night he'd found it, the night he'd been to the hospital and been told of a stranger seen running from the building before the discovery of Grenville's dead body the following morning. He'd always assumed it had been a man who'd been seen; possibly Bristow. Without thinking, he let the folds of the handkerchief fall free and saw again the rust-coloured stains of dried blood.

'You were there, weren't you?' he said. 'It was you the porter saw. It was you who he called. But you ran and jumped out of a window into the road. That's where you lost this handkerchief and where I found it. It was you who killed Grenville, wasn't it?'

Sara's face had paled as he spoke. She put out a hand to steady herself. For a few moments there was absolute silence. Even the horses seemed to have stopped moving about in the adjoining stables.

'Yes, it were me,' she said. 'What will you do?'

Chapter 65

Four months later

John Walter stood on London Bridge looking down through the bustling tangle of barges, skiffs, bumboats and hoys that weaved and bobbed their way back and forth between the quays and the thousand odd ships moored in the Pool of London. A cool breeze rippled the surface of the water, bringing with it the usual intoxicating mix of smells; of hemp, fish, coffee, spices, timber and more. And above it all, the constant cry of the seagulls and the roar of the port as men sang and trudged and carried their way through the working day.

'What happened to the girl in the end?' Walter asked, turning to look at his companion.

'Sara? She stood trial at the Old Bailey for Grenville's murder, was found guilty and sentenced to hang,' said Emanuel.

'Yes, I rather thought that might be the case,' said Walter. 'I knew her trial was coming up but I couldn't get to it. Did you give evidence?'

'No, I wanted to appear as a witness for her, but she refused all help and admitted her guilt. A great pity. I think I could have countered much of the damning evidence given by Bristow but it wasn't to be. She admitted what she'd done.'

'Did she ever tell you why she'd pleaded?'

'No,' said Emanuel, shaking his head. 'But I think Teeling's death robbed her of any wish to go on living.'

'What about Sir Peter?' said Walter. 'I thought the boys from Bow Street were interested in him. Didn't you give them some information about his possible involvement in the plot to shoot Fielding?'

'Aye, I did,' said Emanuel. 'Higgins was the officer's name. I don't think he believed a word. He told me he'd already looked at all the available evidence. In any case, Sir Peter was never prosecuted.'

The two men fell silent, watching the hurly-burly of movement on the tideway.

'And what of Bristow?' said Walter. 'Did he ever discover who it was that saved his life?'

'Not that I'm aware of,' said Emanuel.

'You know he'll never rest until he finds you?' said Walter.

'Don't worry about that. I'll make sure he does,' said Emanuel, his eyes suddenly cold and pitiless.

Historical Note

Very little is known about Emanuel, the central character of this book. He is thought to have arrived in England in about the middle of the eighteenth century from Portugal where he almost certainly studied for (but did not complete) the thirteen-year course for Holy Orders. On arrival in London, he presented himself to the then Vicar Apostolic for the London area (Bishop Challoner) and managed to convince him that he was an ordained Catholic priest. Challoner sent him to look after the Shadwell area of east London.

The political and legal climate of the time meant an almost total absence of Catholic churches in the UK. Certainly this was the case in Shadwell. In the rest of London there existed just five chapels, all attached to foreign legations and all supposedly enjoying diplomatic immunity from outside interference. Outside London, Catholic chapels tended to be confined to stately homes such as Arundel Castle, home to the Duke of Norfolk.

The Virginia Street chapel which features in this book was the result of the tenacity of 'Father' Emanuel who is said to have raised the necessary funds through the Portuguese Royal Court, even having the Royal cypher placed above the main door. Supposedly under the protection of diplomatic immunity, the chapel was nevertheless attacked and burnt to the ground in the 1780 Gordon Riots. A second chapel was built on the same site on the corner of Virginia Street and King's Head Lane (now part of the News International car park). In common with all Catholic chapels of the period – or at least those outside stately homes – the buildings were plain in the extreme and gave no outward sign of their purpose.

Over a thirty-year period 'Father' Emanuel continued his ministry at Virginia Street until questions began to be raised about the legality of his claim to ordination. He was seen by Dr Challoner's successor, Dr John Douglass (Vicar Apostolic from 1790 to 1812), admitted his bogus status and was required to leave his post. Such records as remain suggest Emanuel spent the remainder of his life as an inmate of the Whitechapel Workhouse.

The descriptions I give of the life of a Jew in London are largely accurate, as are the attacks on Catholics during this period. In the main, the Catholic population of east London was Irish, most of whom were escaping the harsh economic climate of their homeland and, since 1798, the consequences of the uprising of that year.

Around these bare facts I have attempted to weave a wholly fictional story. That said, historians may be able to point to one or two figures in the book who lived during this time, including John Walter, who founded *The Times* newspaper, and Lt. Col. George Ramsay, Earl of Dalhousie, who commanded the 2nd Regiment of Foot during the Irish rebellion of 1798, and, of course, John Douglass, the then bishop for London.

Glossary

Alb – see also Surplice – ankle-length white garment worn by a Catholic priest as part of his vestments during the Mass.
Beak – slang term for a magistrate.

Breviary – a book of liturgical text used in many Christian denominations including Roman Catholicism.

Brown coat – this was a form of shorthand used by many in the British army to describe Irish farm labourers during the 1798 uprising.

Capping (or pitch-capping) – a form of torture in which a tightly fitting conical cloth receptacle is placed on the victim's head and filled with boiling tar. When the tar cools, it (and the cloth) is pulled from the victim's head, often bringing the scalp with it. It was in routine use in Ireland during this period.

Castle Street, Holborn – now Furnivall Street. During the latter half of the eighteenth and early part of the nineteenth centuries, 4 Castle Street was the home of the Roman Catholic bishop for London. The building was a three-storey, terraced house known to the clergy as The Castle. It latterly housed an Italian restaurant before being demolished in the late nineteenth century.

Challoner, Richard (1691–1781) Vicar Apostolic (Bishop) for the London area. He it was who accepted Emanuel's word that he was an ordained priest.

Charlie – a slang term for the men employed by the various parishes to act as watchmen, enforcers of the peace before the creation of professional police.

Coffin at Newgate – Men condemned to death at the Old Bailey in the late eighteenth century were expected to attend the prison chapel on the last night, and would gather to pray round an empty coffin.

Committal – A magistrate will commit a case on indictment to the Quarter Sessions (now Crown Court) via the Grand Jury when satisfied the defendant has a case to answer.

Croppies – the term given to the Irish rebels during the uprising of 1798 in recognition of the way they wore their hair cropped short in the style of the French revolutionaries.

Cross-examination – questioning of a witness in court by the 'other' side. The principal body of evidence in known as evidence-in-chief and it is this which is attacked by the opposing side during cross-examination.

Douglass, John, Dr – (1743–1812) Vicar Apostolic for the London District from 1790 until his death in 1812. Removed Emanuel from the church and effectively excommunicated him.

Exchange Alley – now Change Alley.

Grand Jury – now defunct in British law but alive and well elsewhere. All cases committed for trial had first to pass through the grand jury which would mark the Bill of Indictment 'True' or 'Not True'. If Not True, the proceedings ended there.

Grief – London slang for trouble.

Fleet – the River Fleet, a tributary of the Thames. In the time of this story it was little more than a trickle of effluent, colloquially known as the Fleet Ditch and often acted as the disposal point for murder victims. Much (but not all) of its course through London had, by 1800, been ducted.

Hidalgo, Don Diego Beltrán – seventeenth-century Spanish poet and the son of a Jew. He, like Emanuel, is thought to have converted to Christianity.

Jews: attitude to apostasy – many lower- and middle-class Jews of this period would often resort to violence towards apostates, who they regarded as traitors and enemies of their community. Those who converted to Christianity fared even worse, often suffering threats to murder and damage to their homes.

Jews in Portugal, legal position – until comparatively recently, the law in Portugal (and Spain) required the population to follow the Catholic faith. Those of a different persuasion had the choice of becoming Christians or being deported. Faced with such a choice, the majority of Portuguese Jews became

Christians, albeit in name only, and attended Sunday Mass as 'proof' of their Christianity. A few, like Emanuel, embraced the new faith.

King of Portugal – Catholic Portugal was, at the end of the eighteenth century, still a kingdom with an embassy in London. The royal coat of arms above the door of the Virginia Street chapel was intended to reinforce this message.

Lake, Gerard, Viscount – (1744–1808) General Officer Commanding British troops in Ireland in 1798. His reputation rests on his stern approach to the suppression of the Irish rebellion.

Minister – throughout this period of British history, what we now know as the Prime Minister was simply called the Minister.

Mahamad – the elected board of directors of a Spanish-Portuguese Jewish congregation.

Murder, crime of – in the judge's summing up at the end of Bristow's trial, I have been guided by Blackstone, the pre-eminent legal authority of the day when he wrote 'Murder is… when a person is unlawfully killed… with malice aforethought, either express or implied.' (Blackstone Book iv, p.395)

Ordinary of Newgate – the prison chaplain.

Pro bono (publica) – for the public good. Lawyers will sometimes represent defendants free of charge or 'pro bono'.

Ramsay, George, Earl of Dalhousie, Lt. Col., commanded 2nd Regt of Foot at Wexford in 1798 under General Moore who, himself answered to Lake

Rippon, Revd John (1751–1836) was the Baptist Minister at the Carter Lane Meeting House during this period. He was a leading member of the Protestant Association which held strong anti-Catholic views.

Rotten Row – popular in the late eighteenth/early nineteenth centuries with the upper classes as a place to exercise their horses. It was more properly known at the time as the King's Private Road. I've used the modern name in an attempt to avoid confusion.

Sardinian Chapel, Lincoln's Inn Fields – originally an embassy chapel, it became one of the principal targets of the 1780 Gordon Riots. It was subsequently rebuilt and served as a Catholic chapel until the mid-nineteenth century.

Shako – military headgear in the British infantry during this period.

Surplice – see also Alb – a white, loose-fitting garment worn by priests. Very similar to the alb but shorter.

Talbot, the – a coaching inn in Southwark within the Liberty of Winchester, originally named the Tabard from where the pilgrims in Chaucer's *Canterbury Tales* set out. The Talbot was demolished during the late eighteenth century.

True – This term (and its opposite Not True) were used to sign off the deliberations of the Grand Jury prior to trial at the Quarter Sessions (now called Crown Courts). A 'true' Bill of Indictment meant there was sufficient evidence to proceed to trial.

Walter, John (1738–1812) – founder of *The Times*. By 1800 he'd passed the running of the paper to his son, also named John.

Wexford – site of one of the more notorious massacres to take place during the 1798 Irish uprising. The details in the story as it is told in this book are largely accurate. For more details, see *The Year of Liberty* by Thomas Pakenham.

Acknowledgements

In gives me great pleasure to acknowledge the help and support I've received throughout the writing of this book. A great many people gave freely of their time with help and advice on historical and liturgical detail without which the story would have been that much poorer. Among those I especially wish to thank are Father Nicholas Schofield, the curator of the church archives for the Diocese of Westminster to whom I turned for both historical and practical advice on the Catholic Church, Andrew Lewis, the Emeritus Professor of Comparative Legal History UCL who did his best to correct my many misconceptions on 18th Century legal issues and, of course, my editor Liz Hatherall whose keen eye succeeded in rooting out many a grammatical error. That errors remain is entirely my fault.